NOT GUILTY

NOT GUILTY

A Jack Crocker & Jimmy McGuire Mystery

RALPH LANGER

ISBN 0692816844
ISBN 13: 9780692816844

Novels by Ralph Langer
(Paperback or Kindle on Amazon.com)

Personal Verdict, a Civil Rights novel

⅄

<u>THE JACK CROCKER/JIMMY McGUIRE MYSTERY SERIES</u>

HIDE&SEEK (Book One)

NOT GUILTY (Book Two)

For Tammi Lynn Langer Starnes, an amazing mother, wife, daughter, consultant and an inspiring woman.

"Implicit in the concept of sex is consent. Without consent, sexual activity becomes rape."

Kelly Oliver, The New York Times

⅄

"In 1984, John Thompson was wrongfully convicted of two separate crimes—a robbery and murder—in Louisiana...While facing his seventh execution date, a private investigator hired by his appellate attorneys discovered scientific evidence of Thomson's innocence in the robbery case, which had been concealed for 15 years by the New Orleans Parish District Attorney's office.

"Thomson was eventually exonerated of both crimes in 2003 after 18 years in prison—14 of them isolated on death row.

"He sued the district attorney's office and was awarded $14 million, but when the state of Louisiana appealed, Supreme Court Justice Clarence Thomas issued the majority 5-4 decision that the prosecutor's office could not be held liable, ultimately granting prosecutors broad immunity for their misconduct."

From an Innocence Project Report

CHAPTER 1

-----JACK CROCKER----

He startles me the instant I come through the back door; a shadowy dark silhouette against the early dawn, his face close to the glass, peering through the front door of our private investigations agency.

"We may have a potential client extremely anxious for us to help him," I whisper, pausing in mid-step. My partner, Jimmy, bumps into my back and I freeze him with a hand to his chest and a gesture toward the mystery person.

"Or someone's pissed at us for some reason," Jimmy hisses. "Or a burglar is casing our office."

The murky figure turns to leave.

"Aw, hell," I say, "turn on the lights and I'll see who it is," striding to the front, keys still in my hand.

Jimmy hits the switch, I swing the door open and the man turns back.

"Good morning," I say, trying to be welcoming but wondering who he is. "I hope you haven't been waiting long."

A tall, middle-aged man in a black business suit sorta nods while stepping abruptly around me to the middle of our small, two-desk office. He has yet to look at me or Jimmy.

"I need to know if you can help me," he says in a surprisingly low voice. "I need help right now. I'm terrified...my daughter's life...collapsing and...."

He chokes on his words, his throat spasms, tears pool and trickle down reddening cheeks. He stares at his shoes.

I gently guide him to a chair that flanks our two desks. I pass him a tissue box as Jimmy and I slip into our chairs.

Italian shoes? A $2,000 black power suit? $100 tie? Someone who's normally in charge.

He raises his flushed face, eyelids almost closed, as if looking into a spotlight.

"I'm falling apart," he says, finally making eye contact with me, then Jimmy. "I'm not used to being helpless, failing my family. I'm way beyond desperate. Will you help me?"

"I hope so," I say. "We'll certainly do our best. I'm Jack Crocker and this is Jimmy McGuire."

"I know who you are. Everyone in Texas knows you guys. I saw you in the Dallas paper and on TV when you rescued that kidnapped kid."

"My son, Erik," I say.

"Yeah. That was incredible."

He straightens in his chair and despite his scrunched face and red eyes, he still looks like someone accustomed to sitting at the head of the table, comfortably in command.

He looks at Jimmy who's leaning toward him, elbows on his desk.

Then he stares into my eyes for a long moment while he takes three long, lung-filling breaths.

"My daughter was raped Friday night. Maybe several times. She's only 17 and a freshman at McMillan University. Since her rape she's retreated into herself and won't tell us much about what happened. Or who did it. But we know it was horrific from the little that she told my wife the next morning.

"We've discovered she's being bullied by anonymous text messages and emails. She's being taunted with disgusting social media messages."

He pauses and briefly inspects his shoes again.

"And maybe she's being physically stalked. She won't go outside and she's startled by the doorbell or the slightest unexpected sound. We've seen her looking from her window at the street in the middle of the night."

"Where did the attack happen?" Jimmy asks.

"Some kind of campus party. She won't tell us any details."

"Were the police notified?"

"Of course. I insisted even though she didn't want to. But they were worse than useless.

"Meanwhile Robyn is fearful and depressed and closed up inside her own head. She may be blaming herself for what happened. I've heard that rape victims sometimes think it's *their* fault.

"Meanwhile, the sonsabitches who did this are mocking her with vicious, filthy language. And videos."

He looks around the office as if he hadn't noticed it before.

"I need you guys to find out who the monsters are so they can be stopped."

"*Stopped* in what way?" I ask.

"Whatever it takes. We're deathly afraid she'll die," his voice breaks. "Hurt herself. We're trying to watch her 24/7...."

He stares at me, his face pleading, dark blue eyes moistening.

Not used to begging.

"In the next 60 seconds I need to know whether you two are going to help me save my daughter's life or not? I've got to find someone to help me before noon."

I see Jimmy's micro-nod and say, "We're in. We'll help you. And your daughter."

Chapter 2

-----JACK-----

The man briefly holds my gaze then his shoulders slump.

"What's your name, sir?" Jimmy says.

He blinks rapidly, as if waking from a nap.

"Ben Rogers."

"Mr. Rogers, if you're ready to hire us we need some basic information so we can organize our investigation. Are you okay with doing that now or should we meet later?"

"I'm ready right damn now," he mutters.

"We have an hourly rate or we can work on a daily or project basis. We...."

"I'll work that out with you later," dismissing the topic with a hand wave. "Let's get started," he interrupts, taking charge.

We collect his home and office addresses and phones. He's the Chief Financial Officer of an insurance company, headquartered in the LBJ Freeway corridor north of downtown Dallas.

"Do you have any other children?" Jimmy asks.

"Just Robyn. My wife and I have been married for 21 years. After Robyn was born Lauren couldn't have any other babies. Robyn's been a joy. She's very bright, which is why she's a college freshman at barely 17. She's shy and somewhat socially immature for campus life, but she agreed to live at home for at least her first year. We live less than a mile from campus."

"Mr. Rogers," I say, "we should immediately develop a plan to *protect* Robyn from stalkers and internet bullies. And we need to see your house inside and out to be sure it's physically secure. Can we meet your wife and daughter and assess your home's security later today?"

"I don't know if my wife can be ready that soon. I think she's grieving. She's extremely fearful for Robyn. Anyway, I don't know if Lauren has anything to add to what I've already told you. And Robyn..." he pauses, "highly doubtful that she will agree to talk to you."

"We should give it a try, Mr. Rogers," Jimmy says.

"Call me Ben," he says, frowning. "I'll see if my wife's comfortable with talking with you. At home would be easier for her but I'm pretty positive that Robyn won't meet with you. She won't tell us anything. She's just shut herself down. We're monitoring her 24 hours a day to be sure she's...safe," pursing his lips and looking away.

"Can you arrange a time this afternoon that we can meet you, your wife and possibly your daughter, so we can check out your house? We'll develop a full security plan right after that."

"I'll get back to you before noon." he says.

Chapter 3

----JACK-----
We walk him to his late-model black Cadillac at the curb, continuing to assure him we will immediately begin formulating a basic plan. I memorize his license plate as he drives off into the cool May morning even though I know Jimmy is doing the same thing.

Back in the office, I load the coffee pot and mash the button that begins noisily grinding the maximum load of beans I've crammed in it.

Jimmy is already staring at his desk top with what I call his "Clint Eastwood" face. I know his mind is totally focused on the Rogers' family crisis.

I sit across from him at my desk, nose-to-nose with his, and wave a hand in front of his face.

"I'm awake," he says, shifting his squint to me. "We need to jump all over this.

"Let's make a list," I say, pulling a notebook from a drawer and scribbling: 'Immediately help keep daughter safe from bullies and stalkers. And from herself.'

Jimmy adds: "Track down perps, change their attitudes, and usher them into new living quarters, as in *'Welcome to your tiny cells, punks.'* That would make my day."

"You're morphing into your inner Dirty Harry. Take some deep breaths while we plan our interview with the Rogers. And hopefully with their daughter. We need to be thorough but empathetic to their feelings and fears."

"I know how to be sensitive," he fake snarls. "I *am* sensitive."

"Yes you are, but can you develop a smidge less 44-magnum in your facial expression and voice?"

He flashes me the bird and the sight of his bullet-shortened middle finger jerks me back to serious mode.

Sorry," I say. "What info do we need from Mr. and Mrs. Rogers?"

"As many details as they know about the assault on their daughter," he says. "And exactly how she's acting or what she's saying that makes them fear she might be suicidal."

"And if she knows the perps," I say. "And how many were there? Where was this, a frat party or in a car somewhere or at someone's house? Why was she wherever this happened? Was one of the rapists a boyfriend?"

"All of that," he says, "plus what the emails and texts are saying about her that makes her fearful or threatened or whatever she's feeling? Why does she think she's being stalked? Is someone's stalking her? Has she actually seen anyone?"

CHAPTER 4

-----JACK-----

Late that afternoon, Ben Rogers opens his front door within seconds of Jimmy pushing the doorbell. He must have been looking out a window as Jimmy and I exited my Jeep Cherokee on the semi-circle drive to an impressive white clapboard mini-mansion common on the edge of Highland Park, a wealthy suburb surrounded by Dallas.

"Gentlemen," he says, briefly shaking our hands and without another word ushers us through a Mexican-tile foyer to a large, dark-carpeted living room on the left. A graceful curved stairway is straight ahead and a short hallway is visible on the right, probably to the kitchen.

"This way," he says, gesturing to the spacious, but dim room.

Room's bigger than my house!

Heavy drapes keep sunlight at bay outside large windows. I vaguely see a feminine shape in a high-backed chair across the room near a floor-to-ceiling stone fireplace, the smell of a deceased fire faintly lingering.

A post-funeral atmosphere.

"Lauren, these are the private detectives I told you about," Ben says, walking to the woman and gesturing toward us. "Jack Crocker and Jimmy McGuire. They're the men who rescued that kidnapped boy just before Christmas. That was Mr. Crocker's son."

I can see her better now, even though the only light comes from two low-wattage, end-table lamps in opposite corners of the room. She has her legs tucked under her in the large upholstered chair, dark hair brushing her shoulders, wearing gray sweat pants and shirt.

Without getting up, she raises a hand in a half-wave and softly says: "Hello."

"Hello, Mrs. Rogers," I say. "We'll help you, your husband and your daughter in any way we can."

Ben points to a long sofa across from his wife and we sit. Mrs. Rogers seems focused on a single yellow rose in a slim crystal vase on a massive glass coffee table looming between the two of us and her.

"They want us to tell them what little we know about the attack on Robyn and what's been happening since," Ben says, bending close to her face, as if addressing an elderly rest-home resident. "And they'll probably have some questions. You sure you're up for that?"

"Yes," she murmurs without looking at him or us.

Ben straightens and sits in a matching chair a few feet away.

"This all happened five days ago." Ben says, even though he already told us that in our office. "Friday night. We think Robyn was at a party at a frat house on campus. She told us a few details the next morning. She didn't want to involve the police but we insisted."

"*You* insisted," Lauren says under her breath.

"The Highland Park city police told us these *incidents,* as they call campus *rapes,* are usually investigated by the University's Security Department," Ben continues as if his wife hasn't spoken.

"It became obvious that the Campus cops aren't police, they're nothing but public relations agents in cases like this," he declares. "Their primary job is to keep the University out of trouble and out of the news. Protecting the University is obviously their first priority.

"Rapes aren't *incidents.* They're vicious *crimes,*" he snaps, slamming his fist on the table as if executing an invading spider.

"At McMillan University the so-called Campus Police questioned her as if she were the *suspect.* As if she'd hired and paid the rapist herself. I was so furious I terminated their bullshit interview on the spot. By God, it wasn't that way when I was a student there. Everyone respected women then. If one of them reported a rape something would have been done about it."

"No. That's not true," Mrs. Rogers says softly but firmly. "Almost no one reported those things and all of them were hushed up."

"You were at SMU," Ben snaps. "You don't know shit about McMillan."

"Actually I do," she replies, her voice almost a whisper. "Those things happened. And still do at SMU and Mac-U. You think women from both schools didn't talk about these things? SMU's in Dallas, a half-mile from Mac-U in University Park. They're small schools. We heard stuff."

The awkward silence is deafening.

Finally she continues. "What's important *now* is that since she was attacked she has shut herself down and refuses to answer any of our questions. She just stays in her room and mopes."

I shift my gaze to Mrs. Rogers who is looking at me.

"What happened?" I say to her. "What *exactly* has she told you so far?"

"We don't know *who,*" Ben cuts in. "That's the main thing. We're going to find the bastard who did this to her. Or bastards."

"Is that your main goal?" Jimmy asks.

"Damn straight," Ben says. "He…or they're gonna pay big time."

"We're signed up to try finding him," I say. "Making him *pay* is up to the justice system. You aren't thinking about doing that part yourself, are you?"

"Good God, no," Ben says. "We're not vigilantes. We're heart-sick over what's happened to our daughter. We hope that when we get justice for Robyn maybe that'll help her get over this horrible thing that happened to her."

I see Lauren nod, her eyes again focused on the yellow rose.

"Why don't each of you tell us what she's said to you about the attack," Jimmy suggests. "How 'bout you start, Mrs. Rogers.

"There isn't much to add," she says, glancing at Ben, her voice barely audible. "Saturday morning her bedroom door was still closed at 10 so I knocked. She didn't respond so I peeked in and found her lying in bed crying. Her face was red and distorted. She was limp and exhausted, as if she'd just finished a marathon. I stretched out beside her and just held her for a long time. She said nothing and I didn't ask her anything until she'd stopped sobbing.

"When I asked her what was wrong, she shuddered violently and I kept her in a hug. Finally she whispered: 'I was raped last night.'"

"'Oh, honey, I'm so sorry,' I said. 'We need to go to the hospital."

"She said 'No. Maybe.'

"She began crying again and I just held her for a while. Finally she fell asleep and I stayed with her until she awoke a couple of hours later.

"When she sat up in bed I asked if she wanted to talk about what had happened. She said she had a serious headache, maybe a migraine--although she's never had one before.

'After a while she slowly told me she had been at a party with some friends at a house on campus. She said she awoke in a fog and someone was... attacking her. She began sobbing again and I comforted her until she dozed off again.

"When Ben got home, I went downstairs and told him what Robyn said. I went back to Robyn's room and when she was awake Ben and I tried to talk with her."

"She wouldn't tell us anything," Ben said. "Wouldn't even say whether she knows who the sonuvabitch is."

"That's when I convinced her we needed to get her checked out at the hospital. A nurse completed a rape kit, concluded that there had been a...an assault but told us she didn't think there was DNA evidence, so the assailant must have used a condom.

"When we returned home, Ben insisted we file a report with the police and, under serious protest, we all went to the Highland Park Police station. They directed us to the University's Security department. That was awful, just as Ben told you, and we went home."

"Did she say whether the party was in a Greek house or someone's residence?" Jimmy says, looking at Mrs. Rogers.

"No," Ben said. "She won't answer anything."

"You told us she's being bullied and harassed through social media," I say. "Facebook or Twitter or Instagram or what?"

"Don't know about those. Just emails as far as I know," he says.

"Have you seen them?" Jimmy says, looking at Mrs. Rogers.

"Yes. Disgusting stuff," she says. "Emails and text messages and some social media sites I've never heard of before. No decent person could inflict that crap on another human being. It's worse than pornography because it's not anonymous people play acting, it's the actual victim of a sexual assault."

"Did you print copies?"

"No. I don't know how to print from an iPhone and the next time I checked her phone they were gone."

Ben says, "They were calling her terrible names. You couldn't see the guy's face. And you said there was a photo of her screwing some guy."

"Ben!" Mrs. Rogers snaps," raising her voice for the first time. "Stop it! That's not what I said. That wasn't what was happening in that photo. She wasn't *screwing* anyone! She was *being raped*! There's no need to talk about those vicious lies."

"They show what scum we're dealing with," he says angrily. "They have no morals or mercy. They attacked her that night and they're still attacking her. We gotta stop them."

"You mentioned a possible stalker," I say. "Has she *said* anything about a stalker? Has she or you or a neighbor or anyone seen someone hanging around? Has she been out in public at all?"

"She hasn't been out of the house," Mrs. Rogers says, "since Saturday when we went to the hospital and to the Highland Park police, who referred us to the Campus Security Department.

"Her only visitor has been Ashley, Robyn's best friend. Her only really close friend. And Ashley's only been here once since the attack, on Sunday. Her other friends from high school are more casual, not nearly as close as she is to Ashley, who is two years older and already a college sophomore."

"Has Robyn actually mentioned anything about a stalker," I ask again.

"Robyn hasn't said anything about a stalker, but I've seen her at 2 or 3 a.m. peering through her drapes as if looking for someone lurking outside. I've asked what she was looking at but she always says, 'Just looking.'"

"We'll check for prowler reports in the general neighborhood in the last five days," I say. "We have an associate, a former Army Military Police sergeant, who might watch the outside of your house overnight until we have more information."

"What else has she told either of you?" Jimmy says.

They look at each other for a moment.

Ben says: "Look, Robyn's been almost comatose for days and we've told you what little information she's shared with us plus what we're guessing at."

He glances at his wife and she nods.

'That's it, guys, everything we know," he says.

"When can we meet with her," Jimmy says. "Do you think she'll agree to that?"

"We can try," Lauren says, glancing at Ben.

"It might help if Mrs. Rogers explains to her that we're here to help all of you. That might be less stressful for her. Woman to woman," I say.

"Definitely," Mrs. Rogers says. "Less pressure."

A grimace flickered on Ben's face but he looks away without speaking.

"I'll explain to her that we're all trying to help her. I'll call you two as soon as I know her reaction. When can you talk with her if she agrees?"

"Whenever she's ready," Jimmy said. "We'll come back this evening or tomorrow sometime. The sooner the better."

Ben starts to respond but apparently thinks better of it, shrugs and nods.

Chapter 5

-----JACK-----

"It's been a hell of a day," I grunt as we slide into a booth at *Olga's Cafe*, four doors from our office and the only Ukrainian restaurant in the Dallas area.

Jimmy nods without looking up from the menu as if he expects something new there although we've pretty much memorized both the Ukrainian dishes and the "American food" selections during nearly a year of frequenting Olga's.

"What'll it be, guys?" asks Heidi, who always waits on us and is the thirty-something grand-daughter of Olga and Stan who opened the restaurant shortly after World War II.

"Lone Star," Jimmy says.

"I assume you'll have your usual ice tea," Heidi says to me.

"Yep. Any specials?"

"Today, everything's special," she explains.

"Carole is joining us tonight," I say. "She's on the way. Please just bring our drinks and we'll order when she's here."

"Okay," she says. "I'm sure I'll hear her when she arrives."

As soon as Heidi's out of earshot, Jimmy says, "Ben's clearly the dominant parent, isn't he? Talks a lot and answers questions we obviously were asking his wife."

"Absolutely," I say. "His adrenalin is flowing like the Mississippi at flood stage. His circuits may blow out if he doesn't calm down a notch. But wouldn't any parent be borderline crazy under the circumstances?"

"Parents are always borderline crazy," Carole says, taking the last two steps to our booth. She sits next to Jimmy. "It's contagious. We catch it from our kids. And sometimes from a knuckle-headed sibling.

"For example," she continues, looking at her son, "one semester shy of a Computer Science degree and an ex-Marine who worried the crap out of me with three combat tours and real bullets. And now a private investigator living with his uncle in a tiny blue cottage. I think all of that totally justifies my bouts of borderline insanity.

"And you, Baby Brother," she says, looking across the table at me, "have made me a worry-wart for most of your 42 years. A few months ago you two were in harm's way right here in Dallas. There's no mystery why I'm sprouting more gray hair every day."

"Are you pleading guilty by reason of insanity?" I ask. "I thought it was by reason of menopause. Or 'mental-pause,' as I call it."

"All of the above," she says.

Carole is not only my tall Big Sister, she's *big* in every sense. She fully inhabits any space she's in. At almost six-feet, she's automatically imposing at first glance. She runs a small trucking company, operating mostly in the southern tier of states. A former Registered Nurse, she founded the company when her Native American husband abandoned her and their son, Jimmy.

She's a thinner version of Bea Arthur's characters of *Maude* and *Golden Girls* fame, including the husky voice and "no bull-shit zone" attitude.

"Oh, mercy me," she says. "You guys will be the death of me," invoking a sudden southern accent thick enough to deep-fry chicken. She flutters her hands alongside her face, immersed in her periodic Scarlett O'Hara persona.

"Hey, this isn't *"Gone with the Wind,"* Big Sis. We've got serious stuff going on."

"You know I hate being called "Sis," but I'm going to ignore that because you're preoccupied with trying to be *'serious.'* But don't do it again or Heidi will be calling for 'Cleanup on Aisle One.'"

"Yes, Ma'am," I mock. "I'll behave because I love you so much. Not to mention I'm very, very frightened of you."

"As you should be. You better behave."

"I am being *haved*."

"Okay, now, what's going on that's so friggin *serious?*"

Without mentioning any names of people or places, Jimmy briefs her on the Robyn Rogers rape case and explains that we're trying to figure out how to protect her around the clock, while, at the same time, trying to interview her about the horrible experience and not drive her deeper into the dim cave she's retreated to.

"We're thinking we should personally guard the family house 24/7," he says.

"We're considering hiring Mark Easton to guard the house at night," I say. "I'm hoping it's only for a few days, maybe a week. He certainly showed his courage and resourcefulness when that fake cop tried to murder our client last year.

"The parents are monitoring their daughter around the clock and Mark's presence would let them get some sleep. We're going to recommend that to them tomorrow. And maybe we'll come up with more suggestions when we talk directly to the daughter."

"If she actually agrees to talk to us," Jimmy adds. "Her parents aren't sure she will and so far she's kept all the ugly details to herself, which makes it difficult for us to find suspects. We don't know if she knows the perp or perps. She's withdrawn from everyone, hiding in her room, in the dark.

"Hey, Carole," Heidi interrupts, offering Carole a high-five slap. "Haven't seen you in a while. Still kicking butt and taking names?"

"That's my job description around these two."

"I assume you still have your concealed weapons permit."

"Yep."

Heidi nods, takes our orders and leaves.

Unsurprisingly, two familiar gnomes appear, one immediately asking, "How's everything?" as he does every time he approaches his customers.

Heidi's grand-father, Stan Prutko, is, as always, wearing a Texas Rangers ball cap and tee. He is, at maximum, five-two and his suspendered jeans are definitely from the Boy's department. Heidi's grandmother, Olga, is south of five-feet, leans on a cane, her black dress and white apron giving her a miniature Pilgrim look.

We all assure Stan that we're confident *everything* is going to be wonderful. As Heidi's grandparents move to the next booth, Jimmy immediately returns to serious business.

"Let's hope the victim will tell us some things she can't bring herself to say to her mom and dad."

"That may take a while," I say. But maybe two strangers are less off-putting for her than family members."

"Maybe neither of you is of the appropriate gender," Carole says.

That resonates with me.

"Maybe you should come with us? Would you be willing to do that?"

"Sure, but a person trained in traumatic situations would be better."

My cell vibrates and the screen announces "LRogers."

"Robyn agreed to meet with you and Jimmy," Mrs. Rogers whispers. "She didn't commit to anything beyond that. She just said, 'I'll listen to what they say.' I think noon is the best time since she's awake most of the night and only puts together a few hours of sleep after the sun comes up. Can you be here at noon tomorrow?"

"Definitely. And meanwhile, tell her we'll patrol your neighborhood tonight. Maybe all three of you can sleep a little better."

"Probably not," Lauren says. "Robyn got 18 disgusting emails and texts today. I'm staying with her in her room tonight."

CHAPTER 6

-----JACK-----

Early the next morning we're groggily hunching over our desks transcribing and merging notes from yesterday's interview of Ben and Lauren Rogers into our laptops when we hear a polite knock on the front door, the first time anyone's ever knocked before coming in.

My desk faces the door so I see a large man opening the door. Everything about him is black; shoes, suit, shirt and face. Everything except his white clerical collar.

"Excuse me," he says in a deep, rich voice reminiscent of James Earl Jones, as he pauses half-way through the door. "Are you available to investigate something for me?"

"Yessir," Jimmy says, already on his feet. I join him as he introduces us.

The man steps in, bows his head almost imperceptibly and vigorously shakes my hand, using both of his.

"I'm J.D. Finley, pastor of the Oak Cliff Fellowship Community Church.

"I recognize you," Jimmy says. "You took a bunch of your parishioners to Haiti a few years ago to help after that huge earthquake.'

"Yes, we did, but that's not why I'm here. A cousin of mine was murdered last weekend and I want to find out why."

Jimmy gestures him to a chair by our desks but even before he's fully seated he says, "My cousin, Jackson Parks, was found dead in his bed Sunday afternoon. The Medical Examiner says he apparently died from an overdose of a prescription drug, either accidentally or a suicide."

He pauses, studies our faces for a moment and says, "The Medical Examiner is completely wrong. It was neither an accident nor a suicide. Someone murdered him."

He looks each of us in the eyes for a few seconds.

"That's absolutely *not* what happened," he growls, slamming giant hands flat on Jimmy's desk.

"What do you think happened, Pastor Finley?" I say

"Call me *The Rev.* Or *just Rev.* Everyone does."

He flashes an instantly vanishing smile.

"I don't know what happened but I know darn well that he didn't accidentally overdose himself. He wasn't stupid. Or demented. And he definitely wasn't *suicidal*."

Jimmy says: "Sometimes people make mistakes or are depressed but don't show it and folks around them are surprised when...."

"We were as close as brothers," The Rev declares. "I'd have known if he was thinking about suicide."

"Maybe something happened a day or so earlier that caused him to do this to himself," I say.

"A good point, but not relevant," The Rev says. "I was with him nearly all of our waking hours Friday and Saturday. We were coordinating details for a potluck dinner on Sunday late afternoon.

"When he didn't show up at either of two worship services Sunday morning I was worried because he's always there, plus he had things to do for the dinner. I called his house after the 9 a.m. service but got no answer. His wife was in Atlanta visiting relatives and their two kids are both out of college, one living in Chicago, the other in Atlanta.

"When I got another non-answer after the 11 a.m. service, I called 911 but the two cops who went to his house got no response from inside and saw no signs of a break-in or anything suspicious through the windows and left.

"After I heard that, I went to his house--it's only five blocks from the church--and I found him dead. It was a tremendous shock and...I couldn't... it was horrible..." he chokes, blocking his face with huge hands."

"That's okay, sir, we can discuss more details later. What do you want Jimmy and me to do?"

"Find out why Jackson's dead and who killed him."

I say, "Isn't that what the police are supposed to do?"

"I always thought so. But the cops and the Medical Examiner seem convinced that Jackson committed suicide and that I'm just a naive relative in denial. Trust me, they're totally wrong."

"Tell us about Mr. Parks," I say. "What was he like?"

The Rev briefly bows his head.

"Jackson didn't light up a room just by walking into it, but anyone in the room who knew him, respected him. We were de facto brothers our whole lives. We...."

His big baritone fades and I see his eyes moisten as he turns to look at the street. He clears his throat, turns back and dabs at wet cheeks with a tissue from a box Jimmy offers.

"Jackson is...was four months older than me. My mother and her sister delivered us into the world as if by pre-arrangement. Neither of them ever had any other children.

"When the sister and her husband were killed by a drunk driver, my mother and father brought three-year-old Jackson to our house that night and he didn't leave until he enlisted in the Army at 18.

"We were brothers in every sense except for the technical biological definition, even though we were blood relatives. We grew up together.

"Neither of us ever used drugs. Never. We did the teen-age beer gig and we certainly maintained familiarity with the pleasures of a cold beer or two when available in the military and to this day...until last Saturday...but absolutely not to excess.

"All through our school years we often sat together in classrooms and we played on football and baseball teams. We even played brothers in our sophomore-year play. Our last names are different and although everyone knew we lived in the same house, nothing official was ever made of that."

"Naturally, when he enlisted in the Army, so did I. We weren't stationed together, but we wrote letters and tried to arrange for over-lapping furloughs when we could.

"The Vietnam War was officially over by then and in our four Army years each of us had assignments in multiple places, exposing us to more of the world than we'd ever seen before; changed our lives. We got home a couple of months apart in 1982 and we were eager to change the world.

"We weren't twins," he smiled, "but I think we had connections like twins often have. We often finished each other's sentences. Our values and views of the world were similar, even though our personalities are...were different. "I'm a bit louder. Well, maybe a *lot* louder and certainly I talk way more than him. Jackson was definitely quieter...but he always got the job done, whatever the job was. But you might not *hear* him doing the job."

"What did he do for a living?" Jimmy wonders.

The Rev smiles and nods as if reviewing good memories.

"A delivery supervisor at UPS. He started there as a *strong-back* guy personally moving boxes around a warehouse and in less than a year they recognized that he was a *strong-mind* man who made the system work. Quietly. Not much drama. Been there over 30 years."

"What was the prescription drug that the Medical Examiner says killed him?" Jimmy says.

"Oxycontin. It was prescribed after surgery a month or so ago for carpal tunnel damage in his right hand. He thought it was ironic for him to have survived four years in the Army and then suffer bodily injury from typing memos and business forms on a computer keyboard. I saw a bottle of the stuff in his home several days after his surgery and noted that it was nearly full. He said he'd decided to see if he could get through the temporary pain without it.

"I know his medical history as well as I know my own. He and his wife, Shirley, are among the most-active volunteers in our church. We spent many hours a week together, working on one project or another, sharing ideas and chores. Often he'd stop at the church after work for an hour or so before going home. We didn't keep secrets from each other. Someone did this to him."

"He sounds like a wonderful person," I say. "Who would anyone want to kill him?"

His face seems to collapse, his eyes lose their vibrant intelligence.

"I don't know," he says. "It's beyond my comprehension how anyone can murder any human being, let alone someone like Jackson who never harmed a soul."

He stands and both of us do, too.

"I have a pre-marital counseling session in 45 minutes. When can you two start?"

"Right now," I say. "We can work out details later, but our rate is $400 a day, plus expenses. Or we can discuss some options. If you're available early this afternoon, one of us will meet you in your office. We'll need names and contact information for all church members and staff plus a list of his friends. We need to talk to his wife when she's back from Atlanta.

"She's already back, got here Monday afternoon."

"How many church members are there?" Jimmy asks.

"Twelve-hundred and seventy-seven."

OMG!

Chapter 7

-----JACK------

Lauren and Ben Rogers meet us at the door 15 minutes before noon and lead us to the living room. I scan the large space hoping to see Robyn, but she's not there. Mrs. Rogers gestures to the sofa and Jimmy and I sit, looking up at her. Ben is pacing circles around the furniture.

"I just came from Robyn's room," She says in a half-whisper. "She awoke a short time ago and is showering and dressing, which is a good sign because even though she showers five times a day, she hasn't shown any interest whatever in clean or different clothes. This is the first time since this all happened that she's worn anything but pajamas and I've had to remind her to change those."

"We recommend that you hire a security person to watch your property and the neighborhood at night until we can determine if there is any external threat, possibly just for a few days or a week, I say."

"Where would we find someone like that?" Ben asks.

"We have a guy who sometimes works with us," Jimmy says. "He was an Army Military Police sergeant in Iraq. Last year he saved the life of one of our clients when she was attacked in her home by a fake cop. It might be comforting to Robyn and you to know that someone is protecting your house and watching the neighborhood. It might lessen her concern over a possible stalker. And maybe you two can catch up on some sleep."

"Fine," Ben says. "Do it."

"We'll check his availability and try to bring him here later today to meet all of you and have him start tonight. If he can't start right away, one of us will patrol the neighborhood overnight."

"Thank you." Lauren nods.

"Where will we meet with her, Mrs. Rogers?" Jimmy wonders.

"Please call me Lauren," she says, finally sitting down. "She's in her room. It's the closest thing to a comfort zone she has right now. It's her hideaway."

"We've tried to coax her downstairs but she won't do it," Ben mutters.

"She'll come out when she's ready," Lauren says, not looking at her husband. "Agreeing to talk with these gentlemen is significant progress. So far the only visitor she's permitted is her friend Ashley. And that was only once, on Saturday, the day after the...what happened. I'll see if she's ready."

She takes a step and turns back to us. "I assume you two fully realize how fragile she is and that you need to be very careful. And sensitive. And gentle."

"We do," I promise. "We won't pressure her in any way. We'll see how it goes. This might be just a get-acquainted meeting. It might take more than one time to gain her trust and understanding that we're here to help protect her."

Lauren assesses us for a few seconds and heads for the stairs.

Major tension in here and Lauren seems in charge today instead of her Triple-Alpha husband. Mama Bear asserting herself?

Ben continues his hike around the room, silent, frowning, looking like an NFL coach prowling the sidelines. A couple of circuits later, he pauses near us and we stand up.

"Robyn wants us to forget this ever happened," he says softly. "She just wants to move on. I hope she can manage to get most of this horrendous experience behind her. But so far, the fact is, she's *not* moving on.

"And I'm telling you guys that I'm not going to stop until the son-of-a-bitch who did this is off the street."

He's silent for a moment and I see his eyes moistening. He blinks rapidly and takes a step closer to us.

"You find out *who* did this," he whispers but demandingly, "I want that guy behind bars or off the planet," before resuming his journey around the room.

We need to keep our client in the corral.

Jimmy and I drift without talking toward the staircase. A minute or two later Lauren appears half-way down and gestures for us to join her.

"I've reassured her over and over that you two are professionals and good guys and earlier I told her what heroes you were when your son was kidnapped. I think that was the main reason she agreed to meet with you.

"Let's go. I'll introduce you and then leave the three of you alone to get acquainted. I'll keep Ben downstairs," she adds, and turns up the stairs with a slight eye-roll.

Robyn's bedroom is dim thanks to heavy shades over the two large windows.

A young girl-woman sits on the edge of her bed and glances at us as we come in.

"Honey, these are the gentlemen I told you about," Lauren says softly. "Jack Crocker and Jimmy McGuire. They're the ones who rescued Jack's son last December."

Neither Jimmy nor I offer our hands, having decided last night to do so only if she did. We want to avoid anything that might spook her by appearing threatening or over-bearing.

"Hi," she says softly, eyes flitting around the room.

"See you later, Sweetie," Lauren says and disappears, leaving the bedroom door open. An Apple laptop sits open on a full-size business desk with a leather desk chair a few feet from the bed. Two visitor-style chairs flank the desk, dozens of photos almost obscure a wall-mounted cork bulletin board.

"Okay if we sit?" I say, pulling a visitor chair closer to her as soon as she nods.

"Sure," she murmurs, still avoiding eye contact.

I sit closest to her because I'm older and perhaps slightly less scary.

"Hi," I say. "Thanks for talking with us. We realize it's a tough time for you because of some disgusting criminal. Your mom and dad want us to find the men who attacked you. What can you tell us about what happened?"

"I don't care about *finding* them. I just want all of this to go away," she says softly, glancing at me, then at Jimmy, then at a dim window. "I want them to leave me alone."

"Who?" Jimmy says. "Who is bothering you now?"

"Mostly my dad. He wants revenge. He can't drop it."

"Isn't he just seeking justice for you?" I suggest. "Maybe with a *dab* of revenge?"

She closes her eyes but doesn't speak.

Jimmy says, "Had you been drinking that night?"

"You're blaming me," she says angrily. "That's what the police tried…"

"I'm so sorry. I didn't mean it that way," Jimmy says gently. "Miss Rogers, you've done absolutely nothing wrong. You didn't deserve what happened to you. And you don't deserve whatever is happening to you now. Jack and I are here to protect you from whatever's going on now. And to help you and your mom and dad deal with what an evil person has done."

Trying to shift the focus from her momentary anger, I add, "Your mom said you had a massive headache the next morning, do you think your attacker drugged you? Could that have caused the headache?"

She shrugs.

"Are you being harassed now?" Jimmy asks. "By whoever attacked you?"

She seems to shrink inside herself, her face remains expressionless as if she's exited the room, leaving her body behind.

Finally she twitches awake and stares at me. I'm worried that she's about to end our conversation

"Who told you that?"

"Your Mom and Dad are worried that you're being bullied on email or texts or Twitter or whatever," I say. "Is someone doing that?"

She morphs into tears, her body trembling, face reddening, clenched eyes trying to block a world she doesn't want to see.

I leave my chair, sit awkwardly next to her, my hands clasped between my knees, desperately seeking something to do or say that will be soothing instead of unwelcome.

Her gentle crying diminishes and she fist-rubs tears from her eyes and cheeks.

"Let us help you," I say.

"No one can help me," she says, her voice gaining volume. "Can't you see that? There's nothing *anyone* can do. They can rape me again and again in endless different ways."

"Give us a chance to change that," I say.

"Do you know what SnapChat is?" her voice sounding like a young child.

"Yes," Jimmy says. "I'm familiar with it. What are they sending you?"

"Photos and videos that disappear after about ten seconds," she says, her voice almost frail.

"Of the attack...of what they did to me. They send pictures of me being... raped and the photos disappear...but they send them again. They send them to me...and apparently to everyone I know...they can send them to everyone in the world. Over and over and over."

"*Who* is doing this?" Jimmy asks again. "Help us find them and get them punished."

Her eyes close and a slight moan escapes her pursed lips.

"Maybe you should replace your phone--and give the new number only to a few close friends or family. And change your email address and other social media accounts and cancel the old ones."

"I can't do that," she whispers. "I know it's awful to say but part of me wants to know what they're doing to me...even if it makes me want to throw up."

"Is someone *physically* stalking you?" I ask.

"I'm not sure," she whispers. "I haven't *seen* anyone."

"It may help you to know that no one in the neighborhood has reported any prowlers or suspicious people in the past week." Jimmy says.

"Good," she says. "They've threatened to post the photos on Facebook and Twitter and YouTube and everywhere on the internet if I identify them."

"So you know who they are," I say. "Will you help us and the police put them in jail so they can't ever do it again? To you. Or anyone else."

"I'd have to testify in court about everything they did to me. I can't possibly do that."

"We can keep you safe," Jimmy says.

"No you can't," she says. "No one can do that. I'll never be *safe* again."

"If you give us their names we can investigate them and possibly find other crimes they've committed and we can put them in prison without involving you."

"No," she said in a shaky but definite voice. "I can't. And I won't."

I sense that we're losing her and we need to end this on as positive a note as possible and hope to re-interview her later when she might be less traumatized and more open to at least giving us some leads.

"Miss Rogers, we know you've had a terrible experience. And you're under great pressures now. We appreciate your sharing your thoughts with us. We're going to make sure no one can lurk in your neighborhood overnight so you don't have to worry about that.

"Is it all right if we check back with you in a few days and see if we can find more ways to help you?"

After a moment of silence she says: "Maybe. But I doubt it."

Chapter 8

-----JACK-----

Jimmy and I descend the curving staircase without speaking. I see Ben and Lauren sitting near the fireplace. Ben immediately gets up and is striding toward us, Lauren remains in one of the winged-chairs.

"How'd it go?" Ben asks as the three of us converge.

Neither Jimmy nor I respond until we seat ourselves opposite Lauren. Ben, after a brief hesitation, drops onto the other padded chair.

"We got acquainted a little," I say. "But no breakthroughs."

I look at Jimmy who says: "As you emphasized, Mrs. Rogers...Lauren, your daughter is fragile and vulnerable. She's struggling to process what happened to her. And what's happened since."

Ben cuts in. "Did she tell you what happened? Is she being stalked right here in our neighborhood? Is she still getting more harassing and vile emails? Did she tell you who...."

"She told us no details about Saturday night," I say, matching his stare.

"As you know, she's getting disgusting messages on social media. She doesn't know if someone's physically stalking her. She hasn't actually seen anyone. She seemed comforted when we told her we would begin guarding the house overnight."

"She's obviously seriously traumatized. Jimmy and I know some things about stress and trauma from our war experiences. She needs some time to..."

"Did she tell you who did this to her?" Ben demands, again.

"She didn't," Jimmy says, "but she tentatively agreed to talk with us again in a few days. Maybe we'll get more information then. I don't think we should push her now; it just adds to her anxieties."

Good. He didn't mention that she apparently does know the perps.

"Are you considering a rape counselor?" I ask. "Perhaps someone who would come to your house."

"I'm going to work on that," Lauren says.

I say, "It's possible, now that she's talked a little with the two of us, people she just met, it will help her with processing what happened…to start moving on. Just a beginning."

"We want to contact her best friend. *Ashley* is it?" Jimmy says. "We need her last name and contact information. Maybe we can learn something before we ask Robyn to meet with us again."

"Her friend's name is Ashley Scanlon. I'll get her address and cell number," Lauren says as she gets up and disappears toward the kitchen.

Ben says, "Keep *me* posted. You guys find the animal who attacked my daughter. I'll find a hanging tree."

CHAPTER 9

-----JACK-----

Outside we split up and I call Mark Easton and get voicemail. I tell his recorder that we have a job for him if he's available and ask him to call Jimmy.

Now, I'm pulling my Jeep into the circular driveway of my son Erik's middle school.

Erik is already waiting by the building's entrance that is providing shade from the bright sunlight. An assistant principal takes Erik's crutches and backpack and puts them in the backseat while Erik herky-jerks himself into the front passenger seat.

"Hi, Mr. Crocker," the man says. "I can tell Erik's making good progress, getting himself into the car and all."

"Yeah, we're all grateful for how far he's come. He's worked very hard and never complains. We're really proud of him. He's close to walking by himself all the time instead of several 15-minute times a day."

"Yep," Erik smiles. "I've about worn out these crutches and I hope to toss them in the attic soon."

Fifteen minutes later, we're parking in front of *Superior Therapy* in Richardson where the toughest 11-year-old I know has been in twice-a-week rehab sessions for six months, since Children's Hospital doctors decided he could handle out-patient therapy at the clinic near our house following almost a year of extensive two sessions per day, three times a week in their main facility.

"Hey, Erik," Jason, Erik's 20-something physical therapist says, striding across the room as soon as we come through the door. "How's my work-out buddy?"

Soon Erik and Jason are engrossed in the 90-minute session they slog through every Monday and Thursday.

I flash back almost a year and a half and recall how Erik couldn't walk on his own at the beginning and now he parks the crutches and cautiously negotiates a 15-foot path along a back wall while loosely tethered to an overhead safety cable.

The doctors who see him quarterly now seem confident he'll be comfortably walking on his own all day in the couple of months, maybe even running somewhat like a normal 11-year-old in six months. I'll need a full box of tissue when that happens.

He was seriously injured when I accidentally backed my car over him because I thought he was in our house. But he had returned, sprinting from the front door bringing me a fresh-baked brownie. He tripped and fell in the driveway behind my car and I didn't see him in any of my mirrors. His head bounced off the concrete and his right leg was broken, pinned under a tire.

I was departing our house in a huff because my wife, Crystal, confronted me over my long and losing battle with Post Traumatic Stress Disorder symptoms, mostly involving alcohol, that resurfaced after my National Guard unit was reactivated and sent into combat in the second Gulf War.

I'd been in the first Gulf War some years before, but thought I'd cleared my head from the horrifying experience of calling in air strikes on hundreds of retreating Iraqi tanks and trucks. Hundreds of Iraqi troops were trapped in a horrific gridlock on the infamous "Highway of Death" between Kuwait and Baghdad. With my help, many of them died.

The second deployment knocked me into a depression I was unable to wrestle to the ground. I unsuccessfully tried drowning it in booze.

My huge mistake left Erik, then nine-years-old, in a coma for several days and unable to walk without assistance for nearly a year.

Although I'd had only three beers--less than one per quarter--during a televised Dallas Cowboy football game a couple of hours earlier, well before the accident, overall I was drinking too much, too often and generally screwing up, including losing my job as an award-winning investigative reporter for The Dallas News thanks to a stupid ethical breach. I took a short-cut and got caught hacking a prominent Dallas CEO's voicemail, a rookie move I never would have committed before I threw my depressed, self-destructive self over the cliff.

About the same time, my much-younger nephew, Jimmy, left the Marines after three combat tours, one in Iraq and two in Afghanistan.

Using money from my 401(K) and Jimmy's savings from his four years of Marine duty and a good head for poker, we opened *C&M Investigations* together, hoping to earn some money and jointly fight our way through the toxic residue of our separate military experiences.

One of our first cases erupted violently and my son was kidnapped by thugs trying to force Jimmy and me to abandon an investigation. They sliced off part of one of Erik's earlobes and delivered it to Crystal and me. Jimmy and I ended up in a furious warehouse fire-fight with professional killers hired by a corrupt cop.

The intense local, Texas and even national news coverage of our rescue of Erik, boosted our new small private-detective agency. In the immediate aftermath we became at least temporarily semi-famous and our business has increased enough to be viable.

We handle everything from background checks for employers, to Workman's Comp cheaters to deadbeat dads to warehouse inventory theft and bail bond jumpers. Jimmy and I own the company and it's basically a two-person operation but we have several other investigators, all ex-military, who we hire on an as-needed basis.

Now, Erik is finishing his workout session and we head to the Olive Garden for our usual pasta and unlimited breadsticks lunch before I drop him at our house in Plano for his post-therapy nap.

I call it "our house" but I don't live there anymore.

More than a year ago Crystal filed for divorce and tossed me on the lawn. Since then I've been bunking in a two-bedroom rental cottage in a Lake Highlands neighborhood, first alone and then with Jimmy, as we launched our PI agency.

I pop from the car when we're in the driveway, hand Erik his crutches from the backseat, sling his backpack over my shoulder and we trek to the front door. Our newly minted teenager, daughter Carli, answers the bell, smiling at both of us.

"Hey, bro, Mom left us a Twinkie package to share. Our once-a-week junk food treat," she laughs and winks at me. We manage a group hug and the door closes and I'm trudging to my car, moist eyes watching my boots.

Chapter 10

-----JIMMY-----

About a dozen cars are clustered in The Oak Cliff Community Church's huge parking lot when I arrive in the mid-afternoon sunshine.

From the street, the church building is a remarkably well-maintained, classic 1930s or '40s era brick façade with wide concrete steps leading to the sanctuary doors.

From the parking lot in back, I enter what is clearly a new addition to the historic building through automatic, double-glass doors more suitable for an office building or bank.

I see "Pastor's Office" straight ahead and am greeted by a tiny, ultra-thin woman who conceivably could be the original receptionist.

"Are you Mr. McGuire?" her canary voice asks.

"Yes, ma'am. I'm here to see…."

"I know," she says. "You want to interview everyone. I'm Minnie, our church secretary. Most folks call me Church Lady. Follow me. The Rev's expecting you."

She opens the door behind her and waves me into The Rev's office. He is so much larger than Minnie that they could be different species. He's up, walking to me while Minnie vanishes as if scattered like dandelion fuzz in a gentle summer breeze.

"Mr. McGuire," he booms. "There are 11 staff members and volunteers here at the moment. Let's go down the hall. I have a conference room for you to talk with each person."

A rectangular table with six chairs dominates the center of the room. On the right, four upholstered, living room-style chairs face each other over a coffee table holding aluminum coffee carafes and a water pitcher, cups and glasses.

"Minnie will see to it that someone is always ready to come in whenever an interview ends. Sound okay?"

"Sure.

"Let's get started then," The Rev says. "Make yourself comfortable and I'll tell Minnie you're ready to chat with one of our members. Let me know if you need anything. Can we touch base before you leave?"

"Certainly, Sir."

Three seconds later Minnie ushers in a white-haired man in a short-sleeve, white tee shirt under bib overalls that can't hide a significant paunch straining the denim.

"Mr. McGuire," Minnie says, "this is Marvin Miller. He's been taking care of our building for almost 50 years."

She points at the table with coffee carafes and facing chairs.

"Marvin," she adds, "you tell Mr. McGuire whatever he wants to know. Everything," making it sound like the 11th Commandment even without Charlton Heston's voice.

"Hello, Mr. Miller, would you like some coffee or a glass of water?"

He shakes his head and sits rigidly in the chair across from me, focusing on the table between us.

"As you know, Sir, The Rev has asked my partner and me to look into the recent death of Jackson Parks. Did you know Mr. Parks?"

"Of course," he said, finally meeting my gaze. "I've known Jackson practically forever. I saw him several times a week pretty much for 40 years, ever since he returned from the Army. He done a lot of things for this church over the years."

"You may have heard that some people think he accidentally took too much of his pain medications. And some others think he may have committed suicide."

"No way would Jackson do either of those things. No."

"Why do you think that?"

Marvin's face flashes anger.

"He was too smart to accidentally take more pills than he was supposed to. He was a very intelligent man.

"And he wouldna never kilt himself. He wasn't no quitter. People who kill themselves are quitters. Jackson was a fixer. If he saw a problem he got busy and solved it. He wouldna done nothing like that."

"Well, the Medical Examiner said...."

"You stop saying stuff like that," he says, his voice rising.

He stands and points a finger at me.

"It's an insult to Jackson for you to talk like that bout him. He's one of the best people I've ever known."

I get up.

"I understand your feelings, Mr. Miller, but these aren't *my* questions. I'm asking about issues raised by the County Medical Examiner and by the police. Did you see anything in recent times that showed he might have been sad or troubled about something?"

"I already told you he wasn't that kind of person. I'm here all the time and he was in and out of the church three, four times a week, not counting worship times."

He's opening the door and I join him, giving him one of my cards as he steps into the hall. Minnie is already steering a woman toward us and Marvin passes them midway.

"Mr. McGuire, this is Sarah Moore," Minnie says, gesturing to the gray-haired woman and closing the door behind her.

Miss Moore nods at me, sits in the just-vacated chair and pours a cup of coffee.

"Would you like some coffee, Mr. McGuire? I made it myself before you arrived."

"Sure," I tell her, inwardly smiling at her take-charge attitude.

"You don't have to tell me why you're here," she says, handing me a cup. "The Rev told all of us that he's concerned and baffled about Jackson Parks' mysterious death and wants to find out what actually happened.

"I can tell you right now," she continues, her eyes holding mine, "Jackson did *NOT* commit suicide. He wouldn't have done that to his wife, Shirley. And he most certainly did *NOT* mix up his pills.

"I do a lot of volunteering here, including producing the weekly church newsletter. My husband and I were good friends with the Jacksons for many, many years even after my husband died.

"Jackson was...not...careless...or incompetent...or depressed. Shirley, would have known."

"Yes, of course, Mrs. Moore. And just to be clear, the Rev believes that, too. He disagrees, as do you, with the official sources who decided differently. He's asked us to find out what really happened."

"I understand that, young man. Whoever these official sources are they're full of Grape Nuts. And they don't know beans about the real Jackson."

She stands and it feels as if I should leave *her* room. She almost stomps to the door, opens it and advises me.

"Find the truth, Mr. McGuire."

CHAPTER 11

-----JACK-----

Late that afternoon, Jimmy returns to our **C&M Investigations ("We're super discreet")** office where I've been doing web searches for other sexual assault cases at McMillan, SMU, University of Texas at Dallas and other area universities.

Jimmy says, "Mark Easton has agreed to look for stalkers or other creeps in the Rogers' neighborhood starting tonight until we get a handle on what's happening. I gave him night-vision goggles and an infrared camera from my *'Magic Box.'* He'll monitor people and vehicles."

He sees me grinning.

"I know you enjoy mocking me for my love of gadgets, but sometimes stuff from the *Magic Box* in my trunk has been handy. I've got everything in that box from drones to remote-control Tarantulas to tiny cameras hidden in gimme-caps...."

"That makes your toys tax deductible."

He shifts gears.

"We're introducing Mark to Ben and Lauren and hopefully to Robyn, at 7 p.m."

"Did you find any suspects at The Rev's church?" I say.

"Not even a candidate for 'A person of Slight Interest,'" he says, pressing his laptop's on-button. "No one had even a glimmer of an inkling of an idea why Jackson would have been murdered.

"Everyone I interviewed sang from the same hymnal, but sometimes from conflicting verses.

"They were all absolutely positive that he wouldn't have taken his own life. And no one believed that he could have accidentally taken an overdose.

"But just as firmly, in the next breath, none of them could imagine anyone wanting or needing to kill Jackson, a man apparently beloved by everyone.

"The church secretary, a nice lady named Minnie, told me as I was leaving that she had absolutely nothing to say except that 'Jackson Parks did *NOT* kill himself either on purpose or accidentally. Never happened, period,' Minnie said, succinctly summarizing everyone else.

"Jackson seems to have been a nice, low-key guy, dedicated to his family and church. No one I talked to so far knew of any problems, conflicts or bad history with anyone. Of course, I'm going to check everything, but all indications are that suicide would be completely out of character for the man they've known for years."

"Everyone has secrets," I suggest. "Either someone wanted him dead or he was deeply troubled enough to off himself but he hid that from his almost-brother and many friends."

"And from his long-time wife," Jimmy says.

"Did you find any indication he was selling church members shares in fake Montana gold mines or boinking the choir director?"

"No, but I did notice that the choir director is a pretty hot, 86-year-old with a sexy blue, beehive hair-do."

Chapter 12

-----JACK-----

Mark Easton exits his non-descript black Accord behind my Cherokee in the Rogers' driveway and joins Jimmy and me heading to the house.

Inside I introduce Mark to Ben and we troop silently into the living room, Lauren walks to us and extends her hand to Mark.

I briefly summarize Mark's military background and his role in our crisis last December and while we're still in a vertical cluster, tell them: "Mark needs a walk-through of the house."

"I want to check every window and every door," he says. "I'll walk around outside when we're finished in here. I want to be familiar with every tree and shrub, plus find some sightlines from the street for when I'm patrolling the area overnight.

"I know Jack and Jimmy looked at your security system but I want to see how it's wired and if it's vulnerable in any way from the exterior of the house."

Ben and Lauren are listening and nodding, resigned to yet another stranger inspecting their home, inside and out, living in fear for their daughter.

"Is Robyn available to meet Mark?" I say. "We think it could help her feel more comfortable and safe."

"I think maybe she will," Lauren says. "I'll go upstairs and check with her. I already told her about Mr. Easton's role and she surprised me by agreeing when I suggested she meet him.

After Lauren disappears up the stairs, Ben waves at the furniture and seats himself. It takes another minute before he speaks, looking and sounding exhausted.

"I'm so afraid for her," he says, no longer the demanding 'I'm-in-charge' person we've seen before. "Are you guys making any progress on finding the monsters who did this?"

"Without any witnesses or names of suspects, we're having a difficult time," I say. "Our best chance to zero in on a perp is Robyn herself. It's not clear if she knows who was involved, although she might. If she does know, she hasn't told Jimmy and me. Has she said anything to you?"

He shakes his head.

We'll try again today. Maybe now she'll be more comfortable filling in some gaps, even if she doesn't know any names. We hope she can recall a general description, even just a voice or clothing or facial hair…anything."

"We need other details about where the attack took place."

Ben is not cheered by my recitation of failure. He clamps his eyes closed, his shoulders slump, his hands are fists but his energy level seems close to empty.

Lauren appears on the stairway and gestures to Jimmy, Mark and me to come and we're instantly up, heading to the stairs. Before we reach Robyn's bedroom, I pause and quietly ask Lauren: "Has she said anything about who attacked her?"

She shakes her head negatively, too.

Lauren leads us to Robyn's bedroom where she's standing by her desk looking through the window—no drapes this time--and immediately turns to us.

Lauren introduces Mark who instinctively thrusts his hand toward Robyn. She briefly takes it and says, "Hello, Mr. Easton," as Lauren leaves, apparently still hoping Robyn will tell us something she's not comfortable sharing with her parents.

"Hi, Mr. Crocker and Mr. McGuire," Robyn says, stepping to each of us, shaking our hands and making more eye contact in a few seconds than the entire time we interviewed her a day ago.

"Hey, Robyn, let's get past the *Mister* stuff. We're all grownups here," I say. "Besides, it makes me feel old when anyone over the age of 10 calls me *Mister*." I say, venturing a small smile. "Okay?"

She nods and gestures for us to sit. She parks on the edge of her quilted bed.

A tad less sad scaredy-cat posture.

Jimmy again recites Mark's military background. Mark briefs her on his plans to be certain the house is secure.

"Tonight I'll begin patrolling the house exterior and your neighborhood. I have night-vision goggles and you can sleep comfortably without worrying about intruders…or skulkers or people driving by in a suspicious manner."

"Thank you," she says, her voice still soft, but more definite than before. "I appreciate what you guys are doing even if it only helps my father rest easier."

"You're feeling better?" I ask, a tinge of hope in my tone.

"I guess," she responds. "I'm not sure what I am right now."

"What do you recall now about that night?" Jimmy says. "Can you tell us their names?"

Too soon!

She flinches, looks at the floor and the room is so quiet I think I hear my heart valves swooshing.

Robyn looks up, opens her eyes to look at Jimmy, tears moistening her cheeks.

She swallows twice, still staring at him and I know he's desperate to recover from his over-eager question. I'm spinning my hard-drive, frantic to find something to undo the damage, but I got nuthin' in my tool kit.

Aww, shit!

"I'm so sorry, Robyn," Jimmy says, "I don't mean to pressure you. We're working hard to protect you and to find the cowards who attacked you and I just…."

"I know," she says, clearing her throat. "I'm sorry, too. I'm never more than an inch from losing it these days and I'm not sure what I want to do. Or should do. Or can do. It's…it's *everything*, the humiliating texts and emails…

43

the panic attacks blind-siding me several times a day...I can't..." dissolving into tears, shrinking into herself, rolling sideways on the bed, her face to the wall.

I mouth a "let's go," to Mark and Jimmy and we close the bedroom door behind us, traipsing dejectedly downstairs.

Lauren instantly recognizes our body language and runs to the stairs to meet us, Ben trailing a few steps.

"What's wrong? What happened?" Lauren demands.

"She's still overwhelmed with the trauma and conflicting feelings about what to do next," I say. "I'm sure we all agree we shouldn't push her too much. Right now she needs her Mom and maybe, in a few days, she'll have moved on somewhat."

"Or never," Lauren shoots over her shoulder as she sprints up the stairs.

Ben hears everything and silently escorts us to the door.

"Mark will be patrolling the neighborhood tonight," I say. "We'll regroup with you and Lauren later."

The door locks firmly behind us.

Chapter 13

-----JACK-----

The woman answering the doorbell looks very much the widow in black slacks and a dark gray poncho top, no makeup, not even to lessen the dark half-moons under her weary eyes.

"Hello," she says softly, almost as if speaking to herself. The Rev embraces her and the three of us move quietly into a modest living room. He introduces us and we sit, Mrs. Parks on the sofa, her shoulders rounded, The Rev one pillow away from her and I'm in an armchair. The room is from an earlier time, furniture and décor suggesting the 1950s.

"Shirley," The Rev says, "as I mentioned on the phone, Jack needs to ask you some questions about Jackson. Can you handle that?"

She nods, glancing at him.

"Okay then," he says. "Let me know at any point if you're uncomfortable or need a break."

She nods again and turns to me.

"Mrs. Parks," I say. "Thanks for meeting with us. I'm terribly sorry for your loss and we know this is difficult for you."

"I'm ready," she says, straightening her posture.

"In the last few months did your husband seem different in any way, maybe stressed about anything? Perhaps less patient? Or nervous?"

"Not really. You know he had that hand surgery. That wasn't pleasant, the rehab and all, but he was improving. He didn't act strange or different. A little frustrated sometimes. He mainly concentrated on getting himself back to normal and free of the pain that got quite awful before he agreed to have it fixed."

"Did he have pain meds to help him *before* the surgery?"

"Yes, his doctor gave him some strong stuff a few months before Jackson finally said one day: 'Let's get the darn thing fixed.'"

"And after the surgery was the medication changed?"

"No, the doctor told him he could double the dose for a few weeks until he was better. I remember that it went from one pill with breakfast to another one with dinner."

"Did that help?"

"Oh, yes. In a few days after the surgery he could tie his shoes without help. And he wasn't constantly wincing just from using the wrong hand to pick up his coffee mug. Much better.

"But he stopped using the medicine almost right away. The stuff upset his stomach and he said he could tough it out."

"Mrs. Parks, I have to ask, did Mr. Parks gamble, maybe for large amounts?"

"Good gracious, no," she says instantly. "Not at all. I remember once, a few years ago, he mentioned putting $20 in an office pool involving the Super Bowl. I'm not sure exactly how that works but it was unusual enough that he told me about it."

"Other than the damaged hand, was he ill in any way? Any heart problems or diabetes or arthritis? Did he see any doctors in the last year for anything other than his hand?"

"No. I nagged him from time to time about getting an annual physical exam, you know like you read about. He never disagreed, he just didn't do it."

The Rev's been attentively watching her answers.

"Shirley, what do you think happened to Jackson?'

She turns to him but doesn't answer. I think she's holding her breath.

"Oh, J.D., I don't know. I can't at all imagine Jackson committing suicide. He had no reason to do such a horrendous thing and it's something that would have contradicted his entire outlook on life. He had every reason to live. Everyone who knows him likes and admires him. Just in our church alone, his support group is in the hundreds.

"It's a terrible thing to say, but it feels like someone murdered him. But why would anyone do that? And how? I absolutely don't think it was an accident or that he chose to die. Nothing makes any sense."

She pauses and says: "And there's something else that would have kept him from even a stray thought of killing himself."

She's silent again for nearly a minute.

"I feel guilty that I wasn't home when this happened," her voice low and shaky.

"You know I was visiting my sister and son in Atlanta, but I haven't told you why. About two months ago I was diagnosed with ovarian cancer. I didn't even tell Jackson for several weeks, waiting for my doctor to figure out my treatment options. And my prognosis."

"Sweet Jesus," The Rev says, obviously stunned by her revelation. "Shirley, Shirley. You should have told me. You know I'm always here for...."

"Of course I know that," she says without looking at him. "For a while I was trying to absorb and understand what was happening to me. It felt like the right thing to do, even if it wasn't. I just...."

She pulls a tissue from somewhere, dabs her eyes and is silent for a moment.

"He wouldn't have killed himself and left me alone. I absolutely know he wouldn't do that."

She's sobbing now, murmuring nothing I can understand.

Her plate spilleth over.

I get up and go into the kitchen, hoping The Rev can comfort Shirley through her melt-down.

"They've known each other for decades. She needs to dump some of her burden on her unofficial brother-in-law and pastor.

Back in the living room, I sit across from her, leaning forward, my hands on my knees.

"Mrs. Parks," I say. "Thanks for talking with us. When I chatted with others in the last few days, Mr. Parks was universally described as a loving, caring man and a leader at his job and in your church. I wish I'd known him."

Back in my car, we're both silent for a few minutes. Finally I say, "Does her illness prove Jackson Parks didn't commit suicide. Or is it possible that the news knocked him into a deep depression?"

The Rev says, "Someone killed my brother. I don't know why. How on God's earth can that be?"

CHAPTER 14

-----JACK-----

The next morning my cell buzzes while I'm carrying my second coffee to my desk.

"Detective Crocker," The Rev booms, "there's been another death. Possibly a murder and it may be linked to Jackson. Can you come to the church right away?"

"We're heading for the door."

I park among the few cars in the church lot and we find The Rev alone in his office with the door open.

"Oh, good, you're already here. Please close the door."

"Who's dead?" I ask.

"Glen Tarpley. A one-car crash on LBJ freeway near the Galleria. About 10 p.m. yesterday."

"Is Tarpley a member here?"

"No."

"And why do you think it's a murder."

"There was suspicious damage to the car's brake lines."

"How do you know that? This just happened last night," Jimmy says instantly.

"One of our members works in the Dallas Police Impound lot. It's staffed 24/7. When he came to work early this morning he heard a cop and a forensics guy talking about a punctured brake line. And when he processed the paperwork on the car he remembered a long-ago connection between Tarpley and Otis Jefferson."

"I've heard that name but don't remember why," I say. "Who's Otis Jefferson?"

"You probably saw him all over the news a couple of months ago when he was released from prison after 33 years for a crime he didn't commit.

"There was new evidence seriously disputing his conviction. Plus, the District Attorney's office found clear documentation that 33 years ago their office withheld exculpatory evidence. It was obvious that they intentionally railroaded the guy.

"He was on TV with his family rejoicing in his new freedom. He amazed people with his insistence that he forgives everyone from back then and is looking only to the future."

I immediately recall the incredible and tragic story and see Jimmy nodding as well.

"Tarpley was an Assistant District Attorney during the Jefferson trial. He was second chair to the Deputy DA, Carl Weymeyer, who led the prosecution team."

"But how does that link him to your cousin?" I say.

"Jackson was a juror in that 1982 trial. He was the only black juror."

"Holy sh...cow," Jimmy says.

Chapter 15

-----JACK-----

"We've got our hands full, don't we?" I say, late that afternoon, leaning back with my feet on my desk, hoisting a soda can in an indistinct and silent toast to a long day.

Jimmy is pacing around our small office space, apparently not as tired as I am, but he's 15 years younger than his uncle.

"Good grief, Tonto. Is someone killing people from a trial more than 30 years ago? Or is it just a coincidence that two people, out of the many involved back then, may have been murdered?"

"In the same year?" Jimmy says, clearly skeptical. "One coincidence times another coincidence usually equals *highly unlikely*."

"Hey," I say, "maybe it's *not* just this year, maybe other folks involved in that trial have been killed over the 33 years without anyone connecting the dots. If there are any dots.

"We wouldn't be looking into the possibility of a link if one of The Rev's church members hadn't remembered that two recent dead people had briefly crossed paths in a courtroom thirty-some years ago."

"How can we possibly check out everyone who had a role in that trial and what's happened to them since?" Jimmy says. "During the more than 30 years since the trial, it's possible half the people with any connection to that last-century trial have died. I don't think there's an app for that."

"For now," I say, "let's start with the assumption that there *may* be a connection between Tarpley's death and The Rev's cousin's death. We need to talk to this Jefferson guy who just got sprung, plus some of his relatives and friends to see if there's any hint that he or anyone else is taking revenge on people who falsely convicted him."

"That'll take a lot of time," Jimmy says. "Meanwhile, what motivations can we think of for the two murders? If they *are* murders."

I tear off the top sheet of the legal pad I've been doodling on and start a list of possibilities.

"Revenge. Maybe Jefferson is punishing people he blames for wasting 33 years of his life," I say.

"Maybe he's hired someone to kill these people," Jimmy says, "and while he himself publicly rides the high road of *forgiveness,* he's secretly seething at the injustice he's suffered.

"Or maybe friends of Jefferson are avenging their pal."

"Possibly some of his relatives are exacting revenge for the same reason," I say. "Or what if the killer is some random soul with no actual relationship to Jefferson but who became outraged by recent news reports of an innocent man spending 33 years in prison. A colossal injustice."

"Jack, we can't read that many minds," Jimmy says, pushing his chair back and standing up. "This is worse than a needle in a haystack. We don't even know if there is a needle and the line-up of possible haystacks runs to the horizon."

I nod.

"Here's a better idea." I say. "Jackson Parks was the only black person on that 1982 jury. That was unusual back then. It's highly unlikely that he was the jury foreman, although his quiet leadership may have been influential. It was several years later that The Dallas News analyzed the racial makeup of Dallas County juries, proving that the DA's office routinely kept black people off juries.

"That prompted court rulings halting what was then the virtually total rejection of potential black jurors.

"So, why," Jimmy says, "would someone seeking revenge for Otis's conviction kill the only black juror?""

"Maybe someone has been killing other jurors but that hasn't been noticed, I say. "Or maybe the killer blames Jackson Parks for not blocking the conviction. It only takes one holdout.

"Let's find names of all the jurors and see where each one is now; retired, playing golf, greeters at Walmart. Or dead."

"That's doable," he says. "Let's see what we can get, but we may need some help if we want to get all of that done anytime soon."

"And lots of dumb luck," I add.

CHAPTER 16

-----JACK-----

Two hours later, shortly before noon, I'm parking in front of the Jefferson family house and heading for the front door of the modest, split-level home in a neighborhood of mature trees and similar houses.

A balding, late middle-aged black man answers the doorbell.

"Mr. Crocker I presume," he says in a surprisingly soft voice, offers his hand, gently guiding me inside to a living room over-loaded with photographs, more than half of them black-and-white prints from a long-ago era, on every flat surface. Small end-tables flank the large flowery sofa and three matching upholstered chairs, all more or less aimed at a large, wall-mounted, flat-panel television screen.

Not very tall, thin, ordinary. Looks more like a CPA than a guy who's spent 33 years in prison.

He gestures to one of the chairs, sits in another, adjusts rimless glasses and says: "Would you like some ice tea? Coffee? Soda?"

"Tea would be great. Thanks for agreeing to see me."

"If The Rev asks, I can't refuse. I didn't know him growing up but he's ministered to my family while I was gone. I've been to his church and he has come by our house a couple of times since I got back. He has quite a way about him."

A woman, probably Mrs. Jefferson, appears in the archway to the kitchen. A ruffled apron with a yellow rose over her chest and old-fashioned curls framing her face makes her look a generation older than she probably is.

"I'll bring the tea in a minute."

Listening just out of sight.

"Mavis," her husband says, "first meet Mr. Crocker."

She comes in with more of a confident CEO stride than her housfrau first impression.

As she leaves, Jefferson nods toward the big screen where CNN has convened an eight-expert panel on something that apparently needs discussing by multiple talking heads, sometimes simultaneously.

"That TV is unbelievably amazing to someone who's never before seen anything like that. And in someone's home. Thirty-three years ago, TV screens were a lot smaller, not to mention fuzzier. And prison TVs still weigh a ton."

"So a few weeks ago, when you were released, you could watch yourself up there, bigger than life with every pore visible."

"Indeed," he says, "not much fun, seeing this old face up close in razor-sharp, high-def, I believe it's called."

"I've had a little of 'been there, seen that,'" I said.

"The Rev told me about you and your partner rescuing your son from kidnappers and killers. I can't imagine what you and your family went through. Astounding."

"Both of our families have experienced some big-time trauma," I say. "How are you adjusting?"

"Pretty well. You can't imagine how glorious it feels to be able to touch my wife and family after 33 years with glass always between us. To me, a hug is miraculous. I'm still not accustomed to being allowed to go to a restaurant and order anything I want. I'm incredibly grateful."

"And, I imagine, angry at what was taken from you and your family?"

"Young man, if I thought that way I'd be shriveled up and probably dead instead of feeling that I'm where I belong and enjoying what I have."

"Aren't you at least a tiny bit bitter?"

"If I were bitter, it would damage only me. I must live in the present, not in the irretrievable past."

"Yes, but..."

"No buts," he says. "I now have a future that I can somewhat control and participate in. I refuse to live in the *'if only'* world that's gone forever."

"You're a much better person than I think I would be under the circumstances," I say.

"He's a good and decent man," Mrs. Jefferson says as she delivers two frosty glass tumblers of tea. "He always has been that way, no matter what was happening to him."

She leaves the room but I suspect she's lurking in the hallway.

"She's the miracle woman who has kept our family together through all these years," he says.

"Basically a single parent for 33 years, she's worked her way up the ladder at Kroger. She's now the assistant manager. She financed and steered our daughter, Roberta, through North Texas University. Roberta and her daughter, Angel, have lived in this very house their entire lives. Mavis made this old house into our middle-class version of a Jefferson family compound. And it's all due to her innate toughness and self-confidence."

"Very impressive," I say. "You're a lucky man."

Unbelievably stupid. Lucky hardly describes someone wrongly imprisoned for more than three decades.

I watch him stifle a smile at my clumsy word choice.

"I'm sorry. I didn't mean..."

"I understand, Mr. Crocker, but you're right. I have been lucky...even though some of it has been bad-luck," he laughs. "But it's been mostly good-luck so far this year."

"You certainly deserve anything good that comes your way," I say.

"You know, what happened to me actually isn't unusual. It literally happens fairly frequently, much more often than ordinary people know or understand. I'm just one of 325 innocent people freed by new or illegally withheld evidence in the U.S. since 1992."

"Mr. Jefferson, I'm embarrassed to say that I've never focused on this issue. I recall a few news stories from time to time about someone being freed from prison thanks to new evidence or discovery of a corrupt, immoral prosecutor, but I had not realized it's been that many. Really? That many cases?"

"Indeed," he says. "It's always been an unjust system and it still is. People in minority communities have always known that. And it is still happening today. Don't forget that the 325 people freed from prison only includes those who could *prove* they were innocent. There must be hundreds more trapped in cells for years who shouldn't be there. And they will never be free.

"Now, what is it that you want to discuss with me? The Rev just told me it had something to do with the death of an Assistant DA from my trial. Someone named Tarpley. Is that correct?"

"Mr. Jefferson, I have a difficult question to ask you. Please understand that it's something that must be asked and probably will be asked again by the police.

"You want to know if I killed Mr. Tarpley?"

"Yes."

"No. I did not," he says as calmly as if I'd asked if he wanted cream in his coffee. "I have no need for revenge. As I've already told you, I'm living in the present and focusing on the future. I've truly forgiven everyone involved all those years ago and I don't want to think about that period."

"Have you forgiven Jackson Parks?"

"Who's that? I don't know anyone by that name."

"He was a juror during your trial."

"I don't think I ever heard names of any jurors. Never even thought about who they were. They were just the jury."

"He was the only black juror."

"Oh, I remember that. That was definitely unusual back then. What about him?"

"He may have been murdered a few days ago."

His eyes widened. He locked eyes with me for a long moment.

"God in Heaven, what does that mean? Surely no one suspects me of murdering either or both of them."

"The police have no choice but to investigate those possibilities."

He looks pensive, distracted from our conversation, pondering.

"I guess I understand that, but I'm not pleased to have my newly restored reputation crapped on. Not to mention being on a police *murder suspect* list again.

"I wasn't guilty thirty-some years ago."

He hesitates, draws a deep breath. And another

"And I'm not guilty now!"

CHAPTER 17

-----JACK-----

That evening my family seems restored as if the last, two-plus years never happened.

Except that our two kids have clearly aged, Carli now 13 and Erik, 11, even though my almost ex-wife, Crystal, hasn't.

I don't want to calculate how old I am. I know it's more than my chronological 42 years and might be more appropriately expressed in dog years.

The four of us are almost directly behind home plate watching the Texas Rangers struggle to break a three-game losing streak.

But hey, it's the ball park and a new season and it's mashing my nostalgia button with the crisp smacks of 90 mile-per-hour baseballs colliding with bats and triggering undulating waves of cheers and boos and dashed hopes when a Ranger hits a long fly ball that fails to clear the left field fence.

Erik and Carli are finishing off $8 hotdogs while Crystal and I are sharing crispy chips covered in faux cheese, also known as $12 nachos.

I like to imagine that the two of us dining from the same paper tray is a significant change in our seriously wounded marriage, but this is probably wishful thinking. Crystal hasn't actively pursued the divorce she filed for almost two years ago, but she hasn't dropped it, either. And we haven't lived under the same roof since then, although now most weekends revolve around family-oriented activities. Those times feel good but also underline for me what I'm missing every day and night.

She hasn't invited me back into the home we shared for 15 years, before my disintegration. I don't know if that thought has even crossed her mind but every single day I hope that it will and that somehow we'll recreate what we once had. Or at least figure out how to dim the spotlight on those missteps and struggles so we can move toward being a complete family again.

It feels like I'm auditioning for my former life. The life I screwed up. I wonder if I can get a new life more successful than the last one.

Chapter 18

-----JACK-----

At Olga's, Heidi brightens our day with her smile, takes our orders and leaves.

I immediately ask Jimmy: "What do you know about the Innocence Project?"

"Heard of it. Basically a non-profit that tries to get wrongfully convicted inmates out of prison."

"Yeah, that's what they've been doing since 1992. Founded by Barry Scheck and Peter Neufeld, two of O.J.'s lawyers.

"The Project's lawyers and researchers help free people like Otis, although they weren't involved in his case. A local law firm signed on as a pro bono project after multiple requests from Otis's daughter, Roberta.

"I've only been dimly aware over the past few years as these cases came to light but today, after seeing and listening to Otis and understanding what he has suffered, I sat in my car outside his house for several minutes, shaking with anger.

"I came back to the office to research some local and national statistics. When I show you the unbelievable details you'll be outraged, too."

Tonto nods.

"Since 2001, Dallas County has the highest number of exonerations of wrongly convicted felons in the entire United States," I say.

"When the county elected its first black District Attorney in 2001, he created a Conviction Integrity Unit to look into past cases. Already, at least 25 convicts from Dallas County have been freed based on new evidence such as DNA testing that wasn't available years ago. Twenty-five exonerations from just *one* county. At least 325 nation-wide."

"Hard to believe," Jimmy says as Heidi brings our ice teas.

"With you guys, nothing is hard to believe," she says with a grin and a near-pirouette back to the kitchen.

"Here and around the country, an avalanche of evidence is proving egregious prosecutorial misconduct over many decades. I'm really furious after reading some of the cases and what the innocent convicts went through and about the widespread withholding of evidence that could have cleared a defendant, or at least created more than reasonable doubt. Not to mention flat-out lying by prosecutors.

"Otis is just the most-recent exoneree."

"I had no idea things were that bad," Jimmy says. . You were in Iraq or Afghanistan when most of these cases began hitting the news."

Heidi brings our food and as she leaves Jimmy is still staring at me with raised eyebrows.

"Those stats have been in the paper and on TV in bits and pieces as case after case has surfaced. Many of the false convictions in Dallas County happened during the reign of a long-time District Attorney who was in office as far back as the 1963 JFK assassination and the murder of Lee Harvey Oswald. That old DA reportedly operated under the informal motto that any suspect—but particularly black suspects, might not be guilty of the current charge but they were absolutely certain that the guy had been guilty of something, sometime, somewhere.

"It's crystal clear that hundreds of convictions were travesties. Some obtained with false confessions or by planting jail snitches who obviously lied under oath to get softer sentences for their own crimes. Can you imagine how many victims died alone in prison or whose lives were ruined by felony convictions they didn't deserve? Or how many were wrongly executed? Texas has always been an enthusiastic death-penalty state."

I cut a slice of Ukrainian sausage and point my fork at Jimmy.

"In 2007, a father of two was *executed* after two of his kids died in a fire that was ruled arson. It's a virtual certainty that the arson testimony was wrong and the father was killed by the state of Texas while maintaining his innocence."

"Jesus, Jack, I think everyone knows stuff like that probably happens once in a while, but 325 proven cases nationwide and 24 right here in Dallas County? Un-friggin-believable. That's unconscionable. I may sign up for volunteer duty with the people working on these cases.

"But right now, is any of this relevant to solving Jackson Parks' death?

"Obviously it has nothing to do with our other major case; nailing the vicious rapists of a young woman who wasn't born when Otis Jefferson was convicted. We have a ton of manure on our hands already."

"I agree," I say. "Robyn's case is unrelated. But the culture of false convictions may contribute in some way to finding out whether or not someone has killed two people involved in a corrupt trial three decades ago.

"Just so you keep your outrage simmering, a Tulsa woman named Michelle Murphy was convicted in 1995 of brutally stabbing her 15-week-baby to death.

"After 19 years in prison, DNA testing contradicted a prosecutor's *false* testimony and proved an unidentified male's blood had been found at the scene and she was eventually released."

"Okay," he says, spearing a dumpling.... I'll stay pissed off for the foreseeable future but right now I'm mainly focused on sending a vicious rapist or two to prison."

CHAPTER 19

-----JIMMY-----

I'm not much of a Costco shopper. Way too much stuff to wade through to find what I need and always in package sizes that require purchasing a life-time supply of ibuprophen or salad dressing.

Actually, I'm not much of any kind of shopper. Like most guys I know, I'm a *buyer*. When I want or need something I find out where it is, go there, park, buy it and get outta Dodge or Walmart or Ace Hardware.

But today Jack asked me to pick up one of those single-serve coffee ma-chines to replace the permanently stained, antique pot we inherited with our rented office. I'm in Small Appliances spending eight seconds choosing black or red when I see her.

Marsha!

She spots me at the same time and starts walking down the aisle, looking at me.

On their own, my legs are taking me toward her. It's not one of those slow-motion, ultra-romantic-fantasy things in movies or commercials but it sorta feels like that. I haven't seen her in months but I've thought about her every day.

In a few steps we almost collide into an awkward public-place hug.

"Gosh, it's so good to see you," she says. "I've wondered how you're do-ing since you and Jack saved my life."

She notices the coffee maker box under my arm.

"Oh, is that for me?" she laughs in her special way. "I think I'd rather have flowers."

Flowers!

"I can do that," I grin. "Please hold this box while I speed dial my florist. I think she'll deliver to Costco."

We both laugh and I simultaneously realize I have no clue what to say next. It's not like we were ever romantically involved...except in my mind... when Jack and I were trying to protect her from an abusive ex-husband and later from a professional killer.

She says, "Are you still living with Jack in that cute little house in Garland?"

"Yeah, but Jack wants to dump me. He and Crystal are spending lots of time together with the kids and Jack is desperately hoping she will invite him back home."

"I hope that happens for them," Marsha says. "When all the excitement ended back in December I thought maybe they'd get back together."

"Yeah," Mr. Silver Tongue says. "Me, too."

"I wasn't around Crystal much," she says, "but it seemed obvious to me that she still loved Jack but had been disappointed enough times that she was extremely wary."

About an awkward silence, she says, "Well, it really is good to see you. Maybe we'll run into each other again sometime. I come here often."

"I think this is where I ask, 'What's your astrological sign?'"

Her laugh tingles again.

"Let's have coffee or lunch or something, sometime," she says.

"That's by far the best idea I've heard today."

I glance at my watch.

"How about now? It's almost noon."

She hesitates a couple of long seconds.

"Sounds good," she says. "Costco's *Fine Diner* is right over there," nodding toward clusters of plastic tables and chairs.

We pause to study a garish lighted menu board over a walk-up counter.

"What'll you have?" I ask.

"Number 3, the hotdog and Diet Coke."

"Okay, but you realize the minimum order is eight."

Back at the office, I find Jack holding a grilled-cheese sandwich in one hand while punching his keyboard with one finger.

"Hey, you got the new caffeine-delivery machine. And in red. Let's try some samples."

"I had lunch with Marsha," I say, heading for the supply room with the machine.

Jack instantly swivels his chair toward me fast enough to risk whiplash, his face bright with delight.

"You called her for a lunch date?"

"Just ran into each other at Costco."

"And...?"

"And what?"

"And then what happened? Come on. I need all the details."

"I told you the details," I say. "Everything except that we had hotdogs at the Costco lunch counter."

"Your suaveness is at a new, all-time low, somewhere deep in negative numbers. Are you going to see her again, maybe like an actual date?"

"Unless she gets a restraining order."

CHAPTER 20

-----JIMMY-----

I recognize Ashley Scanlon coming through the café door from photographs in Robyn's bedroom. I raise my hand to catch her attention and she nods and joins me in the booth.

"Thanks for coming, Miss Scanlon."

"You said it was important to help Robyn," she says," shifting large sunglasses to the top of her head and brushing stray strands of long, dark hair behind her ear, her attractive, angular face quizzical.

"How can that be? How can I possibly help her?"

"As Robyn's mom explained on the phone, my partner and I are working for Robyn's parents. They want to find whoever attacked her. They hope that might help her recover from the trauma."

A waitress brings menus but Ashley says, "Triple-shot cappuccino," and I say "same."

We stay silent for a minute, both self-consciously glancing around the room, at the front windows and at our table top, until I point out the mid-morning sunshine coming through the window.

Awkward!

"I don't think I can help you," she says, as the coffee arrives. "I wish I could, but she hasn't told me much. Well, nothing really. I've only seen her once, the day after it happened. I was just there because her mom called me to help comfort Robyn, not to pry into what happened.

"Since then she hasn't responded to any of my emails, calls or tweets. Her mom says Robyn's basically hiding out in her bedroom. She may tell me more sometime but she hasn't yet. And I'm not going to put more pressure on her. When she's ready, she'll probably tell me more. Or not."

"I understand," I say. "Did she say anything that might indicate she was drunk? Or drugged?"

"Jesus," she barks, instantly angry. "What part of 'she told me *nothing*' is too hard for you to understand? Nothing means nothing!"

We both glance around the room. No one's looking at us, but I don't know if anyone heard her and might be trying to listen.

"I'm sorry," I say. "Her parents and my partner and I are desperate to find the smallest particle of information to pursue. I didn't mean to imply I didn't believe you. Sometimes people remember something...'

"How about this," she says. "If I say I *don't know*, that's the truth. And if I *know* something, but don't want to tell you, I'll say that. Okay?" She stands up and heads for the street.

"Yeah. I get it," I say to her retreating back.

CHAPTER 21

-----JACK-----

"The bastards are after Robyn again," Lauren says the instant she opens her front door, her voice a mixture of outrage and despair.

Jimmy and I are at the Rogers' house because Robyn has unexpectedly agreed, somewhat reluctantly, to meet with us for a second time. We hope to build some more trust with her and convince her to share more details of the attack she'd suffered; mostly who the attackers were and where it happened.

We're barely inside when Lauren gestures us to the kitchen and continues in a whisper that gradually rises in volume and velocity.

"Robyn told me that they're sending her those disgusting photos and videos again. Plus there are more vicious taunts. Some are apparently new bullies and strangers, jumping in and she's devastated again and..."

"Whoa, Lauren, that's horrendous but you need to take some deep breaths. You're Robyn's anchor. She looks to you for support and if you're hyperventilating it doesn't help her. Or you."

"I don't want your advice," she snaps. "I want you guys to get these vile predators out of my daughter's life. If you think I'm over-reacting, wait till Ben finds out what's happening. He's already paranoid about all of this. He'll hit the nuclear button and God only knows what he'll do."

"We understand," Jimmy says. "Will Robyn still talk with us after what's happened this morning?"

She sighs. "I don't know. She said she would but that might have changed." I'll go upstairs and ask her. Stay here."

Ten minutes later she returns looking even more haggard and I expect the worst but she says: "Robyn wants all of us to talk before her father finds out about these disgusting new attacks."

In the bedroom, Lauren and Robyn perch side-by-side on the edge of the bed.

"We understand the creeps who invaded your life are still taunting you," I say, hoping Robyn will respond. Her face displays the toll the disgusting bullies have inflicted.

"Yes," Robyn says softly. "And others have joined in. Everyone in the world apparently has *seen* me getting raped. Photos and video. And apparently a bunch of perverts in their parent's basement have enjoyed watching and want to judge me," her face scrunching up and darkening.

I see Lauren tighten the one-arm hug she's held Robyn in since they sat. She says: "Oh, sweetheart, don't worry about those..."

"Stop it, Mom. I'm not *worried*, I'm *reliving*. And I'm learning what it feels like to be prey for every disgusting bully with a laptop."

"None of this is your fault," Jimmy says. "These people are sending messages from under the slime pits where they live. They're scum, not worthy of an ounce of your attention."

"No one can make them stop," Robyn says. "And what they've already done can't be erased even if we could put a gun to their heads. And everyone we know has probably already seen the pornographic crap posted by these monsters."

Jimmy says, "How about you turn off your phone and PC for a while and focus on getting on with your life. Get some exercise and sunshine. Take a walk with your Mom. Do you play tennis? Or swim? Jog? Buy some new clothes; anything to move on down the road every day."

Good advice. Come on. Take even one step.

No one speaks and now Robyn startles all of us by screaming, "I can't ignore what's happening." She slumps backward on the bed, sobbing and mumbling, "No one will ever see the real me again. For the rest of my life I'll always be that person everyone saw being raped!"

Lauren is on her feet, gesturing wildly to Jimmy and me to leave the room. She stretches out, putting Robyn in a full-body, Momma Bear hug.

Back in the car, Jimmy says: "Jesus, what kind of sub-humans do crazy, sickening stuff like that to somebody?"

"Ignorant, cowardly losers, predators and sociopaths."

CHAPTER 22

-----JACK-----

Early the next morning, Lauren is hysterical on my cell, her words crammed together without punctuation. I tell her to "slow down and tell me that again."

"Robyn's gone! She's disappeared!" she shouts, putting not even a half-second between each word.

I hear only sobbing now, muffled as if she's dropped the phone. I hold my breath and get up from my desk chair.

Finally she gasps, "I don't know where she is. I'm deathly afraid she might do something horrible. She was so sad this morning. And now she's vanished."

"I'm on the way," I tell her. "Have you called Ashley Scanlon to see if she's heard from Robyn or knows where she is?"

"No. I called you first."

I turn off our "OPEN" sign and lock the door behind me, still holding the phone to my ear, striding to my car.

"I'll be there in 15 minutes. Have you told Ben?"

"No. He's at the office. He'll go ape shit and start calling the FBI and the White House and...."

"I'm in the car now. Who else would Robyn possibly contact or go to? Any possibilities at all? One of her high school friends? Has she mentioned anyone from her short time on campus? Any names come to mind?"

"No."

"I'll be at your house in a few minutes. Meanwhile I'll call Jimmy and ask him to locate Ashley. He talked to her the other day. Maybe she and Robyn are together."

I hang up and order Siri to "Call Tonto."

"Where are you?" I bark the instant he answers knowing he'll recognize my emergency voice.

"Whatya need?"

"Robyn's missing. Very depressed this morning. Find Ashley Scanlon and see if she knows where Robyn is or has any idea where she might be. I'm almost to the Rogers' house. Lauren's melting down."

"I'm talking to folks at The Rev's church. I'll drop that and get on Ashley's trail and call you A-sap."

CHAPTER 23

-----JACK-----

Lauren is ten years older than yesterday. She wordlessly gestures me inside. Her bare legs and feet show under a dark blue, tightly belted, terry-cloth robe. I follow her to the kitchen where the aroma of freshly brewed coffee fills the room.

Still not speaking, she holds up two mugs and I nod. She fills them both, puts them on the counter and slumps onto a tall barstool, staring at the refrigerator with glazed, unseeing eyes.

"She's gone, Jack. She slipped out while I was in the shower."

Her tone is so flat, far from her hysterical voice when she called that I wonder if she's taken an anti-depressant. I sit next to her trying to find something comforting to say. Instead, I take a sip from my mug and mutter: "Have you called Ben?"

"Yes. He'll be here in a few minutes if he isn't arrested for flying too fast and low on North Central Expressway. He shouted something at me that ended with, 'You stupid bitch,' and hung up."

"When he gets here, I'll tell him Jimmy's searching for Ashley Scanlon and will call as soon as he's located her. She may know where Robyn is. What did she say or do that makes you think she might be suicidal?"

"This morning when I checked to see if she was awake she was staring into space, looking like a catatonic rag doll, no energy, mostly not acknowledging that I was there. I tried to convince her to talk with you and your partner again but she refused. I suggested she invite Ashley over, hoping a visit might be helpful. Same reaction. She muttered, 'Nothing and no one can help me,' while hugging her pillow.

"I finally told her I'd bring some her some breakfast but when I did she wasn't here. I almost fell down the stairs running to look in the garage. Her car is gone.

"I've been calling her cell about every 30 seconds but it keeps going to voice mail."

"What was she wearing?"

"Oh, lord, she may still be in her pajamas."

"What kind of car is she driving? Do you have the plate number?"

"Why? Arc you going to look for her car?"

"If we're convinced she's in danger of harming herself I'll contact a Dallas police lieutenant I know and see if he can put out a regional APB on her and her car, although she hasn't been kidnapped. She just went somewhere. But maybe someone...."

We hear the front door open and close with a crash and footsteps running down the hallway toward us.

Ben detonates into the kitchen like a flash-bang grenade, yelling at Lauren, ignoring me. His tie hangs loosely over a rumpled white shirt, his suit jacket clasped in one hand, his other arm waving angrily.

"For God's sake, how could you just let her leave?"

He leans into Lauren's face as if he might bite her. "I told you to watch her every damn minute! Jesus, Lauren, can't you even do a simple thing like that while I'm gone?"

His flaming face is so contorted I hardly recognize him.

"Ben," I say as calmly as I can manage despite the fact that I'd prefer to bloody his face with a quick jab, but I'm trying to divert him from Lauren and re-set his thermostat to below boiling.

"Ben, Jimmy is trying to contact Ashley Scanlon Robyn may be with her or at least she may know where Robyn is. He'll...."

"Well, that's just *super*," he says, sarcasm poisoning the air in the room, his nose still a few inches from Lauren whose eyes remain closed, her chin on her chest.

"Meanwhile my daughter's depressed and scared and possibly suicidal and now she's missing because her *mother* is incapable of keeping her in sight at all times, the way I told her. What a fuck-up."

Last chance asshole.

"Ben," I try again, putting a sharper edge in my voice. "Let's concentrate all our energy on finding Robyn and getting her safely home. Yelling doesn't help anyone and you're close to having a stroke."

He shifts slightly away from Lauren and looks directly at me for the first time. His eyes are flashing warnings and I'm bracing for a physical attack, half hoping he'll take a swing at me so I can justify grabbing his expensive tie and putting him on the kitchen floor.

I see Lauren's head move upward but I'm locked in a High Noon stare with her husband.

Don't blink!

Ben's eyes close, his face looks as if his head is exploding inside his skull. Then he collapses, sobbing and cursing and bashing his fists on the floor, like a frustrated toddler.

Lauren slides off her stool and covers him with her body, murmuring soothing sounds to the creature who cruelly verbally abused her only seconds before.

Chapter 24

-----JACK-----

I blow out my cheeks and inhale and exhale several chests-full of air, my body shaking with anger and a surging adrenalin overdose.

The phone vibrates in my pants.

"Whatcha got?" I demand.

"I'm with Ashley at *The Coffee Shack* on campus," Jimmy says. "I may have a lead on Robyn but it's far from solid. Can you try to follow up by phone while I keep pushing Ashley to recall anything else that might be useful?"

"Sure, what?"

"Ashley says that when she visited Robyn right after the attack she told her about a woman she knows who was raped under similar circumstances about two years ago. The victim cratered for a while, didn't go to the cops, hid out at her mother's home, was embarrassed and depressed.

"But, and this is the good part, she fought her way out of that and for about eight months now has been volunteering at a rape crisis center in Richardson. She may be exactly what Robyn needs. Maybe she's contacted that person and...."

"What's her name and phone," I cut in.

"Pamela Swann." he says, spelling her last name and giving me cell and land-line numbers.

"I'll get right on it. I'm with the Rogers right now. Call if you find anything more."

"I need to make some calls," I tell Lauren and Ben as I disconnect. "I'll be in the living room."

"What has Jimmy found?" Lauren says, still massaging Ben's shoulders.

"No time. Gotta go. I'll fill you in when we have more," already punching in Pamela Swann's home number.

Twelve rings without an answer. I try Swann's cell phone.

On the eighth ring a woman says a cautious "Hello."

"Is this Pamela?" I say. "Pamela Swann?"

"Who's asking?"

"Jack Crocker. I'm a private investigator. My partner and I are working for Robyn Rogers' parents. She's missing and they're desperate to find her. Her best friend, Ashley Scanlon, told her about you, and about your experience. Robyn may want to talk with you. She recently had a similar event in her life. She really *needs* to talk to you. Or someone like you."

"Why are you calling me? I don't know anyone with either of those names."

"Please," I say. "Her parents need to know if she's safe."

"If I'm contacted by this person and if it seems appropriate, I'll inform you," she says.

I give her my cell number and she's gone.

Back in the kitchen, Ben is at the breakfast table holding his head with both hands, his eyes looking out at the backyard, a coffee mug between his elbows. He straightens enough to see me when Lauren says: "What did you find out? Do you know where Robyn is? Is she safe? Can we go get her?"

"Nothing that definite. Ashley apparently told Robyn about a woman who was assaulted a couple a years ago. She staggered for a while, got through the worst and now has a job *and* volunteers at a rape crisis center.

"I called the woman who says she's never heard of Robyn or Ashley but will let us know if Robyn contacts her.

"Jimmy is still hoping to get other possibilities from Ashley. He'll call with updates. Meanwhile, can either of you think of *anyone* Robyn was at all friendly with from high school or even any names she's mentioned since starting her freshman year? Anyone, no matter how remote?"

I'm talking to them as if Ben hasn't just had a border-line psychotic episode right in front of his wife and me.

Lauren sits next to Ben and I see them talking but I can't hear anything. Then Ben glances at me.

"I'm sorry for going off like that. I'm panicked and scared and..."

"I understand," I lie. "Can you come up with any names? Lauren, are there parents of anyone Robyn knows that you can call to see if Robyn's with them. Or if she's been in touch with anyone?"

"Maybe a few," she says. "I would have done that earlier but I was frightened and discombobulated by her disappearance."

I leave them and call Jimmy from the living room.

"Any good news?" he answers.

I fill him in on my brief conversation with Pamela Swann.

"A dead-end?"

"Looks like it," I say. "Ask Ashley if she has an address for Swann. I'm thinking about trying to talk to her in person. Better than spinning my wheels here. And ask Ashley how she knows Swann. She claimed she'd never heard of Ashley."

I hear him talking in the background, then he's back.

"She doesn't actually *know* Swann. She knows *of* her. Actually saw her once. Apparently Swann spoke at a rape prevention presentation at Ashley's sorority several months ago. Ashley kept Swann's card and remembered her story when visiting Robyn after the rape. There's no address on the card."

"I'll Google her and check cross-indexes to see if I can find her. Are you water-boarding Ashley or just using your natural charms?"

Dial tone.

CHAPTER 25

-----JACK-----

I ask Google about 'Pamela Swann' but my phone interrupts.

"This is Pamela Swann and we have a crisis. Robyn Rogers is here and she's deteriorating. I think she needs emergency hospital care."

"Where are you? What's the nearest hospital?"

"Baylor Medical Center on Gaston," she says. "I'm taking her there immediately. It's about 10 minutes from here."

"Her parents and I will meet you there. Go!"

"We're in the car."

In the kitchen I bark orders at the Rogers like the Army sergeant I once was.

"Let's go. Robyn's on the way to the Baylor Hospital branch on Gaston. Follow me there. She's with the Swann woman I told you about. I'll call Jimmy from the car. Maybe he'll bring Ashley, too. Go now, but stay behind me. No speeding. Let's get everyone there in one piece."

I'm out the front door starting my car at the curb when I see the Rogers Cadillac backing rapidly down the driveway.

Ben tailgates me so closely that I can't see his grill. I stop looking in the mirror and concentrate on the half-dozen turns needed on the 15-minute drive to the hospital.

I call Jimmy to tell him where to meet us.

At Baylor, Ben, Lauren and I jog toward the emergency entrance, Lauren still in her robe, having added only slippers. A burgundy Volvo is abandoned under the canopy, the motor running and both doors wide open.

Ten feet inside, a tall woman in a dark-gray business suit is gesturing angrily at a short Hispanic woman in green scrubs.

"Her parents are on the way," the tall brunette says heatedly but not raising her voice. "They'll be here momentarily but she needs attention right now."

"She's being examined," the other woman says. "Calm down. I just want you to stay here until we sort out who's related to whom and who's authorized to do the admittance paperwork. You say you're not family, but you're the only contact person we've got at the moment. Please move your car to the visitor's parking lot and stay in the waiting room while we do our jobs."

A siren-blasting ambulance pulls up outside and staffers are darting through the doors.

"Miss Swann," I say as soon as I'm close enough to be heard. "Are you Pamela Swann?"

She nods and immediately Ben and Lauren surround her and are peppering her with questions, talking over each other.

"Where is she? Why did you bring her here? Is she sick? Was she injured? What happened? What did she say?"

Swann looks stricken, tries to step away from them but they move with her, Ben well within her comfort zone.

She straightens her back, flashes them a time-out sign and when they briefly shut up, she says firmly: "I must move my car. I'll meet you all in the waiting room."

Invoking my inner sheep-dog, I herd Lauren and Ben into an adjacent room where three small family groups are scattered over a large space apparently sound-proofed from the organized chaos in the emergency entrance, the sudden silence almost funereal.

Ben and Lauren go to an empty far corner where two chairs and a pair of sofas surround a low table. They're still arguing, Ben in an angry tone but more quietly now. Lauren's body seems more assertive, each apparently asking the other questions neither can answer.

I flick another glance at the door, looking for Swann.

I hope she's coming back and didn't jump in her Volvo, lock the doors and flee.

My cell vibrates and I recognize my sister's number.

"Where the hell are you," Carole demands. "Are you standing me up for lunch again?"

"Shit," I explain, moving away from Ben and Lauren. "Sorry, I'm at Baylor Medical Center and…."

"You had an accident? Are you sick? What hap…."

"Hey, Sis, calm down. Remember that assault case I mentioned the other day? The victim vanished this morning. Jimmy and I found her. She's semi-conscious and we're at Baylor while the emergency doctors try to find out what's wrong. I forgot about our lunch…."

"Never mind, I'm in Smitty's parking lot waiting for you, less than a mile away. I'll see you in a few minutes."

"Thanks, but that's not necessary, we…." I say to a dead phone.

Pamela Swann comes through the emergency room entrance, surveys the room and heads for Ben and Lauren in the corner. I join them and seemingly within minutes I see Carole striding toward us and I get up to intercept her.

"What happened?" she whispers, shifting back to her years as a nurse.

"The victim was with a volunteer rape counselor, became semi-conscious and was rushed here. "Those are her parents in the corner over there. No info yet from the medical staff."

"I didn't know her parents were here," she says. "I was concerned that you and Jimmy were the only ones with her in the Emergency Room. I was hoping I might know at least one doctor on duty who could be helpful."

I see Jimmy and Ashley coming toward us from a hallway door to our right and now

Halleluiah!

When we're all together I quickly introduce Carole as my sister and a long-time Registered Nurse, probably leaving the impression that she was still on staff. As soon as everyone is introduced and seated, Ben looms over Swann, pointing a finger in her face.

"What happened to my daughter?" he demands. "Why did you bring her here? When…."

"Wait," I say with as much authority as I can muster. "One question at a time. Miss Swann, what caused you to believe Robyn needed medical help?"

Ben swivels, his face flashing a death threat toward me but Swann interrupts, focusing on Lauren as if they are the only two people in the room.

"Robyn called me out of the blue and said she knew of my experiences and she wanted to talk to someone who could understand what she was going through. She sounded confused and desperate and I hadn't left for work yet so I told her how to get to my apartment. She arrived a few minutes before Mr. Crocker called and at that time I didn't have enough information from her to reveal that she was with me. She was in pajamas when she arrived, but had some clothes and shoes in a book bag."

She turns to me. "For all I knew then, you might have been the *problem*, maybe the person who attacked her. So I lied."

"Yeah, yeah, yeah," Ben interjects, finally sitting on the sofa, still frustrated but slightly less furious. "*How* is she? *Why* is she in an emergency room?"

Swann glances at him, scans the rest of us and again looks at Lauren.

"She showed some signs of serious depression, but at first I thought she might be on medications of some kind. She began talking almost inaudibly in short sentences with long gaps in between. She was lethargic and made no eye contact.

"From her fragmented sentences I began connecting snippets about a campus rape, possibly very recent. And references to a young woman, possibly drunk or drugged. But shortly after Mr. Crocker called, her eyelids began intermittingly fluttering. That worsened and I feared she was in some sort of crisis so I drove her here."

"What did the doctors say when you got here?" Lauren said.

"Nothing. One immediately saw that Robyn was fading in and out, asked me a couple of questions and rolled her down the hallway.

"A staff person asked who I was and when I said 'A friend and her parents are on the way,' she told me to move my car and wait."

"Lauren or Ben," I say, looking only at Lauren, "one of you needs to deal with the paperwork plus let the staff know who to update on Robyn's condition. And where you and Ben are."

"I'll handle that," Lauren says.

She's instantly up on slippered feet and retightening her robe's belt for the third time. The rest of us wait silently as she pads to the far door.

"Whoever committed this crime is going to pay big time," Ben mutters to no one in particular.

"I'm sort of an outsider here," Swann says softly, "but I suggest we concentrate on what's best for Robyn."

"Miss Swann," Ben says leaning toward her, "do you think Robyn is suicidal?"

"I don't know," she says. "I'm not a doctor, but unless she's on a medication that's making her almost comatose, she's clearly low-functional right now. Maybe the medical folks will tell us something soon."

"ER Docs are just quick-fix guys," Ben says. "She needs more than a Band-Aid, two aspirins and a pat on the back."

He stands and points at me.

"I've got two things that need doing right away. One, I'm going to get Robyn out of here and into the best place with specialists in trauma patients."

"Where?" I say. "You already have plans?"

"I'll make some calls. I want Robyn in a safe place with experts. So that's what's going to happen.

"And two, I'm going to nail whoever did this, so help me, God."

He points at me again.

"I want you guys to get rolling and find the filthy vermin who raped Robyn."

Lauren reappears, a fist clutching a clipboard of forms to complete. She sits on a sofa next to Jimmy.

"The nurse says one of the doctors will update us soon."

"That'll just be a truck-load of bullshit and blah, blah, blah," Ben says. "We're getting her out of here as soon as I find a place that specializes in this kind of problem. I'll make some calls over there," nodding toward chairs about 20 feet away, "and get some recommendations."

"What are you talking about?" Lauren says sharply. "Robyn's going home with us. We'll take care of...."

Ben says, "She needs more than us watching her every minute while she's getting worse, not better. And your watching skills aren't worth spit."

"We'll hire someone with the right *skills* to come to the house," Lauran insists. "I've already been planning to do that. We're definitely *not* shipping her off to some *institution."*

"We're not *shipping* her off anywhere," Ben says. "We will find her the best possible facility to help her. "I'll let you know what I find," he says, walking away, already tapping on his phone screen.

Lauren appears hypnotized for a moment, then she lurches off the sofa and marches toward Ben, tightening her robe yet again.

I slowly exhale the breath I've been hoarding and see Jimmy and Swann doing the same. Without turning my face directly at the Rogers, I watch Lauren confront Ben. He's waving his phone in the air and they're both talking, although I can't make out any words.

Lauren raises her voice and I hear "...no you're NOT..." and ..."you arrogant son-of-a-bitch..."

Ben glances around to see if anyone's noticing. I see his lips moving but hear only the low rumble of his voice. A few minutes later I see the ER nurse in the doorway pointing at the Rogers and talking to a woman in blue scrubs and a stethoscope who heads for Ben and Lauren.

Jimmy, Swann and I join them just as the doctor arrives, confirms that Lauren and Ben are "the patient's parents" and robotically recites from her clipboard.

"Patient exhibits significant symptoms of depression analogous to Post Traumatic Stress Syndrome. Patient declined explanation of source of severe stress but also exhibits indications consistent with rape or other domestic abuse clusters. Recommend patient be closely monitored for possible self-destructive signs or actions until patient is assessed further by a trauma professional and sources of stress are determined and restoration of equilibrium is established. When patient is fully conscious and judged out of immediate danger, someone will notify you."

She looks up from her clipboard for the first time and makes fleeting eye-contract with Lauren. Then she does a military-quality pivot and mechanically walks away.

I think I hear her knee and elbow joints squeaking, indicating a need for WD-40 if she's going to continue impersonating a homo sapien.

"We're taking her home and hiring expert help," Lauren says firmly to Ben. "We'll find a trauma specialist to come to our *house*. No way in hell are we dropping her off at some institution."

Ben hesitates and hiss-whispers as if four other people aren't standing right next to them.

"We'll talk about it this evening."

"Fine, we'll talk about it when all *three* of us are home," she insists. "Now let's get some recommendations for home care."

"I may be able to help with that," Carole says.

Lauren gestures Carole to two nearby chairs, they lean toward each other and I see them intensely talking.

Ben is pacing around the Waiting Room, periodically sitting in a vacant chair pressing his phone against his ear, probably searching for trauma treatment facilities despite his wife's strong objections.

Pamela says: "Mr. Crocker, I need to get to work. I'll come back late this afternoon if Robyn is still here. I'll do whatever I can for Robyn as long as needed."

Jimmy and I watch her leave and slump into nearby chairs.

Jimmy closes his eyes and blows out his cheeks.

"I think we did a good job finding her," he says. "This has been an extremely tense day and we haven't even had lunch yet."

A few minutes later, Ben motions for me and Jimmy to come closer.

"I want an update from you two every four hours. Find them, dammit!"

Chapter 26

-----JACK-----

Two hours later, another woman with a clipboard, but not robotic, approaches Lauren and Carole, who remain in their long conversation and the rest of us hurry over to hear what we hope is an update on Robyn's condition.

She glances at the group.

"Oh, she says. "Hi, Carole, are you part of the family?"

"Friend of the family," Carole says.

To the rest of us she says: "This is Nancy Brady, a Registered Nurse. We crossed paths briefly several years ago when we were both at Presby.

"This is the patient's mother," she adds, nodding at Lauren.

"Lauren immediately asks, "How is she? Can we see…?"

"Miss Rogers has been conscious for about 20 minutes, slowly responding to visual and verbal stimulation from our staff, as if awakening from deep sleep, similar to someone coming out of anesthesia, post-surgery. She's a little disoriented.

"We think she might benefit from a very *short* and *very* low-key visit with her family."

She scans our group.

"Normally I'd say only mom and dad can go in, but if all of you agree that *only* the parents say anything, I'll permit the rest of you to observe and briefly provide visual support.

"Agreed?"

Six nods and soon we're in a small room and Nurse Brady is retracting curtains and we see Robyn sitting up in bed, eyes closed, head leaning back, her face starkly pale, appearing more dead than alive.

All of us are shocked into silence. Then Lauren lunges to the bed, kisses Robyn's cheek, awkwardly hugging her shoulders.

Robyn's eyes fly open in what looks like fear and pushes her mother away.

"Sweetheart," Lauren's voice panicked. "Honey, it's Mom. Dad's here, too. And Jack and Jimmy, plus Jack's sister, who is also a nurse. And Ashley. All of us are so relieved that you're okay."

Robyn's face morphs from fear to tears of joy.

"Mom, Mom, oh…" sobbing now, clutching Lauren so hard their foreheads collide.

"Sorry," Robyn chokes. "Just hold me, Mom."

A few minutes later, Robyn seems to slip into sleep again and Nurse Brady says, "Okay, let's go. Everyone except Mom. She can stay another few minutes."

She extends her arms to the side in a herding gesture.

"Go back to the Waiting Room."

The four of us retreat to our corner of the waiting room.

"She's so pale and frail," Carole says. "When she closed her eyes I couldn't tell if she was sleeping or unconscious."

"Oh, God," Ben croaked from his slump on one of the sofas. "I swear I'm going to kill whoever did this to my little girl. I don't care what happens after that. I'm…."

Jimmy sits next to Ben and puts his hand on his shoulder, the rest of us silently watching.

"We're going to gather evidence and catch the guy," Jimmy says. "We all want to be sure he and anyone else involved get the justice they deserve. As much as all of us would love roasting whoever it is over a crackling fire, we can't. And particularly you can't let your feelings trap you into trying to provide punishment on your own. You could lose your life and your family in the process. You all need each other now and even more when this is over. You understand?"

Ben seems to deflate on the sofa.

"Yeah, I understand but I *want*..."

He stares at Jimmy.

"I get it...I'll try."

Jimmy pats Ben's shoulder and begins circling our end of the room. The rest of us become a silent group of faces focused on something in the distance.

In a few minutes Lauren returns with Nurse Brady who says in a near-whisper, as if Robyn is in the room: "She's sleeping and we'll keep you advised if there's any significant change and when you might be able to have a longer visit with her."

Brady disappears through the same door and I hear murmurs from our group, discussing the situation, hoping and trying to reassure ourselves and others that Robyn's is on the path to full recovery.

More than an hour later, Jimmy raises his voice and announces, "I'm famished. Who's in for the quick visit to the cafeteria for something edible? We can take the stairs for some exercise, catch a bite and be back in a half hour."

"I'll wait here," Carole says, "in case Nurse Brady has information for us. Jack, just bring me something that won't make me puke."

After some hesitation the rest of us parade through the waiting room and head for the stairwell.

Ashley stops Jimmy with a hand to his shoulder and I see her briefly whisper to him. She heads downstairs, the rest of us go to the cafeteria two floors up.

Chapter 27

-----CAROLE-----

As they leave to assess roadkill in the cafeteria, my hands are trembling with the rage I know I shouldn't express around Robyn's parents.

What kind of sewage-eating animal can attack any woman? There's no such thing as '*Nonconsenual Sex.*' It's *Violence*, plain and simple. I agree with Jimmy's advice to this victim's father but there's no need to grant mercy to anyone capable of what happened. I've seen the victim and I'd like to shoot the subhuman perp in the balls and leave him at the curb for trash pickup.

Do Jack and Jimmy have a specific suspect in their sights? Do they have any convincing evidence against anyone or are they scrambling in the dark hoping to find something or someone? Will they tell me what they have? Or don't have?

"Carole? Carole?"

I turn to the voice and see Nancy Brady gesturing to me.

"Is something new? What's happened?"

"Robyn's awake, seems quite alert. She's wondering what exactly happened that landed her in the hospital. We think it would be good for someone to be with her as she's re-orienting herself."

"The others went to scavenge some cafeteria food, probably back here in 20 or 30 minutes. I can call them to come right back."

"It's probably good for them to get away, even briefly, and eat something. There's no crisis. Can you come with me to Robyn's room just for her to have someone with her for the few minutes her parents aren't here?"

We enter Robyn's where she's visibly more alert than before.

"This is Mr. Crocker's sister," Nurse Brady says.

"I sorta remember," Robyn says. "You're a nurse, too?"

"Not on active duty anymore," I say. "I'm just trying to be helpful. "Feeling better?"

"Yeah, unless this is a dream, I feel awake but a little murky and confused about what happened and how I got here."

"Why don't you chat a bit with Carole," Nancy says. "Your folks and the two others are in the cafeteria getting some grub and will be back shortly. Carole can probably answer some of your questions but even if not, you'll have company until your mother and father are back."

Robyn nods and Brady is gone.

I pull a chair close, put my elbow on her bed and extend my hands to hold one of hers.

"I understand what happened to you," I say, softly. "It's happened to a lot of us. Was it someone you know? It usually is. I imagine you're furious and hoping to send him to solitary confinement."

"I want all of this to go away" Robyn says. "I don't want to think about what happened every waking moment. I'm going to transfer to a different school, maybe on the East Coast or perhaps Stanford in California. I was accepted there but I wanted to do at least a year or two close to home. Now I want to get far away."

Tears form on her cheeks and I realize I've seriously misjudged the situation by assuming she shares my anger and outrage and desire for revenge and justice; otherwise known as my Instantaneous Default Reaction.

She reads my face, looks away then back to me.

"I know that's running away," she says. "But I don't care, I want wipe the slate clean. I don't want to sit in a courtroom telling everything that happened. I'd fall apart. I couldn't do it. I'm not strong enough to do that. I want to run far, far away."

She looks away, her voice weak, defeated.

I understand her feelings but I'm angry with her weakness.

Won't be the first time I've rushed in where angels fear to tread…and are smart enough not to stick their divine noses into other people's business.

"Are you going to live your life as a wimp, getting the vapors and fainting and fleeing tough situations, surrendering to bullies and rapists? Not to mention endangering more victims because you didn't have the courage to stand up and fight?"

I see Robyn's face switch briefly to anger at my blunt question.

"I'm afraid I'm not a fighter," she says.

"I don't mean *'fight like a man,'* "I say. "I mean fight like a self-confident human being, not folding like a rag doll with no spine."

She's crying now, eyes closed, her hand still covered by both of mine.

Nice job. I'll never win the Miss Subtlety Award.

Lauren, Ben, Jack, Jimmy and Nancy Brady come through the door. Lauren sees Robyn crying, shrieks "let go of her" and lunges to the bed opposite me, brushes my hands aside and hugs Robyn.

"What the hell is going on?" Ben says sharply to no one in particular.

Nancy looks quizzically at me, gives me a sideways nod toward the door.

In the hallway, she says: "Robyn is probably still a bit overwhelmed with waking up in a hospital without a clear memory of what happened. I'm going to vacate the room, except for Mom and Dad. The re-entry process is often more a series zigs and zags than a straight line."

I did it again. I didn't just tread, I belly-flopped in the Angel's pond.

CHAPTER 28

-----ROBYN-----

It's happening again. I'm awakening somewhere in a thick fog bank, groggy and disoriented. I don't know where I am, but I know what's happening. I've relived this swirling cloud of confusion many times. And I can't stop it this time, either.

I'm on my back, my body rocking rhythmically and pain surges and surges, matching repeated compressing weights assaulting me from toes to chest.

Absurdly, I dimly hear a male voice counting cadence.

"Hut, one. Hut, two, Hut, hut, hut, hut. Hut, one. Hut, two."

Do I know that voice?

Another voice grunts and exhales in my ears, his foul breath fills my universe.

A disembodied man's face drifts toward me and retreats into the fog. He is smiling. And counting. "Hut, one..."

Do I know him?

Multiple brilliant lights momentarily sear through my closed eye-lids. Camera flashes?

The mocking face emerges again from the fog.

I try to twist or roll away but I can't. I'm as confined as if in a casket, claustrophobia imprisoning me in panic.

I feel like I'm screaming but I can't hear myself. And I know no one else hears me, either.

I know I'm reliving what happened but I can't stop the attack, the dream, the hallucination, this assault as razor sharp as the first one, indistinguishable from the first time. And the endless times in the eternity since.

I feel myself bobbing to the surface of consciousness, a brilliantly white-clad angel hovering above my flickering eyes, saying something to me, then morphing into Beverly, the night nurse I remember giving me something to swallow…minutes ago…or hours or yesterday?

"Robyn. Robyn. You're awake now. Everything's going to be okay."

NOT OKAY! IT WILL NEVER BE OKAY! I WILL NEVER BE ME AGAIN!

Chapter 29

-----JIMMY-----

The next afternoon, Jack, Mark, Carole and I are in Robyn's home bedroom. Ben's at work, Lauren is downstairs interviewing a Trauma Nurse applicant to help with Robyn's recovery.

"Hi," Carole says. "How are you?"

Robyn is in bed, legs extended, back propped against a mountain of pillows, her Minnie Mouse pajamas cheerier than yesterday's hospital gown.

"Hi, Carole. Glad to see you again. Thanks for the candid stuff you told me yesterday."

"How are you?" Carole repeats.

"Frankly, I feel trapped and paralyzed," Robyn says, her face pale, voice soft but firm. "I'm still trying to understand...what's happening...what exactly happened. I'm trying to figure out what I want...need to do. I feel as if I'm in a maze and can't find my way out. I keep running into frightening dead-ends."

"We understand, Robyn, we really do," Carole says.

Jack says. "Everyone in this room has experienced serious trauma in our lives and struggled to get through it. All of us want to help you recover. I'm sure you want to put the attack in your rear-view mirror."

She says nothing, not offering even the slightest nod of agreement.

"We're part of your team, Robyn. Do you agree with that?" Jack says.

She nods, shifting her eyes from Jack to Carole.

"Yes," she says. "And I appreciate it, but I'm struggling to decide what to do. One minute I want to beat the snot out of...out of....The next minute I'm in a fetal position, curled up in bed crying. I'm getting as paranoid as my Dad."

"What you're experiencing and thinking about is understandable and completely normal," I say. "But the plain truth is we need your help. We need to know who we're after so we can take them off the street."

A brief shudder, then downcast eyes.

Gotta try another nudge.

"Robyn, *where* did the attack happen?" I say, hoping for an answer to a less emotional question. "Was it on campus?"

She looks over our heads and nods.

"I don't know much for sure," she says. "It's all mixed up. Blurry. I think I must have been drugged part of the time."

An opening!

"How do you think he drugged you? In beer or some other..."

"Maybe. I don't know for sure, but it seems likely to me."

She closes her eyes, adjusts the pillows behind her, sits a little straighter and finally speaks in a low but clear voice.

"I was in a dim living room on a sofa and this guy sat beside me and he had two long-neck bottles. He gave me one and I took it. I sorta remember he tapped my bottle with his and smiled and we talked for a while. Actually *he* talked and I mostly listened; didn't know what to say to someone so sophisticated compared to me."

She looks down again, breathes noticeably faster, then flicking her eyes around the room and back to me.

"The next thing I think I remember I'm half awake and someone is..." she closes her eyes and coughs as if something's choking her. We're all silent until the coughing subsides and she inhales deep breaths like a drowning person resurfacing from a hundred feet below.

"Let me tell you about a dream I keep having," she says softly and continues in the same whisper, eyes firmly closed, until she's finished.

Her voice is stronger even while describing being terrorized. Maybe it's helpful to say this stuff out loud. Good God in Heaven, how does something this horrible happen?

Chapter 30

"Miss Scanlon, I appreciate your volunteering to talk to me again."

She glances her latte, straightens her back against the book.

"Look, Mr. McGuire, when we met before I didn't think I knew anything that might be helpful to Robyn. And I don't know if that's changed but seeing Robyn looking so pale and fragile in that hospital bed that I was really frightened. That's why I whispered to you that maybe we should talk again."

I nod and she says nothing for several seconds, sighs and plunges in.

"I know and probably you do, too," she says, "that college campuses have many opportunities for casual sex encounters, some meaningless, some under social pressures, at least a few coerced, possibly involving too much alcohol. Some involve date-rape drugs.

"I've been here, in the campus culture long enough to be very careful. When I go out I wear drug-detecting nail polish. Have you heard of that?"

"No."

"I buy it on the internet. It's not perfect but a finger dipped in a spiked drink can change the color of the polish."

"Does Robyn use it?"

"Not that I know of. She's a younger than usual freshman. She handles the academics just fine but she's got a lot to learn socially."

"Who do you *think* attacked her?"

She blinks twice, drops her eyes to the table.

"I don't know," her voice soft and flat.

"I understand," I say. "But maybe you have a suspect or two in mind. A possibility. Someone you wonder about. Any possibility at all?"

I clear my throat and she looks up.

"Who do you think *might* be involved?" I try again. "Even a hint of suspicion in your mind about someone. Maybe someone she might have met, not necessarily *suspicious* but that we can check out. We won't involve you, but we're desperately searching for any possible leads."

She sips the latte and wipes a fleck of foam from her lips.

Hiding behind the big cup?

"Was she seeing anyone?"

"Oh, no. She's really quite shy, probably because she's a year younger than most freshmen, thanks to all the Advanced Placement classes she took in high school. She was class co-valedictorian. She's pretty in an under-stated, almost *little-girl* way. A few guys have tried to flirt with her, trying to figure out who she is."

"Anyone in particular?"

"I've seen two or three guys try to chat her up…maybe. Look, Mr. McGuire, I'm more than two years older than Robyn. I mentored her in a couple of her Advanced Placement classes in high school. I'm a college junior and I have a part-time job. She's barely a freshman and we don't see each other as much as we used to."

"Do you know the names of any of the guys you mentioned?"

A long pause stretches into eternity.

"Sorta."

"I won't mention this to Robyn. Please help us help her."

"Maybe a guy named Randy or Andy. He's kind of creepy."

"What's his last name?"

"I have no idea. Not even sure it's 'Andy.' Might be Sandy or something else. He's not someone you really pay attention to. I know how obnoxious that sounds but he just isn't. He makes you a little uncomfortable. Once I saw him in line ahead of me registering for classes and he asked me: "What's going on?"

"I told him I didn't know what was 'going on.'"

Another time, after a movie Robyn and I and another friend were at Sambuca's over on McKinney. He stopped by our table and said, 'Hi, you girls doin' okay?

"He's not very socially adept. You just want to tell him, 'Yeah, we're doing okay, now go away,' but you don't want to hurt his feelings."

"Who else?"

"Josh somebody. I saw him once when Robyn and I were at The Campus Cup and this tall guy came over and flirted with me for a couple of minutes, gave up and when he started to leave he leaned toward Robyn and said; "Who's the mystery woman?"

She awkwardly glanced over her shoulder, apparently thinking he was referring to someone else. Nothing came of it."

"Andy or Sandy or whatever was at the same table as the tall guy. He acted like he was a friend of Josh's but looked more like a hanger-on to me, not anyone Robyn would be remotely interested in. Josh is way cooler. I think he's on the basketball team. I don't follow sports much and I don't think Robyn even realized he was a BMOC until I told her."

I hold my breath before I say, "What's Josh's last name?"

"I don't know," she whispers as if to herself.

"And this Andy guy, what's his last name?"

She shrugs a 'Don't know' gesture. She's noticeably growing more uncomfortable, shifting on her side of the booth, glancing toward the door to Greenville Avenue.

"Thank you," I say. "You and all of us are trying to help Robyn. You may think of something else later. Anything at all. Please call me," handing her my business card. "I answer the cell number on the back 24/7. Please don't hesitate to call. Any small detail might help Robyn."

She nods and stands, says something about an upcoming class and I jump to my feet. I see her moist eyes blinking rapidly. She pulls her sunglasses down and walks briskly to the street, eyes cast to the floor.

CHAPTER 31

-----JACK-----

That evening, Jimmy and I are in the office, the only light from our two desk lamps. The door is locked, the "Closed" sign in the window.

"I've been researching sexual assaults on Texas campuses and I have some leads that might be helpful," he says, as I glance up from my laptop, hearing our back-room printer stuttering to life.

"It's almost impossible to find information because records of campus police departments at private universities are *not* required to be available to the public.

"Campus cop records at the University of Texas and Texas A&M are legally public documents subject to the state's Open Records law, but the Legislature decided to exempt private schools."

"Gee," I say, in my best mocking voice, "I wonder why they would do that? Could it be that someone representing private schools asked them to? Maybe wrote their point of view on a big stack of hundred-dollar bills disguised as campaign contributions?

"I know from my newspaper career that sexual assault complaints at private colleges often are buried or hushed-up, particularly if it involves a BOMC athlete or someone from an influential family. So, unless it happened at half-time of a football game, witnessed by thousands there still might not be an official police investigation.

"But there would be a police investigation and a public record if the same crime was alleged at a public university or even in a normal neighborhood a few blocks away?

"Who's being protected in that system?" Jimmy says. "Certainly not students, parents and other citizens who have a stake in knowing where predators roam. Obviously the law protects private universities from bad publicity and shields predators but doesn't protect assault victims or the public."

Baylor had a major scandal last year. Several sexual assaults were ignored and covered up, several football players went to prison, and the football coach was fired. The University's president, Ken Star, was fired. You weren't here but, you may recall Ken Starr from Bill Clinton's impeachment trial."

"Still many hidden documents and actions at Baylor. An incredible mess."

CHAPTER 32

-----JACK-----

"On a more positive note," Jimmy says, "I've managed to find McMillan University's Campus Security files of several rape cases that were never reported to city police. Some were partially completed complaint forms that apparently weren't followed up by the University or referred to regular police or pursued by victims. The info was just dumped in a file by Campus Security."

"Do you have an inside source or did you burgle the place?" I ask.

"I *engineered* a digital key into their digital system and looked at some electronic files that are printing right now. They have four unreported rape complaints in a file labeled 'Miscellaneous.'"

"Unbelievable," I say. "So rape is considered *Miscellaneous* by the campus cops?"

"Apparently."

"What's the Executive Summary?" I ask, leaning back and rotating my neck to lessen stiffness from being in the 'keyboard hunch' position for two hours.

"This was a *hack 'n grab* mission. I didn't stay in their computer system long enough to read all the details, but at least one of the rape cases moldering in *Miscellaneous* is a complaint that involves the same fraternity Josh Dixon belongs to."

"Bingo!" I say. "I hope."

I get up to walk little circles and feel my face stretching from a celebratory smile.

"How did you get into the school's files? What's a digital key? Did you get a password somewhere?"

"No, much more complicated than that," he says. "Hacking isn't as easy it looks on TV. In this case, the Security Department's filing software is ancient, so it wasn't nearly as challenging as an up-to-date system. I think I was able to get in and out of the digital files without leaving any obvious fingerprints.

"Fortunately the department scanned at least some of the original hand-written notes of incomplete cases, otherwise there wouldn't be digital files.

"But I think it's possible, even likely, that there are paper documents in plain old file folders in metal cabinets with more cases or more details on the four I found. We need to find a way to see those.

"I also vacuumed up the department's staff roster, including salary information, names and addresses. I'm going to see if any of the officers have personal problems that we might be able to exploit by pressuring them for information and insights into how the department operates.

"But don't pop any champagne yet. Mainly I'm hoping the printouts have some accuser's names or names of suspects. During my quick peek inside I didn't see *any* names, just crap notes such as '...the alleged victim claimed...' or 'when the alleged victim awoke she said she couldn't identify her alleged attacker.'

"One complaint report sounded like it was written by a rapist's defense attorney."

"Nice job. Stay on it," I urge. "I'm hoping this turns into our best--and only--lead we've had since Ashley Scanlon coughed up Dixon's name as a possible perp."

The printer goes silent.

"Yeah, well, I've got some serious sifting to do."

CHAPTER 33

-----JACK-----

Jimmy's six-year-old black Mustang growls to the curb and as we get out I see four cars in the Jefferson driveway. Mavis opens the door, Otis behind her.

"Welcome back, Mr. Crocker," Mavis says and I introduce Jimmy

"Roberta and Angel are setting the table," Mavis says. "Lunch is almost ready."

When I'd called to request individual meetings with Mavis, Otis, Roberta, Angel and Otis's brother, Brandon, Mavis insisted we come for Saturday lunch.

"You can talk to us separately after that," she declares in a tone that I instantly understand is not a suggestion.

An attractive 40-ish woman in jeans and a sweatshirt comes into the room closely followed by a near-clone, obviously her daughter, both with shoulder-brushing black hair.

Mavis introduces them as "Angel, our granddaughter and Roberta Jefferson, our daughter."

Almost instantly Mavis is directing us to assigned places where we find bowls of tomato basil soup next to large Caesar salads.

Only six chairs. Brandon's not coming.

Otis delivers a short prayer that my brain doesn't retain.

I start to pass a basket of home-made bread but Mavis takes over again.

"Brandon couldn't come. You'll have to arrange something separate with him at his place. Now, what is it that you gentlemen want to talk to us about?

Are you going to find a way to put in prison the people who organized that rigged trial over 30 years ago? You know, a year for a year, like the Bible says?"

What I don't want to talk about at lunch is what we're going ask everyone separately. I try to keep the frustration from of my voice.

"We'll get into those subjects after this fine lunch. We really appreciate the home cooking. A lot of our meals are on the run and require a drive-through window."

The laughter works like a detour sign and I catch Jimmy's eye across the table. His face shows no discernible change and that reminds me that while he was in the Marines, he won a substantial amount of poker money, some of which helped launch our fledgling investigations agency.

Roberta, sitting next to me and looking younger than I first thought, says, "Dad told us you and Jimmy are the guys who rescued that nine-year-old boy from actual killers last year. I remember hearing about it when it happened, but what was that about? Why did they kidnap your son?"

I nod at Jimmy and he enables me to get my first sip of soup.

"We were investigating an attempted murder, a suspicious death and a violent stalker. Someone who wanted us to drop a case kidnapped Jack's 10-year-old son, Erik, from a hospital room. They sliced off part of his earlobe and delivered it to Jack's wife. We found where they were holding Erik just before they shot and killed the stalker. There was a bit of a shoot-up and we got Erik back."

"Thank the Lord," Mavis says.

"Did you kill anyone?" Angel asks.

Jimmy hesitates and I try to come up with another detour.

"Two of the kidnappers were killed and the third, a dirty cop, is in prison."

Jimmy and I both fork in some crunchy lettuce and Otis gently intervenes.

"Let's enjoy our lunch and there'll be plenty of time after that for serious questions and discussions. I'm still thrilled just to be eating food that isn't measured by the *glop* and not served on trays with dividers."

∧

After lunch Mavis points at Jimmy and me.

"I'll show you where you can interview us."

We follow her down a hallway and she gestures to a door where I see a home office.

"There are two chairs in there," she notes. "And over here," nodding across the hall, "is a guest room."

I see two metal folding chairs facing each other at the foot of the bed.

"Looks fine," Jimmy says. "I'll start with Angel in here. Jack and Roberta can meet in the office."

CHAPTER 34

-----JACK-----

My folding chair has no comfort zone. Angel apparently already knows this because she moves the other chair aside and sits on the end of the quilt-covered bed.

"Miss Jefferson," I begin, "as we explained to your grandfather, Jack and I are trying to see if two recent deaths are in any way related."

"Related? To what?" she interjects. "From what Grand Papa said, someone thinks he may have murdered two people. Is that true? Do the police actually think he's killed two people in the two months since he was declared innocent and freed?" her voice rising in outrage. "Is someone trying to put him back in prison where he never belonged in the first place?"

"The police must look at all possibilities since both victims were part of your grandfather's trial. Jack and I understand that this could be just a co-incidence involving people with little in common over many years. In other words, two completely separate events not related in any way to the trial."

"Unbelievable," she snaps. "The police and you two guys are investigating a man who was robbed of at least a third of his life. And it's all based on a *coincidence* or on separate and normal things that happened over more than 33 years ago? That's not right and it's not fair."

"You're absolutely correct," I say. "But the police have no choice. Two people from the trial have died, neither of natural causes, since Otis was released. The sooner Jimmy and I can find evidence that your grandfather isn't involved, the sooner the suspicions will go away. But we need help sorting this out...whatever *it* is."

"Why are you talking to me?" she spits. "I'm 20 years old. I wasn't even born when he was *lynched* by the so-called justice system back in the last century."

"We're talking with many people and we need to interview everyone in the family," I say. "Someone may have heard some comments or even speculation that might be helpful. I'm hoping to talk to your uncle Brandon soon since he couldn't be here today."

"Oh, Brandon *could* have been here," she laughs. "But my mom won't let him come here."

"Why not?"

"Look," she says, "I'm just talking about my Grand Papa. I've only been around him for a short time, but I already love him as if I've known him for years. He's smart, loving, forgiving. He forgave the bastards who framed him and locked him in a jail cell for 33 fucking years. He's practically a saint."

"No argument here," I say. "I told him he's a better man than I'd be under his circumstances."

"Please promise me that if you two guys *do* find anything that looks even a little bit negative, you'll keep it to yourselves."

Angel seems to be memorizing my face.

CHAPTER 35

-----JACK---

Roberta sits ram-rod straight in the desk chair, hugging herself and staring at me with arched brows.

"You're wondering why Jimmy and I want to talk to all of you," I say.

"Great," she says. "So now you're a frigging mind-reader?"

I smile.

"The Rev hired us to find out why his cousin, Jackson Parks, was murdered. There's no proof yet that he even *was* murdered."

"I haven't been in The Rev's church in years," she says. "He wasn't at the church when this travesty happened, but the organization couldn't keep my father from a tragic, unjust and bogus conviction and more than three decades in a cage. And they couldn't get him out 10 years later when The Rev arrived.

"I don't see any point in listening to some preacher spout off about 'God's love' and a lot of other crap when in real life I had to travel 172 miles to Huntsville just to look at my father and talk to him through thick glass. No touching.

"He was railroaded into prison despite 'God's love.' The Rev has come by a few times and my mom goes to his church fairly regularly. My father's been to services there a few times since he got out of Hell. I think he prefers one of those old-timey Cowboy churches in Plano. None of that organized religion makes any sense to me."

"You must have been angry every time you visited your father."

"No. I was furious *every* day and *all* day," her lips a thin line of defiance. "And I still am. Every damn day."

What do I say to that?

"I'm sorry. Your father wasn't on anyone's radar when we began looking into Jackson Parks' death. It was only after a second death occurred and someone realized both victims were involved in your father's trial, one was a juror and the other was an Assistant Prosecutor on the case."

"So what? That was decades ago. Why are we sitting here?"

"To help us with these new issues. If we or the police determine that there's no link to the two deaths, just a coincidence, this will all disappear. Do you remember anyone over the years talking about revenge for the failure of the legal system? Anyone make any threats?"

"No," she shoots back. "But even if I did, do you think I would put anyone else in this family in the crosshairs of suspicion? You must be a bigger fool than you think I am."

I see her eyes become lethal and she suddenly lunges to her feet and waves toward the door.

"Get the fuck out of our house," she shouts. "And stay away from us."

She leaves the room and as I get to the door I hear her yelling at Jimmy and Angel.

"Angel, shut up. Mr. McGuire, you get the hell out of here. Angel, go in the kitchen."

She points at me. "And *you* and your partner get your butts in the car and leave us alone. Now!"

Jimmy comes into the hall and we nod to each other and head for the front door amid voices shouting at each other in the kitchen.

As we pull from the curb, he says: "That was weird. She just abruptly went looney tunes. I hope it doesn't turn out to be the highlight of our day."

CHAPTER 36

-----JACK-----

Brandon Jefferson at 54 looks ten years older than his brother, Otis, who is 56.

His odometer's been on fast-forward.

Brandon's long, black-n-mostly gray ponytail, wrinkled tan khakis and a faded *Grateful Dead, New Orleans, 1970* tour tee, plus green flip-flops make him look like the Assistant Professor that he is, but who hasn't completely left his student years and wardrobe behind. He's several inches under six feet and appears fit under the tee. His nearly trimmed Van Dyke and black-frame glasses make it easy to imagine him behind a lectern.

I already know from Jimmy's research that Brandon teaches classes on the Cultural Revolution of the 1960s from Vietnam to Charles Manson and President John Kennedy's assassination and the murders of his brother, Bobby, plus Martin Luther King and other civil rights fighters.

A tall, slender, much-younger woman joins us, drying her hands on a dish towel, bare feet kicking a brightly flowered peasant skirt ahead of her, a white tank top under a muted but multi-colored shawl over her shoulders. Her untethered shiny black hair cascades to her waist.

"This is my wife, Feather."

Her smile is full-face and open, seemingly without artifice, childlike.

Couple of hippies past their expiration dates?

I accept her offer of mango tea, hoping to keep things low key before easing into interview mode.

Brandon had quickly agreed to see me when I sketchily told him we were interviewing family members to help with '*a situation*' possibly linked to Otis. Now he sits on a sofa and sweeps his hand to the rest of the room, apparently inviting me to find a roosting spot, perhaps wherever the Zen speaks to me.

The modest house in the blue-collar suburb of Rowlett is well-maintained inside and out. Two soft gray sofas face each other with upholstered chairs at either end.

I visualize eight or ten people scattered around the dimmed room, on the furniture and floor, toking from a group joint, cocooning, talking softly, New Age music. A mellow congregation of medicated meditators.

I sip mango tea and see Brandon's face turn serious as Feather sits next to him, gathering the peasant skirt around folded knees.

"Exactly what's going on with my brother that brings you here?"

I had told him on the phone only that some issues had developed for Otis and that Jimmy and I wanted to help him.

"Two people who were involved in Otis's 1982 trial have died in the two months since he was released. Both of them may have been murdered."

I'm studying Brandon's face and body language.

As if someone hit the *Pause* button for everyone in the room, Brandon becomes a freeze-dried mummy with a pony-tail and Feather is a life-size sculpture staring at Brandon with a worried face.

I'm not even moving my eyes, locked on Brandon. My plan is to say nothing at this critical point, hoping to force a reaction from him.

I'm mentally chanting 'one-thousand-one, one-thousand-two' to see how much silence is happening. At 'one-thousand-thirty-four,' Brandon says, "Aww, shit. That can't be true. Is there no end to the cosmos crapping on him?"

He begins crying so softly that I see it before it's audible. He tilts toward Feather, who throws her arms around him and kisses his salty cheeks.

It feels like I should leave them alone but I realize my departure might intrude on them even more than if I stayed put, and most importantly, I want to know what he's going to say.

"Damn it," Brandon suddenly roars, shrugging off Feather's embrace. "Otis is a good man. Can't everyone see that? They should just leave him the hell alone. He didn't do anything wrong this time, either. What a fucking mess!"

Feather attempts to recapture him but he stands and gently pushes her down with a hand on her shoulder.

"I'm all right," he says. "It's Otis who's not okay. What are we going to do?"

"We?" she says. "We've only seen him a few times since he got out. And before that, a half-dozen times or so a year since you and I've been together."

He glances at me through red eyes and free-falls heavily back on the sofa.

"Who died?" he says.

"An Assistant District Attorney, second chair at the trial to the top Assistant DA who presented the case," I say. "And a juror."

He frowns. "You said they *may* have been murdered. Why does anyone think they actually *were* murdered?" he says, standing up again, Feather gracefully rising with him, like his ethereal shadow.

"It's been over 30 years," he snaps, staring at me. "I wouldn't be surprised if at least half the people involved in that trial are dead by now. Of natural causes or accidents."

She hugs him, but he gently pushes her away with one hand, strides to the window and as if asking someone across the street, yells: "How about that jailhouse snitch? That pathetic loser who lied through his teeth and testified that Otis told him he was sorry for killing that girl."

He turns from the window, takes a step toward me, still shouting.

"If Otis wanted revenge on someone, wouldn't he go after that little weasel who perjured himself to get a few years off his burglary sentence?" his volume moderating now.

"Joe Bob Spencer. I've never forgotten that son-of-a-bitch's name. Prosecutors planted him in a cell with Otis. Without him, they'd never have convicted Otis. There never was any actual *evidence*.

"Just the lying weasel. No one expected that last-minute, bull-shit testimony.

"My brother's young, inexperienced Public Defender lawyer was caught flat-footed. He didn't make it clear to the jury that the career, low-rent felon was going to benefit from lying about Otis."

"You said someone saw Otis near the girl's house that day," Feather says softly. "Just one elderly witness claimed she saw Otis, or someone who looked like him, in the neighborhood. From half a block away."

"She was three houses away from the person," he says. "Otis's rookie lawyer never attacked attacking that old woman's credibility. I think he was too afraid to look mean go her. She wasn't close enough to be absolutely sure it was him. Probably a case of 'they all look alike to me.

"But Otis had no alibi. He was studying algebra in his bedroom after school and no one else was there."

Brandon's crying again, this time letting the tears waterfall down his cheeks. Feather produces a tissue and dabs at his face.

"Otis doesn't deserve any of this," he roars. "Not one damn bit. Not that first time. Not *this* time."

CHAPTER 37

-----JACK-----

I finish describing the Brandon and Feather interview for Tonto and he says: "Sounds like they're exhibits in the "Beat Generation Hall of Fame.""

He adds: "Feather's real name is Sylvia Brooks. She's 32 and she's a talented, experienced and well-paid flower arranger for a Richardson florist. Seems like a perfect job for a mid-thirties Flower Child.

"I couldn't find any employment history for Brandon other than McMillan University. He started there as an adjunct prof right after his history doctorate from SMU. He's now an assistant prof with tenure."

"Brandon seems devoted to his brother," I say. "Feather says they haven't been together much since Otis was released. I peg him as someone who hasn't matured much, still living inside the academic bubble.

"Feather is a late-comer in Brandon's life. She's only seen Otis a handful of times in prison and a few times since he returned home. She doesn't have much to help us unless she's hiding some family dynamics that we don't know about. She's so ethereal and child-like that she almost seems incapable of deception."

"She's young enough to be Brandon's daughter or possibly even granddaughter," Jimmy says. "That suggests there's an ex-wife or two somewhere."

"Let's find them and try to flesh-out Otis's brother. But let's not ask any family members. We're talking to everyone and I don't want to appear to be concentrating on a single person."

CHAPTER 38

-----JIMMY-----

I'm in my car in the Happy Grape Bistro's small parking lot watching for Marsha.

When I called her after our spontaneous hotdog lunch at Costco, she accepted and immediately said she'd meet me at the restaurant. I recognized that as her effort to avoid the possibility of an awkward situation at the end of the evening that we both realized was a non-date, date. Or a pre-date, date.

I'm usually a pretty good planner but even though I've had several days to prepare for a dinner I've yearned to have for nearly a year, I feel near panic at the possibility of showing up as the socially inept 15-year-old I once was and perhaps still am at times

Now I see her exiting the light-blue, two-seat Mazda Miata that I walked her to in the Costco lot last weekend. She waves at me and we intersect at the front door.

"Hi," I manage.

I might as well have tugged at my non- existent cowlick.

"Hi," she smiles.

Soon, a young man is introducing himself as someone, maybe Elmo, and promising to take care of us and handing us menus large enough to hide behind and blessing our wine selection as "very good, sir."

I feel like a pimple-faced, 17-year-old instead of a 27-year-old ex-Marine.

I look up from the opened menu that I've been staring at as if memorizing the entrees and see Marsha's violet eyes looking at me.

"Well," she says. "Here we are."

We both laugh and I re-inhabit my real self.

"Thanks for coming," I tell her. "It probably feels a little awkward to you, too. Most of our history has been pretty intense…in a seriously bad way."

She grins.

"Yes, it has, but all of that's over and I was glad to see you the other day. And now, too."

Then, Maybe Elmo delivers our wine with a flourish and promises to return for our "dinner selections."

I'm still mentally scrambling for a suitable toast when Marsha raises her glass.

"The past is past, the future is unknown and now is now."

"Amen," I say.

What, exactly, does that mean?

She holds my gaze and says, "I have a question for you?"

"Sure," I say.

"Is it okay if I call you James?"

"Certainly, I get called everything from Jimmy to Tonto to Jim. You'd be the only one using James. That would be fine."

"Good," she says. "I like that. Maybe an occasional Tonto?"

"Absolutely. That was my Marine radio handle given me by my squad. I love it."

We order dinner entrees personally approved by Maybe Elmo, and while avoiding the past, asking each other what's happened *since* The Excitement, the multiple events that have become *The Crises That Shall Not Be Named*, nearly killed us both.

I knew she had considered law school in the aftermath of her abusive ex-husband being murdered and that she resumed her maiden name instead of the false identity she'd created and lived in for the previous 10 years.

She qualifies for free tuition at SMU because she's now the Administrative Assistant to the Dean of the Law school. She says she's finishing her first semester and it's going well so far.

She's fully aware of the 15 minutes of fame Jack and I got.

Marsha personally shot and wounded a would-be killer in her house. Mark Easton was wounded in that attack.

"C&M Investigations still riding the waves?" she asks.

"We're doing fine. Our two main cases right now were sparked by the publicity after all the excitement. We have enough routine stuff to need part-time help, everything from Worker's Comp fakers to employee background checks, warehouse shrinkage, deadbeat dads and the usual cheating spouses. Mark Easton pretty much has a steady stream of special work."

"How about you?" she says, studying my face. "Any life changes in the works?"

Is she asking if I have a love interest? Significant other? Girlfriend? Steady squeeze?

"No, but I'm hoping for Jack's sake that he moves back home. It's all right living with him but obviously it would be great for him to rejoin his family. And I'm looking forward being alone for a while.

"I lived in a college dorm for three-plus years and four years in military barracks with the Marines and now a year with Jack. I'm ready," I say, trying to keep from winking like an idiot.

You think maybe, possibly, sometime you'd like a roommate?

"You mentioned two cases, anything you can tell me about them?"

Omitting names and identifiable details, I brief her on Otis Jefferson's return home and our search for a possible two-time killer.

"Good Lord," she says. "An innocent man in prison for more than 30 years? I think I read about that case. I know there have been several exonerations locally in recent years."

"Our other main case," I say, "involves a young woman raped at a local university and now being harassed by cowardly, simple-minded losers sending disgusting photos, videos, emails and texts from their parent's basements. Some of it shows the actual rape in progress."

"I hope you nail the creeps," she says, loathing in her face and voice.

"We have some leads, How's the Alfredo?"

We chat like old friends catching up on new times for the rest of the dinner and I walk her to her Miata. She slides in, rolls down the window and peers up at me.

"Thank you for the wonderful dinner, I really enjoyed the food and your company. Let's do this again sometime."

"Sure," I say, as I discard any lingering inhibitions and lock my eyes on hers.

"I've had a crush on you almost since the moment you came to our office after someone tried to run you over," I blurt, surprising both of us.

"I know," she says, turning the key and beginning to back out. "Let me know the next time you need anything at Costco."

Chapter 39

-----JIMMY-----
I'm sitting on a campus bench engrossed in a book.

Actually I'm only pretending to be engrossed. My head's aimed downward but behind my aviator sunglasses my eyes continuously scan the three busy sidewalks converging a few feet away, linking classroom buildings surrounding a patch of open space.

Two young men amble toward me from my right, one significantly taller than the other, both in knee-length shorts and tees with SMU logos, backpacks slung over shoulders. I'm similarly dressed except for the flip-flops and my backpack is just a prop.

I recognize the tall one from last year's yearbook that I searched, looking for someone named "Josh" on the basketball team.

There's the sonuvabitch! At least the leading candidate. And is that the other one? Andy something?

As they get closer to me they split, the shorter one heading to my left, the other taking the sidewalk leading to buildings behind me.

I stand after they pass, close the thick book, brush the seat of my shorts and merge into the river of scholars heading for 11 a.m. classes. Or lunch.

I don't look directly at Josh Dixon but he matches the photo I copied from the on-line yearbook. He's striding confidently, almost swaggering, several people ahead of me, backpack hanging from his left shoulder.

As the path veers between two buildings, I close the gap and realize he's passing between two buildings and is headed for a crowded parking lot. He reaches in a pocket and I see tail lights blink on a dark gray BMW. I catch up with him as he reaches for the door handle.

"Excuse me, you're Josh Dixon aren't you?"

He turns to me, his face pleased that I recognized him.

"Yes. Do I know you? Where do I know you from?"

"You don't. Not yet. But I know who *you* are."

His smile broadens as if he's ready to autograph my backpack. Or my forehead.

"How can I help you?" he says.

"I'm researching how sexual assault cases are handled on local college campuses. And I'm trying to determine how extensive the problem is."

"Why would you want to talk to me about that stuff?"

"I'm interviewing people with active campus social lives and who might have information or opinions about current sexual mores and…."

"Who the fuck *are* you?" he says, pulling the door part-way open. "You must be some sicko. Get lost."

"So, you don't recall any rapes at a campus party? Maybe a very drunk woman? Or drugged, unable to resist" Maybe last Friday night?"

"What the hell are you talking about? I know nothing about anything like that. You must be insane. Why would you ask such an outrageous question? Don't come around me again or you'll regret it."

I hand him my card.

"I'm investigating…."

"Shut the fuck up," he snaps, sliding into the car. "If you spread a filthy rumor like that about me, I guaran-damn-tee you it'll be the biggest mistake of your life. I'll kick your stupid ass six ways from Sunday."

He slams the door, the BMW rockets in reverse and I lurch back to avoid the mirror. His car is nearly T-boned by a red Toyota that screeches to a tire-burning stop.

As the BMW barrels away the driver's window slides down and I'm treated to a view of Dixon's middle finger.

Chapter 40

-----JACK-----

Jimmy finishes describing his encounter with Josh Dixon, including the near-miss by the BMW's mirror and Dixon's farewell gesture.

"Sounds like a real jerk," I say.

Jimmy nods.

"Okay, gut-check time. Does your gut think he's a rapist or just an arrogant prick?"

"He's definitely arrogant. I think he's probably capable of rape but that's based on a *feeling*, not evidence."

"We don't know for sure if Robyn knows who raped her," I say, "but when we first talked to her it sounded like she knew who they are but was afraid to identify them. Remember she said 'they' and 'them.' We need to try again to convince her to reveal names. If she doesn't, we're far out on a frail limb concentrating on Dixon based only on Ashley's ultra-thin guessing."

Jimmy says, "Dixon definitely acted guilty when I confronted him about what he was doing Friday night. He changed from being flattered that I recognized him to instantly trying to shut me down and escape."

"Probably not an unusual reaction for big-man-on-campus jocks," I say. "Lot of them are accustomed, even from high school, to being worshipped, not confronted. And being an arrogant jackass isn't a crime, although it should be."

"Well, then, if not Dixon, who?"

"How many males are enrolled this semester?" I say. "Could be any one of them. Or even a non-student or a former student still attending campus parties. You're the computer whiz, is there any way to trace who posted the videos of the actual rape?"

"Probably not. We have nothing to work with. We don't have copies of the photos or videos. They were posted either on SnapChat which deletes them within seconds, or were deleted by Robyn.

"But even if we had the originals, they were probably untraceable, at least by me. I haven't had experience there. I'm a pretty good hacker, but even the Feds can't do some of this kind of research.

"Whoever made the rape video may have shared it via email or text with someone other than the instant-vanishing version to Robyn. Even if that was only one person, he or she could have passed it along and so on and so on. The person who posted it on social media might be far removed from the actual participants. The actual perp *may* have posted it, *may* have sent one or a few bullying emails or texts and the rest of the messages *may* be from anyone and *anywhere* in the world."

"Stop!" I say. "My eyebrows are hurting from frustration. I think we should keep Dixon as the number-one suspect but also go back to Square One to see if we missed anyone else."

"Aarrgghh!" Jimmy says. "I hate Square One."

CHAPTER 41

A woman I hope is Judy Webster kneels and pulls weeds in her suburban Plano side yard as I park at the curb. I'm hoping to get her views of her ex-husband, Brandon Jefferson.

"Hi," I smile and wave when she notices me on her lawn headed her way.

She doesn't smile or wave, just stands and watches me, wariness on her face, her gloved hands motionless at her side. She's slim and looks fit, like someone who has been active for years. I know she's in her early 50s and has been divorced from Brandon since 1987.

I pause at a non-threatening distance from her, say "Good morning," give her a full-face smile and hold up my PI badge.

"Mrs. Webster?"

The barest of nods.

"I'm Jack Crocker. I'm a private investigator helping The Rev J.D. Findley on a few issues. May I chat with you for a few minutes?"

"About what?"

Still no face or posture changes.

I pull a card from my shirt pocket. Handing it to her requires me to take three steps closer to her. I wait a few seconds while she reads the card and looks up.

"I haven't seen The Rev for many years."

"Would you mind if we found a shady place to talk?" I say. "I'd love to get out of the hot sun."

She re-inspects my face, then gestures to follow her to the covered front porch and points at one of four lawn chairs lined up facing the street. I sit and realize she's still standing, her back to the street.

"About what?" she repeats, appearing capable of dashing two blocks away before I can move.

"A very close relative of The Rev's may have been murdered recently and he's asked me and my partner to look into some things that happened years ago."

"How could that have anything to do with me? As I said, I haven't seen him in years and was never close to him. What happened long ago that has *any* connection to me?"

"Well, there are some more-recent things also and we're talking to a few people to see if there's any possibility of a link."

"You either get specific right damn now or you haul your ass out of here while I'm calling the police," pulling a cell phone from her jeans pocket. "I have 911 on speed dial."

"I understand," I say, "You were married to Brandon Jefferson...."

"For less-than two years," she interrupts firmly. "Only one of those years was tolerable with that asshole. That's so far in my rear-view mirror I haven't thought about the experience in years, except for maybe two evenings of wine-prompted depression back in 1999. What the hell are you trying to say? What does Brandon have to do with whatever you're talking about?"

"What kind of guy was Brandon back then?"

"Aren't you listening? I just told you. He was an asshole. I imagine he still is. He was so fucking self-absorbed I had to remind him every day that he was married to *me* and not to the latest *free-love* bimbo he and his hippie friends passed around like a half-smoked joint.

"In the beginning, I was attracted to him because he was interesting and funny and the smartest, best-educated guy I'd ever met. He was a handsome charmer.

"When I finally realized that those qualities didn't make up for the drugs and the booze and the stoned sluts that he couldn't resist, I divorced him. Thank God we never had kids.

"I'm not even slightly interested in looking back now." she says. "I have a good husband, two grown-up kids and a satisfying life. So you trot back to your car and leave me alone before that jerk contaminates my life again. Go!"

I'm up, heading for the porch steps. She moves silently aside, watching me, phone still in her hand.

"I'm truly sorry to have bothered you, Mrs. Webster. We need to gather information from a variety of sources. You probably saw that Brandon's brother, Otis, has been cleared of that long-ago murder conviction and he's returned home after 30-plus years. There have been two murders and once again Otis is…."

"I didn't know anything about the first murder and I certainly don't know anything that's happened since my divorce. I don't want to know anything. Just go. Right damn now."

"Thanks very much for your time," Mrs. Webster."

I walk to my car with no response from her.

Chapter 42

-----JACK-----

"Mr. Jack Crocker?" a woman wonders when I answer our office phone, early the next morning.

"Yes."

"Hold for Mr. Thorndike," her imperial, all-business voice commands.

Who the hell is Mister Thorndike? I despise these power-play calls. Some officious voice telling me to "Hold" because her boss is way too busy to be on the line while she fetches me, an obviously insignificant and less-important peasant.

I hit the speaker button so Jimmy can hear whatever this pompous caller wants.

Best case scenario is that he needs our services and he's willing to pay enough money that we can find a way to tolerate him. Worst case he's selling condos in Florida.

"Hello, Mr. Crocker," says Mr. Important. "I'm Mathew Thorndike from Baker, Adams and Thorndike. We represent someone your colleague, Mr. McGuire, had a disturbing and threatening encounter with recently."

"Then you're representing Josh Dixon," I say, "the arrogant oaf who almost struck Mr. McGuire with his BMW while flipping him off. I assume you're calling to apologize for him. Am I correct, Mr. Thornapple?"

"Thorndike," he says, with an audible sigh. "There's no need for us to be disagreeable. Mr. Crocker. False accusations have been made against our client. Those false statements could subject our client to public scorn and ridicule even though he has no knowledge whatever of the events alleged by Mr. McGuire.

"I demand that you immediately provide me with the names and contact information of every person Mr. McGuire or you or anyone acting at your direction communicated these false accusations either by voice or in written documents or in any other manner."

"Wow," I say, "that's an awful lot of demands for me to remember. Please put them all in a letter, preferably with bullet points ranked in order of priority and with a minimum of multi-syllable words, so we can respond appropriately; you know, considering the limited intellectual capacity of the masses."

"Mr. Crocker, you and Mr. McGuire have no idea of the grief, financial and otherwise, that will befall you if your slanderous behavior doesn't stop. We're prepared to, among other things, sue you both individually as well as your company. I'm betting we would end up owning your tiny little company. Am I being clear?"

"Yes, Mathew, you're very transparent. You're threatening to crush us if we continue investigating your client for being a serial rapist. Why don't you just sue? Is it because a lawsuit would expose the investigation to the public and Mr. Dixon and his family would have to explain what happened. That's *exactly* what they don't want, so don't call here huffing, puffing. And bluffing. You're not going to sue us because if you do we'll explain everything. In the paper and on television. It won't be pretty? Am *I* being clear?"

"I can see that you don't understand the situation you're in," Thorndike snaps. "We'll see you in court. Plan to bring about a dozen very well-paid lawyers. And bring your articles of incorporation. I assume you're a non-profit."

As I hang up Jimmy is staring at me with his *what-the-hell-are-you-doing* face that I've seen before when he thinks I'm screwing up. He's been correct more than once.

"Please tell me why that was a good idea," he says. "Do we really want to poke the big bear in the snout?"

"Why not? He was a condescending jackass trying to intimidate us."

"Sure," Jimmy says. "There's a lot of that going around. Were you just having fun working out on him or do you have an actual plan to avoid seven-figure litigation?"

"Aw, the last thing that asshole wants is to actually sue us. First, we're doing nothing illegal, just investigating a crime against a very sympathetic victim.

"Second, he and Dixon's family don't want *any* mention of what happened or about Josh Dixon's role in it. They want *no* attention at all. Thorndike is trying to intimidate us into dropping the case."

"Neither of us responds well to attempted intimidation," he says. "But you were provoking him. Shouldn't we just let him rant and ignore him?"

"Probably, but he's an arrogant, condescending snob," I explain.

"Agreed," he says. "But isn't he acting exactly as he would if he's certain Josh Dixon is *not* our perp?"

Chapter 43

-----JACK-----

Since Brandon Jefferson's ex-wife kicked me off her porch, I've been in the office cyber-searching for Joe Bob Spencer and finding both too much information and too little.

I turned up several thousand hits on that or almost identical names; depending on use of "Bob" or "B." or no middle name. In the South, including Texas, "Bob" isn't necessarily a middle name, just as likely the second-half of a non-hyphenated first name.

Because some Dallas County court records from 1982 aren't available as digital files, I call a source from my destroyed reporter career and she looks up Spencer's "official" date of birth from his numerous encounters with law enforcement over many years. She faxes me lists of his arrests and convictions and I'm narrowing the search to possible name variations within two years of his apparent age.

But I'm not finding any trace of him in the last nine years. He's somehow managed to avoid getting busted or convicted of anything in Texas. No driver's license since 2006. No indication he owns real estate or even a car.

Leaving Texas seems unlikely. He was born here and has been arrested or incarcerated somewhere in Texas off and on for more than 40 years. But maybe he left for fresh territory.

Maybe he died without any official notice such as a death certificate, not uncommon for bottom-feeding, low-profile career criminals. The only newspaper clip I find reports his testimony in the Otis Jefferson trial when he claimed Otis confided in him that he was "sorry" for murdering the young woman. Apparently none of his other arrests or convictions, all for relatively petty crimes, attracted any public attention.

I hear Jimmy unlocking the back door, returning from dinner with Marsha.

One glance at his face as he slips into his chair across from me and I laugh.

"I assume you're going to explain that silly grin," I tease. "Was the food that good or did she ask you to get married?"

"Yes. And, no. It was a very pleasant evening."

"Pleasant? Pleasant? After a year of being totally smitten by this woman, you had a *pleasant* evening? Doing what, gazing into each other's eyes? Or maybe comparing the Euro's exchange rate with the dollar?"

"So, how was *your* day?" he says, still unable to erase his grin. "What happened with Brandon's ex-missus?"

"She doesn't even want to think about him. Called him an asshole, a lousy husband who didn't know the difference between his wife and an assortment of *bimbos* and *sluts* from his aging-hippie friends who were stoned most of the time. She has two grown-up kids and she considers Brandon someone who briefly contaminated her life before she tossed him in a dumpster and found herself a good and caring husband. Sounds like that was the best trade since the Yankees got Babe Ruth from the Red Sox.

"She says she divorced him after less than two years of wedded non-bliss because he was a horrible father and husband. And then she ordered me off her property."

"Maybe she didn't like you, either," he smirked.

"Quite possible. Meanwhile I'm having trouble finding the jailhouse snitch. He seems to have vanished in the last nine years after a lifetime of arrests, convictions or guilty pleas and endless probations and jail time. Just gone."

"Maybe he died," Jimmy says.

"I just finished trying to find death records anywhere in Texas. I already tried one website that claims to track obituaries throughout the country. Nada."

"There are several sites that claim the same thing but there's one that comes closest and according to some chat-room nerds seems to be the most up-to-date."

"Another advantage of having a partner with a Computer Science degree," I say.

He hands me a scrap of paper with a website scribbled on it.

I key it into my browser.

"How about some details about your *'it's not a date, just dinner'* evening with the lovely Marsha?" I urge, still looking at my laptop screen. "At least one Inquiring Mind wants to know."

"Yeah, well it's really none of your business," he says, "but truth is we had a good time chatting about many things, almost none of them involving hiding for 10 years from a violent almost-ex-husband, or shooting a fake cop trying to murder her. We're going to get together again, so...."

"Hot Damn!" I shout. "I think we just found Joe Bob Spencer, aka The Snitch, aka The Lying Weasel."

"Where is he?" Jimmy gets up to look over my shoulder at a four-paragraph obituary from a weekly newspaper.

"Apparently he's dead in Hugo, Oklahoma. Holy manure pile, he died less than a month ago."

⅄

J.B. Spencer Dies
Joe Bob Spencer, 59, of Hugo, died last Thursday.
He was employed at Mario's Pizza as a delivery driver.
He is survived by his aunt, Virginia Stephens, a life-long Hugo resident with whom he had lived since 2006.
No services were held.

⅄

"Wow, short but not sweet. A four-sentence summary of a crappy human life. We need to find out how he died," Jimmy says.

"Yes. Maybe Otis hasn't actually forgiven *everyone.*"

▲

"Hugo Tribune, how may I help you?"

"I'd like to speak to the reporter who wrote a recent obituary," I say.

"Only one of our two reporters is in the office. I'll transfer you to Donnie."

I explain to Donnie that I'm a private investigator and I want more details on the death of Joe Bob Spencer.

"Oh, gee, that was a handout from Swanson's Funeral Home. I just ran it as it came to us. I don't know anything beyond the news release."

"Would the police have any other information?"

"I have no idea. Is this somehow a suspicious death? Why do you think so? Is there a story here?"

"I don't know," I say. "I'm just wondering how he died. Maybe I should ask the Chief of Police?

"We don't have a police department. Sheriff Davidson and his five deputies handle everything in the county. As soon as I finish what I'm working on, I'll go over there and...."

"That's okay," I say. "I'll check with the Sheriff's department. What's the number?"

He provides it and I thank him for his help, hang up and immediately dial the number.

"Sheriff's office, this is Agnes, what's happening?"

I explain again that I'm a PI in Dallas and want some details about a recent death in Hugo. I hear a click and then a male gravel voice is in my ear.

"This is Sheriff Davidson. You think we have a suspicious death here? Who's dead?"

"Joe Bob Spencer, but I don't know that there's anything suspicious, I'm just wondering how he died. He was a witness in a trial here in Dallas over 30 years ago. I'm updating history."

"I'm not sure what that means, Sonny. J.B. Spencer was just a pizza delivery guy, not famous for anything around here. I doubt that he ever did anything 'historic.'"

"How did he die?"

"Wrong place, wrong time. He made a delivery, was getting back into his rickety old Chevy pickup and was killed when a vehicle, probably another pickup, hit him and his open door, splattering him on the pavement. We don't get many hit-and-runs around here but that's what this was. Probably some teen-ager too scared to stop and risk getting his license yanked. If he even had a license.

"We didn't have any clues, not even any paint scrapings. We suspect the vehicle had an unpainted front grill guard. We sure as hell don't have cameras all over the damn place like you probably do in Dallas."

"Still an open investigation?"

"Sonny, we don't have any *open investigations* unless you count the files that we would look at if something comes along, like maybe we find a suspicious vehicle with scrapes or dents somewhere. 'Cept, of course, pretty much all vehicles around here have scrapes on their bumpers. If they have bumpers."

"I understand, Sheriff. I appreciate your time."

I give him my contact information. He promises to let me know if a clue turns up.

Or if someone strolls into the Sheriff's office and blurts out a confession.

Chapter 44

-----JACK-----

"It's unbelievably, fantastically beautiful," Crystal says, pirouetting, her arms aloft, flowered sun dress flaring. "I've never seen the Arboretum more otherworldly, incredibly stunning than right this minute."

"Even Carli's enjoying it," I smile. "She's already snapped several hundred phone pix even though she's mainly sharing the experience with her Facebook and Instagram friends."

The kids have Friday afternoon off thanks to a teacher's conclave and Crystal left work early so we're getting our annual Dallas Arboretum fix. We've all been on an emotional high since I met them in the parking lot.

We've just finished an all-burger lunch at a small picnic table almost surrounded by waist-high, gorgeous dark-purple Irises.

Anytime I immerse myself in the Arboretum, but particularly in the spring, I can easily believe I'm in Paradise, the biblical one or any other version I can imagine.

Every conceivable shade of green abounds, usually as a background canvas for the entire palette of colors and shades the human eye is capable of seeing. Standing in one place and visually sweeping from side to side is like being in a living kaleidoscope.

I've been told that my mother brought me here several times a year starting when I was a newborn blob of protoplasm in a stroller with fewer stresses than I have now.

I've only missed a spring visit a few years: one as a rebellious 16-year-old and four others thanks to military deployments to places not likely to be mistaken for any kind of paradise.

It was here that I proposed to Crystal and sealed the deal almost 20 springs ago when we both pledged it was for a lifetime. Now we're watching our kids wander the paths winding through a universe of colors.

The family began coming here for an afternoon every May since we became a foursome.

I missed last year's ritual because we became a threesome-plus-one when Crystal tossed my sorry butt out of our home thanks my inability to conquer recurring Post Traumatic Stress Syndrome symptoms without the help of my constant companions and then-BFFs, Jack Daniels and Mr. Bud.

"You remember that Carli's Girl Scout Dads-and Daughters camp-out is tomorrow?" Crystal asks, as we walk a path between ethereal, shoulder-high ferns.

"Looking forward to it."

"So is Carli. She's got all of her gear packed and ready in the garage."

"Good. The only *ugh* part is getting her and her stuff in the car in time to meet the group at 5:30 a.m. and survive two hours in a bus full of cranky dads and hyper teens."

I stand with the bag of garbage and scan the area for a trash can.

"Maybe you should stay over tonight to make it easier," she says without looking at me.

I freeze in place for a couple of seconds digesting her suggestion. An invitation? I haven't stayed over-night in my former home in more than a year.

I spot a trash can, take two steps toward it, successfully launch the bag as if I'm Dirk Nowitzki and, as casually as I can, say: "Yes. That would make it easier. Sure."

CHAPTER 45

-----JACK-----

After the Arboretum, I swing by my cottage and retrieve my cardboard box of camping gear and supplies, then navigate a drive-through for a Family Bucket of the Colonel's best chicken parts and head home where Crystal and the kids live; the house where I lived before Crystal canceled my Husband and Father credentials.

We awaken the tuckered-out Erik dozing on his bed and Carli, sleeping on a living room sofa. They're unaware of the KFC extra-crispy aroma saturating the kitchen and probably already in our blood streams.

Crystal disappears while the suddenly famished kids and I spread paper plates, napkins and drinks on the kitchen table, surrounding the red and white cardboard pail.

Crystal returns, I excuse myself and head for the hallway bathroom. I spot the blankets and pillow awaiting me on the living room sofa that fortunately is long enough to accommodate my 6-3 frame without forcing me into a fetal pose.

It's a start.

By 9 p.m. we're all fading, barely aware of the "Frozen" Netflix movie nearing its end. Neither Carli nor Erik resist when Chrystal suggests they get their pajamas on and "...read in bed for a while if you want."

I'm pretty sure "a while" will be less than 10 minutes.

"I'm heading up, too," Crystal says, standing to turn off the TV. "This has been a fun day."

"Delightful," I add. "I'm glad we've exposed them to the beauty and wonders of the Arboretum over the years. A good legacy."

She holds my gaze for several seconds and I'm wondering if she's thinking about my reference to happier times.

She parks a hip on the sofa arm, looking pensive and uncertain.

My cell buzzes in my jeans and the Marine hymn breaks the spell.

"It's Jimmy. He's on a stakeout. I have to take this. I'm sorry."

"It's okay," she says.

I see her headed upstairs.

"What's up?" I ask him.

"Just checking in. I'm watching the Rogers' neighborhood. Easton had another job tonight. Okay to update you later if anything unusual comes up?"

"Yes if it's important. I have to be up and moving by 5:15. I'll be on an overnight Girl Scout camp-out tomorrow. I'm on the sofa at Crystal's house tonight."

He's silent for a long moment.

"Whoa."

"Yeah."

Chapter 46

-----JACK-----

My phone alarm rudely informs me it's time to join the Girl Scouts. Jimmy calls at 5:20 a.m. to check in and he will gather as much information about the biker as possible while Carli and I are burning a can of beans, hotdogs and S'mores over a smoky campfire somewhere in the East Texas woods.

In the far corner of a Walmart parking lot, Carli and I find the 12-passenger Girl Scout van and soon we and eight other dads and daughters, plus two adult leaders are east-bound on I-30 for the two-hour drive.

The camp itself is a 122-acre, heavily forested sliver of a gigantic Herford ranch set aside for Girl and Boy Scout use by the owners who apparently enjoyed the heck out of their own scouting experiences 60-plus years ago.

We unload our gear at a wall-less roof shielding a bunch of picnic tables. Narrow winding paths sprout in every direction from the shelter, all leading to small individual campsites with two-person, canvas tents not even a 10-year-old can stand up in. Each site has a small fire-ring in front and a path leading to the dreaded pit toilets.

An adult guide, dressed like Carli in jeans and a Scout shirt, introduces herself as Sandra Anderson. She guides Carli and me to our semi-private camp site and instructs us to set up our camp and regroup at the shelter area in 45 minutes. We hustle to stow duffels, unroll sleeping bags in the tent, along with our box of canned and dehydrated foods. From the ground we gather twigs and fallen tree limbs for our fire pit.

The group gathering is relatively brief, to the point and delivered by the high-energy troop leader, a petite brunette amazingly able to convince us that she might have been a tough Marine drill sergeant in another life.

"We have less than two days together," she says, striding purposely inside the circle we form around a large teepee of unlit wood, apparently for the evening group gathering and handing each of us a blue sheet delineating a crammed schedule.

"We will have group and individual activities continuously the rest of today and again tomorrow from breakfast at 5:30 a.m. until the bus leaves at 6 p.m.

"You will have some competitions where each Dad and Daughter team will have to cooperate and coordinate to win.

"You'll have some two-on-two time for each team to prepare a meal for yourselves, using a fire you build, clean your dishes and have some time to talk with each other about anything you want.

"Each team is responsible for all of its meals…except for this one," she says, pointing to the other troop leader who is opening a large cooler on one of the tables under the shelter.

"Your choices are ham and cheese or turkey and cheese, plus Sun Chips, a baggie of baby carrots and water. Consider this a mid-morning snack. As the schedule shows, lunch will be at 12:30 at your campsites. Now go choose a sandwich. You have nine minutes from right now before we move out for the next event."

Watching nine people trying to get outside of a three-piece *snack*, causes me to mentally review my years-ago training in the Heimlich maneuver.

Now it's "move, move, move" from the leaders gesturing us to follow them to a path that ends in a clearing of grass and wild flowers.

For the next 90 minutes we compete as two-person teams in exercises starting with the simple three-legged race that requires coordination between us to three other activities that I recognize from team-building exercises in leadership training at Ft. Bragg, North Carolina years ago.

Then we're dispatched to our various camp sites to prepare our own lunches and return to the shelter for more fun and games.

At 5:30 p.m. we are sent back to our tent to cook our dinner over the fire pit. We mix water into several freeze-dried food packets of brown rice, chicken Tetrazzini and carrots and peas. Then back to the main shelter where everyone now sits on logs bordering the large campfire. We manage to sorta sing a half-dozen traditional campfire songs in the darkening dusk. The leaders pass out S'mores ingredients and utensils and soon the air reeks of burnt marshmallows and graham crackers. Wonderful.

It's fully dark now. Carli and I need flashlights to follow the winding path to our tent where I assemble thin sticks and limbs for a small, temporary fire.

We sit close to the fire. Carli probes it with a long stick, mainly to see the sparks flare and die, her face pensive, captured by "campfire hypnosis" that has fascinated humans for thousands of years.

"If you don't mention it to Mom," I say, "I have a nightcap hidden in my sleeping bag. I didn't know Mrs. Anderson was bringing S'mores but if you have a little room left I'll get us an unhealthy but delicious treat."

She grins. "Definitely."

I retrieve the two packages of twin Twinkies I'd stashed in my day pack and we each open one and toss the wrappers in the fire.

"That's called destroying the evidence," I say. "Now it's our little secret."

She looks at me with a surprisingly serious face and I sense a change of mood.

"Are you and Mom going to get back together?"

And there it is. The absolutely bottom-line question.

"I don't know. I hope so."

She vigorously pokes the fire again, staring into the dancing, sharp-edged flames.

"Doesn't Mom want to?"

"I can't answer that. I've certainly given her lots of reasons not to. I've disappointed her time and again in the last year or so. I promised things I didn't deliver. I hit Erik with my car and..."

My throat closes up, I can't talk and it feels like I'm strangling myself.

Carli drops her stick in the flames, gets to her knees and throws herself at me, hugs my shoulders, suddenly sobbing uncontrollably and breaking my heart, not for the first time.

"Dad, I want our family back. I want *you* back. I want *Mom* back. She can't be the same Mom without you there. Erik wants and needs all of us. And not just on weekends."

Tears are streaming down my cheeks now. We're holding each other so tight it's as if we're a single being, both halves sobbing and shaking. I feel her heart pounding on my arm.

"Please, Dad. Find a way to get us back together."

I've never felt so small or helpless. Or so afraid.

CHAPTER 47

-----JACK-----

Mitch's voice through my cell is hushed, as if he's standing next to me whispering in my ear.

"Smokey Joe's BBQ, 11:30."

"Okay," I say.

The line goes dead.

Since *Smokey Joe's* is our private code for *Chisholm Trail Brisket Shed* in Rockwall, I immediately know something big is happening and we need to meet some place where we're not likely to see anyone we know. Smokey Joe's has 23 locations. The Brisket Shed is east of Dallas, on Lake Ray Hubbard in Rockwall, the Dallas skyline visible about 18 miles away.

Mitch is the Dallas Police Department lieutenant who runs the Homicide Division. He's also been my best friend since grade school. We've been through plenty of scrapes together from pranks in middle school to competing for a defensive-back starting position in high school.

The biggest challenge was when I was a reporter at the Dallas News looking into whiffs of corruption by several DPD officers.

Mitch was widely suspected by many of his fellow officers of being my source for the resulting series in the paper. He wasn't, except for a couple of times when I secretly asked him "Will I be wrong if I write..." something that I already had one or two sources for. He was only able to confirm one specific fact; he was not in the loop of corruption.

Ultimately several officers were fired or went to prison and Mitch remained smudged by suspicions inside the department. Some of his public critics were actually sources who didn't want their help known by others.

Of course, I was, and still am, seriously despised by many officers and unwelcome at police headquarters. Some officers were privately glad to get some bad apples out of uniform but most were not saying that in public, not an unusual part of the price a journalist can pay for peering under rocks on behalf of the public.

Our most-serious crisis together was last year when my son was kidnapped by thugs and killers.

About five years ago, Mitch and I developed some codes for when we needed to privately contact each other. They're not written down anywhere. He has a throwaway phone used only between the two of us for anything significant. We've only used it three times in five years.

My stomach growls as I cross three miles of I-30 bridges east across Lake Ray Hubbard to Rockwall. I slept in this morning after my Girl Scout adventure and haven eaten since last night. I'm curious, close to anxious, wondering what Mitch needs to tell me. Or ask me. Or warn me about.

Inside Chisholm's dimly lighted, sooty-walled main room booths surround a center area with sturdy, well-used picnic tables apparently from the 1955 grand opening.

A waitress who fits the same description nods when I point to a back booth with a single occupant.

My jean-clad butt is still sliding across from Mitch when he leans forward, forearms on the table.

"We have a bit of a problem, mate."

I say, "Oh, you're in your Australian disguise today. I assume you've already ordered the "Shrimp from the Barby" entrée that you get every time we're here."

"We've only been here twice so that's not a pattern. Besides, just shut up and listen."

"Yessir. What's up?"

Before he can answer the waitress appears to take orders.

As soon as she's out of earshot, Mitch leans toward me again and I match his posture.

We probably look like two guys in an AARP chess tournament.

"My guys are finding tracks from you and Tonto every place we turn," he growls. "Too many times when we interview someone even on the fringes of the case we hear some form of: "Oh, those nice officers working with The Rev asked us the same thing.""

"You're not suggesting we're posing as actual police officers are you?"

"Of course not, I know you guys wouldn't do that."

Our chopped brisket sandwiches arrive and I ask, "Then what's the problem?" just before chomping as large a bite as I can.

"Aside from being annoying?" Mitch says. "That's not your fault, although you *are* excellent at annoying people. The problem is there's enough of a rumor in the blue grapevine, not just among my detectives, hinting that maybe I'm slipping you information about what we're doing or planning to do so that you can get a step ahead. You know, a little personal favor between you and me. Everyone knows we're old friends and even though we've played things straight…almost one-hundred percent, you know how suspicious we cops can be. And damn well need to be."

"Sure. Doesn't sound too serious. Am I missing something?"

"This is already becoming a problem that we don't need. We're trying to investigate a case that might be a coincidence spanning 33 years. Or it might not even be a crime at all. But we gotta try to find out. Many of the original participants are dead or incapacitated. A guy spent all those years in prison and he apparently didn't do the deed. This is a nightmare combination of injustice, prosecutorial misconduct, possibly an active serial killer plus a very old cold case. If the Jefferson guy didn't murder that girl, who did?

"It's re-sparking the old conspiracy theories that kept us from even contacting each other for almost a year after your stories put some of my brothers in blue into prison is a distraction I don't want."

"What do you want me to do?"

"How about you and Tonto show good faith by passing along to my team some information or tips you run across?"

"You know we would automatically call you any time we found something significant." I say. "We want the truth about this case and certainly would be happy if the police solve it, with or without our help."

"Yeah," he says, glancing around the room, "but I guess I'm asking you to maybe stretch the definition of *significant* a tad and come up with two or three things you could pass along. It would help me keep my guys focused on the case and not the gossip network."

He's really uncomfortable asking this favor.

"Of course we can do that," I say. "Tonto and I will come up with something in a day or two and I'll give you a buzz."

"No," he says immediately. "Not me. Call Sgt. Carlson, he's got the case. I need you to leave me out of it. Give him two or three calls over the next week or so with anything close to important or significant that you pick up."

"Okay, I get it. I'll find a reason to call Henry Carlson at least once and Jimmy maybe two or three more."

"Thanks, Jack. Carlson's a talented detective and I'm pretty sure he's not one of the guys who think you wrote those stories just to disgrace cops for fun and profit."

"Well," I say, "that's nice to hear, even if you're only *'pretty sure'* he doesn't think I'm a scum-bag, cop hater."

We stand, flash each other our Vulcan split-finger salute from middle school and head separately back to Dallas.

Chapter 48

-----JIMMY-----

As dusk darkens the evening, I'm parked a row behind my Target, waiting for him to clear the front door of the Blue Star Bar & Grill.

Now I'm inside and see him stopping briefly at the right end of the bar along the back of the room, putting something on the bar, speaking briefly to the bartender and heading down a nearby hallway marked "Restrooms."

I pretend to look around the room, glance at my watch as if I'm meeting someone, then saunter to the bar and sit on the stool next to The Target's cigarette pack and lighter, order a beer and wait.

When The Target returns and sits next to me, I barely acknowledge him with brief nod without looking at him. I sip my Lone Star and say, more or less to the mirror behind the bar: "It's been a long damn day. Time for some mellow juice," and take a longer swig from the frosted mug.

"Same here," he says, glancing at me. "I'm just off shift and it wasn't a fun day."

I don't need to ask what his job is because I already know he's the youngest and newest officer on the University's Campus Security police force. I've tailed him here from the University's main parking lot.

"Yeah," I say, "sometimes getting off work is the best thing that happens all day."

For a few minutes we banter about mundane subjects, mostly sports, the way guys do when we're thrown together with strangers in bars or barber shops or elevators.

I sip from the frosted mug.

Time to push this seduction along.

I catch the bartender's eye.

"Another round here," I say, hoping not to hear Target say: "Thanks but I need to head home."

Instead he says, "Hey, thanks. One more might help me forget being pissed off most of the day."

I mentally give myself an enthusiastic high-five but following Asian culture, keep my smile inside my cheeks.

After another swig of fresh beer I up the ante.

"Where do you work? Sounds like you might be looking for a new job."

"Maybe I am," he says as if he hadn't actually said it out loud before. "I'm a campus police officer at McMillan University. You know, parking violations, herding traffic at sports events, plays and lectures. I've only been there eight months and so I get rookie assignments but most everything any of us do is dull stuff."

"I know the feeling," I say.

He tips his bottle and resumes flipping his lighter. He rotates his stool a few degrees toward me, his boyish face seeming out of proportion with his muscular build.

"I took the job to get some on-the-street experience. I eventually want to be on a police force of a medium-size town somewhere. I'm not a big- city guy but I've always wanted to be a cop, you know, helping people, occasionally getting some bad guys off the streets."

"Sounds like a noble and courageous career," I say. "But it's not working out so far?"

We both imbibe more medicine and I stay silent, hoping he'll be compelled to fill the gap.

"Well, I guess I don't think of it in such highfalutin terms. I've got a two-year Criminal Justice degree and want to get more education. I want to be a positive part of some place--maybe even in Amarillo, my home town. You know, raise my kids and go to high school football games. Isn't that the corniest thing you've ever heard?"

"No, I felt something like that when I dropped out of college one semester from a degree in Computer Science to enlist in the Marines. I graduated with the sheepskin three months after I left the military. Felt good."

I drain my mug and he immediately signals for another round.

Perfect.

He extends his right hand.

"By the way, I'm Chris Griffin."

"Jimmy McGuire. Nice to meet you."

"The Marines, huh?" he says. "Where did they send you?"

"One vacation in Iraq and two in Afghanistan," I say softly.

"Wow," he says. "I guess you saw some action, huh?" turning a bit more on his stool.

"Yeah," I say. "Enough to cure me of the idea that I can change the world. The world's too damned big. And in some ways, too screwed up. I need to focus on things that are more doable."

"You okay now?" he says. "I mean...were you wounded?"

He pauses, looking uncomfortable.

"You know," he almost stutters, "physically...or...otherwise?"

"I've pretty much moved on," I say, ignoring most of his question.

He says, "I noticed you're missing the tip of your left middle finger. Was that from Afghanistan or Iraq?"

"No. Actually that got shot off right here in Big D. Ironic, huh?"

His brow wrinkles, clearly curious.

"What the hell happened?"

"My partner and I had a fire-fight with some kidnappers and killers last year while rescuing his young son."

"Wow, you're one of those private detectives I read about and saw on TV last year. Your partner is...Jack something?"

"Jack Crocker. He's my Mom's brother."

"What are you guys doing now?" he says.

I take a couple of long breaths, separated by a modest amount of Lone Star, look him square in his eyes, and leap off a tall cliff without a parachute and no Plan B.

"I'll tell you exactly what I'm doing now if you promise me one thing."

"What?"

"I need you to swear that when I tell you what's going on you will not tell another soul until it's over, no matter what your reaction is to what I say."

He hesitates, his face revealing his inner debate.

"Okay," he says, finally, "I promise to keep your secret...unless you tell me you're about to commit a felony or something obviously immoral."

"It's exactly the opposite of that," I say. "Jack and I are trying to get justice for an innocent person who's being treated very badly, disgustingly actually, by people who should be protecting her. And if that sounds like a comic book plot, so be it."

He cocks his head a little, thinking about it and says: "Okay, I promise I can keep a secret."

I glance around the room verifying that no one is close enough to overhear us at the end of the bar. I reach toward him and we shake hands again.

"We have a deal, Chris," I say. "I'm going to trust you. And you need to trust me.

"This is going to shock you but here's the straight truth. Our sitting here together is not an accident. I followed you here from the campus. I already knew your name and what your job is. We need your help."

His eyes widen and I pause to let him chew on that bombshell.

"Are you shittin' me?"

"Nope. Not now. I sorta was before, just getting to know you. You seem to be a decent guy. I'm taking a big risk right now, telling you this and hoping we can start over and be on the same team. You want me to stop and walk away?"

He thinks for a few seconds.

"No. My God, I'd never be able to think about anything else for the rest of my life wondering what you were going to tell me."

Without revealing her name, I tell him about Robyn and her experience at his Campus Security department, emphasizing how that experience has greatly magnified the horror of her attack. And how she has retreated into herself, withdrawing from family and friends and how the rapists are sending her taunting and disgusting emails, videos and instantly disappearing photos of their assault of this young woman.

And I tell him we believe other rape victims have been similarly interrogated and manipulated into not officially filing or not pursuing complaints.

I'm intensely studying his face and body language for signs of danger. I fear that maybe I've offended his sense of loyalty to his fellow officers. I know that earlier I detected dissatisfaction with his job, but I could have misread the nature or depth of his feelings. I know that attacking someone's family or a group they're part of can provoke sharp anger and defensiveness even if just a few minutes earlier they've been bitterly bitching about the same folks.

What I'm seeing in his body and face is closer to hypnosis. First time I've ever seen someone who actually is "'slack-jawed."

"You see where I'm going?" I ask. "I know you can imagine the horrific consequences of what some officers have been inflicting on victims coming to your department hoping to find justice. And they're putting others in danger. They're leaving future victims of the same perps roaming the streets looking for more victims.

He blinks several times, directs his gaze to the bar top and back to me.

"Yeah," he says. "I get it. I accidentally saw part of an incident like that where it seemed to me the Lieutenant was aggressively questioning a victim about every tawdry detail of the rape. He kept pointing out how the victim would be forced to testify about those details in open court.

"I wondered if this was normal procedure. Were these cases handled differently on campus than in a regular police department? Nothing like this was mentioned in my two-year degree program. Was I just too new to understand what I saw? I was bewildered and angry. I never saw that woman again, but I knew in my gut that what happened that day was wrong. I've tried not to think about it, just learn my job and get established."

He clenches his eyes closed for at least 30 seconds, his hands frenetically massaging each other.

Out damned spot.

"My, God," he chokes, "I'm partly responsible for what happened to the girl you're talking about. And probably others, too. But I just looked away. I've been angry but I never said squat to anyone. I just let it go. What a frigging coward. I've never thought of myself that way but.... bottom line, I haven't done a damned thing about....It's like I've let them rape the victims again."

"Whoa, Chris, this isn't your fault. You're new there and this certainly has been protocol for years. Surely not everyone in the department agrees with what's been going on. Do you know anyone else who's also troubled at being part of protecting the University and the rapists but to hell with the victims?"

"No, but I'm the newest guy and a rookie and if anyone disagrees with policy they probably wouldn't be sharing with me. I think it's like one of those 'unwritten rule' things. It just *is*. No one would want to talk about it. At least not at work."

He's getting more agitated, shifting his butt on the stool, blinking rapidly, breathing heavily, hyperventilating.

I may have to put a paper bag over his head.

"Chris, we want to stop the horror that's happening to these women. Being assaulted by brutal sexual predators is awful enough to recover from without cops terrorizing the victims again, bullying them into silence. Officers are supposed to *protect* victims and put rapists in jail but some of the people you work with are enablers, protecting the rapists. They're border-line terrorists.

"We're all enablers if we don't snuff this system," I whisper. "I don't want that on my soul."

"Exactly," he says, getting off his stool. "That clinches it. I'm getting the hell out of there."

"No," I say louder than I intend. "You need to stay and help us end this crap."

He stares at me as if he's carved from ice.

"Let's get out of here," he says, his lips barely moving, his eyes darting around the room. "I need to talk outside."

"I'll head for the restroom," I say, tossing some cash on the bar. "Meet me in the parking lot. I'm in an eight-year-old, black Mustang."

Outside, the moon is only a sliver as I walk toward my car without turning my head but my eyes scanning the lot. I pause and pretend to pat my pockets for my keys and see a figure detach from the shadows several rows away and head toward me. I get in, turn off the overhead light and Chris opens the passenger door and slides in.

We glance at each other and I wait for him to speak but he doesn't. I wait.

"What are you and Crocker planning to do?"

I hesitate and plunge ahead.

"Somehow we're going to find a way to stop the bullying of victims. And we hope to find a way to destroy the current system that turns rapists loose to assault other women. The wrong people are suffering. The assaulters aren't punished. They remain free to violently do whatever their self-centered viciousness wants. We want to shine the spotlight on the shadows in that department and watch the rats run."

He is silent, not moving.

"We think you can be part of ending this disgusting and immoral treatment. We need information about the names of victims who were bullied and intimidated out of officially filing complaints. And names of those who were frightened enough by officers to never follow up. Or who were manipulated to walk away, leave school or move away.

"We suspect there are files of unpursued sexual assault cases stashed somewhere, not by those names but something to disguise contents. And there are probably other crimes involving influential family members caught driving drunk on campus or theft or beating up roommates or peddling drugs being covered up. If we can find files like that it would strengthen the accusation that the Campus Security Department is really the Campus Public Relations Department.

"Jack and I believe that any officers discouraging sexual assault victims either know what they're doing or they don't. Either way, they don't deserve to be in law enforcement at any level. They deserve to be in prison. They are protecting violent people who are certain to strike again.

"Chris, if you can find files with helpful information then together we'll flush the chicken shit from that corrupt cop coop. Those people aren't like you.

"Obviously this is high-risk stuff. If you get caught looking at or copying files they're trying to hide, you would probably be fired immediately, possibly ending your law enforcement career."

For several minutes he stares through the windshield, his throat swallowing as if he has a mouth full of cotton. His face is flushed and he's breathing heavily, as if he's been running in water up to his knees.

Now he grabs my hand and pumps it.

"Let's nail those sonsabitches!"

Chapter 49

The neighborhood is dark and hushed when I park in our driveway, enter through the kitchen of our little cottage and am greeted by an unexpected, but definitely welcome pizza aroma.

Jack looks up from his laptop.

"It's been a long, post Girl Scout camp day," he tells me. "Gotta brief you on a request from Mitch. Nothing we can't handle, otherwise not very productive."

"Smells wonderful in here. You ordered pizza? Got any left?"

"All of it."

"Let's celebrate," I grin. "I've had a pretty good day."

"You must have hit a home run or at least a triple to be this perky."

I nod and point a folded pizza slice at him.

"I *think* we've now got an undercover agent inside the University's Security department. Someone who might be able to get names of more victims of the department's bullying victims and covering up crimes."

"I'm all ears."

"Remember that rookie Campus Security cop I mentioned the other day? He was on the department's roster and is the newest and youngest officer.

"I followed him to a bar in Oak Cliff for an after-shift beer. I *interviewed* him without his knowing it. I think it might pay off.

"His name is Chris Griffin. I tried to find out whether he knows that some of his colleagues are discouraging rape victims who try to file complaint. Or if he's part of the system.

"I found out he's bored and unhappy in Campus Security and he's been thinking of quitting. He seemed trustworthy, a genuine guy.

"I swore him to secrecy and told him basically what we're trying to do. He's been troubled by witnessing a lieutenant bullying a rape victim and protecting the University instead of the victim that he got visibly agitated when I told him we wanted to put an end to it. He's agreed to help us."

"How?"

"He's going to see if he can find actual names of victims and perps, dates and locations and any other details of what you and I call the *Miscellaneous Files*. I didn't tell him we knew about the four cases.

"He suspects there are what he calls "For Show" files that can be produced if any of the cases are followed up by lawyers for victims and if the department needs to demonstrate that they have actual paperwork. He hasn't seen any files but that jibes with what I saw when I peeked into their files.

"Chris is outraged that there's apparently an unwritten cover-up-policy designed to protect the University and to let the attackers skate, even though they'll probably attack someone else. In other words, to hell with the victims, past and future. He feels personally responsible for not reporting the one incident that he saw happen."

"That has to be sanctioned by University higher-ups," Jack says.

"He told me he was present a couple of months after arriving when a student and her parents came in to file a complaint against a casual acquaintance the night before at a TGIF party.

"The victim he saw was asked if she was certain she wanted to testify in public about *everything* she *claimed* happened.

"He felt the victim interview seemed designed to discourage rather than facilitate and was openly hostile toward the young woman.

"The officer interrogated her in a skeptical tone and predicted in intimate detail the humiliation she faced if she testified in court. She finally ran from the room crying with her parents right behind her. He says as far as he knows, no follow-up ever came from that victim. Officially, nothing had happened; no rape, no complaint, not even a log entry that someone tried to file a complaint.

"That's a version of what Ben Rogers described when he forced Robyn to report her attack," I say.

"Yes and he's the kinda guy who might decide to sue the sox off the University," Jimmy says. "If we tell him there's documentation of intimidation and cover-ups I wouldn't be surprised if he gathered a platoon of lawyers with subpoenas and invaded the "alleged" Campus Security Department," making air finger quotes.

"Any chance this Chris Griffin guy will re-flip or is setting us up? Or maybe he's leading us into a trap?"

"I don't think so, but there's always a chance. We don't need something else to worry about."

"Let's see what we get from him," I say. "We've got an opportunity to make a serious case against Dixon if we can find other complaints against him. If he's the one who raped Robyn I want to personally tack his pelt on our wall."

Jack adds: "Preferably with him still in it."

Chapter 50

I see Marsha coming through the tall, frosted-glass doors to *Sandersons,* an upscale North Dallas restaurant. I've been watching 10 minutes for her, anticipating our first actual dinner date.

We've only seen each other in casual clothes, jeans and slacks and caftans. Except for that first time when she came to our office to hire us after a suspicious, near-miss-and-run. She was hidden in a long black coat, a black scarf over hair in a bun and clothing obviously from some thrift-shop's Granny Department. But that was her disguise.

Now, even from a distance, she's a couple of generations younger in a short, two-strap red dress with silver bracelets on both wrists and a simple silver pendant, her hair upswept with curls framing her face.

She is beautiful.

By the time we're seated, we've encountered valets, the maître d', a guide to our red-velvet booth, and a waiter bringing hard-cover menus and a wine list, three of them in tuxes and one with a French accents.

We order a cabernet. Marsha surveys the subtly lighted room and briefly sniffs the single red rose in a crystal vase next to a flickering candle.

The cab arrives, is poured, swirled, sniffed, tasted and approved.

"I hope," I say, "that you noticed I'm familiar with the required wine ritual. I'm trying to drastically upgrade my *suaveness* rating and possibly dim your memory of hot dogs and fries at Costco."

We laugh and I raise my glass.

"I'd like to propose a repeat of the toast you made at the Happy Grape Bistro.

"'The past is past, the future is unknown and now is now.'"

"Here's to *now*, right this minute," she agrees as we clink long-stem glasses. I gaze at her with delight as we sip.

We cheerfully comment on the tall menu's exotic offerings including appetizers such as Caviar with vodka cream, or entrees up to a 16-oz NY strip for $49.

A Tux materializes and commits our selections to memory and repeats them to us.

"Lobster tacos for two. Veal Milanaise with arugula, artichoke and asparagus salad. Pepper Crusted Tuna Mignon with cranberry-corn galette and braised chanterelle mushrooms."

Marsha leans toward me, smiling, almost whispering, "This is wonderful, James. I appreciate your choice of this place, but I want you to know that you definitely don't need to *court* me in fancy restaurants. Or anywhere else, for that matter."

"I understand," I say. "I view tonight as a *celebration* of our reconnecting, and, I hope, of an opportunity to see if…there might be… something…but, if not, at least refreshing a friendship."

Deduct 50 Suaveness points! Back in negative numbers.

A smile flickers as she looks down, concentrating on realigning two forks on the tablecloth. She glances up and says, "I hear the Rangers have a new pitcher who's looking real good so far."

We both laugh and my relief is bolstered by arrival of the Lobster Taco appetizer.

"Any new developments between Jack and Crystal?"

"Maybe. The family was together a half-day at the Dallas Arboretum recently and Crystal invited Jack to stay overnight at the family house so he could go to a two-day Girl Scout camp-out with Carli early the next morning."

"Overnight?" Marsha's eyebrows soar.

"On the sofa. But it's progress. Maybe. Crystal certainly has seen a pile of disappointments, many promises made but un-kept by Jack. All the family time they've shared in the last eight months or so may have made her less wary, less skeptical and a little more comfortable to take another step forward. I know Jack has tried hard to rebuild her trust. He hasn't had a relapse since shortly after the accident with Erik. Getting back home again is his ultimate goal. "

"Oh, I hope they figure out how to get back together," she says. "They need a fresh start, leaving their bad baggage in their rear-view mirror."

"Maybe you and I should do something similar," I suggest. "A do-over? A start-over?"

I watch her face turn thoughtful, eyes momentarily focusing somewhere over my shoulder, then locked on me.

"We're both reasonably level-headed grown-ups," she says, "You and I have a brief, but *extremely* intense, history together. I shot a man, a professional killer, and I was about to shoot him again. You were wounded in a shoot-out with kidnapers and killers. I'll never forget that you and Jack and Mark saved my life."

"Nah, you'd already wounded the would-be killer before Mark could confront him. You would have shot the guy again if needed. You had things under control."

"Maybe. Maybe not. I hope so. I often relive the stuff that happened, the life-and-death decisions we all made, all the horrific things that could have gone wrong or did go wrong. My husband was murdered. That was a dramatically life-changing time for me. You and Jack freed me from my long ordeal hiding in a stolen identity, hoping my husband wouldn't find me."

"Me, too," I say. "I'm mostly free now from nightmares that dogged me after two Marine tours in Afghanistan and one in Iraq. I feel like a whole person again, *despite* being nostril-deep in two hugely important cases. Or maybe *because* of them."

"I'm wondering," she says, "is there a way we can be friends while we explore what else might happen--if anything--beyond our mutual history?"

"Sign me up," I grin, impulsively raising my wine glass and we ting the crystal glasses again. "You already know I've been attracted to you from Day One, but I can be casual for a while and see what happens."

"I'm intrigued by you," she says so softly that I lean forward, hands on the table, hoping I've heard correctly.

Intrigued? Is this where I wake up still in Afghanistan?

She holds my gaze with her startlingly violet eyes and lightly covers my hands with her own.

"James, you seem so straight-forward, so tough and at the same time *so* gentle, so wholesome and so genuine that you seem too good to be true to someone who spent years hiding from an abusive husband. I want to know more about you."

"It would be wonderful to explore…possibilities," I say.

She smiles, rearranges the forks again and says:

"That could be fun. On the other hand, we don't even know if our tastes in movies or food or travel overlap or are compatible. I might be Felix and you're Oscar."

"Yeah, and I might be heavy metal and you're Ramsey Lewis, not that that would be a deal breaker."

Gotta ask. Too soon?

"This is probably a dumb question at this moment," I say, and see her eyes snap to me. "Any chance you're in a rebound mode? Still recovering from your husband's murder and…."

"Good heavens, no," she laughs. "Anything like that was years ago and it quickly vanished when I fully realized that I had two husbands, one loving and fun and supportive, the other a polar opposite, paranoid, jealous, capable of striking me and begging forgiveness later. I avoided relationships while I was hiding. To say I was *wary* would be putting it mildly.

"But that's definitely in the *past* and we're talking about *now* and about the *future.*"

She closes her eyes for a moment, inhales deeply and says, "James, I'm a clear-eyed, unrestricted free agent."

I barely manage a muffled "Me, too."

Another quick hoist of our wine in a smiling air-toast.

We nibble the lobster tacos saying nothing more serious than "delicious" and "wonderful."

The tacos are dispatched and I put my fork down and engage her eyes for several seconds.

"Okay," I say. "If we're in the *now* while looking to the *future* without lingering in the *past* let's try our own *fresh start*. Let's meet again for the first time tonight."

She slightly tilts her head as if as if asking a question.

"I'd like to introduce myself. I'm Jimmy McGuire, sometimes known as Tonto or James. I'm a private investigator. I got a crush on you the minute you came through the door…less than an hour ago…that door over there, by the maître d'."

Marsha chuckles, her eyes dancing. She extends her hand and I take it for a long moment.

"It's nice to meet you. I'm Marsha Harris, Administrative Assistant to SMU's Law School Dean. I'm also a first-semester law student. I've been known by another name but that's not relevant now. And, I was *intrigued* by you the moment I entered this restaurant. Thanks for asking me to dine with you, Mr. McGuire."

We're both laughing.

"Can we just move on from this moment?" she asks. "We don't need a plan or an outline or a clear path. No commitment except to do whatever seems okay at any given time, even if that's to walk away if either of us wants or needs to."

"Yes we can," I say, raising my right hand in the Boy Scout salute. "I'm in."

"I think this is going to be interesting. And fun," she says.

That's when the entrees arrive and we love them, too.

Later, while waiting for the valets to bring our cars, Marsha says, "Maybe next time we can take another step. You pick me up at home and we'll go to Sonic, which doesn't have a maître 'd or a valet."

CHAPTER 51

-----JACK-----

I park Crystal's borrowed white van near the back of a grass field rapidly filling with cars, SUVs and pickups, large and small.

Outside, I adjust my aviator sunglasses, my dark-gray Stetson and walk toward an old barn about 50 yards away. I don't look back but I know Jimmy is still in the passenger seat pretending to talk on his cell.

He's going to wait five minutes before exiting through the driver's side door. His black felt Stetson shadows his face and like me, he has facial hair and a few temporary tattoos that he didn't have last night.

His black moustache and goatee and his half-Native American skin tone plus a lean ex-Marine body enhances the stud-muffin aura he always radiates.

My slightly gray, Teddy Roosevelt moustache guarantees no one will see my upper lip today. We're both hoping Otis Jefferson won't recognize either of us amongst the gathering congregation. Jimmy and I will be strangers to each other as we try to keep Otis in sight, but at a distance.

I don't need the large *Horseshoe Cowboy Church* sign above the open barn door because I'd seen a photo of the barn-church on its website.

We've come here because Jimmy remembered Roberta mentioning that Otis often attended a Cowboy Church in Plano. She said she'd never been there and that Otis had no connection to it before he was sent to prison.

We followed him in the van this morning to this former farm turned church.

Neither Jimmy nor I knew much about "Cowboy" churches, although we'd heard of them, both of us growing up in Texas. They're mostly in rural areas, but some are in suburban areas around large cities. They are usually fiercely Bible-based, unaffiliated with other Christian groups, services in whatever basic space is available. A web search revealed seven other Cowboy Churches within 40 miles of Dallas.

Since we were making little progress on the case and we wondered why Otis was worshiping at this particular church, we decided to see who he is associating with.

Now, I'm carried along by a human river flowing to the open barn door, couples cradling babies in arms or strollers, toddlers and teens, large men with beer bellies, short men with beer bellies, elderly cowboys, some amazingly reminiscent of photos from 100 years ago, a few with canes, everyone in jeans, most in boots, a few wearing spurs despite no evidence of anyone riding in on horseback, although my nose tells me horses have recently pooped in the vicinity.

We're streaming between two rows of gray concrete stalls, probably 30 in all, lining both sides of the dirt driveway, looking like squat 1950s motel rooms, each with a gated door you can back your trailer up to and unload horses.

Our flow through the front door slows as if encountering a narrow canyon. Every few feet someone seems to recognize that I am a visitor and welcomes me with a smile and a proffered hand.

The interior is much larger than the exterior promised. It's clear that this is a unique place created by folks starting with an old wood barn, adding some new steel construction to almost double the space, but not requiring any fancy-pants architectural assistance. Down-to-earth creative people produced this one-of-a-kind sanctuary organized by many rows of folding chairs without an official color.

Hand-me-down chairs from old school classrooms and extinct dining halls?

I glance around, pretending to admire the space but mostly I'm scanning faces of the growing worshippers milling around, greeting friends, reserving seats by draping jackets over the backs of sturdy folding chairs or tossing a hat or purse on the seat. I leave my sunglasses on an aisle chair eight rows from the raised stage.

From there I count the rows and estimate 200 chairs.

I work my way around the perimeter, taking in the room and watching for Jimmy or Otis. I find myself near a lectern on the concrete floor in front of the stage where nine musicians are lining up, crowding together with guitars, a drum set and microphones in a line.

Left of the lectern, a shiny galvanized steel livestock watering tank awaits the next baptism.

A golden retriever is sleeping curled up by the drums and when I turn back to the main room I see a black Lab, an English short-hair, two tiny Yorkies, a black German Shepherd puppy and other, mostly unleashed dogs, mingling with the assembling congregation.

A dog-friendly, free-range sanctuary. Another first.

Still no sign of Jimmy or Otis. I'm hoping they weren't thrust close to each other in the line outside but even then our professional, hi-def television-quality, faux facial hair should withstand scrutiny.

I'm not worried much about Jimmy's skin-tone since most of the men in here, young and old, have faces indicating they work outside and probably are hunters and fishermen. Very few pale guys, the majority of them displaying facial hair in a wide variety of styles.

Bingo. Otis!

I point my face 90 degrees from where Otis is working his way along an aisle across the room from me, but my eyes track his movements, made easier because Otis is one of very few black faces visible in the crowd.

The band launches into *"That Old Rugged Cross."* the bold-voiced leader singing a rousing version. Apparently this is the signal the service is beginning and the gathering is mostly seated before the song ends.

As I make my way up the aisle to retrieve my sunglasses and reserved chair, I glimpse Jimmy standing in the shadows by the back wall where he can see the whole room.

The band strikes up some introductory notes and a deep-voiced male singer launches into: *"I Met Jesus in a Bar."*

The 80-ish woman sitting next to me mutters, "Good grief, can't we limit that song to once every other leap year?"

An hour later, I've been drawn into the music, drifted through announcements of up-coming meetings and events, followed by a story for youngsters who gather on the floor by the lectern. Most hats come off only during prayers.

The pastor not only has a better Teddy moustache than I do, he could *be* Teddy; short, solidly muscular, small round glasses, wide suspenders providing back up for a wide leather belt. His confident stride, almost a swagger, takes him in and out of the congregation, gesturing, holding dramatic pauses at key points, often sparking a sprinkling of 'Amens.'

I'm keeping watch on the back of Otis's head in the third row, diagonally across from me. When the service is over, Jimmy and I will keep Otis on our radars until he leaves. We want to see if he has any conversations longer than "Hi, how ya doing?" or "Good to see ya. How's Mildred?"

When Pastor Teddy drops to one knee by the lectern all hats come off and heads bow.

Immediately the band is playing and everyone's standing, some heading for the door, others mingling, hugging, laughing and petting the dogs moseying through the crowd checking credentials to determine what the humans had for breakfast.

I don't see Jimmy but I'm confident he's positioned so he has a different angle on Otis.

Fifteen minutes later, Otis is moving to the door. Jimmy is a dozen people behind him, chatting with an elderly woman with a cane and helping her navigate the crowded area.

I merge into the exodus line where Pastor Teddy appears and introduces himself as Billy McDougal, thanks me for coming and assures me I'm welcome at any time.

We emerge into the noon sunshine and others are sidling up to chat with Pastor McDougal.

I step aside and see Otis 50 feet ahead. He's walking close to the row of horse stalls along the left and talking with a tough-looking dude with tattoos on every inch of exposed flesh except his face, framed by long, greasy black and gray hair.

The Charles Manson autograph model hair-do.

They disappear around the far end of the stalls. I see Jimmy between me and the corner Otis just navigated. Jimmy's facing me over the shoulder of a young woman who is, in effect, providing a human shield for Jimmy to keep Otis in view.

I pull my cell, glance at it and bring it to my ear, talking randomly while reversing my direction as if looking for a quiet place to talk. At the near end of the stalls I wander along patchy grass until I can see behind them.

The ground slopes gradually down from the building to a small pond ringed by water willows and cottonwoods. Otis and Tattoo Dude sit on opposite sides of a weather-beaten, rough-wood picnic table. Otis leans forward, forearms on the table. Tattoo Dude pounds his right fist on the table several times, talking directly into Otis's face a foot away.

Angry or frustrated?

I continue strolling in a small circle, lips silently moving, occasionally moving a hand as if making a point.

Tattoo Dude stands and Otis gestures for him to rejoin him at the table. Tattoo Dude waves his arms a few times then sits and they resume talking.

Did I just see Otis slide something across the table to Tattoo Dude?

I know I've stretched the length of a credible phone call walkabout and amble to the end of the building until I can't see the men at the table.

I get to the driveway and don't see Jimmy but I assume he's got Otis in view from somewhere among the cars in the field. I'm holding the phone which startles me by vibrating, the screen showing: "TONTO"

"I see you. Our friend is still talking with the tattoo poster boy. I want to tail Mr. Tattoos and get his license plate. Take your time moseying to the van."

"I'm excellent at moseying," I assure him as the line goes dead.

Now I'm melting in the van's back seat with the air conditioning struggling, the sliding door open, one window down, trying to bleed off the blistering heat.

Jimmy materializes by the driver's side door, gets in, signals me to close the window and I slide the side door shut. We don't speak until we're on a state road headed for Interstate 30 back to Dallas.

"Why is Otis talking with someone who looks like the guy tuning up a chain saw in the basement of every teen horror movie ever made?" I say.

Jimmy says, "Maybe paying off a hired killer?"

"Maybe he's an ex-cellmate from Huntsville?" I say.

"Could you sleep for a single second with that guy in the next bunk?"

"I'd stay awake all night, every night with my sharpened toothbrush under my pillow," I say. "Did you get his plate number?"

"He's riding a Harley. I had trouble getting close enough to read the plate, but I got it. I'll check him out."

"What in hell," I say, "is a guy fresh out of prison after 33 years doing with that Tattoo Dude character?"

"Maybe we'll know when we find out who the Dude is. I don't think he's a Sunday school teacher."

Chapter 52

-----JACK-----

The tiny man is apparently sleeping, curled awkwardly in the wheelchair, looking like a shrunken, balding gray infant.

"I don't think he's open for business," the nursing home manager says. "Those days are far behind him. He doesn't even know what year it is."

She's right but I still don't like her attitude, even knowing that she deals daily with patients who have left the planet in every way except for an increasingly empty human body.

"He looks forgotten but not gone," I say. "A horrible ending."

"The blessing is that he doesn't know that," she says. "Or much of anything else. His son used to visit about once a month, but that's faded to maybe three times in the last year. Mr. Simpson occasionally sorta wakes up and asks questions or says something that he probably originally said in 1973. I don't think he can tell you anything, but if you want to sit with him for a few minutes or push him around the hallways a little, that will be okay."

I nod, tell her I'll stay awhile and she leaves.

I study him. He's breathing so slowly that I at first wonder if he's still alive. Actually he isn't alive for all practical purposes.

The slim hopes that brought me here narrow to zero. But I decide to try to arouse him to something close to a waking state.

"Mr. Simpson, can you hear me?" I repeat several times. "I'd like to talk to you about your legal career. Will you help me with that?"

Apparently not.

"Please Mr. Simpson, I want to get your opinion on a case from the 1980's. Do you remember back then?"

After no response, I say, "Sir, do you recall Otis Jefferson? He was convicted of rape and murder. You were one of the prosecutors."

Three more tries later I step into the hallway, signal an attendant that I'm leaving and when she looks in the room and nods, I head to my car with no notes to write.

Chapter 53

-----JACK-----

Back at the office Jimmy greets me with, "Got him. Tattoo Dude. And guess what, he *was* in a cell next to Otis for two years. He was paroled a year before Otis got out."

"Finally, a link," I say. "What's the guy's story?"

"He's Wayne Watson, a former Army Ranger sergeant, drummed out with a dishonorable discharge for slugging a lieutenant in a Fort Benning, Georgia bar. A couple years after that he got busted by civilian cops for beating the crap out of some biker bully in a bar who called him a traitor. Sentenced to four years in Huntsville, paroled in three, two of them overlapping Otis. A strange sidelight is the guy has an accounting degree from LSU. Now he's stocking shelves at Home Depot in Mesquite."

"So," I say, "our forgiving friend, Otis, is keeping company with a violent, hot-tempered felon once tossed out of the Army and imprisoned for beating up a bully? That looks like a strange relationship that doesn't sound right, but we saw them together and they were quite animated. Did Otis hire him to murder Jackson and ADA Tarpley?"

"Maybe they were close enough friends in prison that Tattoo Dude did the killings out of comradeship," Jimmy says, reluctance in his voice.

"I don't want to believe any of this but it certainly looks bad," I say. "If Otis had been paroled instead of being exonerated, just hanging out with a violent, ex-con felon would be grounds to send him back to prison.

"This is obviously not a healthy relationship. Let's find out more about the Dude's current life. Does he have a wife or girl-friend? Other associates? Are he and Otis birds of a feather or just old friends from the slammer? How soon can you confirm that he lives where his bike is registered? Or, if not, where he really lives?"

"Okay. If it turns out that he *doesn't* live there and I have to try some other sources it may take a little time."

"Okay," I say. "As soon as we know where to start let's set up surveillance on him to see where he goes, who he hangs with, what his daily life is like. Maybe for a few days you and I plus Mark, all using different cars, can watch the Dude for a few hours at a time, handing him off to each other and find out if there are any suspicious people or patterns."

"I'm on it," he promises.

CHAPTER 54

------JIMMY------

Our Tattoo Dude is walking to his Harley parked in a far corner of the huge Home Depot lot in Mesquite, a suburb southeast of Dallas. I'm parked diagonally from him, as far away as I can get. When he dons a black helmet, starts his maroon bike and turns left out of the lot, I let three vehicles trail him out before I fall in behind.

Tailing a motorcycle has its own challenges since they can change speeds more quickly and weave through traffic in ways cars can't. I'm hoping I won't lose him.

The intersection of two interstate highways is only a quarter-mile away and I catch a glimpse of him already accelerating into the northbound traffic flow of LBJ Freeway before I'm halfway down the on-ramp.

I goose the Mustang enough to close some of the gap he's opened but I don't want to call attention to myself, or get busted for speeding, so I merge back into line.

We zip past two off-ramps and suddenly I see the bike's tail lights flash and he's pulling to the side of the road.

What the hell?

I have no choice but to flash past him, not turning my head but with my eyes locked right. I barely glimpse him still astride the halted bike, pulling his gloves off, his face guard pointed down.

An exit ramp is rushing at me, now only a hundred feet ahead and I flip my blinker and lurch right, barely under control, a pickup truck's blaring horn

173

angrily critiquing my driving skills. I'm hoping the brief commotion was not visible to The Dude halted a couple hundred yards away.

Did he notice me tailing him? How could…. But why else would he suddenly stop beside a busy interstate? A mechanical problem? Now what?

I'm riding my brakes on the rising ramp, fast approaching a stop sign at the top. I quickly cross the side road, enter the on-ramp, facing north, back to LBJ Freeway, pull to the side of the ramp and am looking down at the interstate traffic. I decide to wait until I see the Harley pass under the over-pass I'm on and I'll try to fall in behind him.

Five minutes. Ten.

Where is he? Maybe broken down. I could get back on the freeway, take the next exit and try to circle around behind him, somewhere I can see him on the side but not so close that he sees me…Crap, that's not…

I hear the Harley's patented growling

THERE HE IS!

I glance at my side-mirror, see the Harley coming north on the interstate, almost right below me.. Now I'm blowing gravel trying to getting back on the ramp and sliding into traffic, the Harley is nearly out of sight.

Try to close the gap? Risk him noticing? Does he know he has a tail? Maybe try to get at least close enough I'll see him if he exits. THERE HE GOES!

I brake a little less recklessly this time and take the off-ramp without using my blinker so he won't see it. He's out of sight before I get to the stop sign, desperately looking right and left, wondering which way he went.

No clue.

I choose right, hoping he's headed east into north Garland. If he isn't I'll have to start over tomorrow.

Luckily I hit the first three stop lights while they're green and a few blocks more I crest a slight hill and spot the Harley at a red light six cars ahead. I blow out my cheeks, my death grip on the steering wheel loosens. I feel my heart slowing from heavy-metal rhythm toward Simon & Garfunkel.

Red turns green and traffic sluggishly moves out, still congested enough that even the Harley isn't likely to dart ahead. Four more lights and his right flasher comes on. Three of the five cars between me and The Dude continue straight. A half-mile more and his left blinker takes him into a parking lot where a dozen motorcycles are already lined up next to *"Big Nick's Bar & Grill."*

I continue for another block, make three lefts into the same lot, parking by three pickups and one car across from the row of bikes.

I wait ten minutes before walking across the lot, clinking quarters into the newspaper box and pushing through the door.

Nick apparently hasn't aired out the place since 1953. It's dim and dank, a potpourri of smoke, beer spilled over the decades, grease and blended sweat from untold thousands of customers unaware of fundamental personal hygiene products.

Most of the tables and booths have stocky men, and a few women, eating from red plastic baskets. There's a conversational buzz but nothing loud or rowdy.

A primitive bar stretches across the back wall, its sheet metal top hammered into place with nails, some protruding enough to discourage resting elbows

I'm pretty much cured of any appetite I might have had, but I spot an unoccupied table along one side and sit where I can see the entire room, and reach for a one-page, laminated menu where nearly every item has "burger" in the description.

I unfold the newspaper as a pony-tailed, jeans-and-tank-top waitress arrives.

"Hi, handsome stranger," she says, showing nicotine-stained teeth. "Hungry for somethin'?"

I guess her age as north of 70.

"A Lone Star draft and Nick's Famous Big Ass Cheeseburger."

She nods and disappears.

Four men fill a table about ten feet from me. One of them is Tattoo Dude and the other three would qualify for membership in the Association of Tattooed Dudes. I'm glad I'm wearing a long-sleeved tee that hides my otherwise-naked arms.

Bet my lunch money they've all done prison time.

I keep my face in the sports section but I'm not reading, trying to catch a few words from the ex-con quartet, maybe enough to figure out the serious-faced discussion they're having in an undertone, leaning forward between bites. I flick a few quick glances. Tattoo Dude is doing most of the talking, seemingly the leader of the group, but I can't make out any specific words.

Facing away from me a wide-shouldered guy wearing a red bandana as a head cover that at first glance appears to be a paisley pattern but is actually covered in white skulls, is particularly aggressive, repeatedly pointing a finger at someone else's nose, sometimes waving a hand as if erasing a blackboard.

Nick's Famous Cheeseburger arrives with another nod from Pony Tail.

A couple of minutes later, the séance led by Tattoo Dude gets more animated and voices rise enough for me to hear a few phrases.

"…just do it, dammit…"

"Vital…"

"Time's running out and…"

"You're not the only one…"

"We've…pledged…"

I look up just as Tattoo Dude scans the room, presumably for evesdroppers and our eyes meet for a nanosecond before I turn a page and refold the newspaper.

They lower their voices and I hear nothing meaningful in the ten minutes before they all stand and step outside.

I let my eyes follow them while they briefly man-hug each other and three of them disappear toward the parking lot while Tattoo Dude watches from the curb. I hear the bikes start up with the usual throttle-twisting roars that apparently sends testosterone levels soaring.

I hear the bikes driving off and see Tattoo Dude pivot and stride back inside, heading for the bar. I tip up the second Lone Star longneck I've been nursing to make it last, and see Pony Tail at the cash register swiping his credit card.

He says something to her, she smiles and he's heading for the door again while I wipe my lips with a napkin, pretending I'm still reading.

I can't leave for a while. She'd probably tell him that I seemed to be tailing him.

I hear his maroon horse roar to life and appear briefly in the street scooting past Nick's.

I hope he's headed home. I have that address in my phone's GPS so I can resume surveillance without following him directly. If he went somewhere else either Jack or Mark will pick him up after work tomorrow.

Twenty minutes later I drive past his house and see the Harley parked in an open two-door garage, next to the rear end of a white-over-cherry, 20-year-old Chevy.

The surprise is that he's in the front yard with what looks like a four or five-year-old girl trying to pedal a pink three-wheeler. The Dude is guiding her with a hand on her shoulder, the other pushing the back of the tricycle. A mid-thirties woman in jean-shorts and a Dallas Cowboy tee watches from a lawn chair.

He doesn't look as I pass and even if he did my almost-legal smoked windows wouldn't have let him see the same guy he saw at Nick's and I'm pretty sure he wouldn't have seen my Mustang at all thanks to the big pickups and cars surrounding it.

I continue for three blocks and randomly roam the neighborhood, getting a feel for residents and killing some time before seeking a place I might be able to watch his house.

I decide the modest, well-maintained neighborhood isn't conducive to any extended surveillance, at least during daylight. There are too many people and kids outside, washing cars, playing games, mowing lawns plus joggers and walkers. An unfamiliar vehicle is likely to be noticed and wondered about.

I leave the neighborhood the way I came in. Near the highway, I loiter in an Exxon station for a while thinking that if The Dude leaves he'll probably pass by, but he doesn't and I decide to bag it for the day.

I punch my speed-dial list and Jack answers instantly.

"Still on watch?"

"No, the neighborhood's too small for any significant lurking surveillance. I'll fill you in when I get there. Some interesting impressions."

Back in the office, I give Jack the Reader's Digest version of tailing The Dude from Home Depot to Nick's biker bar.

"Then I watched him and three other rough-looking guys who might as well have had "Ex-Con" tats on their foreheads, the only body space not already decorated."

"What were they talking about?" Jack says.

"Dunno, but from overall appearances, I'd bet they weren't planning anything charitable. They all look like walking felonies about to happen."

Just before 6:30 the next morning, I'm in Jack's Jeep turning into The Dude's street as slowly as I can without being obvious. I pass by his house, see some interior lights and continue for several blocks before returning for another pass. He's holding open the passenger door of the old Chevy for the little girl now in a green-plaid skirt and white blouse.

Private or church school uniform?

I continue to the Exxon station and wait for the Chevy. When it passes and is out of sight on the service road, I pull out. I quickly get the Chevy in sight two blocks ahead. When The Dude turns right, onto a residential street I take my time making the same turn. Three blocks later the Chevy swings left into the parking lot alongside St. Mary's Elementary School, a two-story, dark-red brick structure. Three nuns in full habits are shepherding dozens of uniformed youngsters.

I continue past the school and work my way back to the interstate, pondering several stereotypes that just disintegrated.

Chapter 55

-----JIMMY-----

Later that morning, the kid peers at me suspiciously from under dark hair almost surrounding his face, a style that appears to require combing it in a multitude of directions and then coating it with varnish.

"You want to buy me coffee and chat?" he says. "Why? You some kind of pervert? I'm not gay."

I didn't do this right. Repair time.

"Sorry. It's nothing like that. I just want to get some opinions from you. You're a sophomore aren't you?"

"Who are *you?*"

"Look, Andy, I'm a private researcher and I need to understand some things about campus social activities, customs and mores. I should have explained that better."

We're on the sidewalk in front of the Computer Sciences building with dozens of students changing classes flowing around us. Sunshine warms my face and the fragrance of spring grasses and shrubbery acts as aroma therapy.

Andy's brow wrinkles with doubt and maybe a touch of intrigue at unexpectedly being asked for an opinion on something.

Finally he says, "Okay, but the second you go weird I'm outta there."

"Deal. How about lunch on me?"

In a sandwich-coffee shop around the corner we find a tiny table.

"How did you know my name?

"I just asked around that I was looking for a few people with an understanding of the social scene around here. You are Andy Haley and you're a friend of Josh Dixon's, aren't you?"

He nods, clearly pleased at being linked to a BMOC.

"I hope you can help me."

"What do you want to know?" he asks almost immediately, shifting to a straighter posture.

"Tell me how well you think the campus functions as a place to meet people and find common interests. I'm particularly interested in how important your social life is to your overall educational experience."

"You asking me if I'd rather study and write papers or party with my friends?"

I'm glad you see the big picture," I grin. "Do you feel your campus social activities are in a good balance with your studies?"

"Yeah, sure, probably. I'm not getting laid enough, but there's only so much time to party."

I join in his short laugh but don't mirror his smirk.

"Is a fraternity affiliation important to have sufficient access to social opportunities that match your aspirations?"

Hope that sounds sufficiently Academic Mush talk.

He blinks and mutters: "No. Most folks aren't...."

After ten minutes of more blah, blah, blah about party settings, clubs, hookups, he says, "Why do you want to know all this shit?"

"You seem quite knowledgeable about the social scene at McMillan. At the parties I imagine you attend, have you ever seen a rape?"

"Hey, what the hell are you...."

"I'm just interested in the depth of your knowledge of the local social scene. I figure you must have seen it all."

I expect him to bolt, but he looks puzzled, starts to speak, stops. Finally he says, "Is this one of those research projects that get published in obscure academic journals that no one ever reads? Who are you *researching* for?"

"I'm hoping you can tell me more about a party you were at a week ago where a young woman was drugged and raped by two animals, one of them named Andy. What happened there?"

He leaps to his feet, knocking his chair to the floor. Everyone in the coffee shop turns toward us.

"I don't know anything about that," he hisses. "I don't know what you're talking about. You stay the hell away from me."

I pluck a business card from my shirt pocket and hand it to him, expecting a rejection but he's so flummoxed that he takes it as he turns awkwardly to the door.

"When you're ready to clear your conscience of what you did, give me a call and I'll help you."

Chapter 56

-----JACK-----

"Robyn seems to be making modest progress," Rebecca Laughlin says.

She's the trauma nurse hired two days ago to work with Robyn and she's updating Lauren and Ben before she leaves for the day. Jimmy and I are in the Rogers living room because Ben wanted us to hear her assessment. We're all seated around the large glass coffee table.

"Robyn's trying to figure out what to do next," she says. "She has many conflicting feelings and is mulling lots of advice ricocheting inside her head. She's struggling to address the sudden new reality that her life has been changed into something she's never encountered before. In a way, it's like trying to unscramble eggs in hopes of making the Eggs Benedict you wish you had.

"I wish I could say otherwise," the slender, late-40s brunette adds, "but I think she has a ways to go before she sorts out who she is now and what she needs to do to cope with the trauma she's experienced. She has major conflicts over what she thinks maybe she *should* do and what her gut tells her she *wants* to do.

"I've been with her almost constantly yesterday and today. I see her struggling to make sense out of the chaos.

"And, I hate to say this but sometimes she seems to regress. She shuts down more, whenever either Ben or Lauren is around. I think one of the things she's wrestling with is your reactions to what happened to her."

"What the hell does all that mean?" Ben demands. "You're supposed to be the expert and you're saying Lauren and I are the problem, not the son-of-a-bitch who..."

"Please be calm, Mr. Rogers," Rebecca says quietly. "This is a complex situation. There are many things happening simultaneously. I recognize that you're frustrated. Robyn is frustrated. We're all super tense. We need to work on this patiently and analytically. Extra tension won't help any of us."

"What do we *do* now?" he responds, as if he hadn't just been softly chastised in front of his wife and Jimmy and me.

"A crucial question," she says. "I'm going to consult with two of my colleagues this evening and try out an idea I have. Plus I want to see what they might suggest."

"Give us an idea of what you're thinking about," Ben says, his command voice returning with a tad less barbed wire in his tone.

She hesitates but apparently remembers he's the client.

"I don't want to get into a lot of detail right now because I'm still pondering. But I'm wondering if Robyn's experience was even more horrible than we normally encounter in rape cases. By that I mean that whatever happened to her may have registered higher on her *personal* stress meter than it might have been for some other victims. People have different pain and stress tolerances.

"We all know Robyn is younger than her academic peers. She's shy and somewhat immature socially so this experience may have affected her at a higher than normal level. I want to explore that possibility."

"She doesn't know how to handle something like this," Ben says. "That's why we need to decide...."

"NO! THAT'S NOT THE PROBLEM! Robyn screams from halfway down the curved staircase. *YOU* **DON'T NEED TO DECIDE ANYTHING!**

CHAPTER 57

-----JACK-----

I couldn't be more surprised if it had started snowing in the Rogers' living room.

Robyn is leaning with both hands on the railing, glaring down at all of us.

"Stop talking about me as if I'm some incompetent, fragile eight-year-old. You two are the dysfunctional ones."

"Oh, God, Robyn," Lauren moans and starts to get up.

Laughlin manages to whisper, "Wait," barely moving her lips.

Ben is uncharacteristically speechless, staring at his daughter.

"Robyn, please come down and help us understand," Laughlin says gently. "That's all that's going on. Explain what *you're* thinking."

Robyn straightens, tugs at the neck of her pale pink robe but remains where she is.

"Hi, Robyn," Jimmy says. "Good to see you again. Let's get all of us on the same page."

"There is no *same* page," she hisses. "There's only *his* page. He thinks the rest of us have *no* page. But I have my *own* page! I'm trying to write my own book."

"Okay, Robyn," Laughlin says. "Please join us and explain what *your* page is. We'll just listen," shooting an eye-dart at Ben whose own eyes widen but he remains silent.

As far as I can tell, no one in the five-person tableau in the living room is breathing, all of us focused on Robyn.

Finally she takes several deep breaths and floats down the stairs, pausing in the living room entrance.

"Here, take this chair," Laughlin says, rising from it.

Robyn seems to levitate silently across the room and sits on the chair's front edge, bare feet on the soft carpet, the rest of us motionless as if bird-watching and desperately hoping not to frighten this rare, wounded and wary species into flitting back into the dense and dangerous jungle.

Robyn glances around the room at her mother, Jimmy and me for a nano-second each, pausing a tiny bit longer on her father's face, before settling on Laughlin, who nods.

Does Laughlin know what Robyn's going to say? Has she shared more with Laughlin than with anyone else? Do they have a secret script?

"What happened last week happened to *me*," Robyn says so softly that I lean forward, elbows on my knees, straining for every word.

Few moments ago she was yelling.

"I'm the one who must deal with it. I don't want or need any more advice or commands. From anyone."

She's still almost whispering but her tone is determined.

"Revenge won't change what happened to me and I don't want any of you thinking about that, either."

"Sweetheart," Lauren begins, "that's not what we want..."

"*He* wants it," Robyn says in full voice. "Dad does and I don't want to hear...."

"Robyn," Ben interrupts, "I'll take care of whoever did this."

"No! That's *exactly* what I'm talking about. You're not listening to me. You never do. You want things your way and you bully me...and you bully Mom. And she usually lets you. And you do whatever *you* want. Stop it!"

Ben looks as if he's just been hit in the forehead with a two-by-four. Lauren's lips move with a few unspoken words, her eyes glued to her daughter.

Laughlin's eyes are scanning the group as if ready to intercept any potential damage to Robyn.

Jimmy has retrieved his poker face.

I'm impersonating a pillar of salt while wondering if what's happening is a good thing or a bad thing.

The fragile butterfly, formerly known as Robyn, is morphing into a butterfly with a hell of an attitude. Where is that coming from?

Ben tries again. "Robyn, I just want what's best for you. We all do. We want you to recover…back to the way you were."

"You're doing it again, Dad," she snaps. *"I'm* the one who will decide what's best for me. And you need to back off *your* agenda and let me figure out what's best for me. And I'll decide what *I'm* going to do.

She stares at him until he looks away.

"Are you getting it yet? There's nothing you or anyone can do to undo what happened to me. There's no going back to *how I was before.* It's not like restoring a car that's been damaged. There is no *restoration.* I've got to deal with a new reality."

"But," Ben says, starting to get out of his chair, "you've been traumatized and…"

"My God," Lauren shouts, jumping to her feet. "Listen to our daughter and just shut the hell up. Can't you do a simple thing like that?" her tone mocking him now, repeating his harsh criticism of her. "Can you?"

I'm pretty sure I see a smile flicker across Laughlin's face, replaced instantly with the neutral demeanor of a mediator.

Ben stares for a few seconds, makes a *what-the-hell* gesture with his arms and slumps back into his chair. Then he looks at me and the venom in his eyes is startling. He gets up, walks from the room and we hear a door slam, the garage door going up and then down.

"That might work," Lauren says. "For about 20 minutes."

CHAPTER 58

-----JACK-----

"Mom, I want to talk with Jack and Jimmy and Rebecca. They're not as emotionally involved as you and Dad. You can stay if you want, but please just sit back and observe. I don't need any more 'Poor Robyn' help from you although I completely understand and really, really appreciate what you've done for me. I love you more than I can tell you for your reactions and concerns and for you trying to buffer me from Dad's my-way-or-the-highway. But right now I'm trying to understand what choices *I* have to make."

Lauren draws her legs under her and hugs her knees, her face a worry mask.

After a long, awkward silence, Robyn looks at me and says, "Jack, what happens if I do nothing officially?"

"You mean if you don't officially file a complaint with the police and convince them to press criminal charges? Or are you thinking of suing your attackers in a civil court?

"You can do both, a criminal complaint and a civil lawsuit."

Jimmy says: "Are you thinking of putting what happened in the past, moving on with your life and not talking about or thinking about what happened?"

"Something like that," she says. "Maybe I should just move on," glancing at Rebecca. "Maybe start over at a different school where I wouldn't know anyone."

"Then nothing official will happen," I say. "And your attackers will go on with their lives."

"That's what I thought," she says, eyes cast downward.

"And," Jimmy says, "Your attackers will assault another woman. Some other *women*. I doubt you were his first victim."

She looks at her mother for the first time since telling her to stay out of the discussion.

Lauren's arms slightly tighten the embrace of her legs but she shows no other reaction to her newly assertive daughter.

Jimmy and I shouldn't try pushing Robyn toward any particular decision. Her choices, her consequences.

Rebecca may as well have duct-taped her mouth, watching but not recommending any decision.

"Could you live with enabling known sex predators and violent rapists to continue roaming the world searching for victims?" Jimmy asks. "Could you *not* feel guilty when they strike again? Maybe murder someone? Violent people usually escalate their violence."

Nudging her through questions.

I want to catch his eye and warn him away.

She jerks her face to him and stares. I see her eyes moistening, launching salty rivers down her cheeks.

I hope Jimmy takes it down a notch, possibly even backs off somewhat from the direct wording of his questions, but he doesn't. He doesn't offer her a tissue or a comforting word, just continues his eye-lock.

She breaks the stare, turns to me."

"Jack, what would I need to do if I want to put my rapists in jail?"

MY rapists? No abstractions. Definitely personal. Confirming more than one.

"You will need to forget about the Campus Cops and file an official complaint with the city or county prosecutor," I say. "And you must be willing to push hard for a criminal investigation; possibly go public if they don't respond."

I see the smallest of nods as she fist-wipes her eyes and cheeks.

"Also, you'll need to prepare yourself to testify in front of family, friends and strangers about what happened. *Every* detail.

"And you will need to be strong enough to endure an aggressive defense lawyer who will try to destroy your character and make you look like a liar. That person, probably a woman, will do everything, true or not, that she or he can to twist what happened into it being your fault. They will imply the sex was actively welcomed or even invited by you; but that later you regretted it and now you're falsely claiming rape."

Her eyes focus on something far away, maybe imagining the courtroom scene, possibly testing her resolve. And probably experiencing exactly how horrible all of that would be.

Jimmy says, "Will you tell us their names? Was it Josh Dixon? And Andy Haley?"

She continues her unblinking stare and silence, then glances at her mother.

"The truth is," she almost whispers, "part of me wants to declare a scorched-earth war on my attackers. I'd like to convince the police to send a SWAT team to arrest them.

"And I'd like to tell everyone what they did by posting a barrage of detailed accusations every day on FaceBook and Twitter and all the other sites. Maybe I could do a video of me describing everything on YouTube. I might be able to do some newspaper and television interviews."

Shazam! Withdrawn and depressed rape victim considers morphing into pit bull.

"But another part of me wants to walk away, *run* away actually, and try to never think about it again."

"Could you do that?" Jimmy says. "Erase your hard-drive or create a new one?"

I glance at Lauren, still locked in a self-hug, staring fixedly at Robyn as if hypnotized.

Should we give Robyn time to ponder her choices or give her another nudge toward the blitzkrieg scenario?

"What does your heart tell you, sweetheart?" Lauren says, startling the rest of us, partly just by joining the discussion but mostly because of what she said.

Is she suggesting Robyn should go into attack mode?

Mother and daughter focus on each other as if they're alone in the room. I decide to stay out of this exchange and I'm hoping Jimmy does, too.

"Mom," Robyn says almost inaudibly. "Mom," she says again and Lauren jumps up and lurches to her daughter, now standing. They embrace, burying their faces in each other's shoulders. I hear someone crying but can't tell if it's Lauren or Robyn, or, more probably, both.

"It's okay either way," Lauren says. "I'm with you *whatever* you decide."

"What about Dad?"

"He'll accept whatever your decision is or…. Don't worry, I'll get him on our team…or out of the way…whatever your goal. I promise."

Rebecca's face says, *'Not likely.'*

I say, "What more do you need in order to decide?"

"I want to talk with you and Jimmy and Ashley. And Carole. She gave me a lot of straight talk to think about when I was in the hospital. I want to explore some ideas with all of you."

CHAPTER 59

-----JACK-----

Robyn calls Ashley with a cryptic request to "meet and brainstorm." Ashley immediately agrees and offers her apartment. A few minutes later, Robyn, Jimmy and I are in my car for the two-mile trip. Jimmy is on the phone from the shotgun seat inviting his mother to join us.

Now, Robyn, Jimmy and I are in Ashley's apartment, Robyn's first venture away from her home since the attack. She's far from exuberant but compared with her near-comatose demeanor a few days ago, she seems more like a young college freshman than a trauma patient. This confirms our impression that her new relative assertiveness is genuine and that she's progressed significantly since our first interview with her.

Still pulled in several directions but definitely determined to make her own decisions.

Robyn is on the floor, back against the sofa, legs stretched in front of her. Jimmy and I sit loosely flanking her.

The two-bedroom apartment is larger than the typical one-person student rental. A large-screen TV is wall-mounted and the furniture is a few notches above cement blocks and planks and even better than second-hand, Swedish knock-offs for sale in every edition of the campus newspaper.

Ashley is the only one in a chair. She finger-combs her long, dark-brown hair. "Okay, Robyn, what's going on?"

Before Robyn can respond, the doorbell rings and Ashley welcomes Carole to the gathering and sits on the carpet, legs extended parallel with Robyn's, facing the opposite direction.

"Hi, Carole," Robyn says, as Carole takes Ashley's abandoned hair. "I appreciate your willingness to help me sort out some things. You've already given me other perspectives that I hadn't thought of."

Carole nods. "What's happening?"

Robyn gulps some air.

"I'm trying to decide if I want to put my...my *rape*...behind me...get out of here...go somewhere new, some fresh place."

She pauses, swallows more air and restarts.

"I'm having a war with myself. One brain lobe wants to find a different universe, wants to delete the part of my brain that keeps replaying my attack. And find a new campus. Or maybe join the Peace Corps and dig wells in Burundi.

"My other lobe sees my only other choice as mounting up, locking and loading and trying to destroy the dick-head fuckers who attacked me."

She surveys us, waiting through a mutual silence.

Ashley says, "Those are definitely wildly conflicting goals. You're the only person on earth who can decide."

She waits for a response but Robyn seems lost in space.

"By the way," Ashley says, "when did you expand your vocabulary to include 'dick-heads' and the F word?"

"I know I used to sound like super-naïve, Miss Goody-Two-Shoes," Robyn says, "but I wasn't living in a nunnery or in *The Sound of Music*. I was aware of reality. I *am* aware...I was shy and introverted. Actually, I mostly still am, but I'm thinking about some important things differently now. Part of me understands that I have an obligation to other victims, past or future, of these sons...of...bitches," stretching out the word I suspect she has never-before uttered aloud.

Was that a smile or a grimace flickering?

"Which way are you leaning?" Ashley wonders.

Robyn hesitates, her face showing stress.

"I didn't want my Mom or Dad here," Robyn finally says. "They have opinions I've already heard over and over. And particularly with Dad...you know what a black or white, fire-ready-aim guy he is. And he won't change.

"Before I say anything more, what do each of you think I should do?"

She looks around the room, pausing briefly at each of us.

New-born pit bull still has insecurities and doubts.

No one volunteers and Robyn fills the silence.

"Ashley?"

"Wow, Robyn," Ashley says, "I'm amazed at where you are now. You've obviously been processing what happened last week and have clearly recognized your conflicting feelings and choices. You go girl!"

"Go where?" Robyn insists. "What would you do?"

"Only you can answer that," Ashley says again. "The right answer is whatever's best for you. One person's *correct answer* could be completely wrong for someone else."

Robyn shifts her gaze to me.

"What's your bottom-line advice, Jack?"

"Ashley's absolutely right and I don't have any advice, either. But I hope our answers to the questions you asked back in your living room gave you a realistic forecast of what you'd probably face if you decide to go after the evil predators who assaulted you. We can explore that more if you want."

"What about your 'let's *destroy* the'…uh, evil people option?" Carole interjects, even before Robyn turns to her.

"That's what you think I should do, isn't it?"

Carole says, "I agree with your mom and Ashley and Jack that you should do whatever you believe is best for you. But I'll go a step further. I believe that, in the long run, if you help get your attackers off the street you will benefit for the rest of your life. You'll look back at this over the years and be glad and proud that you had the courage to help save other women from being assaulted."

Robyn rubs her temples as they stare at each other for a minute, apparently in some kind of mind meld.

Jimmy says, "Robyn, no one has the right to judge you for whatever you decide. But I agree that this is a defining moment for your life."

She sighs and closes her eyes for a long moment, chin on her chest. She straightens her spine and studies each of us for nearly a minute, her eyes moist, expression unreadable.

"I know what I want," she says, sadness shading her soft voice and her gaze grazing each of us in continuous short glances.

"I want to get out of Dallas and I want two men in black suits to hold a magic device in front of my face and delete my memory of last Friday night. And I want them to wipe clean the memories of anyone who saw the pictures of my rape in progress. That's what I want. I want all of this to go away. Completely. And forever."

Any fair-minded person understands that choice.

Okay,' Ashley says, getting to her knees and putting Robyn in a comforting, back-patting hug.

"Let's make some plans for putting this behind you and moving forward again," Ashley murmurs.

Robyn's hands on Ashley's shoulders push a little space between them.

"That's what I really *want* to do," Robyn says, "but it's not what I'm *going* to do. I've been mulling some things Carole said.

She looks at Carole.

"You upset me but now I'm convinced you're right."

She glances at the rest of us again.

"Carole bluntly told me I was being a wimp and putting other possible future victims in harm's way.

"But mostly she said I was setting myself up to live as a coward. If you will all help me, I'm going to go after those monsters. Jimmy and Jack told me the same thing...but slightly more gently.

"Anyone here have any tough pills?"

"I think you just demonstrated enough toughness to make pills unnecessary," I say. "We're all with you. To this Gang of Five," raising my right hand, which is quickly joined by four fists.

Chapter 60

"Now what?" Ashley says a few minutes later, diverting our bubbling enthusiasm toward practical logistics.

"We need to figure out e*xactly* how we are going to put down these vicious predatory beasts? How we're going to team-kick some butts into prison cells?"

"What's our first move?" Ashley asks.

"Other than designing our *Gang-of-Five* tee shirts?" I say, "I suggest we list our primary goals."

"I'll get my white board," Ashley says.

Ashley-the-Organizer!

Two minutes later, Ashley has set a large white board on an easel and is brandishing a red dry-erase marker, writing GOALS in the top left corner and underlines it with a dramatic flourish.

"What are our goals?" she demands.

"Put two rapists in jail," Robyn suggests.

"Publically humiliate and disgrace them," Carole says.

Ashley writes on the board and immediately adds to the list in bold, block letters.

"Expose Campus Cops intimidating victims and covering up campus sexual assaults," Jimmy says.

There's a pause and Ashley begins another column with the heading:

POSSIBLE ACTIONS

"We must find proof," Jimmy says. "We don't have any proof and we probably can't trace the emails, tweets or any of the electronic taunts or pictures."

Ashley writes: **Find Evidence** and asks, "What else?"

Jimmy says: "We don't know who sent the *original* taunting emails and videos and photos, although one or both of the perps almost certainly started it. They have the video and photos. But it appears several others have joined in.

"I don't think I can track the cruel cowards who do this stuff...how many guys living in their mother's basements are out there with keyboards? Each one with multiple identities. And these creeps could be anywhere in the world."

"Have you tried tracing any of the postings to actual creeps?" Ashley says.

"Not yet, but it's somewhere between extremely difficult and impossible, depending on how sophisticated the posters are. I'm going to see if any of my friends from computer science classes have more experience and expertise in following tracks of anonymous internet stalkers. I wouldn't count on any success."

"Okay, what else?" Ashley says.

"Will we need a lawyer to file a criminal complaint?" Robyn says.

"No, although it might be helpful," I say, "but we definitely need one to put together a civil suit. And it's always helpful to have an expert pushing the process along, not let the system stall."

"Robyn, would your dad pay for an attorney?" Carole says.

"I don't know. I don't want to tell him what I'm doing till it's over. I hope that's not unrealistic. If Mom actually does sign up for whatever our plan turns out to be, maybe she can bring Dad along. Or *shove* him along," she says. "Thing is, he's obviously more of a shover than a shovee."

"Let's go back to the top," I say. "We've got to tie these guys to a specific crime. We can't just waltz into the cop shop and file a she-said, he-said complaint with no witnesses or evidence and expect much to happen.

"Robyn, do you have any evidence at all? Any chance there's DNA on the clothes you were wearing?

"Ashley, can you list everyone you saw at the party? We can talk to them and maybe come up with witnesses."

"I'll try," she says.

Robyn stands, and walks behind the sofa, putting it between herself and the four of us, looking over our heads.

"There are no clothes from that night," she says. "While I showered for about an hour, Mom bagged what I was wearing, including my shoes, and tossed it all in the trash. She knew I'd never wear any of that stuff again."

Here I go.

"Robyn, I'm sorry to have to ask this, but do you feel comfortable sharing the entire story? Tell us everything starting with who invited you to the party, how you got there and what happened? How you got home? If you don't….."

"Would it be easier if you wrote it down and not have to say things out loud?" Jimmy suggests.

Robyn closes her eyes, puts her hands on the sofa's back, looking like someone at an altar or podium about to deliver a speech.

"One day I met Ashley for coffee at The Java Cup. We each had 50 minutes between classes. I noticed this tall guy eyeing us while we were in line. A few minutes later, the guy stopped by our patio table and said 'What's happening?' It was casual, kinda corny. He was charming in a low-key way. It was kind of fun, actually. He asked for my name and phone number, but I didn't give them because I thought he was being rude, leaving Ashley out of the conversation.

"He grinned, said, 'Maybe later,' saluted and walked away.

"When he was gone, Ashley told me he was some kind of BMOC. A jock. I think she said basketball."

"Did you know Dixon before that?" I ask Ashley.

"No, but I vaguely knew who he was. I had seen his photo in the campus paper."

"The next time I saw him," Robyn says, "was at a TGIF party several weeks later. Ashley had been invited by someone she knew from a mutual class and asked me if I wanted to go with her."

Ashley nods agreement.

"Ashley and I got separated for a while at the party and I was mostly just watching people from a sofa when the same tall guy appeared. He had two plastic cups of beer and handed me one, sat next to me and said, 'Glad to see you again, Mystery Woman. I've been thinking about you.'

"That was flattering, of course, but totally obvious. He introduced himself and I told him my first name. He has a nice way of making you think you're the only person in the room with him. Charming even when simultaneously using obvious pick-up lines. It was fun, not scary in any way. Just flirty.

"We chatted for a while, he asked if I liked basketball, what I was studying, what kind of music I liked, you know, everything but the weather.

"I sipped less than half the beer he gave me. I don't particularly like the taste of beer. That was the fourth or fifth one I've ever had; never finished any of them, just stretched them out at parties because everyone else was doing it, everybody trying desperately to look as insanely happy as the people in beer commercials. Stupid.

"He stood up, took our beer cups, said 'these are getting flat, I'll get us some fresh.'

"When he returned, I think we talked about some recent movies…and then I was crying on Ashley's shoulder and she took me home."

Her voice is softer now, her body trembling.

"For a couple of days details from that night were hazy. Then I began to remember a few things in a foggy way. I'm still dreaming about it every night."

She returns from the back of the sofa and stands, her eyes closed for a moment, all four of us silent.

"That's pretty much all I can remember," she says, heading for the kitchen. "I need to dunk my face in a sink-full of cold water."

A few minutes later, Robyn returns, face flushed but seemingly refreshed.

"Okay," she says, "let's figure out what we're going to do next. I'm tired of re-living the past, I'm ready to go after these inhuman, violent sociopaths."

"Amen," Ashley whoops, pumping her fist. "Let's put the bastards in prison."

Jimmy says, "To do that we need *legally obtained,* persuasive evidence. We don't have that in Robyn's case…and we probably never will unless Dixon or Haley decides to confess.

"So, we need evidence from other assaults, if we can find additional victims. Possibly from names in the Security Department's files. If not there, maybe we need to be present when Dixon attacks again."

After a brief pause as all of us realize what Tonto is suggesting, Ashley says, "I'll do it. That's perfect. I want to do that."

We all hear Jimmy's cell vibrating on the coffee table.

He answers and holds it toward me and I hear: "Jimmy, it's Chris. We gotta talk. Sarge caught me reading the For-Show files. Denny's at Greenville and Royal in 30 minutes?"

I nod, Jimmy says, "We'll be there," and we're moving toward the door.

I pause to face Robyn, Ashley and Carole.

"Sorry, we gotta go. It's an emergency.

"We've been working on this project for hours and maybe taking a break now is a good thing. Let's get together tomorrow after some rest and time to think. We can start fresh then."

"I like that idea," Ashley says. "Can everyone make it back here tomorrow at, say, 5:30?"

All heads nod and I ask, "Chinese food okay with everyone? Hearing no objections, Tonto and I will deliver."

In the car, Jimmy says, "Another truckload of manure is at our front door. It's starting to pile up. This sounds like big trouble and could cost Griffin his job."

CHAPTER 61

-----JACK-----

I've never met Chris Griffin but even without Jimmy I could have found him; the only occupant of a far-corner booth.

"You must be Jack Crocker," the dark-blond, sturdily built man says as Jimmy and I slide in. A waitress takes our "three coffees" order and Jimmy immediately says, "What happened?"

Chris surveys the room.

"After I got off shift, Sarge caught me reading what I think are the For-Show files.

"Things started after I clocked in today and was putting on my gear. A middle-aged couple and their early-twenties daughter came in. I heard the father tell Sgt. Wilcox that they wanted to file charges against a male student. They said the guy 'drugged and assaulted our daughter.'

"I was at the key rack right behind Wilcox getting keys to a patrol car. I froze when I heard 'assaulted our daughter.'

"Sarge waved to Lt. Ferguson who took a clipboard from Sarge and invited the family to follow him to a "quiet room where we can talk."

"I tagged along into one of our interrogation rooms. When Ferguson noticed me, he said, "It's okay, Griffin, I'll handle this."

"Maybe I can help," I said, making no move to leave. "The perp may be someone I've run across on patrol."

"Ferguson gave me a look that could have fried bacon but it was awkward for him with the family members already sitting down.

"After a few seconds of angry-face but silent messages aimed at me, the Lieutenant took the last chair and I continued leaning against the door.

"Ferguson asked for their names and contact information. The father gave him a business card and he copied information on a plain pad, not on an official complaint form.

"'I'm Julie Norton,' the daughter told him.

"Then Ferguson said, 'what happened, Miss?'

"One of your students attacked me two nights ago," she said.

"Sexually," her mother added.

"We want him arrested," the father said. "His name is Ross Worthington. Here's his address," handing the Lieutenant a scrap of paper. Ferguson glanced at it and stuck it inside the pad.

"*Exactly* what happened, Miss?' he repeated. 'Where were you? What were you doing? In detail.'

"Julie Norton stared at him for a few seconds but didn't seem intimidated or anything. She spoke clearly and firmly

"'Six of us were watching Netflix movies at Marion's apartment. We had burgers and some beer. We were eating and laughing and commenting on various actors. Nothing unusual.'

"'What drugs did you have? Or was it just pot?'

"'Hey,' her father said. 'She didn't mention pot or any drugs. She said there was beer. Watch your attitude, mister.'

"The Lieutenant smiled but said, 'Please answer my question, Miss.'

"' No pot, no drugs,' she said a little louder, her eyes locked on his. 'Nothing like that.'

"'So, there were six of you at this party. Were you all hooked up? Did you know each other before that night?'

"'We all knew each other from sharing classes or meeting elsewhere. Only Tony and Beth are sorta dating, the rest of us are just friends. We weren't paired off in any way.'

"'How does any of that have anything to do with our daughter being attacked?' the father said, standing up. 'What kind of operation are you running here?'

"'We need to know all of the circumstances, sir,' the Lieutenant said. 'These are easy questions compared to those that she will be asked in a court hearing and trial. Now, how did this little gathering end up in an alleged rape?'

"'*Alleged?*' the father shouted. '*Alleged?* There's no *alleged* rape here, you son of a bitch, I ought to punch the shit....'

"I saw the mother begin to cry, wiping her eyes with a tissue and staring at her knees.

"'Explain why you think you were raped,' Ferguson said.

"Julie stood up then and pointed at him. 'Are you some kind of perverted voyeur?' she said. 'I'm not going to recite the intimate details so you can have your second-hand jollies. I'm making a complaint that this guy I barely knew slipped me a drug of some kind and raped me. He needs to be held accountable. Do you understand what I'm saying?'

"'Sure,' he said, almost smiling. 'I'm just getting your side of the story. In court you'll be asked for all of the *intimate* details you're trying to avoid now. It'll be much more detailed later. Are you sure you want to put yourself through that?'

"She stared at him.

"Finally he broke the silence. 'Were you injured in any way?'

"'Yes. Twice. Once two nights ago by a rapist and again *just now, by you.*

"'Let's go,' she said, going to the door and gesturing to her parents to join her. 'We're wasting our time here. These people aren't going to investigate anything.'

"She briefly turned back to the Lieutenant. 'Goodbye. We'll let you return to your home under a rock with the other worms and grubs.'

"Good for her," Jimmy interrupts.

"I moved to the side, as the three of them left," Chris continues. "The daughter stomped out in straight-spine defiance, the mother was still crying, her head bowed. The father attempted to comfort her.

"I followed them from the room, escaped to the parking lot and left for my patrol shift. I don't want the Lieutenant to think I was disturbed by what I saw, but he probably already suspected me of being a problem at that point."

"Julie sounds less traumatized and vulnerable than you'd expect," I say. "Maybe we can sign her up to help take these sleaze bags off the map. Did you get an address or phone number?"

"That's partly why I wanted to see what, if any, paperwork went into a Complaint or Incident file; even if it's only the few notes Lt. Ferguson wrote on the legal pad and the victim's contact information."

"Julie Norton and her parents," I say, "could be major trouble for the Campus Security Department. They sound like folks who won't drop the issue. They seem like people confident enough and angry enough to go to the regular police or even the District Attorney's office."

"You're right," Chris says. "I didn't see any signs that they're easy to intimidate."

"Let's track them down," I say. "I hope we can recruit them to our cause."

"On it," Jimmy says. "We already have the daughter's name. Should be a piece of cake."

"Yeah, well," Chris says. "Here's the really bad part."

Chris visibly and audibly inhales and I see Jimmy eyes narrow and Clint taking over.

"Later tonight the Security office was nearly deserted when I returned from my shift, just the usual one guy on the far side of the main room manning phones, which are seldom busy. He waved at me and went back to the book he was reading. That time of night there's only one other officer on duty, replacing me driving around in what we call *patrolling*.

"I went down the hall into the file room and checked a drawer of a battered file cabinet without a label. I'd seen the sergeant putting a folder in that drawer after the earlier time when I arrived during his successful attempt to discourage a young woman from filing an official Rape Complaint against her boyfriend.

"There were several folders in the drawer. The one in front had today's date penciled on the tab. The folder held only the single page with the contact information the father gave the Lieutenant.

"The second folder had a partially completed Complaint Form from the woman I saw humiliated and intimidated out of the building the second week I was there.

"As I bent down to replace the folder Sarge yelled at me from two feet behind me. '"What the fuck are you doing in here? You're lucky I even saw you, I was about to lock up and go home. You'd have spent the night in this room. Keep your nose pointed at your job and not snooping around old files. You understand what I'm telling you? Now git, so I can lock up in here.'

"I messed up, guys," Chris says. "I had no idea Sarge was there. He's never been in the office that time of night. He must have had to do something that couldn't wait and parked in front where I didn't see him when I parked in the back lot. I don't know where he was when I got to the Duty Room, maybe in the restroom.

"I'll be under suspicion now, particularly if Sarge mentions to Lt. Ferguson that he found me in the File Room. What a disaster! I might not be able to stay there until we get whatever evidence there is, if any. I might be fired tomorrow."

"Yeah," Jimmy says. "Any chance you were followed here?"

"Damn! I was so upset I didn't even think of that. What a rookie doofus."

"Why don't you just keep your head down?" I say. "Focus on your regular job while we work on other possible information sources."

"If at all possible, I need to line up another job before leaving. I've got a family to support."

"You want to quit any way. Maybe, if you're not fired, you can do a last-minute *burglary* when you find another job and gather whatever documents you can on your way out of there for good. Think you can you do that?"

"I don't know."

CHAPTER 62

-----JACK-----

The next morning while dropping two frozen waffles in the toaster, I mutter to Jimmy, "I've been wondering about Roberta suddenly kicking us out of Otis's house minutes after she and Angel and Mavis served us lunch. Why did she freak out like that? At the time, we thought it was an emotional over-reaction but the more I think about it, the more bizarre it seems."

"Yeah, that *was* weird," he says. One second I'm explaining why we wanted to talk to all of the family members about what they remembered and ask if any of them had ever indicated they wanted revenge for what happened to Otis. The next second she explodes into a yell-fest, screaming and tossing our fannies into the street."

He stares at me as I join him at the kitchen table.

"But why are you thinking about that now, with everything else that's going on?"

"I guess because of the unanswered question. Roberta says, 'Hi, we've home-cooked a lunch for you and then we'll be glad to answer any questions you have. Blah, blah, blah,' then inexplicably morphs into a banshee banishing us from her family. The more I replay that scene, the more I wonder what was going on that day.

"Something's not right. We need to consider her a suspect…for something."

Chapter 63

-----JACK-----

I'm pulling boxes of Chinese takeout from two large bags and putting them on the table in Ashley's kitchen. I see the board still on the tripod in her living room from last night. Tonto and I brought enough food for a Gang-of-Eight, even though there are only four of us. Carol is still at work. Robyn stayed overnight.

"Seeing that most of the Gang has assembled," Jimmy announces, "fill your plates and let's get started."

Soon we're all clustered around the board balancing heaping paper plates on our laps, and I say, "If everyone agrees, I suggest we brainstorm all the ways we can imagine to get some kind of proof that Josh Dixon is a cold-blooded rapist. After we have a list we can assess all the options and decide what to do next. Okay?"

Nods and affirmative noises from hungry conspirators.

Ashley says, "I'll make notes while we're eating and transfer them to the board later."

"Here's one," Robyn immediately says. "I wear a secret recorder and confront Dixon and get him to acknowledge that he raped me."

"Yes, but…" Ashley says before Jimmy cuts her off.

"We're not debating anything yet," he says. "For now we're just listing, without criticism or analysis or discussing logistics. We want to see all options we can dream up. After that, we'll analyze, compare and decide what our best choice is."

I see Ashley scribbling in a notebook in between forks-full of cashew chicken.

"Okay," Robyn says. "Here's another idea. I wear a wire and confront that weakling, Andy, and frighten him into a confession implicating himself and Dixon."

Jimmy says, "Jack and I could talk to some of Dixon's friends or hangers-on and see if any of them heard him saying anything about his abuse of Robyn. He seems like someone who would boast to his buddies. Maybe some people in his social circle know of other possible victims."

"But that would get back to him and…." Ashley says, then looks sheepish. "Next idea, please."

"This one has some problems, too," I say, "but we could talk to anyone we can identify as being at the party who might have witnessed or heard something. Maybe someone took photos or videos that could help us. We all know almost everything gets photographed these days. We might get lucky."

Ashley stands up, flips the board over and writes in red.

1: **Robyn confronts Josh**
2: **Robyn confronts Andy**
3: **Someone baits either or both**
4: **J&J talk to both perps' friends, acquaintances**
5: **J&J interview party guests, seeking witnesses & photos**

"And from yesterday's discussion," she says as she writes:

6. **File criminal complaint**
7. **File civil suit**

"Any other ideas?" I ask.

"What if we kidnap Josh and I use my Leatherman tool to make him eligible for a middle-school boys' choir?" Jimmy says.

Eight hands reach for the ceiling in a unanimous *Hell, Yes* vote.

While laughter's still rippling through the room, I toss everyone a wrapped fortune cookie.

"Maybe the right choice is in the cookie," I say. "Let's take a 5-minute break to get more grub or fresh beverages."

Ashley touches my elbow.

"Let me show you something," she says softly, gesturing for me to follow her toward the hallway leading to the two bedrooms.

In a combination bedroom-office she points at the left wall. A large version of the iconic theatrical twin-masks symbolizing comedy and tragedy is surrounded by dozens of framed Broadway Playbill covers.

"I've seen all of those plays at least once."

She turns 180 degrees where multiple photos of what look like high school or college or community theater productions blanket the opposite wall.

"I'm in all of those photos," she says. "I'm a drama major. I've even been accused of being a 'thespian,'" she grins. "I can play predator bait. I just wanted you to know while we're deciding what to do."

"I'm impressed, but I assume not one of these roles involved real and dangerous pirates or actual rapists."

"Keep an open mind, Jack."

"I promise."

Back in the living room we're all staring at the board, considering the options we've identified. I'm trying to visualize how each would work. And how each could go seriously, possibly catastrophically, bad.

I suspect others are doing similar mental gymnastics. I know Tonto is. He and I are the only two here who have actually planned and carried-out risky plans. We know that once a planned operation begins it always changes depending on what the opposition does. Every damn time.

"Well," Tonto says, "shall we go around the room and each of us nominate our first choice and see if we're close to a consensus?"

"I definitely want to look in the face of one or both of the creeps who attacked me," Robyn says immediately, her face determined.

Our fragile little wounded bird has become an eagle bristling for a fight.

"It would feel terrific and I believe an unexpected encounter could discombobulate either of them into saying something incriminating."

Jimmy turns to Ashley, who says, "My favorite option is offering Dixon an opportunity to attack another victim while we document as proof of an actual crime he can be punished for. And it would support the idea that he's probably raped others, including Robyn.

"I explained my acting background to Jack. Robyn already knows about it and I can show you my Memory Wall, too, if you want. I'm confident I can handle a role like this and I have the improvisation skills it would require.

"Robyn told me what Jack and you did last year when Jack's son was kidnapped by thugs and killers, so I'm comfortable that you two *heroes* can protect me if you decide to help us."

Jimmy turns to me with eyebrows raised.

"I respect both of you for your passion and courage," I say, trying to sound analytical and not reveal the depth of my fears of helping either of them get into a dangerous and unpredictable situation.

"Sometimes the best approach is straight ahead at full speed. In this case that might include gathering information from every source we can; people at the party, friends and anyone with any connection to the perps to hidden police or campus cop records. Plus, try to find other victims.

"Then we file a civil suit with that as ammunition. A civil suit would be about establishing Dixon's liability and seeking financial damages."

"And then," Jimmy says, "we'd probably want to aggressively go public every way we can, keeping pressure on Dixon and his family. "A civil suit would generate lots of publicity," I add, "exactly what Dixon's family must want to avoid despite their threats to the contrary."

"Or," I say, "you *could* file an official complaint and try to force a criminal investigation leading to charges."

"Robyn says, "My dad would have to be in on any legal stuff and I don't know what his attitude would be and I don't want him involved. And by the way, Jack, I don't know if he will pay you and Jimmy for what you're doing right now."

"We're off the clock," I say. "We're trying to help you because we support your cause, not for money."

"Right," Jimmy says, "but that raises the point that we may need to notify your father of what we're doing. We're kinda in no-man's land right now."

"Yeah, we need to figure out which hats we're wearing."

A snake pit of ethical conflicts and differences of opinion.

I think I see indecision on Jimmy's face and gesture to him for more discussion.

"I'm of two minds," he says. "Personally, I'd absolutely love to see a personal confrontation between Robyn and Josh-the-creep that totally nails these guys and no one gets hurt. Except them. That would be an adrenalin rush, fist-pumping victory."

He looks at each of us for a second or two.

"Baiting Dixon into another attempted assault would be right out of a TV drama but definitely off-the-chart scary in real life."

"I can do that, Robyn insists. "I *want* to do that."

"But both those options are extremely high-risk operations," I say, "and could easily go totally off the rails. I don't think we should risk those."

"With all due respect, Jack," Robyn says firmly, "it's not up to you or Jimmy. Ashley and I can decide to do these things on our own. We don't need your *permission*."

Crap! Asking our advice but apparently not valuing it much. Naïve young women way, way over-confident! Taking the helm from the captain and sailing right into a typhoon.

"Think about what happens if we try a confrontation and things don't work perfectly," I say. "Anything we gather could be ruled inadmissible. It would be worse than just wasted effort."

"Dixon's family is wealthy and influential," Jimmy says. "A high-powered legal team might turn the effort completely against us.

"It is obviously entrapment, your Honor," he says in a stilted courtroom voice. 'These people should be criminally prosecuted and we're filing a civil suit today for millions of dollars in damages done to our client's and his family's reputations.'

"They could entangle all of us, including your family, Robyn, in years of back-breaking legal fees. And even with all of that, the issue might never be settled. No closure. That's the opposite of what you and all of us want."

"It couldn't end like that," Robyn's raised voice is certain. "Not in the United States of America. That would be totally unfair. That wouldn't be justice."

God help her. Was I ever that young? That naïve? Did I ever believe so completely in the fabled justice system of civics textbooks? Definitely not after years of reporting from courtrooms!

"I think either a direct confrontation or an attempt to provoke another rape attempt is way too risky," I say. "Legally, financially and physically."

"I don't care about all of that," Robyn snaps. "I want them behind bars and I'm willing to take risks. I'm not afraid anymore."

Gotta get this runaway train gently back on track before it runs over them.

"Let's return to our Gang-of-Five mode," Jimmy says, smiling cheerfully, "and come up with a plan that doesn't put anyone in serious danger."

Good, it may help that Jimmy's closer to their age. I'm closer to their father's age and at least Robyn's father's not in good standing right now.

"I'm not hiding anymore," Robyn insists. "I want their scalps and I want them in prison."

"I'm not afraid, either," Ashley adds. "I think we should attack these assholes head on."

"We can't let you do that," I say. "These guys are dangerous. Date-rape drugs can be dangerous. And we couldn't protect you from every awful thing that might happen if you try tricking them into committing another crime.

"It's not as easy as it looks on TV cop shows. If it's not done precisely correctly, within all of the legal rules, any evidence, even if it demonstrated guilt, wouldn't be admissible in court because it was obtained illegally. In effect you could give him a Get-Out-Of Jail card."

I see determination on Ashley's face. She turns to Robyn and I follow her gaze.

Robyn rises, defiance radiating from her hands-on-hips stance, looking as if she's ready to draw two guns as soon as it's High Noon.

"Well, Jack and Jimmy, are you two *heroes* going to help us or not?"

CHAPTER 64

-----JACK-----

As we're driving back to the office, Jimmy says, "That was a replay of the first morning Ben came to our office. He asked us the same question she just did.

"Remember how distraught he was over what had happened to her and demanded: "I need to know in the next 60 seconds. Are you two going to help me save my daughter's life or not?"

"Maybe she learned it from him," I say.

"She's also mirroring Ben with her new-found aggressive determination to crush her attackers. That's still his goal, too."

A few minutes later, we're in desk chairs, boots atop facing desks, a single desk lamp casting light in the otherwise dark room.

"So, Kemosabe, what we do now?"

"I thought Tonto was the smart one now that Johnny Depp made the Lone Ranger look like a buffoon in the latest movie."

"Hmmm, Tonto ask *you* cause Scout parked at curb and I heap exhausted by white women's dilemmas and plans."

"Seriously," I say, "we've got important decisions and almost no time for debate. If we don't help Robyn and Ashley, they're going to try at least one, and possibly two, dangerous *missions,* as we called them in the military."

"Absolutely they will," he agrees. "And if we try to stop them I'm not sure how we could actually do that. Should we tell Ben or Lauren? I don't have good feelings about that. Probably Lauren and Ben would disagree with each other. She said she will back Robyn on whatever she decides to do. It's highly likely that Ben would try to force his own plans on his family. And on us.

"If we tell Ben and Lauren what Robyn's planning to do, that would be a huge violation of trust with Robyn and Ashley," I say, "but what's our obligation to our original clients? Ben and Lauren have trusted us to help protect their daughter. Could we possibly claim, even to ourselves, that we're not obligated to them because both Ben and Lauren heard Robyn's strong and clear declaration of independence?"

"That sent Ben fleeing to his car," I say, "while Lauren promised to support Robyn's decisions, whatever they turn out to be...although I doubt mom was imagining her daughter in close, face-to-face confrontations with her attackers.'"

"Maybe technically Ben and Lauren aren't our clients in this situation," Jimmy says. "We're trying to help Robyn and Ashley. That's a separate, pro bono project."

"Are you really comfortable with that distinction," I ask, hoping he can convince me. "If something goes wrong could you look at Ben and Lauren and convince them we didn't have an obligation to give them a specific head's up about this?"

"On the other hand," Jimmy says, "Robyn asked for our advice in front of Lauren, who knew Robyn was considering options that could be risky. I'm pretty clear on the problems and conflicts we face, but what the hell are we going to *do*, Jack? There is no walk-away option for us."

"I think the bottom line is *if* Robyn persists either she or we are ethically obligated to inform Ben and Lauren that their family's future could be incredibly affected. If Robyn doesn't do it, then we need to do it."

Jimmy says, "I think if we can't talk Robyn out of a potentially dangerous confrontation with Dixon or Andy Haley, then we need to do absolutely everything we can to make it successful, and at the very least, physically safe for everyone involved."

"And," I say, "*if* she and Robyn decide on the even riskier idea of attempting to tempt Dixon into another assault, we must try to protect her."

"In other words, we're in quicksand up to our eyeballs." Jimmy explains.

Chapter 65

-----JACK-----

The next afternoon, we're back in Ashley's apartment.

"I'm calling this meeting of the Gang-of-Five Conspiracy Club to order, minus Carole who has a trucking business to run," I say, from my seat on the floor, my back against the sofa next to Jimmy.

"Robyn, what are your thoughts now that we've all had a few hours to ponder the ideas we talked about?"

Robyn and Ashley exchange a quick glance and Robyn says: "Guys, I…we are going after my attackers in every way we've discussed if our first attempt doesn't work. We plan to start by trying to get him to attack Ashley and document everything on video."

She looks at Ashley again, finger-brushes her hair back, her eyes boring into mine.

"Our only question now is whether or not you and Jimmy are going to help us."

Before I or Jimmy can respond, she adds: "Either way, we're fine. We understand the pressures and conflicts you guys have and we're both totally cool with whatever you've decided. We just need to know if you're in or out."

Our High Noon moment.

Jimmy flicks a glance at me and says, "We'll help you if we can agree on a *reasonable* and *safe* plan to accomplish what you want."

Ashley nods from her spot on the other sofa, facing us. Robyn jumps up and now the four of us are in a group hug with everyone talking at once, then we all take a step back, abruptly breaking up like an NFL huddle.

Robyn says, "I can't tell you how much we appreciate your support. The four of us are going to drag that arrogant sociopath to the curb and flush him down the sewer."

She gestures us to sit as she hands out foot-long Subway sandwiches.

"Now," Ashley says, "let's work out a few details."

OMG! A few details. Understatement of the week.

"What's your plan so far?" Jimmy asks, unwrapping his sandwich. "How do you visualize this going down?"

"Umm, well," she says, "it's pretty simple. I find out when the next casual social event is happening at Dixon's frat. We think the parties aren't every Friday, more spur-of-the moment, not planned very far in advance, sometimes on Saturday, sometimes just word-of-mouth on party day, At best the word goes out a day in advance.

"I plan to get myself inside one of those, find Dixon and give him the opportunity to think I might be easy prey. We'll see if he tries to drug or otherwise attack me. We'll get everything on video. As soon as that happens, I break free and we go to the cops with the evidence."

Robyn brushes a few crumbs from her sweatshirt and nods agreement.

"That's it?" Jimmy says in a voice I recognize as an attempt to disguise doubt.

"That's the basic outline," Robyn says. "We'll need to find out how to record what happens and how to signal for help if things get out of hand, but we assume you guys know how to do that kinda stuff. Do you?"

"We can work it out," I say, "but the devil is always in the details. Jimmy knows a lot about equipment for something like that and may even have what we need in his Magic Gadget box. But we also have to plan for all of the stuff that can go wrong."

"Sure, fine," Ashley says. "We feel very confident about this, but what else do you guys recommend?"

"Okay," Jimmy says, "let's discuss some very *specific* options, such as who else we need for backup and to help pull this off."

"And *precisely* what gear we need to capture Dixon in action so we can prove he's a predator," I add.

"And what I'm going to wear," Ashley says. "I want to attract his attention without looking like a tramp."

"Maybe just trampy enough to be sure he'll try something," Robyn says.

"Robyn, you weren't dressed provocatively," I say. "He probably attacked you because you seemed vulnerable, don't you think? Or was it something else?"

She leans back against the chair as if I'd slapped her. I see her moistening eyes blinking rapidly, her hands forming fists.

"I don't know why he did what he did," her voice choked and barely audible. "He probably saw me as a weak, naïve target, because that's what I was."

"Nothing that happened is your fault, Robyn" Jimmy says immediately, trying to undo my unintended implication that she had somehow brought the attack on herself.

Still super sensitive.

"I know," she says, "but it's incredibly painful to even think about…"

Ashley hugs her and Robyn goes still for a few minutes while Jimmy and I try to blend into the carpet.

"We can't have Ashley alone at any time," I say. "We need someone else inside to watch and record what happens and be able to alert us if there are sudden dangerous developments."

"That's fine," Ashley says. "Nothing like that's likely to happen, but we understand that we should be a little cautious."

Bless her heart. Yeah, here's my plan. I'm aiming to trick a vicious, poisonous snake that has already bitten other victims, but heck, what could go wrong?

"If possible, we might get our new friend involved," Jimmy says, looking at me, referring to Chris Griffin.

Turning to Robyn and Ashley, he adds: "We know someone who works for the University and is furious about how rape victims are treated and cases are covered up. He looks and is young enough to be a student. If he's willing, maybe he could be inside to watch over Ashley and record Dixon's activity.

"And maybe we can recruit the latest victim we just heard about yesterday," I say, "It would be nice to have as many inside folks as possible, but, on the other hand, the more people involved the greater the risk of blowing our cover.

"Keep in mind that if our friend helps, he'll be putting his job, and possibly his career, in serious jeopardy. We would need to protect his identity."

"We have a lot of *ifs, shoulds, woulds* and *maybes*," I point out.

"We can do this, Jack," Robyn says. "Justice is on our side."

I wish I could be as blindly confident that the Good Guys always win. They don't.

"Robyn," I say firmly, "here's something we absolutely must agree on."

She and everyone else catches my no-compromise tone and stares at me.

"What's that?" she says.

"Before we launch ANY plan, whether giving Dixon an opportunity to attack another victim or trying to confront Dixon or Haley into a recorded confession, you *must* notify your parents before it actually happens. We have no way of predicting when that will happen."

"No," she says, standing up, her face reddening with anger. "No damn way. My father will try to stop us."

"This isn't negotiable, Robyn," I say softly. "You're putting your family's future at risk. Your parents have a right to know that. And in time to get involved if they decide to. If you won't, Jimmy and I will."

Her shoulders slump and after a pause, she looks up and says, "Okay, Jack. I'll take care of it when the time comes."

Chapter 66

-----JACK-----

An hour later, Jimmy is spooning chocolate ice cream into two coffee mugs

"Well, we have a basic plan," I say. "How confident are you that it will go down close enough to the plot line to be effective? And safe?"

He puts a mug on the kitchen table in front of me, sighs and sits.

"Less confident than Ashley and Robyn, that's for damn sure. They're at two-hundred-and ten percent. But if we get the details nailed down it *could* work. No matter what, we gotta do everything we can to keep Dixon from hurting Ashley.

. "If he tries to drug her we won't be able to intervene because that would blow the whole project. She's okay with drinking a spiked drink, and confident that we'll be able to rescue her before it's too late. Me? Nervous."

"Yeah," I say, napkining chocolate off my lips. "Lots of things could go very wrong. If he drugs her, we might not be able to know where he takes her next. How can we keep her under close-enough surveillance that we'll be able to instantly intervene?"

"Despite Robyn's and Ashley's massively naïve, over-confidence, we have a lot of stuff to figure out," he says.

"Yep," I say. "Tomorrow. Right now I'm totally tuckered out from trying to make them understand the very real and serious dangers they're confidently jumping into."

Chapter 67

-----JACK-----

Thursday afternoon, Ashley calls to enthusiastically announce "Party, party, party."

As if she's been invited to the White House.

"At Dixon's frat house?"

"Yes. Just got the word from a guy in my English Lit class. A party at Dixon's Greek House of Horrors starts Saturday, any time after 4:30. Twenty bucks per head to cover tickets for "bar drinks or BYOB.""

"That gives us two days to be ready. We need to get everyone together tomorrow to rehearse. Our place at 11 a.m. okay? Jimmy and I will get pizza."

"Sounds good," she says. Can you get your mysterious friend there?"

"I'll try."

"And the recent victim you mentioned, is she on board?"

"We'll try to get her signed up today. She may or may not be interested or available."

"We have lots to arrange to be ready to rehearse by tomorrow. We'll need a couple of run-throughs on Friday, and maybe one or even two, on Saturday just before Party Time. Same time and place? You and Robyn available both times?

"Yup, see you and Jimmy and possibly the other two recruits Friday at 11."

I call Jimmy who is at The Rev's church, interviewing more members.

"Tonto, we have a party to attend Saturday. Has Chris agreed to help?"

"Yeah, I briefed him on the plan yesterday. He's in. I'll double check that he's available Saturday."

"And," I say, "we'll need him Friday from 11 a.m. to about 3 p.m. to practice with the team. Also, I know it's short notice, but can you contact Julie Norton, the victim Chris saw being mistreated last week and ask her to join us?"

"I told him we might want to do that. I already got her phone number. I'll call her right now to see if she will join us. It may be a long shot and we don't have much time but we need several people inside to film any moves Dixon makes on Ashley."

"From this minute," I say, "all the way through *Show Time* Saturday, we're in total crisis mode."

"Yeah," he says. "Gotta get the details settled and practiced so we're all on the same page…at least until we get to Page Two when it will probably be mostly improvisation…by amateurs."

CHAPTER 68

-----JACK-----

That evening, I'm about to risk triggering a response the opposite of the one I desperately want. I've teetered on the edge of asking this question several times, but always veered away at the last second.

Crystal and I are loading popcorn bowls and soda glasses into her dishwasher. We've just finished a Netflix movie. Carli and Erik have been upstairs asleep for an hour and I'm about to head for my little house in Garland.

I try to speak but I can't.

I peer into her quizzical eyes, clear my throat and try again.

"Crystal."

I clear my throat again and my feelings blurt out in a high-speed, out-of-control, non-stop, no-punctuation, raspy voice.

"Crystal, I'm on a tightrope with no safety net totally excruciatingly scared to hear your answer but I've got to know if there's *any* chance any path any way any possibility we...can...*might* repair our marriage and get our family back together and put a lot of bad stuff behind us and...Hon...you *know* what I'm asking...I love you more than I can say and more than I've demonstrated sometimes and I'm so sorry for my past multiple screw-ups I've always loved you and I want...need...more than anything in the world...a fresh start if there's the teeniest tiniest slimmest sliver of a chance you...we...."

Her eyebrows momentarily flick up, her eyes widen and shift to her hands.

My eyes moisten, her face goes out of focus and I clamp my eyelids shut.

I've messed up again. Big time.

"Maybe." A whisper.

Maybe?

"I don't know," she says. "I've been struggling with that question for a long time."

Struggling! At least that's not HELL NO!

I fist-rub my eyes and try to read her face. She's crying silently, cheeks wet and red but we see each other.

"I know your demons from two wars are real and not your fault," she murmurs. "But there have been so *many* promises and *endless* disappointments."

There it is again. Her trust eternally ruptured?

"I completely understand that I damaged your faith in me," I say, "and I'm definitely not saying I *deserve* forgiveness."

She takes a deep breath, then another.

"I know you're basically a good person, but I wonder if you can truly, absolutely, positively follow through and crush your demons."

"Have I repaired *any* of my credibility with you in the last six months?"

"Yeah," she says, still having trouble looking at me for more than a few seconds. "But I know that every previous time you've pledged to do what you need to do, *you* believed your promises were true. They just never got done. The truth is, Jack, I'm wary of counting on you. I'm afraid to hope one more time. I've already taken too many up-n-down rides on the One-More-Time roller coaster."

I need to beg.

"What do I have to do to convince you to trust...and love me again?"

She pats her tear-stained cheeks, blinks and looks at me for a moment. She reaches for my hand and gently pats it in what I feel is a *'there, there'* way, plummeting me to the bottom of the despair scale.

."Oh, good grief, Jack. I love you. I've loved you since your fourth-grade, hand-made Valentine declaring that I was the most-interesting girl in class.

"In the past two years, even when I was screaming at you and ordering you out of the house, on some level I still loved you. It was just too painful to be *in* love with you, watching you destroying yourself and your family and unable to stop. I was furious with you for failing over and over despite the love and help of your main support group; me, Carole, even Carli and Erik. And when you backed your car over Erik, I couldn't…I *had* to get you out of our day-to-day lives."

I'm crying…no, sobbing, my entire body trembling, mind racing.

"We've had almost normal family times in recent months," she says. "We're just not living in the same house."

She gently squeezes my right hand and I'm gasping for air in between sobs.

Of joy?

I flick one eyelid open for a few seconds and see she's crying, too.

I cover her hand with my left, she completes the stack and we sit like that for several minutes, eyes assessing eyes, hands sandwiched.

"Convince me that just like you've recovered from the bullet wound you suffered rescuing Erik, you're also now the man I married nearly 20 years ago. Are you?"

Am I correctly hearing what she's saying? If not, please don't wake me from this dream.

"Yes," I declare immediately. "Yes, I am. I desperately miss our former life. I want to tuck the kids in bed *every* night, not just once in a while. I want to help get them to school and not just take Erik to therapy sessions. I want to wake up with you.

"I want that life back and I'm a thousand percent prepared to get there. We've had tons of trauma in recent times with Erik being injured and kid-napped…and everything else that happened.

"I want us all to have a fresh start. I absolutely swear I won't let you and the kids down. Are you willing to try?"

She bites her lower lip, still probing my eyes, absorbs two deep breaths and adjusts her arms so that we're now clasping hands across the table in a circle I chose to interpret as hopeful.

"Let's try," she says softly. "Maybe we can work it out. I'm willing to try. Let's try together."

Chapter 69

-----JIMMY-----

"Miss Norton? Julie Norton?"

"Who's calling?"

"Jimmy McGuire. Chris Griffin called you about an hour ago about the experience you had when you tried to file an assault complaint with McMillan University police. I'm one of the two private investigators he mentioned are trying to change how the University handles these cases."

"Yes, he called. I knew he was in the room when I was there with my parents but I didn't realize until today that he disagreed with how I was treated. I didn't even know his name. He said you and your partner want me to help with some kind of sting operation? Is that true?"

She sounds skeptical.

I briefly explain our basic goal is to get a predator on video attacking a new victim. I tell her a few details of the plan.

"It's a risky idea and may not work…or it could even backfire. Will you help us?"

It took her less than 10 seconds to decide.

"Hell, yes. I'd love to help nail one of those bastards!"

Chapter 70

-----JACK-----

Next morning, I'm either dreaming that I'm awake, or I'm awakening from a nightmare. When I last checked my bedside clock it said 2:34 a.m. Now it's 4:47 a.m., either for real or in my dream.

I must be awake. I'm gasping for breath and my heart is trying to hammer an escape from my chest. I'm desperately afraid of what might happen tomorrow. The plan I just dreamed about ended tragically.

No point trying to get a few more hours of sleep, I'm going to be a mess until Saturday is behind us.

I'm up now, padding barefoot to the kitchen. Soon the coffee maker is making sounds akin to an upset stomach, while I slump at the table, barely conscious, definitely not focused.

Tonto materializes without sound and heads for the coffee.

He brings two filled mugs to the table, sits and stares at me for a while, and says: "Are you in there or have you left the building and abandoned your human husk?"

"Um…ah… mmm…shut the hell up."

"Thanks for the explanation. Obviously you're wound a little tight this morning."

"I've been nearly paralyzed since Ashley called yesterday. I'm vividly realizing that two days from now someone we needed to protect might be hurt. And I might be ending another career in our risky attempt to prove Josh Dixon is a sex predator.

"I've already crashed and burned once, losing my journalism dream job by crossing the line between common sense and breaking rules. I was pursuing a good cause but not in the *right* way. Déjà vu, anyone?"

"I get it," he says. "We're both nervous about this idea. Let's go for a run. That'll smooth out our physical and mental kinks so we can focus on our mission. We need to be the calm guys today, Friday and Saturday."

Later, we're showered, dressed, fully caffeinated and reviewing for the umpteenth time every detail of what we hope to pull off on Saturday.

"Okay," Jimmy says, glancing at his watch and rising from his kitchen chair," I think we've memorized the plan. Now let's hope it *works*. Everyone will be here in 45 minutes so I need to pick up the pizzas for the Gang's rehearsal lunch."

"We need enough for our newly expanded Gang-of-Eight. It's scary that we were worried about involving one or two folks beyond our group of four, and now, with Julie Norton, Chris Griffin and Pamela Swann signed up, we're double the original four if you count your Mom, aka my sister."

We look at each other for a moment.

"What's your confidence level right now?" I ask.

"Ah, probably a seven out of ten. You?"

"Somewhere between six-point nine and seven-point-one. Every time we go through the plan I'm intensely aware that no mission plays out perfectly and requires on-the-fly changes caused by unpredictable events and reactions. And that's true even when *professionals* are doing the planning and *well-trained troops* will try to execute the game plan."

"Yep," he says, turning to the door. "And that's the way it is. We can re-visit our confidence levels later after some practice drills with our rookie partners. Gotta go."

The kitchen door closes with an ominous finality that's far outside my comfort zone.

Chapter 71

-----JACK-----

Before 10 a.m. I'm crouching in the back of a borrowed van, unfolding a small camping table and arranging several small monitors for live video feeds from sun glasses that will be worn by Ashley, Julie, Chris and Pamela.

Another monitor will display video from a camera in the small helicopter drone Jimmy is assembling on the floor behind me. The drone's rotors are almost two feet long.

The table and three folding chairs occupy most of the limited space in the window-less back of the black van.

"I hope there'll be enough oxygen when Robyn joins us back here," Jimmy says.

"I may hyperventilate before then," I say. "The rest of our gang will be here in a few minutes for equipment and practice runs. I plan to push them rapidly through everything we hope happens.

"We've only got today and tomorrow morning before actually launching an inexperienced assortment of young civilians into a risky situation. It's going to feel like a month before tomorrow is over."

"You got that right."

At 11 a.m., our Gang is newly enlarged to eight by Julie Norton, the most-recent victim turned away by the McMillan University Security department.

She joins Chris Griffin, Pamela Swann, Ashley Scanlon, Robyn, Tonto and me, clustering silently around our dining room table, unwrapping sandwiches, no one saying anything even vaguely related to why we've gathered together. Carole is at her trucking company office, on standby if needed. Possibly to post bond for us if bad things happen.

I break the conversational hum.

"Okay, everyone listen up. Keep eating but pay attention. It's absolutely critical that all of us get not only on the same page, but that we all know *exactly* what our roles are. And also exactly what *everyone else* is going to do. Any questions so far?"

"None? Good. Here's your surprise pop quiz. Ashley, what will you be doing at 4:30 Saturday?"

Ashley abandons her sandwich, her face displaying uncertainty and anxiety. She straightens her spine, breathes in and says: "Julie and I will arrive at the frat house, merge alongside or close behind other people that we won't know, but we'll try to make it look like we're with them."

"Okay, enough for now," I interrupt.

"Chris, where will you be at 4:30 p.m. Saturday?"

He finger-smooths a new moustache.

"A similar beginning," he says. "Pamela and I will join other arriving guests, blending with them until we're inside."

"What else?" I bark.

He hesitates, then snaps his fingers.

"When we're approaching the party I'll try to see if Dixon's bedroom window is open, or if the blinds are open. Mark showed me a phone-photo of the side of the house."

"Robyn," I say, "where will you be?"

"In the back of the van with Jimmy and you."

Jimmy says: "Julie, thank you for agreeing to help this project. Do you have any questions about we're about to do? You okay with the details so far?"

Julie is sturdy with a curly cap of close-cropped reddish-brown hair. She plants her hands on her hips and makes eye contact with all of us. Her voice is strongly confident, matching Chris Griffin's description of her confrontation with the lieutenant in the University's Security Department.

"As Ashley just said, the two of us will slip into house and once inside we'll try to locate the psychopath and hope one of us looks like prey to him."

"Pamela?"

She smiles and shrugs.

"I'm Chris's date and we're each other's cover. Our job is finding Dixon and providing video evidence of whatever happens."

"Also to sound an alarm if anything goes dangerously bad," Jimmy says.

Jimmy helps us set up a speed-dial group that includes all of us.

"Everyone bring freshly charged batteries in your phones tomorrow," I say. "Anyone want to tug Chris's brand-new moustache to double-check that it won't fall off?" he grins.

"I already did that," Pamela says. "It passed."

"I decided to try it out right away," he says. "I'm getting used to it. I may grow a real one when this is over."

We all agree that it looks genuine and changes his appearance enough that he's unlikely to be recognized, particularly out of uniform.

"Ashley and Julie," Tonto says, "are you both wearing the drug-detecting fingernail polish?"

"I'll bring some for Julie tomorrow," Ashley says. "I've got mine and so does Pamela, just in case although she's not likely to get hit on by anyone since she's with a date."

"Any questions or concerns from anyone?" Tonto asks.

"I'm a little nervous," Ashley says. "I didn't expect to be but now that we're within two days of actually trying to *do* all of this, I'm realizing the risks we're all taking."

"If anyone wants or needs to drop out, this is the time to decide. No one should feel pressure to stay. The stakes are high and we have no guarantee of success or that this won't blow up in our faces."

The room is silent.

"Okay, let's get started," Tonto says.

He, Robyn and I move outside where we test the video feeds from the cameras in special sunglasses Jimmy found on the internet. Each has a tiny camera that can transmit video about 200 feet, depending on how many walls are in between. Pamela, Ashley, Chris and Julie will wear them when they arrive at the party in the afternoon.

The miniature chopper's camera is also displaying on its monitor.

We'll test everything again tomorrow before heading to the frat house.

Shortly before 2 p.m., my cell screen announces a call from 'Jackson Parks.'

"Hey," I tell Jimmy, "I think Jackson Parks' widow is calling."

I punch speaker phone and as soon as I say "hello," Mrs. Parks says, "Mr. Crocker?" in a near-whisper.

"Yes," I assure her. "What can I do for you, Mrs. Parks?"

"Mr. Crocker, I want…I *need* to talk to you. Can you come to my home?"

"Of course. Unfortunately we're right in the middle of a critical project right now. May I call you in a couple of days to set up a time that's good for you? Would that be all right?"

After a momentary pause, "Yes, that's okay. Thank you."

Jimmy nods as I disconnect.

"I'm checking off the last box on our list," Tonto says. "Everything's working now. I have eight battery packs for our Bird in the Sky. Each battery gets about 15 minutes of fly time and we can't predict how long we'll need to deploy it, if at all."

Back inside, "Anyone have remaining questions or concerns?" I say.

"I think I've got it," Chris says. "I'll feel better when we've reviewed everything again tomorrow. Knowing we have to do this stuff for real in just two days is a bit scary. And exciting!"

I see several nods of agreement and hear a firm 'Amen,' from Pamela.

"We all feel that way," Jimmy says, "Everyone please be back here Friday at 11 for a couple more *walk-and-talk* through rehearsals for Saturday."

Twenty minutes later, everyone except Jimmy is gone and I'm in stretched out, eyes closed, in my battered recliner. As I did before every military mission during two deployments, I'm trying to visualize every aspect of our operational plan. So far, none of my mental reviews have been successful.

I mentally restart our plan from the beginning. And again. And again.

I awake with a start, and a queasy feeling that haunts me the rest of the day and for most of a restless night.

CHAPTER 72

-----JACK-----

At 4:34 Friday morning, I give up seeking sleep, take a quick shower and am scarfing two-day-old, cold pizza with one hand and sipping coffee with the other.

"Man, you're the cat on the hot tin roof," Tonto says, watching my legs jiggling under the kitchen table. "Are you going to force me to hide all caffeine products today so you don't disintegrate into tiny fragments while we're practicing our attack plans for tomorrow?"

"Maybe."

"Give me that coffee cup," he demands. "I'll warm a quart of milk to settle you down."

"Ha, ha," I mock. "Go to Hell."

"Time for another run?"

"Good idea," I agree. "Might help my focus until the Gang's all here and we're practicing our game plan."

Just before 11 a.m., the Gang is arriving, Jimmy, Robyn and I are firing up the monitors in the van and I'm feeling slightly less jittery.

Chris parks at the curb and he says he wants a 'peek at the tech stuff." Ashley chimes in and now we're all crowding inside the van and Jimmy is explaining what's showing on the monitors; and demonstrating the small drone's camera.

Close to noon, Jimmy catches my eye and I nod and he takes the helm.

"Everyone inside. Grab a beverage from the cooler in the kitchen. You know where the bathroom is. Sandwiches are warm in the oven. Rehearsal in 15 minutes. Put on your game faces."

By 2 p.m. we're fed and each of us has recited our plan aloud at least once.

Jimmy says, "Thanks. That's enough for now. We're all tired but you all did pretty well. Same drill tomorrow before we pull the pin on our Saturday surprise at Dixon's frat house...."

I say: "If for *any* reason we need to end this project quickly, we will send everyone a text with the word 'football' in it. Remember, 'football' means everything is shut down. Meet up back here.

"And if any of you need to bail out for *any* reason use the same code to let us know you're leaving."

Ashley's cell interrupts with a couple of bars from a Taylor Swift song.

She scurries to the kitchen before answering.

Jimmy says, "Giving Dixon the opportunity to wander into our rat trap is...."

We all hear Ashley shouting in the kitchen. "No. That can't be right!"

Robyn and Chris sprint toward Ashley in the kitchen, but she bursts into the living room, yelling and waving her phone. "Are you're absolutely friggin' positive? Really?"

She listens for a few seconds and clicks off to announce, "The party is NOT tomorrow! It's today! TODAY!"

I hear my own voice booming.

"Holy Damn Moley!"

CHAPTER 73

-----JACK-----

The Gang silently assembles in the kitchen, Robyn, Ashley, Pamela and Julie in chairs, Jimmy and Chris leaning back against the cabinets, me sitting on the counter by the sink, wondering if I should feed our plan to the garbage disposal.

"Well, Gangsters," I say, "we need a quick, smart decision. Should we scrub our game plan and hope to try again at some future time? Or, are we sufficiently prepared to launch *Project Kick a Predator's Ass* in less than three hours from now?"

'Do you and Jimmy think we're ready?" Chris says.

"Do *you* feel ready?" I ask him.

He shrugs. "I guess so."

"No one's ever completely comfortable in this kind of situation," Jimmy says. "But we don't want to screw it up because we weren't ready."

"It's now or never," Julie says. "It's mid-May, the semester's ending. Final exams are beginning in some classes. People are focused on studying and finishing. Some are already turning in papers or having early finals and leaving campus for the summer."

She looks around the room.

"I think we do it today or it's unlikely to ever happen."

Seems like everyone is taking a silent timeout.

"I vote for today," Ashley says. "Some of us may not be here in the fall."

233

She glances at Robyn who is studying her hands.

"I think we're ready," Chris says.

"Let's vote," I say.

If it's not unanimous we shouldn't go.

"All in favor?"

Every hand, some of them fisted, lift toward the ceiling. Except mine, but I vote with the rest. We all realize what that means and, just that quickly, we're as committed as seven skydivers who have left the plane with one marginal parachute per person.

Chapter 74

A blurry, chaotic frenzy.

There's no other way to describe the next two hours. Everyone except Jimmy and me scattered to their residences to change clothes, some applying makeup, two adding drug-detecting nail polish.

Pamela has donned a UCLA tee over white shorts and sandals to support her cover story that she's a visitor from California, visiting her grandparents in Garland and her old friend, Julie, from high school.

Ashley returns in a McMillan tee and denim shorts.

Julie's pony tail extends through a blue, Southwest Texas University hat that we hope signals she's from a less-sophisticated, small school, possibly making her appear more vulnerable.

Robyn is in all black jeans and tee, looking like a short Ninja, needing only a black ski mask to complete image.

A little after 4 p.m., we're all in the kitchen again. Jimmy whispers to me, "I think we're as ready as we're going to be. Time to dispatch the troops."

He calls for attention.

"Our infiltration squad needs to head for the frat house. Ashley, Pamela, Julie and Chris, are you ready to infiltrate a party and maybe nail a future prison inmate?"

"Hell, yes," Julie says and the other three agree.

"We've talked about it, now let's all mount up and go," I say.

"Okay, is *everyone* ready?" Jimmy asks.

A unanimous cheer.

"Okay," I shout, "Last group hug before we attack."

We all stand and link arms over shoulders in a loose scrum. I sense the pent-up tension in the air and feel it in the tight shoulder muscles of Chris to my left and Ashley on my right.

"Okay, Gang," I say. "Let's go kick some rapist ass."

CHAPTER 75

-----JACK-----

We're parked on a side street two blocks from the frat house. Robyn, Jimmy and I are crammed together in our Situation Room, aka The Van, the windshield blocked by sun screens, the driver and passenger door windows so darkly tinted that no one can see inside even if leaving nose prints on the glass.

We're in full operational mode, activating signals from Chris and Pamela, approaching the frat house from the north and Julie and Ashley, coming from the south.

"Done," Jimmy announces.

"Julie's feed is a little pixelated but usable. I'm ready. As soon as there's something we need to monitor from outside, I'll send my chopper to sneak up on the house. Chris's feed isn't clear on whether the blinds are raised in Dixon's room."

"Roger that, Tonto," I say in my most-serious voice and everyone laughs, I hope reducing the stress level a notch.

"What's the intel from inside the house," Jimmy asks Robyn, drawing a brief smile.

"Mostly I'm seeing arriving guests mingling in what looks like a gigantic living room or rec room, a gathering place of some kind," she says softly but in a business-like tone.

On that screen I see Chris in his Dallas Cowboys tee following Pamela into the large room.

"Oh, good," Robyn says. "Chris and Pamela are inside and just found seats near the glass doors that slide open to the backyard. It's good that our people got there early," she says. "The place is filling up already."

Via Pamela's video feed, we see Ashley and Julie claim seats on a dark leather sofa against a wall adjacent to Chris and Pamela, their feeds now panning the room on another screen.

"This is great," I say, "seeing what they're seeing in real time, showing us the room plus where everyone's sitting, standing or passing through."

I lean closer to the table and from Julie's point of view I see a bar on the large patio outside, guests clustering nearby. People are going outside and returning with large red paper cups of beer and disappearing from our monitors.

With all four videos we see the entire large room in side-by-side monitors. Most of the space on four sofas, eight chairs and even the carpet is already occupied.

This must have been a ballroom when it was an oil baron's mansion.

An hour and a half later, we've seen nothing unusual.

"I hope we don't end up with nothing more than five or six hours of video showing only soundless people we don't know, wandering randomly around a party we weren't even invited to," I say.

"Yeah," Jimmy says. "We're way over-prepared for that."

A half-hour later, I say: "Time to adjust the plan," I say. "Robyn, text Ashley to take Julie and mingle in the backyard to see if they can spot our target. We still don't know if he's in the house."

Robyn's thumbs fly over her phone.

I watch Screen One and see Ashley casually glance at her phone and show it to Julie. Both laugh, as if sharing an internet joke. Neither moves immediately but a couple of minutes later they get up and stroll outside.

"Tonto, text Chris to take a slow mingling tour of the house looking for Target One."

On Screen Two I see Chris check his phone and put it back in his pants, still chatting with Pamela, who's sipping wine she got almost two hours ago.

Video from Ashley and Julie now show unsteady images as they approach the crowded bar. No Josh Dixon.

Chris stands up, tips his cup toward Pamela as if he's leaving for a refill and casually exits the main room, not looking at all like someone who is risking his job and possibly his entire law-enforcement career.

His screen is an ever-changing kaleidoscope of faces, backs and tops of heads as he pushes slowly down a crowded hallway into another room, smaller than the main gathering area, perhaps a former dining room. He moves through the room slowly, partly because it's crowded but mostly so he can send us images of everyone within range.

"Anyone see a familiar face?" I say.

Tonto adds, "Not even Andy Haley, that star-struck dweeb who hangs out with Dixon. He's probably not Greek material anyway, a little too creepy to invite, although he was part of the original attack. Robyn, you see anyone you recognize?"

"Not yet," she says firmly but so softly I barely hear her. "If I see anyone I remember, you'll damn-well instantly know about it."

I'm trying to monitor the two feeds from members of our gang who are on the move outside and a third scouting other rooms.

Nada.

I say, "We knew it could be a long night, that's why we have a bag of granola and energy bars and the cooler full of Diet Coke."

"Oh, my God," Robyn shouts. "That's him."

"Holy cow! There he is!" Tonto exclaims.

Dixon's face almost fills Pamela's monitor. He's standing right in front of her, leaning down to her.

My body on full alert, heart thumping much too rapidly, breaths coming in gasps. I'm hoping Pamela has already mentally switched from *observer* to *bait* and that the shark is circling his prey and not just passing by.

"Tonto, text Ashley, Julie and Chris that the scumbag is in sight but to stay where they are for the moment."

"He just sat next to her," Robyn hisses. "See, she's not looking up at him now. The son-of-a-bitch is sitting in Chris's spot, probably excreting fake charm."

"We need a wider view," I say. "Text Chris to stay away from this room for a few minutes. Dixon must not have seen him and Pamela together, so presumably he doesn't know she's with someone."

"Tell Ashley and Julie to stay near the bar in case he goes for fresh drinks, which is his best opportunity to spike her wine."

"If he tries something like that," Tonto says, "it probably won't happen immediately. He'll need time to assess her vulnerability before trying to set her up. Or he might just move on."

"Wow," Robyn says, "A big change of plans. We didn't expect he would hit on Pamela."

"Pamela's a grown-up, she'll be able to handle this," I say, desperately hoping it's true. "We knew there'd be adjustments, we just didn't know what they would be. We'll soon find out if he's actually considering going after Pamela."

"Or maybe he just spotted someone new," Robyn says, "and is exploring possibilities. Or maybe he's just practicing his flirting skills. Or showing off."

"For everything to work for us," I add, "he's gotta be attracted without her openly welcoming his advances. She must appear unwilling, but he must think a dab of Date-Rape drug will knock her out enough to get her upstairs in a semi-conscious state."

"Yeah," Tonto says. "If they leave together and go to his room on the second floor, I'll launch the helicopter so it can be close by if he attacks. We need video evidence plus we want to have help available to rescue Pamela if that's needed."

"We knew it was a difficult and risky plan," I say. "Right now it looks like it might work but it still could end with him walking away and we pack up and leave with nothing useful. Robyn, text Chris to ease back into the main room, but stay as far from Pamela and Dixon as possible, out of sight."

"Even if he doesn't try anything with Pamela," Tonto says, "we need to keep our electronic eyes on him till the evening is over because he might attack someone else and we could document that. Even if we don't get evidence against him, we need to protect any other possible victims."

I'm still scanning the screens, but primarily the one showing Dixon's animated face apparently flirting with Pamela.

"He's been chatting her up long enough that I'm getting optimistic he's going to try something," Robyn says. "He must be interested or he wouldn't be investing this much of his precious hunting time."

"Is this sparking any memories for you?" I ask.

"Sorta," she says. "Murky. I feel like I've seen this before but can't clearly visualize the outcome unless my horrifying dream *is* that ending. I guess it must be but I wasn't fully conscious. I don't know...."

I hear her voice choke and she can't speak but her eyes remain locked on Dixon's face. Pamela shifts her head for brief moments and the camera shows glimpses of the room. No one seems to be paying attention to her or Dixon.

Just another fleeting encounter at a party between two adults. Could be significant or forgotten an hour later.

Chris's screen shows what he sees as he re-enters the room and sits on the floor in a corner diagonally across the room from Pamela and Dixon. He's behind other carpet sitters, largely shielded from Dixon's view, not staring at the two-some, glancing around the room, slowing enough as he pans past prey and predator for us to see Dixon holding a red cup, sitting closer to Pamela than before, both of them alternately laughing at something the other says and Dixon leaning even closer and seemingly speaking softly and seriously, so close that her screen displays only half of his face.

The longer view from Chris shows Dixon putting his hand on Pamela's knee for a few seconds before she casually removes it.

"A good move by Pamela," I say. "She's playing her role perfectly, staying somewhat aloof, not letting him move too rapidly, but not making a fuss that might send him away looking for a different victim."

"I can hardly watch this," Robyn mutters. "To me, he's already assaulting her, touching her without any encouragement from her except what I'm sure has been nothing but small talk."

Tonto says: "But the big picture is that even if he's trying to seduce her, that's hardly unusual in this kind of setting," Tonto says. "And even in a legal sense, he's done nothing wrong yet, so we have to give him a little benefit of the doubt at this stage."

"No we don't," she spits. "No, we damn well don't owe him that, or anything else. The justice system may not judge him yet on his behavior tonight so far, but he's got a history of violence, he just hasn't been officially caught yet."

"Yes," Jimmy says, "but right now he may merely be trying to charm her into a seduction and will resort to drugs or force only if that doesn't work, so there's nothing legally nefarious happening."

"That's nonsense," Robyn says. "He *prefers* violence and drugs and rendering his victims helpless because he's a sicko pervert. He's not a rejected suitor. He *enjoys* exploiting a totally controlled captive. This isn't romance, this is sadistic terrorism."

Jimmy and I are silent, watching the monitors.

Probably true, but not yet provable.

Finally Jimmy says, "I think you're right about that. It's just that he hasn't yet crossed into any criminal territory."

Transmissions from Ashley and Julie in the back yard seem innocuous, people mingling in small groups, laughing and having conversations we can't hear but that are probably not discussions of the global economy or astrophysics, just young college students having fun, checking out the dating or mating pools, getting buzzed, some probably aiming for blotto.

Fifteen minutes later, the three of us remain silent, our universe narrowed to monitors displaying other people partying. I feel a tinge of voyeuristic guilt amidst growing frustration that so far our rapist has done nothing even remotely improper.

"Damn it, you asshole," Robyn shouts, causing Jimmy and me to flinch. "Make your move. Show your true, piece-of-shit self!"

"Amen, sister," I murmur, trying to lower the volume inside the van.

"Sorry, guys," she says. "I may explode before his mask comes off. He's more patient than I am."

"We've all been all day," I say. "That's okay. Something will happen, even if it doesn't help us prove Dixon's a psychopath. Either way, this part of trying to bring him down will be over. We can't force him into anything. We'll keep after him."

"I want to go in there and scream at him and bash his face in and…." Robyn says.

"Ninety-nine bottles of beer in the wall," I begin, "Don't make me sing the whole song. Deep breaths, everyone."

"Nooooo!" Tonto begs, grinning.

"Yeah, what he said," Robyn half smiles. "I'll stop whining…and threatening."

A few minutes later I'm unwrapping two more sticks of gum so my teeth have something to do besides grind each other.

"He's up!" Robyn yells. "Something's going down. He's either giving up or he's going into attack mode."

We all see Dixon's face peering down at Pamela her camera, till smiling and talking.

From across the room, the video from Chris shows Dixon standing and pivoting toward the doors to the bar in the yard.

"He's on the move!" I say. "Robyn, text Ashley and Julie that he's coming to the bar and they need to split up to record two angles of everything he does out there!"

"Jimmy, text Chris to get outside for a wider view of the bar. When Dixon goes back inside, Chris needs to be close behind so we can record whatever happens next."

We see Pamela briefly texting until Chris is up and he heads to the patio and gets stationary in a head-on view, about 15 feet from the bar where Dixon is already talking to the bartender.

Pamela's text arrives. "I'm fine. Think he's closing in. I'm okay with Full Monty."

The "Full Monty" refers to Ashley and Julie each volunteering to actually drink something that might contain the Date-Rape or some other drug. They planned to drink only white wine that would be less visible than red wine if dumped on the carpet.

"But if I can't discard it, I'll drink up and count on you guys to rescue me if I end up Full Monty and comatose," Ashley had said and Julie also took the pledge. They planned to try avoiding any drink that Dixon might have spiked, but were willing to take the risk. Pamela hadn't joined in because none of us saw her as a possible target for Dixon.

Now her text alerts us that she's willing to risk being drugged into unconsciousness.

"I get it," Jimmy says. "She's trusting us to intervene if things go bad."

We're all silent. I'm holding my breath, zeroed in on three views of the patio bar, desperately hoping to see Dixon tampering with Pamela's wine.

Julie's point of view is from several feet beyond the left end of the eight-foot, roll-around bar. Ashley is at the other end, but closer to the bar. She's talking with an unidentified male whose image floats in and out of her video feed, momentarily blocking our view of the bar, the bartender and the table behind him holding a variety of wine and hard booze. The bartender fills a large red cup from one of the draft beer nozzles and puts it on the bar in front of Dixon.

"Shit," Robyn says, anger in her voice. "He's just getting himself a fresh beer. He's moving on. We've lost him."

We see the bartender pouring white wine into a smaller cup and setting it on the bar.

"Wait," I say, "that's not for him, it's for Pamela. He's still stalking her."

Julie's and Ashley's video angles on Dixon show him moving the wine cup to the edge of the bar with one hand and, at the same time, leaning forward, chest against the bar, grabbing two napkins, spreading them near the wine and moving that cup to one napkin while simultaneously shifting the beer cup to the other.

What just happened? Was that a magician's sleight of hand distraction?

I say: Did either of you see what the hell happened there?"

"Maybe," Jimmy says. "There was a lot of over-lapping movement but...."

"I'm not sure *exactly* what I saw, but I know *absolutely* what happened," Robyn says, certainty in her voice and on her face. "He dropped something in that wine glass while those napkins were moving around."

"Robyn, call Mark Easton and tell him we need him here right-damn-now."

"We can replay the video in slow-motion later," I say. "For now, let's assume he's trying to drug Pamela."

Jimmy interrupts. "I'm sending the chopper right now to Dixon's bedroom window on the side of the house."

Through the van's windows he checks all four directions before opening the rear door, stepping into the parking lot and quickly launching the copter and hurriedly ducking back in the van with the remote control in hand, images already appearing on the previously blank screen.

Two mornings earlier, we sent Mark Easton to the house disguised as an AT&T repairman who told the House Mother he needed to "...find and fix the problems reported by several of the residents." She unlocked the three bedrooms he listed and paced the hallway while he "tested" the lines with a meter designed for evaluating car batteries.

In Dixon's room he managed to install a tiny, lip-stick shaped video camera with a wide-angle view of the room from the corner opposite the bed, before declaring, "All fixed and good to go."

Now, Mark is at a Dunkin' Donuts shop about two miles away, waiting to join us if needed.

Now, my pulse beats are so strong and close together they sound like distant automatic weapons fire in my ears.

Robyn, Jimmy and I are clustered so close to the monitors in the van that our shoulders touch.

Two screens show angles of Dixon heading away from the bar. Ashley's and Julie's cameras track Dixon from the back and he disappears from their feeds as he gets inside and turns right.

Less than a minute later, Chris returns to the back of the room and his camera shows Dixon sitting close to Pamela sipping from the wine cup.

"She did it," I exclaim. "She's showing us that she's drinking the wine, assuming that's it's spiked. Her clock is ticking, and it'll speed up if she can't avoid drinking more of the stuff."

Fifteen minutes later, thanks to Chris's camera we're still watching Pamela and Josh Dixon chatting, sipping, laughing.

Ashley and a young man come through the patio door, glance around and squeeze into an open sofa spot more suited to one person than two. She's closer to Pamela and Dixon than Chris and I'm trying to read Pamela's lips on the monitor but having no luck.

They look like any other young couple enjoying each other's company, but I know she despises the sonuvabitch.

"Somethings gotta happen soon," I say. "I can't tell for sure if she's slowing down. Any opinions?"

"I definitely think so," Robyn says. "Every so often she sorta stares into space for a few seconds. I think that's real, although she could be pretending. She's drinking the wine slowly, stretching it out, but it's either taking effect or she's a wonderful actress."

"Let's remember to nominate Pamela for an Oscar," I mutter, sparking an "amen" from Jimmy.

"Robyn," I say, "text Mark Easton to activate the bedroom cam immediately and get here to infiltrate the party as soon as he's here.

"He's been sending a "Still here" every half-hour, from the donut shop." Robyn says.

"I'm bringing the chopper back for a new battery," Jimmy says. "It's got about five minutes left and I can freshen it and get it back to the house by the time Mark's inside."

As if he heard our conversation, Josh Dixon stands up, thrusts his hand to Pamela who takes it and slowly stands, pausing momentarily before following Dixon from the room, out of sight of our cameras.

Pamela's feed shows an unsteady journey down a crowded hallway.

Then her monitor shows a stationary view of a snow storm.

"What the hell?" Jimmy says, silence the only answer.

"Maybe her glasses fell off or he took them from her and put them on a white shelf or a white table cloth."

"Whatever happened," Jimmy says, "we're blind now until they get upstairs to Dixon's room. We don't even know for sure that's where he's taking her. Let's hope Mark is close enough to activate that camera damn quick; and that it actually works, we never had a chance to test that one."

"Robyn, call Mark and update him. How long before he's here?"

"She seemed shaky," Robyn says. "Still can't tell if she's faking it. If she's not acting... she's definitely in danger."

"Mark's at least four minutes away. He's in heavy traffic from a soccer match that just ended. He must be within 100 feet of the camera to activate it."

"Damn!" I spit. "I'm going in now!" and open the van's rear door.

"Tonto, Call Mark and update him. Text me when we have video of what's happening in Dixon's bedroom!"

CHAPTER 76

-----JACK-----

I'm running down a sidewalk, dodging a few walkers, a jogger coming right at me. I veer right, aiming for the alley, sprinting as fast as my lungs permit, my feet each weighing 50 pounds, crossing another street with barely a glance for traffic.

One block. One more. Go! There it is!

The party is easy to hear, even with a six-foot concrete wall shielding the property.

I lunge for a wood door set in the gray concrete hoping it's unlocked for the party. It isn't. I twist the unmoving doorknob, trying desperately to shake it loose, simultaneously pounding on the faded dark wood and shouting: "Open up!" Deep breaths. "Open the door, dammit!"

It opens a crack and I see a large, bearded young man blocking the door, peering at me.

"Let me in," I half gasp, half shout. "I've got to...."

"Whoa, pal," he grins. "You're supposed to come through the front door. What's so urgently burning your butt to get in? You can...."

"There's a girl...."

"Isn't there always?" he says, smiling and swinging the door open. "Are you worried she'll find someone else before...."

"Something like that," I say as calmly as I can, forcing a smile.

He looks at my burnt-orange UT tee and at my face.

"Aren't you a little old for…"

"Adjunct faculty," I say, slipping past him, fast-walking through the crowd, trying to attract as little attention as possible, moving past the bar to the sliding doors into the house.

I slow to a casual walk and step inside, scanning the room, trying to slow my breathing. I see Ashley and Julie but we don't acknowledge each other.

Chris is immobile against the wall opposite the doors. I glance at him, flash him a nano-nod to my left and head down the hallway to stairs visible at the end.

I'm at the top of the stairs gulping air and Chris joins me. No one in the second-floor hallway.

"Anything change while I was running over here?" I whisper.

"No," he says. "Pamela and Dixon are gone. We think they went upstairs to Dixon's room, but we don't know for sure."

I tell him, "Her glasses are AWOL, possibly discarded, but Pamela wouldn't do that voluntarily so she might be drugged and not aware, but we don't know.

"Mark is trying to get here. He can't activate the camera in Dixon's bedroom until he is closer. Traffic leaving the stadium after a soccer match delayed him for more than 10 minutes that we didn't factor into our plan."

He points to the door behind me. The brass label says "Anderson."

"According to Mark, Dixon's room is the third one on the left," I say. "Let's see if we can hear anything…and hope everyone else stays downstairs at the party.

We move quickly down the carpeted hallway, splitting to flank the door labeled "Dixon," and lean in, ears touching the door. I see Chris clenching his eyes closed to better focus on sounds and I follow suit.

A long minute later I straighten and glance at him. He hasn't moved. I tap his shoulder, his eyes flash open and he shakes his head negatively. I nod, shoot a look down the still empty hallway and step back.

He joins me and whispers, "Nuthin. Maybe they're not in there."

"Where else?" I say. "God help us if he's got another playpen…"

My cell vibrates, Chris and I read the text screen: "Bedroom camera activated. Pam restrained on bed. Underwear only. Seems unconscious, eyes fluttering, head moving, body twitching. Resisting? Recording. Can't see perp. Rescue time NOW!"

I text back. "GOING IN."

Chapter 77

-----JACK-----

I step closer and unleash a door-breaking kick to its center, but the door suffers only minimal damage and doesn't open.

Chris pushes me aside, does a quick martial-arts hop, smashes his shoe near the door knob, demolishing it and the door caves in.

I throw myself against the ajar door and half-stumble into the dim room. As I regain my balance, I sense Chris pushing past me to the opposite wall. Then I dimly see Pamela to my left in the darkened room, almost naked, both arms and an ankle lashed to the bed frame with soft cuffs, her head moving slowly from side to side.

"Gun!" Chris shouts. "He's got a gun!"

Left of the bed. Dixon is franticly waving a black, semi-automatic pistol as if fending off a swarm of bees. His face is so flushed it looks like his flesh is on fire, his features distorted by an insane fury, screaming "Get out, goddammit, get out!"

He stops wildly waving the pistol and now I'm looking straight into its bore. "Who the fuck are you two? Get out!"

When neither Chris nor I move, Dixon shouts: "You're both gonna die. You're attacking me in my own room and I'm defending...."

"Listen, asshole," Chris commands, his soft voice belying his words.

Dixon and I turn to look at him just as he suddenly floods the room with daylight by yanking down so fiercely that the venetian blind clatters to the floor.

"Do you see that helicopter hovering right outside this window?" Chris says. "It's streaming video of you and this room to a police server. Do you want it recording you committing a *murder*? You *do* know Texas is an *enthusiastic* death-penalty state, don't ya? You're too much of a narcissist to want the lethal needle. Am I right?"

I see a moment of indecision flash on Dixon's face but the pistol remains aimed at my nose.

"Fuck you," he screams, pivoting, holding the gun in both hands, aimed at Chris now.

I lunge two steps alongside the bed, arms outstretched, hands grasping for the gun. My momentum slams him backward into the wall.

A thunderous gunshot an inch from my ear silences my world, my nose clogs with gun powder, my mouth tastes the metallic, acrid residue.

I head-butt Dixon's face and simultaneously feel the gun crack into the back of my skull. I grab his gun wrist, thrusting it toward the ceiling, the gun fires again and I feel it more than hear it.

I'm shoved to my left, jerked to the right, battered in a whirlwind of frantic punches. I dig my fingernails into his wrist and he drops the pistol. I swing his arm down, simultaneously pivoting to put my butt against his belly and throw myself backward, crashing him into the wall again.

I fall on my side next to the bed and someone is stomping on my stomach and ribs and I'm trying not to vomit, but the kicking stops. I look up, see Mark Easton with a knee on Dixon's back, yanking his arms violently toward his head as if trying to dislocate his shoulders, attaching flexi-cuffs. Dixon's nose is dripping blood on the floor.

I'm struggling to stand by using the bed for support, my legs shaking, balance uncertain, feeling that I might topple back on the floor. My vision is blurry and I feel sweat on my face. I try wiping it away then realizing when I see my hand that it's blood from my forehead. I try to blot the blood with my sleeves.

I'm regaining some hearing but can't clearly decipher much from background noise that t sounds like 50 voices shouting inside my head at the same time, no specific words, just muffled confusion. I have a pounding headache and am dizzy enough to need one hand on the bed to stay vertical.

The room is full of people, spilling into the hall in unknown numbers. Most of the ones I see are holding up smart phones aimed at Mark, Chris and Dixon and me.

And at Pamela, seemingly unconscious, helpless, tied to the bed and exposed.

Holy smokes, we've got dozens of actual witnesses!

"Stop," I croak, my throat sore, voice unrecognizable even to me and completely unheard by the invading crowd.

Chris rips sheets from the mattress and covers Pamela toe to chin and releases her restraints.

I spot Ashley and Julie roughly pushing people aside to get to Pamela, hugging her, stroking her arms, shoulders and forehead, whispering comfort.

I look for the drone but see only a shattered window.

Did he shoot down Jimmy's drone?

"Hey! Hey! Please shut up! Now!" Mark, the former Army MP Sergeant, attempts to create a group out of a mob. His age, size and demeanor begins to focus everyone's attention on him and the chaotic chatter begins to fade.

"Thank you. Thank you," he says in a voice suitable for a much larger space.

"As you can see, we've had an attempted sexual assault here."

He pauses for a few seconds of complete silence. I look behind me and see Chris sitting close to Dixon, also on the floor, hands and ankles cuffed, his face sideways on the floor, bleeding from a forehead cut and from his nose, probably from my head-butt. His eyes are clenched and I can't tell if he's conscious.

"Everything's under control," Mark says. "We need your help right now. And this is vitally important."

He pauses and scans the room. "We need all of you to share photos or videos you've taken of this incident."

He shouts a Hotmail address that I can't absorb.

Will you do that? "

"Absolutely. Yes," a young woman shouts. "He can't get away with this shit."

"Great," Mark says.

"This is unbelievably disgusting," a young man yells, sparking murmurs of agreement from the crowd.

Mark says, "Please focus on sharing your photos and videos. Please, everyone, do it now."

He recites the email address again.

A booming voice interrupts from a tall guy barely inside the doorway. "*Who* the fuck are you? *What* are you doing here?

"I'm a former Army MP, we're.... "

"Who is *we* and why is an ex-Army cop here?"

"We're gathering evidence on that rapist over there in the corner. You saw what he just did to that woman who was drugged and held against her will, tied to the bed. He's attacked other women before and he just did it again."

"Hell, no," Mr. Big Voice shouts. "That's not true. "This is an obvious a set-up. Some kind of entrapment. We're not going to fall for this bullshit about Josh."

Basketball team mate of Dixon?

I see several people again holding up cameras, capturing the argument, probably at least some of them on audio and video.

"Please let me through," a woman's voice comes from the hall and everyone turns to see who is speaking.

"Move out of the way," a 50-something woman in a blue medical smock and matching says. "I must get in there."

She squeezes through the crowded door and past the Big Voice, to the bed.

She is a colleague of Pamela's from volunteer work at domestic violence workshops. Pamela recruited her to be nearby to collect a blood sample from Ashley or Julie, the targets our plan envisioned.

Ashley steps back, the nurse unzips a small black pouch, removes a syringe and an alcohol patch.

Julie continues massaging Pamela's other arm and shoulder.

Nolan briefly examines Pamela's hands before she rubs the alcohol patch on Pamela's inner elbow, then inserts the needle into a vein and we see the syringe fill with blood.

The on-lookers are deathly silent as if witnessing an autopsy.

She caps the blood vial, fills a second one and puts everything in the zipper pouch and turns to leave.

"Who are you? What the hell are you doing?" Big Voice demands.

She stares at him for a few seconds and says, "I'm Samantha Nolan. I'm a registered nurse at Presbyterian Hospital. I'm drawing blood so I can test it for the Date-Rape or other drugs. You have a problem with that?"

He shakes his head and drops his eyes.

She leans across the bed toward me and whispers: "A positive fingernail."

She disappears through the door, the crowd parting like the Red Sea for Moses.

The mood in the room is notably changed, almost somber now, no loud voices, just people talking quietly among themselves.

Now two cops come into the room. The older one shouts: "Someone tell me what the hell's going on here!'"

Still leaning shakily against the bed, I raise my hand.

Chapter 78

-----JACK-----

Before the older cop reaches me, shouts erupt again from the hallway and diverts his attention as all of us turn to look.

"Out of the way! Move back! Move!"

Two paramedics with a stretcher barge into the room.

"Hug the walls!" one of them yells as the other flips a lever, four legs drop and the stretcher morphs into a wheeled gurney.

"What happened to her?" a uniformed EMT asks the room, as she applies a stethoscope to Pamela's chest and neck.

"She was drugged," Chris says. "Probably the Date-Rape drug but we're not sure."

"Pulse slow but strong," the other EMT recites. "Both eyes dilated, flickering side to side. Blood pressure low but not critically. No obvious physical injuries. No medical alert bracelet. Touch responses present but faint."

They lift Pamela onto the gurney and push-pull her to the door and vanish in seconds, Ashley, Julie and Mark Easton close behind them.

The cop is almost chest-to-chest with me.

"Who are you?" he demands, spewing coffee breath in my face.

"Jack Crocker. I'm a private investigator."

"Is that so?" he snaps. "What's the story here? What do you have to do with an unconscious woman and a bunch of half-drunk kids standing around? This some kind of sicko Greek initiation ritual?"

"I have a client whose daughter was raped by that piece of crap on the floor there," I say, gesturing to Dixon.

"Who cuffed him?" the cop asks. "Is he conscious?"

He drops to a knee and presses two fingers against Dixon's throat.

"Heart's beating fine. Is he drugged, too?"

"I don't know. Maybe. His face may have collided with something and he's groggy."

"Why didn't you tell the paramedics about him? I don't think they saw him on the floor over there."

"It never crossed my mind," I say. "I was only worried about the victim."

"I've called for an ambulance," Chris's voice comes from behind me. "That shit-head will be okay."

"Stay right there," the cop says, turning and gesturing for his partner, still in the doorway, to join him. I hear fragments of a brief whispered consultation, the sergeant instructing his partner to call for reinforcements and have them seal off the property, identify everyone still there and interview anyone who had relevant information. The partner heads for the door and the older cop turns to glare at Chris.

"I'm Sgt. Mike Fletcher. Now, who the hell are you? Another PI?"

"I'm Chris Griffin, a friend of Jack's," he says, almost to himself, then pauses as if he's rethinking his response.

"Also, I'm on the University's Campus Police Department."

"Are you saying this is some kind of *official* investigation?" Sgt. Fletcher says, doubt soaking his voice. "Who else is part of this...whatever *this* is?"

The room is emptied of spectators now, only Chris and me plus the crumpled Josh Dixon on the floor.

I flash a time-out signal to the cop and stagger to a black leather desk chair, looking and feeling like someone trying to walk up a steep hill.

"Okay," I begin, "here's the deal..."

Two more paramedics and a gurney intrude.

"That the patient?" one says, nodding toward Dixon, still curled on the floor. "What happened to him?" kneeling to put a stethoscope on his chest.

"He tried to break my elbow with his face," Chris says. "I think he's just sleeping," then adds: "there's a Glock under the bed. I found it after the scuffle but haven't touched it. Sleeping Beauty there threatened us with it and fired through that broken window at a helicopter drone that was filming what happened here."

Sgt. Fletcher's eyebrows almost leave his forehead.

"He also fired a shot into the ceiling," Chris says, pointing at the overhead bullet hole.

"Don't touch the gun," Sgt. Fletcher orders the EMTs. The medics quickly determine there are no obvious wounds except Dixon's bloody nose that one of them declares "broken."

"Let's get him outta here," one says. Then, looking at Fletcher, "what about the cuffs? Those yours?"

"They're mine," Chris says and quickly removes them.

The sergeant says, "When you get downstairs tell Corporal Hinojosa to send an officer with you in the ambulance and to stay with this guy until we sort out what we're dealing with. Tell him to call me when he's at the hospital."

"Will do."

The gurney departs and the sergeant kneels to peer under the bed, pulls a pen from his pocket, snags the Glock's trigger guard and pulls the black and silver semi-automatic to him, dropping it into a plastic evidence bag.

He turns to me. "Okay, Mr. Crocker, start again at the beginning."

Twenty minutes later, I'm exhausted and Sgt. Fletcher slumps on the bed's end, his eyes glazed. Chris leans against the wall, arms crossed.

Fletcher heads for the bedroom door and pauses as Chris and I join him for the trek downstairs. I'm dabbing at my forehead with fresh tissues

"Holy Joe DiMaggio," Fletcher says. "This is so bizarre, I almost *have* to believe you."

Chapter 79

-----JACK-----

A muted chaos greets us in the first-floor room where an hour earlier Dixon drugged Pamela and guided her upstairs.

Party-goers chatter softly in clusters, many engaged with social media on phones. Cops are blocking exits to the street and patio, getting identifications and brief interviews.

I see Jimmy in a far corner and he simultaneously waves Chris and me to join him.

"Holy shit, guys, we *did* it!" Jimmy whispers as we back thump each other. "Ashley, Robyn, Julie and Mark are with Pamela at Presby," Jimmy says. "Latest text update from Ashley is that Pamela is slowly coming out of the drugged state, not talking yet but responding to touch. The doctors think she'll be fine in a few hours. "Well, not *fine* exactly, more like conscious but probably with a dreadful hangover."

"Obviously," I say, "all this social media exposure might change our original plan of posting our own video over the next few days. We need to rethink our options later tonight or early tomorrow morning.

"Let's retrieve the van, drop Chris off at his car and head to the hospital to see how Pamela is doing."

Chapter 80

-----JACK------

Pamela is surrounded by angels with Julie and Robyn seated along one side of the bed, Ashley and nurse Nolan on the other, all extending arms to gently massage Pamela's arms, wrists, shoulders and calves. Her eyes are closed.

Asleep or still gripped by drugs?

Jimmy stands behind Julie, documenting the scene with video on his phone-camera.

Ashley is softly murmuring reassuring sounds close to Pamela's face.

"Pamela, I think you can hear me. You were *so* brave. We're all totally proud of you. You're safe now. Everything's going to be okay."

Nurse Nolan goes to the door and whispers, "She's improving, pretty much on schedule now that we know she tested positive for an unknown dose of date-rape drug. She'll probably be talking to you in an hour or so. I'm not on duty but I need to check in with my supervisor and brief her on what's going on."

Pamela moves her head to the side, her eyes blink open and shut several times and we all focus with hope on her.

My cell vibrates in my pocket and I see "Baker, Adams LAW" on the screen.

Sonuvabitch! Thorndike.

I show my phone to Jimmy who frowns questioningly and I mouth a silent "Dixon's attorney."

He nods and I slip into the hall.

"Hello, Mr. *Thornapple*, I hope you're not calling to invite me to a round of golf 'cause I'm really kinda tied up right now."

"You listen to me, you penny-ante bull-shitter," he snarls.

Can I really hear spittle hitting his phone?

"You're already neck deep in legal horse apples," he continues, his volume still set on maximum. "You and your partner are defaming my client and his entire family. That whole episode was entrapment and you know it. I demand that you cease and desist and delete these ridiculous social media hoaxes that are damaging my clients. Your financial liability already far exceeds your pitiful net worth. And your tab is growing by the minute."

"Gee, Thorny, I think that bell has been rung. As the saying goes, even you can't un-ring it. The whole world knows your client drugs and rapes women. The Dixon family needs to find new country clubs."

"I demand a meeting with you and your partner in my office within the hour!"

"Just so it's clear on your recording of this call, you're not in any position to *demand* anything. The reason I'm *tied up* right now is because that's what your client did to a young woman today. And we have it all on video. Everything from 'Hi' to 'have a drugged glass of wine' to restraining her half-naked in your client's bedroom. And, he had gun and he fired it. Twice."

I wait but he doesn't immediately respond.

"Do you get it yet, Thorny? What *you* need to do *within the hour* is invite your clients to join you for one of your multi-thousand-dollar-per-hour séances so you can run up your billing invoice by explaining that justice is about to change their lives in a huge and permanent way. You know, man, changes like going from living on a pedestal made of money to the septic tank."

"I know a million ways to take down big-time folks, let alone bit players like you, Crocker," he hisses. "We'll hit you from so many directions you'll…"

"Goodbye, Thornapple. Right now I'm at a hospital watching your client's victim struggling to regain consciousness. That's a lot more important than listening to your expensive bullshit."

Probably not productive but wow, that felt really, really wonderful!

⋏

Robyn joins me in the hallway and says: "Photos and videos of the bed-room scene are already *everywhere*. Pictures of Dixon collapsed on the floor and Pamela practically naked, tied up on the bed are all over YouTube and Facebook and Instagram and every other social media site we know of. It's being posted everywhere in the country; around the world actually!"

"I'm calling my mom to let her know I'm okay, hopefully before she sees any news coverage about this. I'll go home after we're sure Pamela's okay.

"They're going to freak out," she says, punching her speed dial. "Dad will be totally bat shit. I hope Mom can help calm him down but I don't want her to have to do that by herself.

Then it hits me. She didn't warn Ben.

"I'll take care of it," she had promised.

"Hi, Mom. I need to fill you in on something that happened this evening.

"No, no, everything's fine. I'm fine. It's been exciting but everything's okay.

"Yeah, it's a long story and I'll tell you all about it. We have a few loose ends then I'll be home right after that."

"No, Mom, I'm absolutely okay. "There's nothing at all wrong with me, not even a bump or a bruise. Please be patient. See you soon. I'll call when I'm on the way."

"Is she going to fall apart before we get there?" I ask.

"Probably," Robyn says. "I need to be with her as soon as possible, but Pamela comes first. Cripes, I really need to be in two places at once."

"You didn't notify your mother or father, did you?"

She gazes at me for a long moment.

"No. No, I didn't. I'm sorry. When we had to scramble because the party was suddenly two hours away, not on Saturday, I totally forgot about that."

We stare at each other.

Do I believe her? Either way, Jimmy and I are probably nothing but soup ingredients now.

"Jimmy and I will go with you to meet with your parents."

CHAPTER 81

-----JACK-----

Later that evening, as the three of us pile into the van, I hear her cell ring and she says, "Darn, it's my Dad calling. I don't know which is worse, answering or not answering." She puts the phone away. "Either way, I'm sure he's already on the moon."

"Or Pluto," I mutter.

Ben Rogers is eerily and un-characteristically quiet as Lauren ushers us into the living room. He's in a wing-back chair, a crystal, old-fashioned glass with golden contents rests on a round side table, a cut-glass decanter next to it.

He looks at us, sips from the glass, his heavy-lidded eyes following the three of us to seats on the adjoining sofa, Lauren curls her legs under her in a chair matching Ben's.

Enroute from the hospital to Robyn's home, we brainstormed possible responses to Ben's expected anger, hostility, histrionics and low-level atomic explosions, but so far no sign of any of those.

A ticking time bomb? Depression? Boozed?

"Hi, Dad," Robyn says, from two feet away. "We've had quite a day."

She forces a small, brief smile as if inviting him to ask what happened.

He sips again, holds her gaze for a long moment and finally says softly, *"Precisely* what happened and why didn't I know about it?"

"Several friends went to a party at a frat house, where we thought one of my attackers would be. He was there. He drugged one of my friends, tied her to the bed in his room while she was semi-conscious and unable to fight him off. We have it all on video and…"

"Jesus H. Christ, Robyn," Ben screams, lurching to his feet, "what in hell were you thinking, taking risks like that?

"Video tapes? The whole thing sounds like entrapment to me! We're probably going to get sued Big Time. We might lose everything we have. Can't you understand that?"

No longer a ticking bomb. He's detonated!

He downs the rest of his drink, refills it to the rim from the decanter, takes a swig and steps toward Jimmy and me on the sofa.

"And you two incompetent, unprofessional knotheads went along with this idiocy?" he shouts. "Letting my daughter be involved? And you didn't try to stop it? You actually *personally participated* in it? You're both toast. When I'm through with you, you won't even be a grease spot on your driveway. You won't even have a driveway."

Lauren is up, stepping between Ben and Jimmy and me.

He roughly shoves her sideways, toppling her back into her chair.

Robyn leaps into the gap, pushes her father with both hands to his chest and he staggers back two steps, regains his balance and glares at his daughter, his arm pulled back as if to deliver a slap.

Tonto and I are both up, not advancing on him but clearly prepared to handle any further violence.

"Mr. Rogers. Everyone," I say as gently as I can, trying to appear non-threatening.

"Please. We need to stay calm. Please, everyone take a seat and we can discuss the whole situation."

Every nerve I have is vibrating Red Alert.

Ben appears ready to launch himself, and all of us, into outer space, but he hesitates, looking from me to Jimmy to his daughter, who remains standing in his path.

Finally his face begins to disintegrate, scrunching and reddening. He looks as if he's going to cry. He slumps heavily into his chair and reaches for the decanter.

I step forward and take the decanter and half-full glass.

"Not now," I whisper.

As Robyn, Jimmy and I sit, Lauren is quietly crying in her chair, eyes closed, her body shaking and seemingly wrapped onto itself, reduced to a fraction of her normal size.

A silent moment stretches past awkwardness, all of us wary and unsure of what to say, where to start.

"How about some coffee or tea…or…" Lauren says in a genteel tone suitable for a book-club gathering at a retirement home.

"Coffee," Ben surprisingly grunts. Jimmy and I quickly agree. Lauren heads for the kitchen and the uncomfortable silence re-grips the four of us, no one making eye-contact with anyone else. Ben is staring holes in the far wall, Robyn isn't responding in any visible or audible way.

Lauren reappears with a coffee carafe, mugs, a porcelain tea pot and two tea cups on saucers, everything balanced on a large silver tray. She begins filling mugs.

Maybe a major caffeine jolt will stimulate my brain into a hint of how to proceed. Maybe just a straight-ahead, full speed review?

Lauren hands a mug to Tonto who sips, leans forward and waves a hand before Ben's thousand-yard gaze.

"Okay," Jimmy says, "let's walk through how this sting operation began and specifically, what happened today."

Thanks, Partner!

He scans Ben, Lauren and Robyn's faces before adding: "And we need to discuss what the next few days are likely to bring all of us."

He pauses again.

"Everybody on board?"

Ben straightens his posture, his face still flushed. Lauren looks up, wipes her eyes with a tissue. Robyn raises her hand as if asking a classroom question.

Tonto hesitates, finally nods in her direction, his face uncertain.

"Dad," she says, "this was all my idea. I decided to stop being sad and instead I got mad. I want justice…along with a helping of revenge and that's how this began."

"You should have told me," he says softly, but firmly.

"You would have tried to stop me," she answers. "You know you would have."

Ben turns to me.

"*You* should have stopped her. You should have told me."

"Dad, listen. Jack and Jimmy tried to talk me out of going after the creep but they couldn't change my mind. I was so angry. I *am* fiercely determined to put my rapist in prison. No one could have…or *will* stop me. Besides, that's history. I think we got him."

"That right, Crocker?" his voice harsh, eyes heavy-lidded, still threatening.

"I believe so," I say. "Jimmy and I had concerns but eventually realized Robyn and her friends were definitely going to try exposing this guy and the two of us decided we needed to be as protective as we could and develop a credible plan that might…possibly result in his butt landing in prison."

"You had a professional obligation to inform me of this," he insists through hostile lips.

"Another tough call," Jimmy says. "Technically we weren't acting as your client, we were pro bono providing security to Robyn and her friends plus some ideas on how to pull it off."

"I think that's a bowl of mumbo-jumbo and twisted legal bullshit," Ben snaps.

"I want what Robyn wants," Lauren whispers barely audibly. "I support her and I'm proud of her determination and courage."

"That's because *you* have no damn clue what the dangers are and what the ramifications are for our entire family," Ben snarls. "No clue whatever."

A phone rings on the small table between the wing-back chairs. Ben retrieves the cordless handset, reads the screen and quick-walks out of the room.

Over his shoulder he says, "This is probably the opening blast."

The rest of us freeze in place for a moment, Lauren rises, Robyn follows and they embrace in a lengthy, intimate mother and daughter moment. Jimmy and I glance at each other, then focus on the far end of the room, anxiously awaiting Ben's return.

My cell vibrates and I read Ashley's text.

"Pamela has been released from the hospital," I say.

"Great," Robyn says.

"And Dixon is out, too. No charges filed, so not even any bail."

Ben returns and sinks into his chair, still clutching the phone.

"I knew it," he says. "That was Mathew Thorndike, a top partner in a big-time Dallas law firm. I've met him a few times. He's represented the Dixon family and their oil company for many years. The Dixons are 'old money.' They bought large chunks of land that turned out to be a major West Texas oil field before anyone else fully realized what a big deal that was going to be.

"Thorndike claims young Josh Dixon is the victim of an entrapment created by Robyn, several friends plus Crocker and McGuire. Thorndike says the entire Dixon family is being defamed by these actions and a resulting tidal wave of social media.

"They want the defamatory postings to stop. And they demand that Robyn and her friends admit it was a setup, an entrapment scheme, and apologize for illegally creating the situation. Otherwise, he says he will sue us for millions of dollars for the damage to this important family. He could tie us up for several expensive years trying to defend ourselves.

"He demanded that I meet with him tomorrow morning."

"He *demanded* a meeting with me and Jimmy, also," I say. "I told him no."

"So he said," Ben says. "He said he promised to crush you two like bugs.

"You guys are officially fired. You need your own lawyer. Your interests and my family's interests are completely different and not compatible. Good bye. Get the hell out of my house!"

As Jimmy and I head for the front door, we hear Robyn pleading, "No, Dad, you're making a big mistake. You...."

"Shut up," Ben yells. "It's *you* who made the huge mistake. Now I gotta see if there's a way to keep this from being a total disaster."

Outside, says, "I know it's almost midnight, but what's your plan now, Kemosabe?"

"I may change my mind by morning, but right now I vote we continue full speed ahead until Josh Dixon is getting his dinner on a tray slipped under a prison door.

"I hope we can ramp up the public exposure of him as the disgusting, predatory sexual attacker that he is. We must intensify the pressure on the University to fix their cop department. And we need to lean on the county prosecutor to indict the bastard. And..."

"Yeah," Tonto says. "Doubling down sounds smart. What could go wrong?"

Chapter 82

-----JACK-----

At 5:15 Saturday morning I'm awake but exhausted after only three or four hours of interrupted and uneasy sleep. My elbows on the kitchen table prop up my face.

I'm seriously worried, maybe depressed, about my plan for "doubling down," that was a much better idea at midnight than it seems now.

I'm wondering how Ben, Lauren and Robyn are handling the major legal threats to their family's future.

Too many things are beyond our control now. Pamela's semi-conscious bondage video has been posted by multiple witnesses. Jimmy and I couldn't retrieve and delete those world-wide, third-party posts even if we wanted to. And we don't want to.

At 6 a.m., Jimmy is scheduled to post a video of Julie Norton describing her sexual assault and explaining how she was brushed off by University cops.

We have two more victims of the University's system on video for release in coming days. And we're promising more soon, all by women who came forward using their real names after learning of the attack on Pamela and seeing some of the video from Dixon's bedroom

It feels like we're running out of control at full speed downhill toward a cliff without knowing what's over the edge.

My head throbs with an ache reminiscent of my drinking days.

I've got to stop head-butting predators.

I put another coffee pod in the machine and wait impatiently for the 58 seconds it takes to fill my mug.

"Hey, Jack," Jimmy booms, as he often does as a card-carrying *morning person*. "Drop in a dark-roast Columbian for me."

"Do it yourself," I say. "I'm not actually conscious yet."

"Any reason to wait till 8 to post Julie Norton's video?" he wonders. "I can just as easily do it right now."

"Sure, go ahead," I mutter. "And please see if the paper is here yet. I've already checked three times."

He's back in a minute, slipping Saturday's newspaper from its plastic sleeve and we're spreading it on the table.

"Nothing in A-section," he says, still standing.

"Here it is, front of Metro," I say.

Together we read the short story on the bottom of the page.

⅄

Park Cities police are investigating an altercation at a fraternity party on the campus of McMillan University Friday evening. A woman and a man were transported to Presbyterian hospital. It was not clear whether either of them is a student at the University.

No information was available last night concerning possible injuries. Other details couldn't be confirmed early Saturday morning. The hospital issued a statement saying only that both unidentified patients had been discharged shortly after midnight.

Police are investigating the incident. Unconfirmed reports indicated the incident may have involved a firearm being discharged in a fraternity house.

⅄

"Okay," Jimmy says. "I'll launch one of our surprises and let's see what happens. Julie is very credible and because her case doesn't involve Dixon, her story should expand the University's problems and probably prompt a police investigation, particularly since we're promising that more sexual assault victim videos are coming."

By 10 a.m., the YouTube video of Julie Norton describing her treatment when she and her parents tried to file a complaint with the McMillan Campus Cops already has more than 22,000 views and sparked several thousand Twitter Tweets in response.

Right now, I'm losing control of my own kitchen. As if every news organization in the region just finished reading the short story in The News, our landline and both of our cells are ringing non-stop, my email alert dings a constant chorus of new deliveries.

Now someone knocks on the front door and impatiently rings the doorbell.

"Probably a newspaper or television station reporter," I say, striding through our small living room.

"Jack Crocker?" a short, middle-aged man in jeans and blue blazer asks.

I nod and he hands me a manila folder with two sheets of paper,

"The hearing is 10 a.m. Monday. Don't be late," he warns as he trots to his curbed car.

"Did he say 'hearing?'" Jimmy says from behind me.

"The document notifies us that a Temporary Restraining Order has been requested by the Dixon family via Thorndike.

"They're trying to stop us from posting any more videos," I say. "And they want the court to force us to delete from the internet all of the present postings."

"Can they do that?" Jimmy says.

"It's usually not difficult in Dallas to find a judge who'll sign nearly anything. Look, on a Saturday morning, Thorndike found a judge willing to order a hearing. I'm almost surprised the hearing isn't Sunday morning since they're so anxious to get the videos stopped and erased.

"If, on Monday, a judge signs a *permanent* Restraining Order, we will have two choices.

"One is to comply with the Order and stop posting, while arguing in court that the Order should be lifted. And we can bet that the subsequent court argument will be lengthy and involve a mini-trial; time consuming and damned expensive.

"The other choice would be to defy the Order by immediately dumping all our videos into YouTube and other social media sites, so everything would instantly be public. If we do that, there's a pretty good chance you and I will be tossed in Dallas County jail on Contempt of Court charges, probably with daily fines until we capitulate or the case is concluded."

"But if we dump everything," Jimmy says, "the details of the other attacks will already be public, out there, everywhere on the internet. There's no way for us or anyone else to delete them."

"Yes," I say, "the details would be *'out* there' but *we* could be *'in* there,' meaning jail."

"We need a lawyer right damn now," Jimmy says.

"I know who we need. Paul Wilson is the paper's First Amendment attorney. He's as good as it gets on these issues," I say, reaching for my cell.

CHAPTER 83

-----JACK-----

Just before noon, my cell dings and caller-ID signals Joann Hillman, a former colleague from my deceased newspaper career.

"I hear you're the spokesperson for the group that recorded an attempted rape at McMillan University, last night," she says. "What's the rest of the story?"

"Hi, Joann. I'm fine. Thanks for asking, it makes me feel warm and fuzzy."

"Sorry, Jack. I'm chasing after facts. You know how it is. Running hard to get it right and still be first."

"Yes, I remember. Who gave you my name?"

"Pamela Swann. I called her because she was admitted to the hospital about the same time as the Dixon guy. She referred me to you, said you were the spokesperson for something called the *Gang of Eight*. Is that right?"

"Pretty much."

"I want every detail," she says. "This is a going to be a big-ass deal. Talk to me, Jack, while I try visualizing you as a *gang* leader."

I answer as many of her questions as I can because this is an opportunity to get the basic story well written by a fine reporter in a credible newspaper.

Chapter 84

-----JACK-----

By 9:30 Sunday morning, Jimmy, Paul Wilson and I have ordered unhealthy IHOP breakfasts and I'm backgrounding Paul on Robyn's case, starting with the original rape and through the sting that she, her friends, Jimmy and I pulled off.

Wilson says: "I read the stories in the paper this morning. Sounds like there's lots more to come. Obviously, this is a big damn deal with ramifications for the University on several levels, particularly its campus cop operation.

"On the immediate issue, the TRO request tomorrow, we can argue that most of the toothpaste they want to hide is already out of the tube. The fact that dozens of party-goers saw Dixon and a semi-conscious, half-nude woman in restraints on his bed is devastating. And since many witnesses posted online their own photos and videos of that nasty scene, the argument is limited to further actions by you two and the others in your so-called Gang-of-Eight."

"Sounds like our chances are pretty good," Jimmy says.

"As close to a slam-dunk as I can imagine," Wilson says.

"We wonder why," I say, "they're even asking for a TRO that seems unenforceable on us, let alone the world-wide social media network."

"Could it be some kind of trap?" Jimmy says.

CHAPTER 85

-----JACK-----

It's 5:45 a.m. Monday. Jimmy and I are plowing through the Dallas and Ft. Worth newspapers, both of which have several stories explaining developments from Friday's Date-Rape case. The most complete of these is Joann Hillman's narrative of how and why the Gang was formed.

Local TV news channels this morning have 30-45 seconds devoted to "the Date-Rape case at McMillan University" with promises of "more developments at 5, 6 and 10."

"Essentially the outline of what happened to Pamela is getting out in public," I say. "The University leadership, the real police and the Campus Cops and probably the Dallas County Prosecutor's office are all going to be in a huge public pressure cooker as more details become known."

"We're under pressure, too," Jimmy says, "from Thorndike's threat of a massive civil suit that's supposed to devastate us in every way he can think of."

"Well," I say, "we'll jump off that bridge when we get to it."

"That's comforting. You're my favorite wordsmith not named Yogi Berra," he laughs.

"Please call Robyn to check on Pamela this morning, and ask her if the official results of the blood test are in. Unofficially we already know it's positive and we need to get that reported in public. The finger-nail polish part will intrigue everyone."

"I'm on it," he says.

A half hour later, Sonia Nelson, editor of *Campus Watch,* the student paper, calls to "clarify a few things." She asks a few questions and gives me as much new information as she gets.

"Thanks, Mr. Crocker," she says as we are ending our phone interview.

"You'll be glad to hear that we've had several students come to us in the last two days to recount their horrible experiences with the University's Security Department. Two of them happened almost 10 years ago."

"Can you share their names with me?" I say.

"Sure," she laughs. "Their stories will be in tomorrow's *Campus Watch.* All of them okayed using their real names."

"Tomorrow we'll have a front-page editorial demanding that the Administration start answering questions and decide what they're going to about this outrage. Protesters are organizing to besiege McMillan University President's office and his home, starting today. They want him to fire the Security Department Chief.

"Thanks for all of what your Gang of Eight did to gather this devastating evidence. That has launched this huge media coverage follow up. It's definitely going to force radical changes on this campus."

"About damn time," I say.

Chapter 86

-----JACK----

That afternoon I remember Mrs. Parks Friday call just as we were about to spring our trap.

"She said she wanted to talk, then changed it to *"I need"* to talk," I reminded Jimmy. "I have no idea what's on her mind, could be something mundane or something important. She seemed quite sharp when The Rev and I met with her."

"Maybe we're catching a break," he says. "We sure could use one. Either way, we need to focus more on The Rev's case as soon as the dust settles a little more in the sexual predator project."

I call Mrs. Parks and she's available. We reach the Parks home ten minutes early and almost immediately see a window curtain moving and a face peering at us.

I introduce Jimmy as soon as we're inside. She welcomes us into her living room, reminding me again of the 1950s. She gestures for us to sit on a flowered sofa in front of a low table displaying a silver coffee carafe and a plate of cookies.

"Can I offer you gentlemen some coffee and chocolate-chip cookies?"

"That would be wonderful, Mrs. Parks," Jimmy says and we both see the delight in her eyes as she sits opposite us.

I take a sip and a bite while she clasps her hands in her lap and closes her eyes as if she's about to pray, but hesitates and looks at us.

"What do want to tell us, Mrs. Parks," I say.

She glances at her hands, then up.

"I remembered something," she finally manages to say. "It may not be anything significant or relevant to your investigation."

She pauses again, lifts the cookie plate, offers it again and we both enthusiastically accept.

"My husband absolutely did *not* kill himself," she declares firmly. I am completely certain of that. I know what kind of man he was. He would never kill himself. Or hurt anyone. He wouldn't leave me alone like this.

"And I don't think he *accidentally* overdosed on the medication he'd been taking. He was totally familiar with it and it wasn't complicated. One capsule at breakfast, another with dinner. And besides that," she says like an accusation, "he wasn't taking any medication for the previous two weeks. None. He said it upset his stomach and he could manage without it."

She pauses briefly, readjusts her hands and takes a deep breath.

"So, in case this in any way helps you find Jackson's murderer, I want you to know something."

"We appreciate any help you can give us," I say.

"A few days ago I suddenly remembered something Jackson mentioned years ago, before Otis was accused of...that terrible crime.

"After an evening church board meeting Jackson and Otis had a beer or two on the way home and when he arrived I remember him looking a little somber as he took off his coat. I asked him if something had gone wrong at the meeting.

"He said 'No. I'm thinking about something Otis said as we headed for our cars. We were talking about Roberta running off and marrying that Stiles guy and how Otis didn't like him even though he only met him once before suddenly Roberta is pregnant and elopes.

"Otis said he wondered if his brother, Brandon, somehow knew more about the situation than he was sharing with Otis.'"

She looks at us expectantly.

"What do you think he meant by that?" Jimmy asks."

"I don't know. I just knew Jackson was bothered by the comment and felt that Otis wouldn't have said anything if it hadn't been important to him. Jackson never mentioned it again and with all of the excitement after that, with the trial and everything, it never crossed my mind again until recently."

A few minutes later it's clear that Mrs. Parks has nothing more to tell us. She declines to speculate any further and stresses that she just wants to pass along something that, at least briefly a long time ago, had bothered her husband. And Otis.

We thank her, urge her to call us again if she remembers anything else and return to our car, each of us with four still-warm cookies wrapped in napkins.

"Did we learn anything that might possibly help us find Jackson's killer? If there actually is a killer," I wonder aloud, parking in front of our office.

"Maybe," Tonto says.

"We've definitely discovered where to score great cookies."

Chapter 87

-----JACK-----

We leave the lights off in the office, Jimmy slouches in his desk chair, boots braced against his waste basket. I bring him a long-neck Lone Star and a Diet Dr Pepper for myself and mirror his posture.

He sips and says, "We need to interview Otis about this, find out what was happening back then and figure out if it's important. Why did he tell Jackson he thought Brandon knew things about Roberta's quickie marriage to that guy who left town when their daughter was born? I don't know how that could be relevant but…."

"I agree," I say. "And that reminds me of the last time we tried interviewing the family, Roberta booted our butts out of the house and told us to stay away. Maybe she knows something. She may still be hostile and will try to keep us from talking with Otis."

"Yeah," he says. "We need to talk with Otis first without Roberta finding out, perhaps meet him somewhere other than his house. Mavis might help set up a meeting. I don't think she approved of Roberta's over-the-top tantrum."

"Roberta may have been threatened by questions I was asking and wanted out of the situation," Tonto says. "And depending on what Otis tells us, we should try to talk with Brandon immediately afterwards to see if their stories match."

"After Brandon," I say, we should attempt to talk with Mavis and Angel. With luck, Roberta won't know what we're doing until we've talked to the others, and we can try Roberta last. What ya think?"

"It's a plan. Might work. We're gonna be swamped for at least a few more days dealing with developments in Robyn's case, new videos, street protests and not to mention, threats aimed at us from a big-time lawyer who wants to wipe us off the map."

"Yeah, and the fragment of new info about Otis that Mrs. Parks gave us has been forgotten for more than 30 years. And it may not be relevant, anyway. I guess it can wait a few more days."

Chapter 88

-----JACK-----

It's always a bit scary walking into a courtroom dreading that you'll soon be under oath and some highly-paid, smarty-pants lawyer is going to try to trip you up if you use one wrong word or remember or describe some tiny detail slightly differently than you did months ago.

As a staff reporter I've been in lots of courtrooms reporting on many news-worthy cases, but the hand-full of times I was there to testify myself, it was always on behalf of the newspaper, sometimes trying to quash a fishing-expedition subpoena from over-zealous prosecutors or criminal defense lawyers seeking to force a journalist to turn over private notes or to reveal sources.

On a few occasions I was under oath in a courtroom answering questions because someone was suing the paper, claiming we'd libeled someone, usually by revealing facts that they didn't want the public to know.

A few times, the under-oath testimony was a pre-trial deposition in a lawyer's office and some lasted an entire day or even more. Either way, it was always a tense experience.

This Monday morning, I'm wound extra tight as Jimmy and I are bypassing the actual courtroom, walking with our attorney, Paul Wilson, to Judge Marjorie Bennett's chambers.

When the judge's receptionist escorts us down a hallway, Mathew Thorndike and two other Dixon family attorneys are 15 feet ahead of us. The six of us enter the judge's chambers together, acknowledging each other with polite platitudes, nods and poker faces.

Judge Bennett stands by her desk in her black robe gesturing for everyone to sit. A court stenographer and her recording machine are almost invisible a few feet to her left.

"We're on the record," she tells us and the court reporter.

"Mr. Thorndike," she says, "who are your associates?"

He introduces his two, stern-faced dark suits.

Probably moonlight as funeral directors.

Paul Wilson says, "Your Honor, I have with me, my clients, Jack Crocker and Jimmy McGuire."

She looks at Thorndike.

"None of your clients wish to attend this hearing?"

"No, Your Honor."

"Mr. Thorndike, please explain the case behind your request for an emergency TRO."

"Your Honor, we are petitioning the court for an immediate, permanent and *sealed* restraining order directing Mr. Crocker and Mr. McGuire to cease and desist posting false and defamatory accusations against a member of the Franklin Dixon family. These postings defame the entire Dixon family, a well-known and long respected Dallas family.

"And we request that Mr. Crocker and Mr. McGuire be ordered to immediately and completely remove all such false and defamatory postings. And…"

"Okay, Mr. Thorndike," Judge Bennett interrupts. "Am I correct that your clients are seeking a TRO blocking all future internet postings referring to a Josh Dixon?"

"Yes, Your Honor, and…."

"And you want me to order Mr. Crocker and Mr. McGuire to delete any and all *previous* postings pertaining to Josh Dixon?"

"Yes, Your Honor. We want immediate deletion of any traces of those vicious and false defamatory postings by Mr. Crocker and Mr. McGuire and by others responding to Mr. Crocker and Mr. McGuire's damaging social media messages that are libeling this widely respected family. Postings are coming from all over the country, even the world."

She cocks her head as if puzzled. She pauses before looking at the three of us.

"Mr. Thorndike, do you and your associates understand how the internet works?"

The three lawyers look at each other and Thorndike says, "Yes, Your Honor, at least somewhat."

"Then you should know that your request concerning *previous* postings is impossible to be effectively accomplished. Things posted on the internet are effectively published to the world. They may exist on millions of other devices and computers, all of which are beyond the control of Mr. Crocker or Mr. McGuire. Beyond the control of anyone."

Thorndike doesn't flinch, shows no signs that he's just been rejected on one of his two requests.

"Your Honor, we also want to forbid any future postings."

"Mr. Thorndike, I don't think this hearing in my chambers is the proper place for a request to disregard the First Amendment. Prior restraint on someone's right to free speech is unlikely to survive any venue I can imagine."

The room is awkwardly silent, no one moving, talking or breathing.

"This petition is dismissed," Judge Bennett declares, rising from her chair, dismissing all of us as well.

Paul opens the door, Jimmy and I follow him down the hallway. I pause as we get to the exit and see Dixon's lawyers trailing behind.

"Was that as good an outcome as it feels," I whisper to Paul as we walk in the sunshine to our cars.

"Definitely. The system worked. I didn't know Judge Bennett was so tech-savvy. And wasn't I brilliant in there without needing to do anything except introduce you two?'

CHAPTER 89

"That was quite an evening," Jimmy says.

"The frosting on a truly amazing day," I add.

We're driving home from a celebratory Gang-of-Eight pizza party in Pamela's apartment.

"I'm glad Pamela has recovered so well," Jimmy says. "Seeing her in her own digs was a big relief. She's normal, maybe even feistier than before she was drugged. She's thoroughly pissed now."

"Except for significant sleep deprivation, the whole Gang is doing well," I say. "I think everyone's inspired by Pamela's courage and rapid recovery. We all realize we've got some serious challenges ahead with possible civil lawsuits against us and probably some nasty attempts to personally discredit all of us, but no one was visibly shaking in their boots."

"I don't think any of them fully understand the range of possible bad outcomes."

"I agree. I'm much more worried than they are about a huge, expensive civil suit consuming us for a year or more."

"I'm trying to stay optimistic," he smiles. "We're the good guys in this."

"Yeah," I say, sarcastically. "Neither of us has ever seen good guys defeated by folks with more money and more clout. We could end up winning a drawn-out case but end up bankrupt."

"Then you can write a book about it and rake in some big bucks."

"Okay," I say, "that's now our *official* Emergency, Worst-Case, Lots-of-Poop-Has-Hit-the-Fan, Fallback Plan."

CHAPTER 90

-----JACK-----

"There's a feature on the front page explaining how the special nail polish detected the Date-Rape drug, now confirmed by Pamela okaying release of her hospital records. By tonight, the TV folks will all be real excited over diagnostic nail polish," I tell Jimmy as he joins me for a 5:10 a.m. caffeine fix.

"And," I grin, "the letters-to-editors column is full of demands for the University to fire the chief and reform or disband the Campus Security Department.

"One letter suggests Josh Dixon is the victim because the writer claims he knows entrapment when he sees it and, you know, 'boys will be boys.' Another letter urges the 'immediate arrest of that rich Frat Brat.'

"I don't think there'll be any charges or arrests happening soon. Police investigators and the Prosecutor's office have lots of interviews to conduct and they'll want to be absolutely certain they've got enough evidence to convict."

"Good lord, Jack, law enforcement has *video* of the attack and not just from us, from a couple dozen people at the party. What more do they need?"

"They'll sort it out. We need patience. They gotta verify everything. We all know photos or videos can be misleading. Instant-replay video of NFL games doesn't always convince everyone, sometimes even after multiple, slow-motion screenings."

"I'm going to post Robyn's video describing how she was treated," Jimmy says. "That will ratchet up pressure on the University to publicly respond."

Chapter 91

-----JACK-----

By noon Wednesday, three TV channels are live, covering a spokeswoman announcing a "thorough and fair investigation of this matter by the University.

"President Daniel Montgomery is appointing a ten-person committee of community leaders to get to the bottom of this situation. Panel members will be announced by the President tomorrow at 10 a.m. The University takes these accusations very seriously...."

"That's a start," Jimmy says, waving his BLT sandwich in approval.

At 1 p.m., he posts our third video by a previously unknown victim of the Campus Police scare tactics. This one includes the young woman's mother who was with her daughter when she tried to file a complaint. The mother emotionally recalls leaving campus crying from fear, fury and frustration. She and her daughter called me as soon as Pamela and Robyn's case became public.

Chapter 92

------JACK-----

Between sunrise and sunset Thursday, the spotlight shining on the University's disgraceful treatment of victims of sexual assaults is growing by the hour.

"Not only the feathers, but the whole damn chicken has hit the fan," Jimmy says after finishing the News and surfing the web to read three more large regional newspapers, Chicago, Los Angeles and Boston, all with CNN chattering in the background.

"The local and national TV coverage has suddenly shifted from endlessly repeating clips from the Josh Dixon videos and decided to focus on the aftermath. The local channels are feeding their networks and two national anchors have already parachuted into Dallas, to front coverage."

"Student and faculty protestors are still picketing and hampering traffic," I say. "That group has been growing every day. TV reporters love protesters because they can stand with their microphones in front of sign-waving, chanting people wanting change of some sort."

Jimmy points the remote and switches to a Dallas channel.

"This is terrific," he says, "seeing not only local students, but professors, staff, women's-rights groups and even the AARP crowd all demanding huge changes in University policies and practices and particularly in Campus Security Department procedures. Most of them want the school to dismantle the department altogether."

"According to the News," I say, "some large donors are angrily insisting on answers from the University Administration. And they want public release of files relating to sexual assaults on campus, even from the Counseling Clinic run by the University's Health Services. Apparently no one actually knows how many assaults there have been on campus because the data has never been collected from medical or counseling or campus police records. And even if someone compiled school records, we know damn well the Campus Security records are deliberately bogus."

"Hey, look at this," he says, turning up the TV volume.

The University spokeswoman says "…President Montgomery has suspended McMillan University's Security Chief, Samuel Whitaker, effective immediately, pending outcome of the Special Panel's investigation."

"Yahoo," Jimmy shouts. "Now *that's* progress."

My phone vibrates on the kitchen table.

"Hey, Jack," Pamela says. "You're not going to believe what's happened."

"Yeah, we just saw announcement of the chief's suspension."

"That's not it," Pamela says. "This is even better."

Chapter 93

-----JACK-----

Talk!" I demand, punching speaker so Jimmy can listen.

"Robyn filed a criminal complaint with the Park Cities Police Department. And get this, she gave the cops a video of Andy Haley confessing that he and Dixon raped her."

"Why would he confess?" Tonto interrupts. "Why would he do that? How did she get him to spill his guts?"

"She surprised him coming out of a class in a crowded hallway, got right up in his face and described how she has suffered from being drugged and raped. Less than two minutes into it, the little creep was sobbing and apologizing. At the end he was hysterically begging her to forgive him."

"Why didn't she tell us she was going to confront him? We should have been there for protection."

"She was afraid you two would try to talk her out of it and once she made up her mind, she just went into action. Julie, Ashley and I recorded everything from a few feet away. The four of us could easily have put that twerp on the floor."

CHAPTER 94

-----JACK-----

"Hello, Mr. Crocker," Mavis answers before I say anything, the benefits of caller-ID.

"Hi, Mrs. Jefferson. "I know it's fairly early on Sunday morning, but I hope you have a moment."

"Gracious, Mr. Crocker, I've been up for hours. I'm leaving for church in a few minutes."

"Okay, I'll be brief. Jimmy's here with me so I have you on speaker phone if that's okay. We're hoping to speak with Otis. Is he available?"

"We've been expecting your call," she says in a soft voice. "We owe you an apology. What happened when you and your partner were here was rude and unnecessary. Roberta was very emotional at that time, so soon after her father returned, and while we understand that, we're all somewhat embarrassed. Even Roberta. Otis and I figured you would let the situation cool off a little and then try again."

"Thank you, Mrs. Jefferson. Both Jimmy and I are aware of the stress you've all been under, even though Otis's return home is a wonderful thing. But I'm sure his presence reminds all of you of the irreparable loss of all those years."

"You said you wanted to speak with Otis, may I ask why?"

"We've run across information that he may have had some concerns shortly before the incident that led to the charges against him and the subsequent trial."

"Well, I can't help you with that," she says. "And I'm not going to answer any questions without talking with Otis first. I think he's willing to talk with you."

"I'm very glad to hear that, Mrs. Jefferson. Is Otis there?"

"No, he's not. He's in Alaska for another two days. When some high school classmates heard that he'd always dreamed of fishing for salmon in Alaska, and that while in prison all those years he often imagined he was wading in an Alaskan river, several of them raised enough money for them to take him on that dream trip. He's there now, with two old friends chasing salmon for a week. And enjoying absolutely everything about it, according to his call to me last night."

"That's fantastic," I say. "Do you think we could talk with him as soon as he's back?

"Probably. I'll let him know you want to talk with him and we'll see what he wants to do."

"Thanks so much," Mrs. Jefferson. We…"

"Mavis," she says. "Please call me Mavis, Mr. Crocker."

"Sure. And please call me Jack," I say.

We both laugh.

"Are Angel or Brandon available? I ask? "We would like to check a few things with each of them."

"I'm the only one here. Angel and Roberta left separately earlier this morning. I don't know where either of them is at the moment or when they'll be back."

She's silent for several seconds.

"And as for Brandon, I don't have the slightest idea of where he might be or what he's doing. Have you called him at his home or office?"

"Not yet, but I will. Thanks again, Mavis. We're pursuing every idea or angle or sliver of information we can. We look forward to seeing you again.

"And Mavis?"

"Yes?"

"Mavis, by any chance is one of the people with Otis a guy with tattoos pretty much everywhere?"

"Oh," she said, laughing. "Yes he is. Have you met him? He sure stands out, doesn't he? That's Rodney Forester. He goes by 'Rod.' He and Otis have known each other for years. Otis helps out with Rod's AA group ministering to ex-con alcoholics. Rod used to be an alcoholic but he's been sober for many years and puts in lots of time helping members of the group. So has Otis since he returned home."

Chapter 95

-----JACK-----

As I hang up, Jimmy shrugs.

"Looks like a dead-end on Otis for a while," he says.

"But that certainly clears up the relationship between Otis and Tattoo Dude. We've been chasing the wrong dude."

"We still have time to join the rest of our Gang for brunch at Arnie's Cafeteria. We're going to brief each other so we'll be up to date on new developments and be aware of any plans for the next few days."

"Thanks for the reminder. Go to brunch and I'll catch up with you. The comment Mavis just made about Brandon echoes something Angel said before Roberta evicted us from their house. I remember Mavis telling us then that 'Brandon couldn't join us' for lunch.

"Later, Angel laughed and told me, "Brandon *could* have been here, but my Mom doesn't allow him here.'

"I'll see if Brandon's home and if not, I'll head for brunch. If he is home and agrees I'll zip over there and ask him what he knew about Roberta's marriage that he hadn't shared with Otis. Shouldn't take long."

"Okay," Jimmy says, "I'm outta here. I'll take good notes if you're delayed."

Chapter 96

-----JACK-----

Feather answers on the second ring.

"Hi, Jack" as if we're old friends instead of having met only once before under stressful conditions.

"Hi, Feather," I say, hoping her greeting heralded cooperation.

"Is Brandon around? I need to check something with him."

"He's not here and I'm not sure when he'll be back. Some woman, one of his students, called a while ago wanting to meet with him in his office. This happens once in a while when a student requests help with a project, although not usually on Sunday."

"Has he ever gone to the office to meet a student on a Sunday before?"

"Not that I can remember."

"When did he leave?"

"About 20 minutes ago. The meeting was for noon."

12:15 already!

"Okay, Feather, thanks. I'll check back later."

"You're welcome to come over now and have some tea while we wait."

"Sorry, I gotta run to a meeting. Bye."

Please, don't let this be what I think it is.

I'm dashing to my driveway, clicking to unlock the Jeep, throwing myself inside, mashing my left hand between my knee and the steering wheel.

The nearly deserted Sunday streets tempt me to ignore the speed limit on North Central Freeway but the last thing I need is a cop pulling me over, so I reluctantly resist the urge to floor the accelerator.

Should have called Jimmy for backup. Can't handle blood-pounding crisis-driving and trying to hold my phone with painful fingers. I'll call the second I get to campus.

I zip up an exit ramp and two minutes later I'm on campus. Unlike weekdays, when finding parking is a daily exercise of masochism designed to create students who remain hostile for the first 20 minutes of every class, on this Sunday there are only a half-dozen cars in the lot near the History building.

I jump from the Jeep and sprint to the main entrance, hoping it's unlocked, wondering what I'll do if it is.

I yank at the door bar and it's unyielding.

Damn! I don't have time for this. I...

I pull the left bar of the split door and...it opens.

I'm running to the elevator, boots sending staccato clackings on the marble floor. The elevator is "Not in Service."

I check the building's roster for Brandon's office number, pivot right, spotting what looks like a mile-long staircase.

At least it's only one floor up.

At the top, I rest my hand on the railing and pause to slow open-mouth gasps and figure out if Brandon's office is right or left.

Call Jimmy!

I slip my phone from my jeans and....

A sharp **POP** that *might* be a gunshot, echoes from the right hallway.

My phone ricochets off the floor as I pull my pistol from the holster in the middle of my back and move along the hallway as quickly as possible without sounding like a tap dancer practicing in the hallway.

Only one shot so far.

At Brandon's office I press my ear against the wood door for half a minute. *Nada.* I try opening the door but it's locked.

Did the sound come from here? Gotta get in there.

I step directly in front of the door, take a chest full of air and kick as hard as I can on the doorknob. The hollow door splinters. A second kick demolishes it so easily that I half-stumble into the office, eyes sweeping the room, pistol extended in both hands.

What I see shocks and freezes me in an uncertain crouch.

Chapter 97

-----JACK-----

"Hi, Jack," she says, with a slight smile. "That was quite an entrance."

I slowly straighten my body, my gun still aimed at her.

"What the hell happened here?" I demand.

"Justice sorta happened, Jack. Finally."

I slide down the wall behind me. She's facing me, sitting on the floor, both of us with backs to a wall.

"He deserved a lot more and worse punishment than he just got," she says. "He was a *despicable animal* who unforgivably betrayed his brother twice. And his niece and everyone else in our family."

Angel speaks matter-of-factly, eerily calm considering a dead man's body and a pool of his blood are on the floor and she's holding a pistol.

She seems unaware of the semi-auto Beretta pistol she's holding in her lap or that she's sitting on the floor and blood is slowly spreading toward her jeans and shoes from the crumpled, obviously dead body two feet away.

I rest my gun on my thigh, still pointing in her direction.

"There always was obvious tension in our house if Uncle Brandon was there.

"For years I thought everyone's reluctance to be in the same room with him was the family's intense and total disapproval of his never-ending, hippie lifestyle, his daily alcohol and pot intake *plus* his eagerness to sleep with any woman at any time and calling it 'free-love.'

"There's not an ounce of *love* in what he did."

Calm. As if she's describing a movie she saw.

"But there was another cause for my Mom shunning him. Know what it was?"

She looks at me as if I'm supposed to guess.

"When Grand Papa returned home, Mom over-flowed with conflicting emotions. She'd be ecstatic one minute, sobbing the next.

"I realized she, like all of us, was overjoyed that her father was finally cleared of that horrible crime and freed from prison, but at the same time, she was deeply depressed by the incredible injustice he'd suffered. She kept thinking about everything she had…that he had…that all of us had missed for more than 30 years.

"All of us have been sharply and painfully reminded every day of the suffering inflicted on our family by unscrupulous and unethical legal officials. We all know those years are gone forever, can never be relived. All of our lives were forever changed in unforgiveable ways by people who shouldn't be walking around free. They deserve to be behind bars for 33 years. Grand Papa didn't deserve a single day in a cell.

"I thought I understood what she was going through. The more I was around Grand Papa, getting to know him for the first time, the more I loved him for the wonderful, unbelievably forgiving person he is.

"Then one night, about a month after he was released, I heard Mom in bed hysterically sobbing. I climbed in with her, held her tight, trying to bring her out of her desperate sadness. When her crying eased somewhat, she vaguely hinted at some secrets.

"A few days later, Mom shocked me with her deepest secret. Late in the afternoon, she and I were kneeling in flower beds alongside the house, pulling weeds and stirring the soil. She suddenly toppled face forward onto all fours, weeping and shaking.

"I half-crawled the three feet between us, helped her sit up and hugged her from the side. She was clutching herself with dirt-covered hands.

"'Oh, Angel,'" she gasped, her voice raspy. "'Grand Papa and Gram Mavis are visiting Uncle Brandon and Feather. They're having dinner there. They don't know…what he's actually…what he…for years, he….'

"And right then I *knew*. Even before she finished a few staccato sentences, I knew what had haunted her for all this time. At that moment I began to understand the conflicting emotions that engulfed her.

"She told me she rejoiced when Grand Papa's release was near, but she feared Brandon would inevitably be part of the celebration and impossible to avoid. Her past was becoming her present.

"Then she told me the horrible secret she'd hidden all these years.

"I decided right there, kneeling in the dirt, to crush that evil bastard for what he'd done to my mother when she was a child.

"The next day, as I began to fully imagine the details of these unbelievable family secrets, I asked her if Brandon was the real killer of that young girl years ago. She hesitated and whispered, 'I don't know. Not for sure.'

Angel stares unblinkingly at me, face defiant, one small hand fisted, the other still holding the gun in her lap.

"Now you know why my mother shuns Brandon," she snarls.

"That pig fucked an eight-year-old child," she spits. "A child! Just a pure and innocent little girl, one day playing with dolls, another day she's an aspiring princess with a dime store tiara, or a free-form artist creating refrigerator art or dancing her one-of-a-kind dance."

Angel glances at the body to her right.

"But because of that now-dead turd right there, she never had a real *childhood*. He stole it. Destroyed it without a single thought of her as a human being because he is…*wasn't* human. He was a selfish, narcissistic *pervert* preying on a child. Probably several children."

"Angel, you don't have to explain now," I say. "We need to call 911 and get you some medical attention. You don't need to talk about this now. You've just had a big-time trauma. We can discuss everything later."

"No, I'm fine. I'm not wounded. I'm just tired," her body sags, raising both hands slightly, and I briefly look down her Beretta's barrel. She seems surprised to see the gun, stares at it for a moment and drops it to the floor by her hip, almost in the blood pond.

Slipping into shock?

"Jack, I need to explain *everything*. And right now. I can't live with these toxic secrets inside any longer. I need to get them out into the sunshine so everyone understands what happened over these many years. Maybe my last chance."

What does that mean? Planning to kill herself next? Got to get that gun without spooking her.

I stand, holster my pistol and begin pacing a tight circle, hoping to make her comfortable with me moving. I want to ease into position to grab or kick the pistol out of her reach in case she's thinking of harming herself. Or me.

She glances again at Brandon's body.

"She told me that for many years, after becoming her adult self, she deeply regretted not knowing how to end Brandon's sexual assaults on her. She didn't know what a *sexual assault* was. She was too young to understand that she had options until it was too late, but it still looms over her. She never told her mother or Gram Mavis and Grand Papa.

"Besides, who knows what might have happened back then if she'd told anyone of his attacks? She had no concept then that what he was doing to her was a crime. She was just a child being used by a soulless adult who threatened to kill her mother if she told anyone about *'our special secret.'*"

Angel's face fades, her body appears to run out of energy and slumps as if she needs new batteries.

She straightens her posture against the wall, locks eyes with me and with steel in her voice says, "He repeatedly fucked an eight-year-old child, Jack. Don't you *ever* forget that fact! Imagine the details of what happened to that child. Visualize that happening to your daughter over and over. Then you tell me if you'd be reluctant to erase every damn trace that he ever existed."

She's right. Everything I believe in would probably dissolve into volcanic fatherly rage. Into instant insanity. A rational reaction would be impossible at that moment.

"Does my language offend you, Jack?" she says, in a normal voice now, watching my face. "If so, that's too damn bad because that precisely describes what he did to that little girl who is now my Mom. And that's why he didn't deserve space on this or any other planet."

I nod, not wanting to divert her from her soul-searing story. The blood flow from Brandon has slowed but now touches her pink and white sneakers.

"When I understood the horrific truth and thought back over the years," she says, "it was obvious that Mom had *always* tried to protect me. I was never alone with Uncle Brandon. He never baby-sat me, or took me to the zoo or out for ice cream. When I was born she created a barbed-wire barrier between that monster and me.

"After Grand Papa had been home a couple of weeks and I got to know him. I flat-out asked him if his brother killed that young girl in 1982.

"He was shocked by my question. He said he didn't know who the murderer or murderers were and that he was focused *only* on the future. And I should be, too.'

"But I knew in my gut that it was Brandon. And it turns out my gut was right."

"Did you kill him?" I say, looking for the first time directly at Brandon's body for more than a few seconds. I'd glanced at him enough to know he was dead when I first invaded this room of death.

"No. I didn't kill him. The cowardly pile of shit killed *himself* when I confronted him. I wanted to tell him in excruciating detail what a narcissistic predator he'd been his entire life before I punched his ticket to Hell.

"I told him I knew he'd killed that girl.

"You can't possibly know that," he said.

"I ignored him and berated him for ruining his brother's life and my Mom's life just to satisfy his perversions. I wanted him to understand why I was going to execute him. He didn't respond, just looked at me quizzically, as if he'd never thought about what he'd done to everyone.

"I had no idea he had a gun. He pulled it from his pocket and we had a stand-off, pointing guns at each other. I think now that he *wanted* me to kill him.

"I continued telling him what a twisted, inhuman monster he was. In my mind, I had issued an indictment of him and I couldn't stop reading it. But before I ran out of shit to dump on him, he jerked the gun to the side of his head, said something I didn't understand and blew his brains out. He's definitely dead. I double-checked. Now someone needs to sweep out the trash."

"What did he say just before pulling the trigger?"

"It was something like, 'For the proof, go to the light.' I was so shocked at the blood all over the wall and how his face looked and…I didn't even re-member that he said anything until I was telling you what happened."

"Where's his gun?"

She briefly looks at the body.

"Dunno. Probably fell on it."

Could be behind her.

I slightly expand my pacing circle but am still too far from her.

"Did you kill that juror from 1982?"

"Not exactly, but it's definitely my fault."

I raise my eyebrows as I circle.

"It's a long story."

"We can save it for later. We've got to call 911. Do you have a phone? I dropped mine in the hall."

There's a land line phone on his desk.

I reach for it, but her flat, report-reading voice restarts as if she's pressed her 'play' button.

"Mom briefly married an older guy named Albert Stiles when she was barely 17. She wanted to escape our house because of *him*," nodding toward Brandon's body. "He lived next door until about 20 years ago.

"Mom quickly realized Stiles wasn't what he claimed to be. He told her he was a mechanic at the Chevrolet truck plant in Fort Worth. Actually, he was a bottom-rung drug retailer who tried to hook Middle- and High-schoolers into becoming loyal customers. He apparently wasn't very successful even at that disgusting career.

"She calls him 'the biggest mistake I ever made except for giving her me.'

"When I was born, Stiles showed absolutely no interest in being a father. Apparently he had no idea what being a *father* even meant.

"Between discovering that he peddled drugs to kids and his emotional non-involvement with his daughter, Mom divorced him less than a year after I was born. She told him to never contact her or me again. Despite that, Stiles shows up every few years.

Always refers to him by his last name.

"Mom always sent him away and re-issued her command to, 'Go away. Stay away. We have nothing to say to each other.' I've heard it word-for-word several times.

"A month after Grand Papa came home, Stiles showed up again; probably prompted by the publicity. Mom was in Austin at a two-day teaching workshop. I came out of Krogers on the way home and saw him leaning on my car, as if he'd been beamed down by Scotty.

"I tried to deflect him but he begged me to have dinner and then he'd leave. I followed him to *Waffle House*.

"He began with the regrets he said he always had for not being present in my life. He knew it was too late to repair that, but he said he couldn't stop thinking about how things could have been different and, gee, was there possibly *any* chance we could have some kind of relationship once in a while?

"I cut him off at the third recitation of that happy bullshit and asked him what he was up to now.

"When he hesitated, I said, 'Still marketing drugs to kids?'

"His silence and obvious discomfort were the only answer he could muster.

"'Still crazy after all these years?' I asked him, quoting my favorite wise sage, Paul Simon, to mock him as I prepared to bolt without finishing my pancakes. I was about to tell him to 'Go away. Stay away. We have nothing to say to each other and we never will,' when it dawned on me that he probably knew someone, who knew someone, who knew people, who would kill strangers for money.

"After some hinting and exploring his attitude, I told him I needed someone like that. It seemed like a good idea at the time," she sighs. "I was seething over what happened to Grand Papa and wanted revenge. I wanted the fires of Hell to rain on everyone involved."

She seems to notice her blood-stained sneakers for the first time, shutters and scooches her fanny a foot farther from Brandon's blood pool.

The room is so quiet it seems impossible that lethal violence exploded here a few minutes ago.

"What did he say when you told him you wanted to hire a hit-man to murder some people?"

Her eyes flick up to me.

"He stunned me by saying, 'I'll do it myself. As a favor to you. I'll consider it a down- payment on my debt for being such a shitty father.'

"'You've never been any kind of father,' I told him. "And you've never been anything resembling a loving husband. You're just a stranger who's a pain in the ass every few years, before your next vanishing act.'

"I could tell that stung but he didn't offer a defense, just stared at me.

"I asked him if he'd ever killed anyone before.

"'Maybe,'" he said, showing me a wicked grin Jack Nicholson would be proud of. 'Either way, I can get it done.'

"He surveyed the restaurant for nearby ears, leaned across the table and whispered: 'Who do you want me to whack, Sweetheart?'

"Maybe a juror or two," I said, still not quite believing that I was arranging for someone to die.

"Every one of those jurors voted to send Grand Papa to prison. They were all horribly wrong. There even was a black juror, not usual in those years from what I've read. He could have blocked the verdict, but he didn't.

"By far the guiltiest person," I told him, "is Carl Weymeyer, then an Assistant District Attorney who presented the case. Grand Papa was exonerated partly because old files showed that Weymeyer was the snake who withheld evidence that could have cleared Grand Papa. He also planted that snitch in the cell with Grand Papa and who lied in court to get a lesser sentence for his latest burglary conviction.

"He hasn't even had the decency to admit what he did or to apologize for Grand Papa's years locked in a cell. He's gone. When I tried to find out where he was, Courthouse rumors were that when Grand Papa got out of prison, Weymeyer sold his house, packed up and left in the middle of the night.

"There was been speculation that he's hiding somewhere in Idaho or Montana or Oregon, because someone remembered that he occasionally vacationed in what he said was a family-owned cabin in a Northwest state. Or, maybe it was Wyoming or it's *anybody's guess*. He's been retired for years but he's definitely the main son-of-a-bitch who manipulated Grand Papa into prison. He personally framed Grand Papa into a cage.

"All of the other key officials who railroaded Grand Papa are dead, except an old coot named Lawrence Simpson, one of the assistant DAs, who deservedly is spending his few remaining demented days in a wheelchair with no idea where he is or who he is or used to be."

She looks at Brandon's body again, blinks a few times, inhales twice, and resumes.

"Then, Stiles became oddly business-like.

"'Do you want these people to just quietly die, as if from natural causes or accidents?' he asked me. "'Or, do you want to send a public message that someone's avenging Otis?'"

"No public messages," I told him. "I want the Deputy DA to die knowing why he's being executed but it needs to *look* like an isolated incident, maybe a random road-rage case. Or a screwed-up drug deal. Or a home-invasion.

"I don't want anyone connecting dots to 1982. That would point an arrow directly at Grand Papa.

"I know he would never harm *anyone*, but he would immediately be the first suspect if that DA is an obvious murder victim. And God knows, Grand Papa doesn't need another shit-load of injustice if anyone suspects he's murdering people who lied him into prison. But I definitely want some people severely punished for what they deliberately did to him."

"So," I said, watching her face, "did Stiles somehow provide the narcotic overdose that killed Jackson Parks?"

"I think so," she says, "but I'm not sure. I never heard of Jackson Parks until you came to our house and linked that Assistant DA's death to this obscure juror that not even Grand Papa knew by name."

She folds her legs, bringing her feet back, looking like a pint-sized Buddha.

"I realized that Stiles probably killed Parks without telling me. I don't know how or why he chose him.

"I am pretty sure Stiles killed the ex-ADA, Tarpley.

"I tried contacting Stiles when I saw the news of the death, but he was nowhere I could find. He disappeared. God only knows where, hopefully non-stop to Hell. He had one of those toss-in-the-lake, disposable phones that's a dead number now. I don't expect or want to ever see him again. She glances again at her bloody shoes, then over at the body."

"Do you think Stiles may still be hunting people?" I ask. "Is anyone from that trial still in danger?"

"I don't know," she says.

"I'm wondering about Carl Weymeyer, the old Assistant District Attorney who you particularly blamed for railroading your grandfather. Could your father still hunting for him?"

"No way for me to know," she says. "I have no way to contact him or know if he can locate Weymeyer."

Then, as if to herself: "What I wanted to do to Uncle Brandon was spend a week cutting off his fingers and toes. And then his arms and legs. And his dick.

"Then I wanted to slam what would be left over into a four-foot by four-foot cage for 33 years. If he survived that long or died, I wanted to run him through the garbage disposal. I've often visualized doing all of that."

I believe her.

"I wanted to eliminate that pile of crap for my Mom, to set her free from his crimes."

"Do you think," I say, "that she'll appreciate what you've done? Don't you think she knows how to cope with Brandon? I'm absolutely certain she doesn't want to lose you. Surely she doesn't want to see *you* in prison instead of her father?"

"She's never going to know and I don't plan to be in prison."

"Then why are you confessing? Doesn't that pretty much guarantee that you'll do lots of prison time? Or worse?"

"I don't know what you're talking about."

"Just now. You just told me everything."

"Are you going to turn me in? I came here with a gun so I could tell him what a creep he's been. I didn't know he would pull his gun and then shoot himself. *Himself.* He shot himself."

"Yes, but you *planned* to kill him. Two other people were probably killed by a hitman you unleashed. Even Brandon's death is suspicious. You could have taken his gun from him and then shot him."

"You're the only person who knows any of that. I'll deny it. Are you going to tell someone?"

I hesitate.

"I don't know. Certainly if I'm asked by police or in a court room, I won't lie."

"Fine," she says. "Why would anyone ask you if I confessed when this is an obvious…and *actual* suicide? He has gunpowder on his hands. There's none on mine."

"Yes, but this puts you on the short list of suspects in the search for the person who killed the juror and the retired Assistant District Attorney. You apparently hired the killer who murdered those people."

"Stiles killed those people," she says. "No one knows about him."

"I do," I say and lunge for her discarded pistol.

I expect a scuffle with Angel but I get the blood-slippery pistol in my hand and she maintains her yoga-like posture on the floor. I put her pistol on the floor in the corner near the door.

"Did you think I was going to kill you?" she says. "Or myself?"

"Maybe."

"You still don't understand," she says. "I've avenged my Mom and Grand Papa and that's the end of this song. Uncle Turd killed himself. A mystery person may have killed the juror and the old ADA, if they were murdered at all.

"And don't forget," she says firmly, "*only* guilty people are dead in this story."

"What about Jackson Parks, the juror? He was just one of 12 votes and there's no evidence that he or any of the jurors did anything did anything wrong considering some crucial evidence was withheld. Mr. Parks seems to have been a terrific person, dedicated to his family and his church. He wasn't guilty of anything that harmed your grandfather. He's dead because of you."

"He voted to convict Grand Papa. He shouldn't have."

"What will your Grand Papa say if he finds out what you've done?"

She avoids looking at me.

"He must never know. No one can know. And, unless you decide to claim that I confessed to certain things, which I'll deny, I'm in the clear. I don't think you'll rat me out, but if you try, I promise you I'll convince everyone I was insane at the time.

"And when my worthless biological father offered to kill some people for me, I didn't believe him because he has never, *ever* kept a promise to me in his entire life. Other than his mindless sperm donation, he never participated in my life...except for two murders. Maybe. As a *favor!*

"Gosh, thanks, Dad!"

Chapter 98

-----JACK-----

Sirens are arriving in the parking lot. Within seconds, I hear shouts from the stairwell. I keep my eyes on Angel, who is still seated and staring at her hands. I don't know for sure that she doesn't have Brandon's gun.

I raise my hands toward the ceiling seconds before two uniformed cops with guns drawn materialize, peer in, and carefully step around the damaged door into the room.

"POLICE! DON'T MOVE!

The taller officer takes a shooter's stance targeting me, the younger officer confronts Angel, still sitting on the floor.

"I'm a private investigator," I say as calmly as I can. "There's a gun in a holster at my back."

"Don't even blink," the nearest one says, stepping closer and lifting my shirt to pull the pistol from the holster before patting me down from neck to shoes.

Shoulder patch: University Park Police. Name tag: Sgt. Pachino.

"Someone in this building called to report hearing a possible gunshot. Was that either of you?"

"Not me," I said.

Angel shook her head, eyes focused on the bloody floor near her feet.

"My ID is in my wallet," I tell him, my hands still skyward.

He pulls it from my back pocket and flips it open.

"Jack Crocker," he says. "I've heard of you. What are you doing here?"

"My uncle committed suicide," Angel says, to no one in particular, not raising her gaze from h''r bloody sneaker.

"Are you injured, lady?" Sgt. Pachino asks.

"No," finally looking at him.

"Do you realize you're practically sitting in blood? And you've got blood on one of your shoes? Can you stand up?"

"Yes, I think so," she says, starting to push herself up.

"Freeze!" he yells.

"Ray, help her up but first check her for weapons."

"There's another gun on the floor in the corner to my right," I tell him. "And there may be another one under the deceased man."

"What was this, a three-way OK Corral?" he says. "Jesus, that's a lot of blood."

Two more uniforms enter so now there are two guns pointed at me and two more at Angel.

"Tony, call for an ambulance," Pachino orders. "And tell the Lieutenant there's a dead person and we need a Crime Scene team."

"Ray, check the pulse on the guy on the floor, just in case he's still alive, although it would be a miracle with all that blood. Don't step in it."

Ray steps as close as he can, leans over, moves fingers over Brandon's throat.

"No miracles today. He's definitely gone. No pulse, entry wound by left ear. And Sergeant, I see the butt of a gun partially visible under his left arm. Should I lift it out?"

"No, leave it for the Crime Scene team."

"Sgt. Pachino, can I put my hands down?" I say. "Everything's under control now."

"Everything's under control when I say it is," he explains, watching Ray gingerly step clear of the bloody pond.

"Crocker, you can put your hands down now but don't make any sudden moves. I'd definitely get a medal for shooting you."

Oh, great, now I'm a trophy. This guy probably wants to lash my dead carcass to his fender.

Chapter 99

-----JACK-----

By the time I sign my statement to the police, it's late Sunday afternoon. A steady rain blurs the windshield and I'm slumped against the passenger door of Tonto's Mustang in the police parking lot. I've been telling him everything that happened in Brandon's office after I burst through the door and found Angel with a gun and Brandon dead in a blood pond.

He listens without a single comment or question until I say, "That's how my day has been so far."

"Holy Toledo," he says. "One humongous surprise after another. You sure you haven't been hallucinating because you had only a Pop Tart all day? You missed buffet lunch with our Gang."

"Maybe. I'm definitely drained by everything that happened. today. Let's get cheeseburgers on the way to retrieving my car from campus."

The car starts and I spot Feather walking out of the police station, head down, no umbrella shielding her from rain, heading for a Honda Civic parked alone on the far fringe of the lot.

I lower the window, shout "Feather" and climb out of the car waving at her.

She turns, peers at me and stops as I jog to her, Jimmy following.

"I'm so sorry for your loss," I say. Jimmy pauses ten feet away, not wanting to intrude.

"I can't believe what's happened," she says, fresh tears on her cheeks, rain beading on her long hair.

"I…identified…him…his body. Then the police wanted me here and I've been answering a bunch of questions until just now."

"This is my partner, Jimmy McGuire," I say, gesturing for him to join us.

"Hi," she acknowledges him through blurred vision.

"Let's get out of the rain," I say. "I can drive you home. You've just had a horrible shock. Jimmy can follow us."

She nods without argument and 20 minutes later we're parking in her driveway.

Before opening her door, she says: "You were there? When Angel killed him?"

"I don't think Angel killed him," I say. "But I don't know for sure how he died. The cops are investigating, probably for quite a while."

"Can you come in for a few minutes? Maybe some tea or coffee? I need to know more than the police told me. I don't understand why he would have… how he could have…could be…gone."

Inside, Feather silently heats a tea kettle as Jimmy sits and I semi-collapse on kitchen chairs.

"Why don't you think Angel killed Brandon?" she says, bringing tea and joining us at the table. "There's no way I can imagine him committing suicide, he was always so *alive*. He enjoyed life and was interested in *everything* from music to books, politics and movies. And history, that's what he taught, you know."

She stares at me for a moment.

"Why did you go to his office when I told you he was meeting a student there? Why did that alarm you?"

I'm silent, knowing I can't reveal what I'm thinking. I had thought Roberta might be after Brandon because we knew she had something against him. She'd banned him from the family home. I only told the cops that I reacted to Feather telling me it was unprecedented to meet a student on campus on a Sunday. But I'm sure they will want more details at some point.

"How did he die?"

"That's what the cops are trying to figure out."

She continues staring but says nothing,

"Feather," I say, "he died before I got there. I'm not a witness to his death."

"What did you actually *see*?"

"I saw Angel sitting on the floor and Brandon deceased a few feet away. That's about all I can say at this point."

She sips her tea, looking everywhere except at me.

"Did Brandon own a pistol?" Jimmy says.

"Yeah, he's had it forever."

She looks quizzically at me, then at Jimmy.

"Were you there, too?" she asks him.

He shakes his head.

"We went to a gun range once, a long time ago, he taught me how to load and unload it. And how to aim.

"Feather," I say, "was Brandon right or left-handed?"

"Left," she snaps, eyes boring into mine. "What does *that* have to do with anything?"

"He apparently had a gun with him," I say. "He may have shot himself with it. The police found it by his body."

She glares at us, clenches her eyes closed for a few seconds, gets up and sprints from the kitchen.

Jimmy raises his eyebrows and shrugs a *'now what?'* face at me.

She's really upset. Still in shock? Too soon for this conversation. Should we leave?

Feather returns carrying a metal box the size of an unabridged dictionary. She drops it on the table and flips the lid open.

"The gun's not in there," she says, almost inaudibly from two feet away. "There's only a partial box of bullets. He always kept the gun locked in this box. It's been years since we took it to the range, that's the last time I saw it."

Her shoulders slump, her face distraught, her loose hair obscuring part of her face

I exchange glances with Jimmy.

"Feather," I say, "Brandon apparently said something a moment before he died. Maybe you can explain it."

She instantly straightens in her chair.

"What did he say? Tell me!"

"He *may* have said, 'For proof, go to the light.' Does that mean anything to you?"

"No," she snaps. "Must be something Angel *claims* he said. She was the only one there and I certainly don't trust her about anything. Why was she meeting with Brandon?"

Jimmy says, "That phrase, 'Go to the light' is sometimes used in various ways as death approaches. I heard it in Afghanistan. A Marine told his critically wounded friend: 'Go to the light and see Jesus.'

He's trying to divert her from that question. I can't tell her Angel was confronting Brandon about his betrayals.

"And a character in the famous movie, *Poltergeist*, said it," Jimmy continues. "It's also a song title."

She shrugs.

"Any idea what '*For the proof*' means?" I ask.

Feather shakes her head, her hands rubbing her temples, her brow furled. "Proof of *what*?" she murmurs.

Proof of his innocence? Or proof of his guilt after Angel confronted him? If he actually said it. Can't tell Feather anything more yet. None of us know what it means.

Feather stands and waves us away without looking at us, just pointing at the kitchen door and leaves the room.

Back in the Mustang, I tell Jimmy: "Get me to a cheeseburger drive-through as fast as you can. I want two of everything!"

Chapter 100

-----JACK-----

At home, my strawberry milkshake has disappeared up my straw and I'm tossing the balled-up paper wrapper from my second bacon cheeseburger toward the kitchen sink.

"Swish!" I celebrate. "Now we need a figure out what Brandon's damn *light* is. Or *where it is*. Or what he *meant* with his last words."

"He was either sending Angel a message or he was talking to himself, knowing he was about to die," Jimmy says, trying to stifle a yawn. "Don't people normally tell the truth on their death beds? We've thought about this from every perspective we can think of. Let's hand the problem to our subconscious minds by getting some shut-eye."

"Okay," I mutter. "I can honestly say today ranks in my top-five most incredible days."

I linger in the shower before switching off my bedside lamp and slipping nude between the sheets.

Now I'm wide awake again and the bedside clock says 3:28.

"Holy shit," I say aloud, jumping out of bed, sprinting down the hallway to Tonto's room and throwing his door open, hitting the light switch.

"I think I've figured it out!" I say a little too loudly for the hour.

"Great news," he says, sitting up and shielding his eyes from the sudden light. "But I'm always skeptical of shouting, naked men appearing in the middle of the night with an announcement. And please either get some jam-mies on or turn off the light."

I tell him what I'm thinking.

He's silent for a brief moment.

"Sonuvabitch!" he says. "That *might* be it!"

CHAPTER 101

-----JACK-----

Monday morning Feather's phone is ringing for the 12th time but she hasn't picked up.

"Too early?" I say to Jimmy, both of us staring at my cell on the kitchen table. "Maybe she's not taking calls the morning after her husband dies? Surely she's not working today."

"Who?" her bleary voice sounding unused yet today.

"Feather, it's Jack and Jimmy. We know it's early but we have a theory about what Brandon said just before he died."

"I don't give a damn...what he said...if he actually said *anything*. That bitch Angel murdered...."

"Feather, we understand how you feel, bt this *might* be important to understanding what actually happened yesterday. It's only a *guess* and it might not be correct. Or even relevant. But what he said must have meant something to him. We need your help."

"What are you asking?" she says, sounding exhausted.

"Will you let us check a few places in your home?"

"You want to search our home? Why would I agree to that? What are you looking for?"

Jimmy shoots a raised-eyebrows glance at me.

I leap off the cliff.

"Feather, it's possible that Brandon was referring to something that would somehow explain what led to the confrontation with Angel. And to his death."

We hear her breathing.

"What time is it?"

"Nine-thirty."

"Be here in an hour."

Dial tone.

⋏

She looks as if she's been run over by a rampaging herd of Hummers.

She peers at Jimmy's cardboard tray of three coffees and a half-dozen donuts.

"I never eat crap like that," gesturing to follow her to the kitchen we left a few hours ago.

"Let's get done whatever it is you want to do," she says softly but it's definitely a command.

"We think that *maybe* Brandon was referring to something he stashed that reveals why he and Angel met yesterday. And why the meeting resulted in a bloody confrontation. And it's possible that his telling Angel 'Go to the light' has something to do with light here or at his office. Could be light from windows, light fixtures, maybe even switches or skylights if you have any."

"We have two, one in our bedroom and another in our bathroom."

"Did Brandon have any special places where he liked to read because it's comfortable or has good light?"

"We often read in bed and we have matching lamps on bedside stands. And he often reads books or student papers in his favorite recliner. It has a floor lamp next to it."

"Okay," Jimmy says, "let's start in the living room. Then the bedside lamps."

I unplug the brass floor lamp and Jimmy pulls a small plastic box of small screwdrivers and opens the lamp base.

"Nothing unusual in here," he reports as I peer over his shoulder.

He removes and examines the conical shade. Then he gently tugs the electrical cord that runs from the base up through the cylindrical pole to the LED bulb, but there's barely two inches of slack.

He hands me a small, super-bright flashlight and I shine it into the bottom of the brass support tube while he squints into the top.

"Nothing hiding in there," he says and begins reassembling the lamp.

We repeat the process on both bedroom lamps with the same results.

An hour later, we've also found exactly nothing in the guest bedroom, bath and kitchen.

"On to the garage," I say with more enthusiasm than I actually have.

"Not much to see here," Jimmy says, "just one fluorescent ceiling fixture."

"There are lights in both garage door openers," I note. "As long as we're looking we might as well check 'em all."

We check the fluorescent fixture and examine lights in the garage door openers on the ceiling. We remove several panels in the hanging ceiling and survey the space. Other than the accumulated dust that makes me sneeze non-stop for several minutes and some assorted dead bugs, we find zip, and not a bit of doo-da.

Feather has watched us remove dozens of small screws to take lamps apart only to reverse gears and reassemble them.

"Anyone not want tea? Feather says and heads to the kitchen without waiting for answers.

I whisper to Jimmy: "Are we just wasting time here? I'm starting to feel like a fool."

"Not me," he says, grinning. "But as you know, this is *not* my idea, so I'm not the one being humiliated."

"Thanks for always having my back," I grumble. "I'm feel much, much better now."

"I think we're done here," he says. "I don't suppose we can get access to his campus office any time soon, since it's a fresh crime scene."

We leave the garage and return to the kitchen where Feather has orange tea in porcelain cups and a plate of oatmeal cookies.

"Thanks for allowing us to test our theory," I tell her. "I guess we struck out."

"You might want to check the pantry before you go," Feather says.

"Pantry?" Jimmy says.

"It's not much of a pantry." she says. "Brandon has a little office in there."

She opens a louvered door revealing a narrow, shelf-lined space partially blocked by a small, portable table holding a laptop computer, a tiny adjustable desk lamp, a coffee mug and a phone charger plugged into a wall socket under the row of shelves on the right.

"I can barely squeeze through there to get pantry stuff," Feather says. "You big guys couldn't get the Wheaties or the spaghetti sauce without knocking over the table."

"Unplug the desk lamp," Jimmy almost whispers, pulling his screwdriver set and clearing space on the kitchen table.

The lamp base is a six-inch inverted black dish designed to support the adjustable arm of the high-intensity bulb.

Jimmy engages two almost-invisible screws and pries off the bottom plate revealing the two wires bringing in electricity.

"We're becoming experts in lamp wiring," I say. "But no hint of a clue of any…."

"What's that wad of black electrical tape behind the wires?" Jimmy interrupts.

"A sloppy wiring job in a Chinese sweatshop?" I suggest.

He unplugs the lamp and uses needle-nose pliers to tug at the discarded tape blob, maneuvering it around the electrical wires to the table.

I lean in for a closer look as if we've captured a rare moth.

"It's not a glob of left-over tape," I say, using one of the small screwdrivers as a pointer. "I think it's a layer of tape covering something else. There's a teeny-tiny glimpse of something white, possibly paper, at one corner."

Jimmy hunches over the object, grunts and uses his pocket knife to lift a tape edge, then excruciatingly slowly uncovers a tightly folded sheet of onion-skin paper covered with small, precise, blue-ink, hand writing.

"Quick, look at this," I say to Feather who is making more tea.

"Is that Brandon's handwriting?"

She bends over, nose inches above the table, her hands flanking the wrinkled document

She silently reads the top few lines, skips to the bottom of the page.

"Oh, dear God, yes. And that's his signature."

Chapter 102

Since someone is reading this, I'm probably finally where I belong, burning forever **in** Hell for betraying my brother, Otis, and his daughter, Roberta, and the remainder of my family and pretty much everyone I've ever encountered in my cowardly, fraudulent, disgusting life that should have ended decades ago, before I infected so many innocent souls.

Over many years, as I've grown older, lived an academic life and found true and pure love with sweet, gentle, wonderful Feather, I've slowly fully realized the devastating impacts of some of my horrific sins. It has taken decades, but I've gradually absorbed that reality into every cell of my body.

Sometimes it feels as though someone else, not me, did those indescribable things. I couldn't have been involved in any way. At the same time, I know parts of the old me still inhabit this mortal, sinful body. Somehow, I've been able to deeply bury my guilt even as I was changing as a human being and recognizing what my former self had done. What I did.

Seeing my forgiving brother return from 33 undeserved years in prison because of me has made it impossible for me to harbor the monster I used to be in the new person I have become.

It's been an unforgivable three decades and I don't know how much longer I can live with the vivid awareness of the unspeakable cruel pain that I've caused.

I don't want anyone to say Satan made me do those horrendous things. That's a cop-out and untrue. I did what I did for my own narcissistic gratification. I absolutely don't believe in a Satan who supposedly makes us do things that we know are evil. But I definitely believe there is a Hell of some sort, probably completely unlike the various versions organized religions have described, but I believe there is some form of eternal punishment for inflicting pain on someone for my own selfish reasons.

I don't know if humans have what we call souls but I hope and pray that they do, even if I apparently don't.

Pray? Who or what am I praying to? Any god I can imagine would have struck me down years ago before I destroyed so many lives.

Certainly no one who severely damaged so many others can't possibly have what we think of as a *soul*.

I brutally raped and accidentally killed an innocent stranger, barely an adolescent.

I stole more than 3o years of my own brother's life by watching silently as he was sentenced for my crime. I was so terrified that I never said a word while he wasted his middle years caged like a pet rattlesnake. Until today when he came home.

I intimidated little Roberta into keeping silent about what I did to her when she was a child.

I can't possibly adequitely apologize for the things I've done. No one could. No apology could possibly be appropriate. It would be like Hitler saying "'Gee, I'm sorry for what I did to the world and for those millions of murders. Please forgive me."

As for me, I can't begin to explain, I can only totally regret what I did without a speck of empathy or remorse back then.

I should remove myself from this life. I need to send myself to my highly deserved eternal punishment. Or to oblivion.

Even that's probably the ranting of the cowardly, narcissist I've always been.

Other than my total and uncomplicated love for Dear Feather, have I ever had a thought that wasn't completely self-centered?

⅄

"What the hell do we do with this?" Tonto asks.

"Give it to Otis," Feather says.

CHAPTER 103

-----JACK-----

At 5:45 the next morning, I'm at the kitchen table alternating bites from a peanut butter-covered English muffin with coffee swigs from a Dallas Cowboys mug. Tonto crunches the last spoonful of his favorite granola and leans back.

"Wow," he says, "we've had our own Lollapalooza the last few days with Brandon apparently shooting himself, almost miraculously finding Brandon's confession that puts a final bow on the case. I'm ready for a week on Cancun's white sand beaches staring at the deep-blue Gulf of Mexico."

"Would that include the lovely Marsha?"

"Maybe."

"There's one last loose end," I say, "that I think we should try to wrap up."

"What? Josh Dixon and his creepy friend have been arrested and face criminal and civil trials."

"Otis, and maybe his family, now know what happened."

He puts his bowl in the dishwasher.

"Don't you think our clients will be able to move forward now?"

"Yep, but there's a corrupt, rogue former Assistant District Attorney living freely somewhere. He knowingly put an innocent man in jail for 33 years. He was the primary prosecutor. He should be in prison."

"He was disgraced and he ran away," Tonto says. "He's not a wanted fugitive, no criminal or civil suits were ever filed and he's probably legally immune from everything anyway. Seems like that's the end of that story."

"He's mostly escaped accountability for stealing much of a man's life," I say. "There were a brief few *moments* of public disgrace when Otis was released.

"But most of that was barely mentioned or noticed during the flurry of stories about Otis being exonerated and leaving prison and how he and his family were rebuilding their lives.

"The plain fact is that son-of-a-bitch committed an unforgiveable crime against Otis and he hasn't been held accountable or punished. Sure, in the middle of the night he slithered out of Dallas where he was born and became a big damn deal. But he had no family here anymore and he's still drawing a hefty government pension check.

"Personally, I think he should be in prison for the next 33 years."

"That would be a good outcome," Tonto says, "but I don't think we can get that done."

"I agree, but what if we can track him down, confront him on video tape, and try to get him to explain what happened and how he feels about it now."

"And then what? If we find him, why would he even say 'hello?' More likely he'd flip us off and slam the door."

"Possibly. But what if the only thing that happens is we locate him, spark some shaming news coverage of how he's living. That could focus attention on what he did to Otis, and on the flawed and corrupt system that needs fixing. At the very least there should be consequences when officials violate legal and moral standards."

"What's the best outcome we can seriously hope for?" he asks.

"It would be mostly symbolic, but attention gathering," I say.

"What if we got the bastard disbarred?"

CHAPTER 104

-----JACK-----

"You think he'd use his own name?" Tonto wonders.

He's jotting possible search parameters on a legal pad. We're looking for any mentions of a Carl Weymeyer. It's mid-morning and we're at our office, the "CLOSED" sign in the window.

"Quite possibly," I say. "He's not a fugitive although he's probably trying to keep a low profile, wherever he is. Let's start with his real name and we can try some variations if that doesn't work. It helps that his last name isn't *Smith*."

"Angel said the courthouse rumors mentioned Oregon, Montana, Wyoming or Idaho?" he says. "That's a lot of territory."

"Yep, and that may or may not be true. And his name *now* might be Smith or Jones or...."

"Okay, I'll start with those states and with his real name and see if anything turns up."

A couple hours later, he sighs, looks at me across the desk and says: "I've searched on his name and all the variations I can think of within those states. The good news is I'm not getting thousands or even hundreds of hits to cull through. The bad news is I'm not getting any solid matches at all."

"You think he's using a completely different name? Is it possible that he's dead under another name? Could we be hunting a ghost?"

"Possibly," he says. "I'm wondering if we're trying to find a person when it might be easier to find a *place*."

"Look for the real estate?"

"The courthouse talk was that he occasionally vacationed at a family cabin or house. Maybe we can find where he's living."

Then I figure it out.

"We've been looking for variations of *Weymeyer*," I say. "See if you can find his wife's maiden name. Maybe the real estate is from *her* family."

A minute later, Tonto has Carl Meymeyer's deceased wife's obituary on the screen.

"Katrina *Zelineck*," he says.

For several hours he searches real estate records in Oregon and Utah then switches to Montana. Because real estate records are county responsibilities it's evening when he yells: "Got the sumbitch! Park County, Montana. Original owner John Zelnick. Katrina must have inherited the property from her grandfather or great-grandfather."

His high-five stings my hand but I don't mind.

"He may or may not be there, but we know where the family real estate is."

I plug the information into Google and determine that the nearest airport to the property's address is Bozeman.

"Start checking for flights to Bozeman, Montana."

CHAPTER 105

-----JACK-----

Looming over us is a 3,000 pound grizzly bear, six-feet tall. And that's while he's sitting down.

He's a spectacular bronze sculpture in the Bozeman airport. We'd already been accompanied down the escalator from the gate to baggage claim by a v-flock of geese sculptures hanging from the ceiling.

"I love Montana already," Jimmy says, "even if Weymeyer is not here."

We roll our carry-on bags to the rental car bus and an hour later we've driven 25 miles east to Livingston and collected a box we shipped to ourselves at the local UPS store.

Now, we're eating paninis at Chadz, an eclectic and eccentric café on Main Street in the center of Livingston. Our compact, black hybrid SUV at the curb.

We're about 30 miles north of where we think Weymeyer is living on the family property.

"After this, let's check all the grocery stores in town," I say. "If there's any chance we can find out where he buys groceries, maybe we can find him."

"Or maybe he frequents one of the local bars. That might be preferable to unexpectedly dropping in on him at some cabin tucked back in the woods off that gravel road we saw on Google maps."

"Let's get a couple of espressos to go and tour the town before interviewing bartenders and grocery clerks," Tonto suggests.

At the counter, our espresso orders are taken by a 70-plus man with a pencil-thin moustache, denim shirt and jeans securely held up by both a leather belt and bright-blue suspenders.

"Been around here for a while?" I ask.

"If all my life counts as a *while*," he smiles, "I'd say yes."

I pull a photo from my shirt pocket and show it to him.

"This is my grandfather 30 years ago. I'm trying to find him...or at least discover what happened to him. Any chance he looks familiar if you can imagine him a lot older?"

He focuses on the photo before shaking his head and looks up.

"Nope. Don't think I've ever seen that feller. What happened?"

"About 1985 he left Texas saying he wanted to find a job in Montana and would move the family when he could. No one ever heard from him again. I decided to see if I could find him...or any trace of him."

"Sorry, sonny."

In less than an hour, we've seen many highlights from our Google research including multiple historic buildings displaying construction dates from as early as 1901, but restored and looking brand new.

We found a couple of the highly rated restaurants listed on the internet, plus the architecturally wonderful old Railroad Depot, now a museum, next to the closed railroad Roundhouse where for many years massive locomotives were maintained and repaired until the company shut down railroad functions in the 90s.The city assessed its assets and brilliantly reinvented itself as a tourist destination amidst some of the best trout fly-fishing in the world.

And as a cultural outpost, advertising itself as "Livingston:14 Art Galleries, two stoplights."

It also has three bookstores, three community theaters and numerous painters, graphic artists, sculpters, actors, writers and photographers, many many making handsome fulltime livings. The interior scenes of the movie, "A River Runs Through It" were filmed in the town's Civic Center.

It took the rest of the afternoon to bar-hop along Main Street, even though we weren't actually drinking. I unsuccessfully showed the old photo of Carl Weymeyer and told my grandfather search story to bartenders at The

Mint, The Livingston Bar & Grill, The Stockman Bar & Grill, The Murray, The Sport, plus The Hiatt Hotel bar and several more within a few blocks of Main Street.

"I've heard more C&W music today than all of last year," I say as we walk into the Whiskey Creek Saloon. The woman bartender, likely in her 60s, looks at the photo and right away thinks the photo is of a much younger guy who now "sports white hair and an extensive white beard.

"He comes in from time to time. Pretty sure it's him. It's the eyes, Hon," she tells me. "The eyes are individual, almost like fingerprints. The U.S. and British were able to identify that terrorist who was cutting off heads, partly by studying his eyes, even though he always wore a ski mask.

"The beard your grandfather has now covers his entire face except for the eyes and they look a lot older than in the photo. They're similar. But sadder. If he's your grandfather, he looks like he's had some really bad times in his life."

"Is he a heavy drinker?"

"Not that I know of. I've only seen him a few times. You probably thought that at my age I've been behind this bar for decades but I moved here from Denver only two years ago."

"What's this guy's name?" Tonto asks.

"He's never said his name here that I know of."

"Is there any pattern to his visits? Like every third Friday or something?"

"Not that I can tell," she says. "Just every once in a while."

I thank her, drop a $10 bill on the bar and we head for the street.

Tonto says: "I saw two grocery stores as got off the Interstate. Let's try them both. He's got to get food somewhere."

We show the photo to four Albertson cashiers and two folks behind the meat counter, but no one recalls seeing him even after hearing the full description.

At the employee-owned, bring-your-own-boxes and bags, two cashiers think they've seen him when I describe his hair and beard.

"Could be a guy who comes here from time to time."

"How often?" Jimmy asks.

"I don't know, maybe once a month off and on for at least a year," says a short, balding middle-aged man in a red-plaid flannel shirt. Don't know his name or anything, always pays cash."

"Does he come on any particular day that you've noticed?"

"Uh, no way I would know that. I see a lot of people through here every day. Well, six days a week. I'm here Tuesdays through Sunday. I can't keep track of their schedules."

Back outside, I push the key-less button and the hybrid is ready, but completely silent.

"We can't camp out here or at Whiskey Creek Saloon hoping to see him *sometime*. Tomorrow we need to find his hideout cabin in the woods and hope he'll talk with us."

As the car starts moving, Tonto says: "That could be easy…or could go very wrong."

"Yep. Let's find a motel. And a restaurant with Bison Burgers on the dinner menu."

CHAPTER 106

Early the next morning, after cholesterol-bomb breakfasts at The Beanery, a restaurant frequented for decades by railroad employees working at the near-by Roundhouse, we head out of Livingston, driving south on State Highway 89 along the Yellowstone River, the longest un-dammed river in the lower 48.

The river begins south of Yellowstone National Park, flows north through the park to Mammoth, the park's north exit, continues 50 miles through the Paradise Valley to Livingston, makes an eastward turn for 115 miles to Billings, where it merges with the Missouri.

We follow the river about 40 miles, veer right onto Tom Miner Basin Road, where the pavement quickly vanishes, replaced by a gravel and dirt road with twists and turns, climbing up the mountainside. We're looking for the driveway to the cabin. From the real estate records we know the property's address but after about five miles, driving slowly and seeing only an oc-casional pickup truck while scanning the widely spaced roadside mailboxes, we realize his driveway must not have a mailbox and we backtrack.

Entries to all properties are required by law to have a small sign display-ing numbers for emergency responders such as volunteer firefighters, police or ambulances.

"There it is," Tonto says. "Right there by that path."

The eight-inch square sign is almost totally obscured by weeds and bush-es left of what appears to be a footpath. I make a k-turn and we stop at the path and get out. Immediately after the path leaves the road, it turns sharply and is invisible to anyone driving by.

"Anyone driving off the road onto this so-called driveway would have scratches on their vehicle at any speed," Tonto says.

He disappears for several minutes.

"Faint tire tracks are visible about 20 feet from here," he reports. "I think this path/driveway is infrequently used and someone brushes the first 20 feet or so each time to almost erase the tracks unless you're close to them in good light."

"Let's squeeze through there and confirm there's a cabin at the end," I say.

We slowly maneuver the SUV through the shrubbery and continue silently in our stealth vehicle.

I hit the brakes at the first glimpse of a clearing, a weathered log cabin at the far end, the entire area surrounded by tall and densely packed fir trees. The odometer shows we're eight-tenths of a mile from the road.

"We can walk up from here," Tonto says.

"Let's drive closer and get out," I say. "We're not trying to sneak up on him. We're going to tell him who we are and we should act normally even if the setting is a bit mysterious."

We decided last night to leave our guns in the car trunk, still in the unopened UPS box.

"It leaves us more vulnerable," I told Tonto, but it might add credibility when we tell him we only want to talk to him."

Now, I stop about 20 yards from the cabin's front porch, respecting the rural custom of unexpected strangers giving advance notice before getting too close or knocking on the door.

I have my left foot on the ground when I glimpse two huge Rottweillers dashing from near the right side of the cabin, coming 90 miles an hour right at us.

"Dogs" we shout simultaneously, scrambling back in the car and slamming doors.

"Holy shit," Tonto says as the dogs circle the SUV snarling and snapping menacingly.

I roll my window down a few inches and test my dog-whispering skills.

"Good boys. We come in peace. Good boys. It's the soothing tone that counts," I tell Tonto, "not the words."

The dogs ignore me.

"They're not buying it," Tonto points out. "Maybe you should try German…"

A piercing whistle comes from somewhere in the woods and the Rottweillers slam their butts to the ground, still staring at us but eerily silent now.

"Put your guns on the dashboard and get out of the car," a gruff male voice orders.

"We don't have any weapons," I yell through the window.

"Get out of the car," the voice says.

"Please restrain the dogs first," I yell.

"They *are* restrained," the voice growls, sounding closer. "They do what I tell them. Now get out facing the cabin. Don't make any sudden moves."

We look at each other, I take a deep breath, we both nod and get out, arms at our sides, leaving the car doors open.

"Don't turn around!" the voice commands from behind us. "And don't even twitch. The dogs hate visitors even though they find them delicious."

The dogs remain sitting and panting a few feet away. Pine scent wafts gently on the breeze.

"Who the hell are you guys and what you doing creeping up my driveway in a rental car?" the still unseen man demands.

"We're from Dallas," I say. "I'm Jack Crocker and my partner's Jimmy McGuire. We want to…."

"Crocker?" the voice interrupts. "You the guys who rescued that kid, killed one of the bad guys and put that crooked cop in Huntsville?"

"Yeah," Jimmy says. "That *kid* is Jack's son."

"I know about that," the voice says. "I may live in rural Montana mountains but I got satellite TV and Wi-Fi."

Nothing happens for a long minute.

Trying to figure out what to do with us?

"Keep your hands where I can see them and turn around."

We pivot into fierce brown eyes assessing us from behind a bountiful white beard and unruly white hair jutting from a green John Deere gimme cap, a black Glock semi-auto pistol pointed between us.

"Why are you two here?"

"We're trying to understand what happened during Otis Jefferson's trial," Tonto says. "We wondering...."

"Are you both crazy?" he explodes. "You think I want to talk about that shit? From more than 30 years ago? Not gonna happen! You get back in that car and haul your sorry asses back to Texas before I decide to feed you to my dogs."

"There have been three recent deaths of people who were part of the trial," I say.

"Three?" he asks. "I saw that my former assistant, Glen Tarpley, died a week or so in a one-car accident on ...."

"That wasn't an accident," Tonto says.

"Why do you think it wasn't an accident?"

"His car was tampered with," Tonto says. "A brake line was punctured."

"Why would anyone kill Glen? And after all these years?"

"Well," I say, "Tarpley helped present the case in court. That could be a motive. Plus, a juror from the trial died of an overdose of prescription drugs last week." I add.

"Which one?"

"The only black juror," I say. "Jackson Parks."

"I don't remember the name but of course I remember him. I tried to keep him off the jury but I ran out of options and in the end he voted to convict."

Tonto says, "And a few weeks ago, the snitch you planted next to Mr. Jefferson was killed in a hit-and-run in Hugo, Oklahoma."

"None of that makes any sense," Carl says. "All of that was decades ago. Only the court freeing Otis Jefferson has changed."

He pauses, his face freezes.

"Holy shit, is Otis Jefferson tracking down people from way back then and killing them for revenge?"

"No," I say. "We don't believe Otis Jefferson is involved."

I capture his gaze and say: "But maybe someone else is. Whoever it is could have you on his target list. It would be logical that if someone is killing people from the trial, he would probably target you. *You* may be in danger."

His eyes refocus beyond me, seemingly to infinity.

Or to Hell.

Tonto and I remain frozen in place not wanting to provoke the Rottweillers.

Finally, Carl says, "I can't believe this crap. I...."

"Can we discuss things," I interrupt, "without seriously hoping your dogs aren't getting hungry?"

He stares at me, glances at Tonto, blows out his cheeks and looks at the dogs, still sitting, big tongues hanging from mouths filled with glistening, saliva-covered gigantic teeth.

"Kennel-up," Carl orders and the dogs trot toward the house.

"Okay, you two," Carl says to us. "Let's go sit on the porch."

He stays behind us until we get to the cabin. The dogs are lapping water from a galvanized tank in a heavy-gauge, wire fenced area.

The porch runs the width of the cabin and holds a single rocker and small table. Tonto and I sit on the steps.

Carl sits rigidly in the rocker, Glock in his lap, his head slightly tilted, as if assessing us but it's unclear, thanks to his hair and full, bushy beard serving as a white ski mask revealing only his eyes.

"Okay" he says, looking straight ahead, "here's the deal. I've never thought highly of Private Snoops who scratch out a living following stray spouses and Workers Comp cheats or bail-bond skippers. You two have a little more credibility after that kid's rescue last year, but I don't want you here and I don't ever want to see you again after today. You and everyone else, are going to stay away. Leave me the hell alone."

Neither Tonto nor I respond.

"I have no family anymore," Carl continues, his voice softer but eerily threatening. "There's absolutely no one I want to see or talk to. Ever. Get it? I don't have a phone. I don't even have a mailbox."

"Why have you exiled yourself?" Tonto asks. "You were pretty big 'taters for years in Dallas."

"Long time ago," Carl says. "But I've been betrayed over and over. This is as close as I can get to being on a different planet."

"*You've* been betrayed?" I ask way too loudly. "*You've* been betrayed? By *whom?* How do you figure that?"

"Betrayed by those week-kneed, second-guessers." His voice is cold steel. "Those cowards who wanted to be safe but who got real queasy when the chips were down. They didn't want involvement in what needed to be done to keep society's vermin from their neighborhoods. I helped keep the scum behind bars where they belong.

"'You do what you have to,' those chicken-shit, stuffed shirts said. 'But please don't tell *us* about it, we don't want to *know* anything about it. Just get it done,' they squealed,' like the piglets that they were.

"And now some politically correct court decides Otis Jefferson shouldn't be in prison and lets him out.

"You think any of those guys in their thousand-dollar suits backed me up? Hell, damn no. As soon as Jefferson was released, those guys *discovered* that they were *horrified*. Retroactively horrified! Disloyal shitheads!"

"What happened back then?" I say. "How did the exculpatory evidence raising serious doubts about Mr. Jefferson's guilt get withheld? Did you know about it?"

"Ah, shit, man, that wasn't much. He was going to be convicted. We just simplified that case a little here and there. He did the deed."

"What about Joe Bob Spencer, the snitch you planted in the cell next to Mr. Jefferson? Didn't you bribe him to lie in exchange for a lower sentence?"

"Hell," Carl says. "I just provided an opportunity for Jefferson to confess to someone; get his guilt off his chest. He didn't have to tell anyone what he'd done."

"So, you believed Spencer was telling the truth?"

"He was under oath. Why wouldn't we believe him?"

"Good God, Weymeyer, you screwed around with the evidence and sent an innocent man to 33 years in prison," Jimmy yells, standing up, towering over Carl who still holds the Glock and stares into the woods.

"You're so damn naïve," Carl says. "I never did anything that didn't benefit society. Those folks all upset about protecting the *so-called* rights of criminals should worry about the *actual* rights of victims. We got justice for victims and put dangerous people behind bars, away from civilized human beings, details be damned."

"That's not how America works," I say, knowing he doesn't want a civics lecture.

"Get in that car, go back to Texas and never come back here. If anyone else comes, I'll know you told them and I'll find a way to make you and your families pay a price. And if I ever see you around here again you'll deeply regret it, but only for the brief time it takes to turn you into Rottweiler kibbles or fertilizer for those trees," gesturing to the woods surrounding the cabin.

We walk to the car without glancing back. As I make a tight U-turn we see Carl still in his rocker with the pistol, not moving, like a tragic, lonely mannequin propped up in a diorama far from any members of his species.

We're silent while negotiating the faint path to the gravel country road. When we get back to the paved state highway and turn north back to Livingston, I hand my hat to Tonto.

"Check to see if we got all of that on our hat-cams."

Five miles later, he slides off a headset and says: "We both recorded what we saw. Much of it is staring away from him, some good video of the dogs. The audio is marginal in a few spots but it's all there."

"Enough to try for a disbarment hearing?"

"I think so but we'd need a lawyer to look at it."

"I have another idea," I say.

I think we should just end everything now."

"And let that sumbitch…" Tonto slaps the dashboard with a fist, his voice incredulous and angry.

He inhales several chests full of air, glances at me, then at the road before starting over.

"You're willing to let that unrepentant, immoral, totally unethical turd escape punishment for what he did to Otis and who knows how many others? I can't believe you want to drop it now."

I watch the road disappear under our car for several miles.

"We just left a dead man back there. A dead man in a rocking chair. Even if we got him disbarred he wouldn't care. That means nothing to him now.

"Unless we want to go back there and shoot him, here's the reality now. He has sentenced *himself* to life in solitary confinement. Maybe some time in the future, some elk hunters will find Carl's bones on that porch, slumped alone in a self-created, private prison cell.

"There's a ton of justice in that."

Chapter 107

-----JACK-----

The day after our return from Montana, Jimmy and I attended Brandon's funeral, actually a secular 'Celebration of Life,' organized and conducted by a faculty member with short anecdotes about Brandon and nostalgia music from the 1960s.

Otis, Mavis, Roberta and Feather were there. None of them spoke and Angel wasn't there, even though the police have concluded the death was a suicide because Angel had no gunpowder residue and the weapon belonged to Brandon.

News coverage has reported the police department's conclusion to the public.

⚊

Now, Jimmy and I are sitting in the Jefferson living room with Otis.

He reluctantly agreed to meet when I called him the day after the funeral. I told him a public place wasn't suitable for the subject we need to discuss.

He almost refused to meet at all when I insisted that not even his wife, Mavis, be present.

He hasn't spoken, let alone smiled, since we arrived.

"So, what's this all about?" he demands. "Are the police after me again?"

I glance at Jimmy next to me on the sofa.

"No," I say. "Nothing like that."

I lean toward him, look him in the eyes and exhale.

"Otis, we know who actually killed the girl you were convicted of murdering. We have proof. Do you want to know?"

He doesn't blink, or even appear to be breathing.

"How could you possibly have proof after all these years?" His voice is flat, almost inaudible, his face blank as a dead man's.

"We have a confession," Jimmy says. "In writing."

Otis remains unchanged except for his eyes becoming eerily unfocused. He says nothing for at least five minutes of the most awkward silence I've ever experienced.

Maybe he died but is still sitting upright.

Then his hands form a prayer tent to cover his eyes, his head bows.

Tears begin seeping under his hands and his body trembles.

Tears of joy? Fear? Relief? Does he already know?

"Show me," he whispers, finger-rubbing his wet cheeks. "Show me your proof."

I hand him a legal-size tan envelope and he extracts the onion-skin paper still showing multiple creases from being folded.

Otis reads the letter in Brandon's tiny, precise handwriting excruciatingly slowly, as if he doesn't want to get to the signature that by then he certainly must know who wrote it.

Has he known that Brandon was the murderer for all 30-plus years?

.When he finally finishes, he gently puts the letter in his lap and closes his eyes for several minutes.

Then he reads it again.

"Where did you get this?"

"It was hidden but Brandon hinted at it just before he…died."

"Who else has read it?"

"Only one person who will never mention it."

"And what am I to do with it?"

"We're giving this to you to do whatever you want to do with it. As far as we're concerned, you can give it to the police or share it with some or all of your family. Or burn it."

He flicks a glance at Jimmy and back to me.

Assessing us?

I hold his gaze.

"Have you known this ever since 1982?" I ask, so softly I wonder if he heard me.

He rises. And so do we, heading for the door. As I open it I turn back to him, still standing by his chair.

"Otis, there are no copies of the letter and we will never speak of it again."

Epilogue

A couple of days later, Lauren calls to invite Jimmy and me to a "backyard cookout" at their house the next day.

"It's to thank everyone who helped get evidence against Robyn's attackers and kept everyone safe.

"Don't you remember we were fired?" I ask.

"That was temporary," she says. "Ben wants to do a *'reset.'* Actually it was my idea but he's is fully on board and may, by now, think it was *his* idea. Please come. Six-thirty?"

I glance at Jimmy, who's been listening.

He nods, eyebrows raised.

"We'll be there."

"Bring your significant others."

⋏

Lauren escorts Crystal, Carole and me into the Rogers' backyard where the late May evening flirts with the high 80s but a dozen mature oak and maple trees shade the area with a leafy tent.

Robyn, Ashley and Pamela cluster around one corner of a square table created by two jammed-together folding tables. Two large, ice-filled coolers bristle with bottles and cans.

The women are all in shorts, sandals and tees of various colors. Their laughter infuses the atmosphere with a sense of fun and light-heartedness.

Robyn spots us and the trio jumps up and runs to us. I introduce Crystal to everyone, including Ben who is apparently supervising a short black man in jeans, a white apron with a caterer's logo and a red forehead bandana, arranging charcoal briquettes on a large professional grill.

Lauren returns with Jimmy and Marsha, sparking more handshakes, hugs and chatter. Crystal and I join Jimmy and Marsha as an audience few feet from the others.

"Ah, the enthusiasm of kids," Marsha says, gently swinging Jimmy's hand.

Jimmy hasn't shared many details but I'm aware that he's returned to our rental house in Garland several times recently with the clock closer to breakfast than to midnight.

The chatter briefly changes to shrieks when Julie Norton arrives and Robyn, Ashley and Pamela greet her.

"You guys have created one heck of an enthusiastic Gang," Crystal tells me and Jimmy as we watch the young women enjoying their reunion, even though it comes less than a week after Josh Dixon and Andy Haley were arrested on criminal sex assault charges.

Crystal hadn't hesitated a second when I asked if she would accompany me tonight. "Of course I'll come. This is a huge victory for you. I want to be there to cheer for you."

I'm hoping this is another step toward our family's reconciliation and reconstruction.

About a half-hour later, Ben shatters the festive ambiance by banging a large metal spatula on the steel grill cover. Everyone stops talking, staring at him and I see the caterer glaring while inspecting his grill for damage.

"Everyone," Ben booms, as he moves to the end of the table. "Take your seats and we'll get this show on the road."

Show?

When we're all at the table, Ben, still standing, looks at each of us for a moment.

"As I'm sure you all know," he says, "I absolutely would have been completely against the extremely risky sting operation you all launched...*if* I'd known about it. And, to be honest, I was totally infuriated when I found out about it *after* it was over, when it was on TV and in the papers and we faced massive financial and legal threats from that scumbag's family."

He walks behind my chair and stands there for a moment. I can't see his face.

"Jack, I fired you and Jimmy because I was furious that you guys helped my rebellious, traumatized and naive daughter put herself...and others, in a very dangerous situation. And you guys helped them form this *gang* to disrespect me. Except for Ashley, I didn't know these people until I met them tonight.

"I was tremendously angry that I couldn't control this vital family crisis. My own wife supported your plan but didn't tell me."

He pauses, looks around the table at all of us stunned into silence by his remarks.

Crystal is sitting next to me. She reaches for my hand and squeezes it.

Did he invite us to dinner so he can air his grievances?

Ben pats my shoulder.

"Yesterday the Dixon family lawyer made an indirect inquiry about a possible settlement of our civil suit against them. The case seems headed for exactly the resolution you expected from the start.

"I owe you guys an apology."

I didn't think he ever uttered that word.

He pulls a white envelope from his back pocket and hands it to me.

"You haven't sent me an invoice, Jack, but I think this will more than cover it. Let me know if it doesn't."

Ben returns to the end of the table.

"My goal for tonight is...*our* goal, Lauren's and mine...is to show our deep and sincere gratitude for what all of you accomplished recently, particularly getting such vivid video evidence leading to criminal charges and arrests of the two sonsab...attackers.

"And we appreciate that everyone involved is safe, especially you, Miss Swann. You showed enormous courage by knowingly putting yourself in danger from unidentified drugs and whatever perverted plans that creep, Dixon, had in mind."

"Thanks, Mr. Rogers," Pamela says. "I'm totally fine physically and all other ways except maybe a little chagrined at photos and videos of me unconscious, restrained and mostly undressed. Overall, I'm fine even with that if it contributes to scraping those two pieces of crap off the sidewalk and into prison cells."

"Wow Pamela!" Julie Norton shouts. "You go girl! Pamela. Pamela. Pamela," waving her arms upward, a cheerleader urging all of us to chant along. And we do.

Robyn rises next to Ashley's chair, takes a deep breath and says: "Ashley, your friendship and mentoring have often helped me navigate some of the mysteries of growing up. I'll never forget your advice and guidance starting back in high school, plus you unhesitatingly took on the dangerous role of bait to a violent predator."

Robyn's voice quivers and her eyes moisten before she can speak again. "You are my volunteer Big Sister."

As applause ripples around the table, Ashley jumps up to embrace Robyn, both of them crying happily.

I suspect every person is having the same difficulty I am trying to swallow or speak, not to mention a mass outbreak of blurred vision.

Julie Norton waves at Ben like a student with the answer to a classroom question.

"This is all wonderful," she says, to nodding heads around the table. "But there are many more violent sex predators out there.

"Is it possible that we can all *remember* how we fired up we feel right now and look for ways our Gang or any one of us can amplify that message?"

Ben has to repeat himself when he tries talking over the applause for Julie's challenge.

"I'm going to remember...." He says.

He walks to Robyn's chair where she's pretending to focus on rotating a paper cup on the table.

"I need to *remember* that my daughter is much stronger than I've given her credit for."

Robyn brings the cup to her lips, still not looking at her father.

"I realize…mainly Lauren helped me understand…at least somewhat, that Robyn may have been the really smart, somewhat naïve daughter that I saw her as, but…Lauren showed me that Robyn was more complicated than that, I just was too rigid and controlling to understand. I frankly didn't get it.

"Now, even I can see she has demonstrated growth and toughness that I overlooked. In some ways she's shown more maturity than I do sometimes, particularly when I'm in my micro-managing mode.

"Robyn," he says, "I promise to *try* remembering who you've become. Who you are *now*."

Robyn gets up and hugs Ben.

Everyone's up now, applauding, watching father and daughter trying for a fresh start.

"Chris," Jimmy says, "you've been quite quiet so far tonight. What's up with you?"

"Mostly rethinking and reorganizing my life," Chris says. "I'm sorry Jennifer couldn't be here for this but our son has an ear infection. She and I are considering a move to some place far from Dallas or the Texas Panhandle where we both grew up.

"When McMillan University's president suspended the Security Department's Chief, every staff member from the Captain and Lieutenant down to me, a rookie cop, shifted focus to the future. I figure all of us will be replaced but even if not, I don't want to be there.

"I've checked out several advertised positions in some western states and already have responses from two. Jennifer and I are particularly interested in an opening in Oregon for a certified law enforcement officer.

"I fit the specs okay and we're hoping that comes through and we can start over in a new place. I know some police chiefs might view what I did as disloyal or would worry I'd be a rabble-rouser inside the department.

"But we're optimistic we'll find a good place."

After applause, Lauren gestures across the table.

"Carole," she says, "I can't tell you how much your instant friendship meant to me when I met you while Robyn was unconscious in the hospital. Your experience and advice seriously lowered my stress during that time."

Carole sips her Diet Coke.

"I remember waking up in that hospital," Robyn says, "and this unfamiliar woman was sitting there watching me. A short time later her common sense counsel clarified my situation and pointed out some new options for me to think about back when I was so conflicted and depressed.

"You helped channel my anger toward trying to keep what happened to me from happening to someone else.

"Everyone here has helped me in different ways. I'm taking a semester off before transferring to UT Dallas in January. Between now and then I'm volunteering with Pamela's group that helps victims.

"Bottom line is that I feel damn good about finding out who I am."

---------THE END------

Thank You Notes

I'm grateful for the support of family and friends throughout the writing of *NOT GUILTY.* Your support and encouragement are always appreciated.

Special thanks to Joann Byrd, a friend and former colleague, who devoted many hours to reading the manuscript with her agile and analytical mind, giving me significant feedback and suggestions.

And special thanks to Kathy, my live-in (56 years!) consultant who read uncountable versions of the book in progress as well as smaller parts whenever I needed her keen eyes.

And thanks to readers who post reviews of *Not Guilty* on Amazon, Facebook, GoodReads or other social media sites. Reviews are critical to independent publishers and are seriously helpful to authors.

My website is *Ralphlanger.com*

Made in the USA
Lexington, KY
11 February 2017